Stealing Venus

Richard John Mitchell

Copyright © 2011 Richard John Mitchell

ISBN: 1467906476
ISBN-13: 978-1467906470

The right of Richard John Mitchell to be identified as the author of this work has been asserted by him in accordance with the Copyright, Designs and Patents Act 1988.

All rights reserved. No part of this publication may be reproduced, stored in or introduced into a retrieval system, or transmitted, in any form, or by any means (electronic, mechanical, photocopying, recording or otherwise) without the prior written permission of the publisher.

All the characters in this book are fictitious, and any resemblance to actual persons, living or dead, is purely coincidental.

STEALING VENUS

For Viv, with love.

RICHARD JOHN MITCHELL

ONE

The model is not to be copied, but to be realized.
ROBERT HENRI

Will Bentley's painting of Ladies Day at Ascot had encountered a setback – his chief model had flounced out. Yesterday he had drawn in the lines of the foreground girl, floating her on a sea of background heads, but then she had departed following an imprudent remark about her weight.

He sipped from a mug of very hot tea. Long hair framed his features and every now and then he swept it back with a flick of his head. He had done all he could to the background drawing. He had dressed the heads in top hats or exotic millinery according to gender, working from a patchwork of his own photographs. Now he needed the girl but she was just a hint of faded perfume hanging in the air.

He leaned against the table edge and examined his studio, which had evolved over the years to its current magnificent clutter. It had been closed for his long months in prison, and nothing had given him greater joy than removing the heavy padlocks and flinging open the windows, blowing away the cobwebs of his past folly. The studio resided in an ugly red-brick building, once used for the manufacture of ball bearings. Its walls were painted black. There was an ancient industrial heater which kept out the cold of Cambridge in the winter months, but now in the July heat its creaking and clattering was mercifully silent. Stacked against the walls were dozens of paintings and the open loft space held still more of them. The far section of the studio was given over to wood and machinery for framing, and Will employed a reserved young man called Ian who came in once a week to make frames.

Somewhere above Will could hear a buzzing sound, and presently a bumble bee lumbered into sight and circled the room. Its wings caught the golden beams from a skylight and motes of dust scintillated around it. Will walked over to the window, remembering an old man painting in a prison cell. A bee had flown in from the outside that day, and the old man had stood frozen with his brush in his hand, watching it intently.

"He can come and go as he likes, my boy."

Will's memory of Alfred was oddly clear in his mind, triggered by the bumbling insect and the familiar smell of paint. They had vowed to keep in touch when they came out of prison, but Will had never heard from the old man again. He felt a little hurt by this and he wrinkled his chin.

A car outside tooted a reprimand at a devil-may-care cyclist, bringing Will back to earth. Through the glass he could see occasional cars passing by, and further away the spire of a church which tolled a bell on Sundays to summon the faithful. The bee bumped impatiently on the glass. Will unhooked the casement latch and let it tumble out into the English summer. He leaned after it and watched it diminish into the distance, feeling the sun hot on his face. Then he looked down and watched the pedestrians, noting the play of light and shadow; solitary figures in poses; animated couples talking; complementary colours.

A young brunette stopped and looked in the window of his studio. Will had put an advert for a new model in his window that morning and he realised that she was reading it. A tantalizing glimpse of skin was exposed at her midriff. She was wearing a yellow skirt and a white top which had spaghetti straps to expose her brown arms. She glanced up as if feeling his eyes upon her and he toasted her solemnly with his mug of tea. She smiled but then spun on her heel and walked away.

He stepped back from the window and put his tea down on the table beside the easel with undue force so that it slopped over a little. He looked at the unfinished picture crossly. He would have to take a break and paint something else.

He riffled the brushes in their jugs; long flats, thick rounds and 00-grade riggers. There was a pot of spatulas for mixing paint on the palette, and a bottle of turpentine. There were drying enhancers and various oils, some of which he used daily; others that he had bought on a whim and never opened. An array of large oil paint tubes lay next to a battered biscuit tin filled with smaller ones, some of them squeezed empty. Beside a large mirror on a wooden stand there stood a vase of yellow freesias that his friend Anna had brought to the studio. He glared at them, wondering if he should paint them instead.

The door banged downstairs and the stairs creaked – it would be Anna, popping in after her morning surgery. He would ask *her* opinion about the painting. But someone knocked on the door so it wasn't Anna.

Will crossed the studio and opened the door to the girl in the lemon skirt that he had seen on the pavement. She had come back.

"I'm looking for the artist," she said a little breathlessly.

Will stepped back.

"You've found him," he said. "I'm Will Bentley."

"My name's Sandy Lennox," she said. "I saw the advert in your window for a life model and I thought that's me! I could do that."

She was nervous.

He stood aside to let her in.

"Have you done any modelling before?"

"Not as such, but I thought, how difficult can it be? My friend used to do modelling for the art classes over at King's. She said it's all right once you get used to it; you don't have to do anything except keep still. And take your clothes off, obviously."

He scrutinised her until she began to appear uncomfortable.

"Good face," he said absently, picking up the bonnet from his recently vacated model's chair. "Just pop this on and we'll see how you look in it."

"Have I got the job then?"

"Not until I see if you can sit still. You have to get used to me staring at you. People find it peculiar at first."

She giggled shyly.

"Loads of blokes stare at me."

She put on the bonnet and tied the silk ties in a bow beneath her chin. She looked very sweet in it. Will handed her a pair of racing binoculars to hold. Then he realigned the model's chair with the chalk marks on the studio floor, sat the girl down and looked critically at her.

"You need to sit back and relax," he said. "You're perched on the edge of your chair like it's red hot." She shifted her position obediently and he nodded. "That's better. Make sure you're comfortable and we'll try a five-minute sketch."

She blushed.

"Don't I need to change or anything?"

"Not for this picture because we're just practising. Now then, hold up the binoculars and look at me. Can you look impish? A little cheeky and try to flirt a bit. We want the person looking at the picture to think you're flirting with them."

She was a natural. She dropped her face and looked up at him with raised eyebrows, a smile on her lips.

"That's *perfect*," he said, hearing his voice as if it was not his own. "Now all you've got to do is hold the pose."

He raised the easel clamp and swung the large wet canvas out of the way, replacing it with a board on which he swiftly taped a sheet of paper. Then he grabbed a stick of charcoal and stared intently at Sandy for a few seconds.

"Can I talk?" she asked.

"Not to start with for a portrait," he said. "You can for figure work but not while I'm catching the lines of your face. Fix your eyes on something – it's easier to keep still."

She sat demurely on the chair, looking at him coquettishly, holding up the field glasses. It was a strange experience for her being drawn; very intimate with just the two of them. He began to draw with swift, confident strokes using the point of the charcoal, rubbing with his finger to soften and smudge lines and turning the stick on its side to block in the darks. After five minutes he stopped, as good as his word.

"Relax."

She stood up and stretched.

"It doesn't half make your bum ache sitting so still."

She came round and looked at the drawing, her mouth falling open.

"You've got me spot on," she said in genuine wonderment. "That's amazing!"

Will was not immune to flattery and an hour later Sandy had her first modelling assignment. She wore the black dress of the girl at Ascot, and it fitted her better than Will's previous model, emphasizing her bust and the curve of her hips. She stood as if she had been modelling all her life. The hat shaded her eyes from the bright daylight spot lamp that illuminated her. She held a champagne flute with water in it.

"Aren't you going to fill it up with bubbly?" she had asked with mock innocence.

"This time I'll just paint the bubbles in," he said solemnly. "But if I sell it I promise I'll buy you a bottle."

He held a clutch of paintbrushes. There was a large flat loaded with a mixture of ultramarine and burnt umber. He was using it for various background darks. Then there were two thinner flats with pale blue and pale grey for dress highlights, and another loaded with yellow. Once he had the dress blocked in he switched to skin tones, starting on the cheek with a mixture of Naples yellow and alizarin crimson, and spreading down the face, adjusting the skin tone with ochre and cadmium orange so that it was never constant. Frequently he would take a skin colour and touch it into the background, or drop it into the paler folds of the dress. He also echoed the dark of the dress onto top hats in the crowd. Every half an hour he paused to let Sandy stretch her legs, and in these intervals they would talk, chiefly because Sandy was turning out to be very inquisitive.

"How long have you been doing this then?" she asked during the first break, looking at the emerging picture in awe.

He was cleaning a pair of brushes, ready to reload them with fresh paint.

"I started when I was 14," he said. "Sold my first painting and never looked back."

She slyly examined him while he cleaned the brushes. He must be in his late thirties – she was only 28 – but he certainly was good-looking in an arty kind of way. She quite fancied him, but more than once her boyfriend Barry had slapped her for even *looking* at another man, or had taken someone outside for staring at her in a pub. She would have to keep this job to herself or Barry would be around here and half murder him, especially if he found out about her having to take her clothes off. Which was plain stupid, because Will Bentley was a perfect gentleman and hadn't given her the eye; or at least no more than most men did.

They learned more about each other as the morning progressed. If she moved and upset the line or the angle then he would rage at her, but forget it all immediately and be so charming that she quickly forgave him. When he was painting he forgot about everything else, and as she was "looking out of the canvas" she was able to stare at him just as much as he stared at her.

He had tied his dark hair back into a loose ponytail to keep it out of his eyes while he worked. He had naturally tanned skin, as if Spanish blood ran in his veins. He had high cheekbones and a chiselled face, with a dark growth of stubble on his unshaven chin. He wore a silver stud in his ear. He wasn't quite big enough or muscled enough for her taste, and was only her height, though she was tall, nearly six feet. When she asked him if he had a wife he told her he had nearly married a girl called Fiona Ruskin, but they'd split up. He'd done some paintings for her old man and then had ended up in jail on a charge of forgery.

"Best year of my life," Will told Sandy as he carefully painted a curve. "Not the prison, that was bloody awful. But I met a bloke in prison who was a *real* forger. A man called Alfred."

She noticed that when he was concentrating he stuck his tongue out and licked his lower lip, and it reminded her of her dad, who used to do the same thing when he was picking the winners for his Saturday flutter on the races. It was rather endearing.

"Were *you* a forger, then?" she asked curiously.

"I certainly was not," he said, but then smiled sheepishly. "Though of course we all say we didn't do it."

"How come you got locked up for it then?" Sandy persisted, not one to give up that easily.

"Because Fiona's father swore blind that I did it and he didn't know anything about it," Will said in bitter memory. "And they all believed him because he was Lord Bloody Ruskin. That was when I realised that everyone's corrupt. Innocent until proved guilty my arse. If he'd been some old tramp and I'd been the eighth earl of whatever, it would have been the other way around."

"A real *lord*," she said, impressed but then noticing his expression and rearranging her features hurriedly.

"So what was it like in prison then?"

"I'll tell you later," he said, adjusting the canvas before him so that the light didn't shine on the wet paint. "First we've got to get a bit further with this little beauty."

TWO

It is a wonderful moment in the life of a lover of art when he finds himself suddenly confronted with a hitherto unknown painting by a great master, untouched, on the original canvas, and without any restoration, just as it left the painter's studio! And what a picture! Neither the beautiful signature...nor the pointillé on the bread which Christ is blessing, is necessary to convince us that what we have here is – I am inclined to say – THE masterpiece of Johannes Vermeer of Delft...
DR. ABRAHAM BREDIUS, Mauritshuis Museum, November 1937

Lucy Wrackham was sitting in her office at Hoffman and Courtland, which was located in an elegant six-storey block in Bishopsgate, London, just down the road from Liverpool Street station. She was carefully slicing a lemon with a black-handled paring knife. When she had picked the pips out one of the slices, she lifted it carefully on the side of the knife and dropped it into a glass of iced mineral water. She sipped from the glass, and then frowned. A droplet of water had splashed out of the glass, ejected by the arrival of the lemon, and had landed on her framed photograph of David. She picked up the silver frame, took a tissue from the box on her desk and wiped away the droplet. She rarely looked at the picture any more, but removing it would seem like betrayal. Her husband had died three years previously, and she had run through a common pattern of those suddenly bereaved: first shock and disbelief; then appalling months of grief followed by growing anger and bitterness at being left alone, and finally despair. After nine months she had emerged slowly from her depression and her employer had taken her back from her leave of absence. Ordinarily they may have been less generous, but her husband had worked for them as a fraud investigator prior to his untimely death, so they were constrained not by law but by the stronger bond of moral obligation.

Hoffman and Courtland insured fine art. The company was started by two gentlemen, Mr Hoffman and Mr Courtlandt, who came to England from the Dutch East Indies in 1897. The "t" was dropped from the end of Courtlandt's name in 1908, because the English gentry misspelled the name and it was deemed bad for business. From the start the company had insured art and had prospered. Now it occupied the entire fourth floor of the stately old building, and Lucy's exclusive office faced out onto Bishopsgate as a reward for her unparalleled efficiency in recovering lost or stolen works. The irony was that she now had David's job.

When he was found dead she had been an assessor for Hoffmans, valuing works of art all around the country. She and David had been married then for almost two years. David had been Hoffman's investigator of insurance fraud, a role in which he worked hand in hand with the Art and Antiquities department of the Metropolitan Police. He and Lucy had been contemplating children, but like all newly-weds they were struggling with the problem of going from two salaries down to one, and Lucy didn't want to abandon her career. She sat at her desk with the picture of David in her hands and shook her head a little, remembering. How he had not answered his phone and she had eventually called the police and reported him missing. The discovery of his body in the Thames, and having to identify his bloated corpse from his single remaining shoe because he was unrecognizable. She had been sick on the floor from the smell of him. The DNA analysis had subsequently confirmed his identity, and the post mortem had identified his death not from drowning but from a severe blow to the head. They'd found his car up river and his blood on the stanchion of a nearby bridge, as if he'd taken a dive off, or been pushed. The police had been unable to prove foul play and the coroner had returned an open verdict, though the media had invented many lurid explanations, ranging from suicide to murder. They had followed Lucy every day for weeks, printing long-lens photographs of her stricken face, starting with her as victim and then accusing her of his murder.

She put down the photo frame in a measured way and stood up as if physically to disconnect herself – she hadn't gone back over it all like this for many months and she felt a little light-headed, as when at the height of her stress and anger she had experienced palpitations. She gulped down the entire glass of iced water and placed it carefully on the desk, then looked around the room, seeking to clear her head. She breathed deeply and made herself relax, deliberately focusing on everyday objects in the room. It was a pleasant enough place to work. She had two framed prints of old masters on the walls; a pretty Mary Cassatt "At the Theatre", and the Frans Hals of a young man with a skull; the outstretched hand demonstrating the artist's mastery of foreshortening.

In the centre space on the long wall, Lucy had with a touch of irony placed a print by the Dutch forger Han van Meegeren. It was "Christ at Emmaus", which van Meegeren considered his greatest work, painted on genuine 17th century canvas in the style of Vermeer. It recounted the story of the newly resurrected Christ appearing before two of his disciples in the village of Emmaus. Van Meegeren's forgery had been authenticated in 1937 by the renowned museum director Abraham Bredius, nicknamed "the Pope" because his opinion was taken as gospel in the pre-war art world.

A rare signed limited-edition Picasso print took pride of place on Lucy's inner wall, opposite the window. It was screwed to the wall and only she knew that it was genuine, for she felt sure that Security would insist on its removal had they but known its value. Below the wall of pictures there was a long wooden bookcase full of art reference books and price guides. Next to it was a round table. Beneath the window and to one side was her desk, bearing a docked laptop computer and a very large screen which she used to examine digital images of paintings. Next to the computer was a phone, a flip-catalogue of business cards and a wooden pot filled with sharp pencils and fine-pointed pens. Everything was perfectly aligned and the room was spotless. She had always been a tidy person, but since David's death she had been obsessively tidy – it was as if keeping her life in order would eradicate that terrible period of loss after his death, when she had spoken to no-one for weeks at a time and had let herself go.

Lucy sat down at the desk again, feeling calmer. She opened her post. The only item of interest was an invitation to a private view at the Limerston Gallery in the Kings Road. She put the invitation in her bag to consider later and opened the green file in front of her, but before she could take out the first page her secretary Vicky Bowles appeared in the doorway.

"Is your phone on divert?" Vicky asked. "I've got Hugh Davies from the Met on the line and he says you keep going into voicemail."

Lucy looked at the phone and pressed two keys.

"Sorry," she said. "I'm trying to avoid that awful man from Sotheby's. He won't accept that we've nothing in common and keeps calling me."

Vicky rolled her eyes and disappeared.

Lucy had recently broken up with her boyfriend Sam, with whom she had been living for the last seven months. The relationship had been the first since David, and she had kept Sam at arm's length, as if falling in love might be a betrayal. It had been a bitter parting – she had found him in bed with her best friend Millie, so Sam was now off the scene and since that awful night she hadn't spoken to Millie either, though she missed her terribly. She missed Sam too, but somehow she had known that this first new relationship was never going to work out. Sam was too much like David, but time and trauma had changed her and she couldn't be the woman she was then.

The phone interrupted her thoughts and Lucy answered it to hear a loud Welsh voice.

"My God, woman, you're a bugger to get hold of."

She smiled into the mouthpiece. Davies was a policeman, charming and a little scruffy. He worked for the Metropolitan Police's art crimes investigative unit, and he was married to Carol; an overweight Englishwoman whom he adored. He was very genuine and tended to lighten her mood, so she was fond of him although his messiness irked her.

"Hello Hugh," she said. "My phone's on divert because I'm trying to avoid a frightful lawyer at Sotheby's that I went out with *one single time*." She spaced out the last three words. "I'm sure he must want to auction me off since he can't have me."

"Don't get me started on the subject of auction houses," Davies said darkly, and then he cleared his throat. "I want to talk to you about something else. It's a bit odd, really."

"Fire away then."

"Do you remember the Alma-Tadema that was stolen a few months ago?"

"I was going to say no," she said, wrinkling her brow. "But you don't mean one of *ours*, do you?"

"Not a Hoffman, no. It was covered by North's. It was nicked in transit from America, on loan to one of the London galleries. We never found the culprits and it was a bit embarrassing."

"So what's the big mystery?"

"It turned up," Davies said. "In a gents' toilet in Islington, wrapped in a brown-paper parcel. The local coppers got a tip off."

"That's nice for you. Any idea who did it?"

"None at all. They managed to pick the only bit of London left which doesn't have CCTV."

Lucy thought for a moment.

"Well, so far as North's are concerned, the picture is back so they're happy," she said pragmatically. "They won't have to pay out so they'll just breathe a sigh of relief."

"I won't argue with you on that. But you know what occurred to me while I was looking at the picture? What about that Frans Snyders that Hoffmans paid out on last year?"

"We didn't pay out on it," Lucy said automatically. "Well we *almost* did, but then it was – oh, I see what you mean."

"Then it turned up, didn't it?" Davies said. "Wrapped in brown paper, found in Harrods with a note saying 'Sorry'."

"Brown paper packages tied up with strings," Lucy said thoughtfully, running a pencil through her blonde tightly-pinned hair. "That's a coincidence."

"That's what I thought too," Davies said. "So I did a bit of detecting for a change instead of filling in forms. I managed to get hold of the paper that the Frans Snyders painting had been wrapped in. They had it in a box in the depths of Cannon Row nick. I sent it off to forensics, and they had a look at the fibres under a microscope. It turns out it's from the same roll."

She frowned. "How very peculiar. So someone is stealing famous pictures, hanging on to them for a while and then giving them back. I don't suppose you've still got the Alma-Tadema?"

"As it happens I have. North's asked me to lock it up until Tuesday because their authenticator has gone off for a weekend in Bruges, if you please. Do you fancy popping around to my office for a bit of an art show?"

THREE

To tell the secrets of my prison-house,
I could a tale unfold whose lightest word
Would harrow up thy soul, freeze thy young blood,
Make thy two eyes, like stars, start from their spheres
WILLIAM SHAKESPEARE, Hamlet

Will painted Sandy until early afternoon. Then he paid her from an old metal box full of cash. She changed back into her ordinary clothes behind a screen in the corner. For a moment as she dressed he glimpsed naked thigh and yellow underwear, and his blood quickened. She had an interesting face, with a long neck, mid-length straight brown hair and a frequently mischievous look. She could look happy or sad. He knew that once he got to know her she would be a great model, because she had that rare and perfect quality that is essential; a good figure and a captivating face.

To the casual observer the painting of Sandy in her black dress and bonnet was complete, and it was only the sea of heads in the background that still revealed glimpses of the original charcoal drawing. But Will knew better. Once the first layer was dry he would be making fine adjustments for another week or so, though he would continue with other work in between.

"That's it for now," he said, surveying the picture. "Besides, I need some coffee."

"Want to go out for one?" Sandy said. "I never sat still for so long. Let me sort out your face though. It's covered in smudges."

She picked up a cloth and cleaned away the charcoal smudges from the side of his nose. It was a strangely intimate gesture for someone who had just met him, but he said nothing.

He locked the studio door and they walked through the Cambridge streets to her favourite coffee bar.

"So what actually happened, then?" Sandy asked him as they walked. "I mean, call me nosey, but you said you didn't do it. Seems a bit much if your girlfriend's father stitched you up."

"*Fiancée's* father," Will said darkly. "We were engaged. I first met Ruskin as a client. He wanted some *trompe l'oeil* done in his house."

He sensed her blank look rather than saw it.

"Where you do wall paintings that look like something real, such as painting a window on a blank wall. At Chatsworth House in Derbyshire there's a *trompe l'oeil* of a violin hanging on a door which was painted nearly 300 years ago. I saw it once – it's pretty amazing."

"Doesn't it just look like a picture though?"

"You'd think so, but this guy didn't just paint the violin; he painted the hook it was supposed to be hanging from and the shadow it cast on the door."

"Bit of a clever clogs."

"Yes. So Ruskin contacted me, and I thought, why not? I went to see him and discovered that he was richer than King Midas. He lived in a great big mansion set in two or three hundred acres, with a banqueting hall and a chapel and everything else you can think of. It was old as well, it had a priest's-hole in the chapel; he showed me once. And the house was supposed to be haunted, I remember. A young housemaid had been crushed under the wheels of a carriage, and she used to be seen in a certain corridor at night."

Sandy's eyes were round again.

"Did you ever see her?"

"Not me, but I talked to people that swore blind they'd seen her. Anyway, I painted the panels in the banqueting hall for his lordship, and then I did some religious pictures for the chapel. It took me months and Fiona used to pop in to see how I was getting on. One thing led to another."

They arrived at the street café Sandy had been thinking of. It was luring people off the street with the aroma of hot pastries. They ordered and sat down outside. There were two female students and a young man of about twenty at the next table, drinking iced coffee and earnestly discussing Dionysian rites and their relationship to Greek tragedy. You could tell you were in Cambridge. Next to them were a man and a woman with a very old Scottie dog. A third table contained two elegant women in their thirties, festooned with shopping bags. A father and his teenage son sat at the fourth table, casting surreptitious glances at Sandy as she and Will sat down. Will glared at them until they looked away, and when he looked back Sandy was smiling at him.

"Want a bit of my Danish pastry?" he asked, for she had taken nothing with her coffee.

"I'd love to, but I've got to watch my weight," she said. "Can't have a fat bird as a model!"

They sat and watched Cambridge pass by, and Will felt the flagstones radiating stored heat into the soles of his shoes. To one side of them was a blue and gold railing, beyond which the dark waters of the Cam slid languidly by. A "No Bicycles" sign shimmered with reflected light from the river.

"So one thing led to another with this Fiona, did it?" Sandy prompted, stirring the foamy milk topping into her coffee.

"Pretty much," Will nodded, smiling inwardly at Sandy's apparently insatiable curiosity. "Fiona was a good-looking girl but she spent money like water, and I started to worry that I couldn't afford her. She had a private plane, for God's sake! I was getting into debt trying to pay my share, so I don't suppose it would ever have worked out."

Sandy tutted in sympathy.

"Probably a blessing in disguise," she said. "So tell me about forging. It sounds dead exciting."

"I did it for her old man," Will said, looking into the middle distance. "He asked me to copy an old painting. He even gave me an old canvas to paint it on so it would look authentic. He said he wasn't sure I could do it, but he'd like to see how I got on. I suppose it was a challenge to my pride, so I painted the best damn copy of that painting you ever saw in your life, and he took it away and gave me a lot of money for it. And I mean a *lot* of money. I didn't sign it with the original name, I signed it with mine, but I dare say he had someone scrape off my signature and put on a copy of the original. I was pretty stupid, looking back."

"So it was just the one picture?" Sandy said, her mouth a little open as she listened.

"Oh no, I did loads of them. I should have asked what was happening to them, but I was doing these copies and enjoying it – you learn a lot from copying the masters – and the money had sorted out the debt problem, so I was fine whichever way you looked at it. Ruskin told me he was flogging them to a gallery owner in London, and he forgot to mention they were passing them off as the real thing. He gave me this story about how people pay a lot of money for high-quality copies, and I never suspected a bloody thing."

"Well, you wouldn't when he was all lined up to be your father in law," she said sympathetically. "He sounds like a wicked old sod. So when did it all go wrong, then?"

"One Christmas," Will said. I'd just finished a painting and it was sitting there on the easel, still wet and not yet signed. It was freezing cold even though the heater was roaring away; I remember I was wearing fingerless gloves, like Fagin. So there I am in the studio, when suddenly it's swarming with policemen. They took away a ton of my work and arrested me for forgery. I couldn't believe it. Ruskin visited me and was full of outrage. He'd get me out in a jiffy, all that sort of thing. He set me up with a lawyer he knew and like a fool I accepted. Well, the next thing I know I'm in the dock swearing blind I never signed the pictures, and his lordship has a very different story and two witnesses lined up to agree with him. He got off on some legal technicality because he had the best defence in town. My lawyer turned out to be a complete idiot and the next thing I knew I was sent down for two years.

"You got well stitched up," Sandy said.

He nodded.

"It was only a year in the end though," he went on. "They let you out halfway through if you behave yourself."

They finished their coffee and strolled through the streets, ignoring the cyclists that weaved expertly between pedestrians. Sandy Lennox made men stare, Will observed, and he felt an odd male pride to be with her. The sun was hot on their backs, slanting down between the stately college buildings. There was the thrumming sound of cycle tyres and the hum of traffic, and the occasional cadence of mobile phones. A siren wailed in the distance. They passed a candle shop and the pungent odour of citrus assailed their nostrils. Sandy stopped and enthused over the shop's contents, but Will disliked the heavy scent and wouldn't go in. They crossed the street and entered one of the colleges, soothed by the quiet cloisters, but the cobbles were uneven under their feet and Sandy was wobbling on high heels.

"My feet are killing me," she moaned, gesturing at a wooden seat. "Can we sit down for a minute?"

So they sat down and she took off her high-heels and stretched out her naked toes, while Will looked at her wiggling them and chuckled.

"So what happened with this Fiona?" she said, wanting to know how the story ended.

"She walked out on me straight away. The moment I was sent down she broke off the engagement. Then Ruskin took out injunctions so that I couldn't even *see* her without being in breach of something or other. Not that I wanted to see either of them ever again. It took me the whole year to calm down."

"What happened to your friend you mentioned though; the forger bloke?"

"Alfred," Will said. "He was what made it worth going to prison, but that was later. The first six months were hell because I was locked up with all these blokes who were either nutters or as vicious as they come. At one point I thought I wasn't going to survive, but I got a bit of a reputation for doing pictures and that got me off."

"How come?"

"Well, I was in trouble, to tell you the truth. A few of them started calling me a bloody nancy boy and deliberately picking on me. I can hold my own all right, but not against five ugly blokes who want to kill you. I was beaten up a couple of times. It was looking bad. Then I met a man called Lewis."

"Who was he then, another prisoner?"

Will nodded, gesturing wide with his hands.

"A big guy. About six foot eight and an ex-bouncer, but with a temper if someone got `unreasonable'. He was in for GBH."

"Sounds charming," Sandy said with irony.

Will chuckled. "Yes, but the funny thing is that he was an old softy really. His mum was in a nursing home in Bexhill and of course he couldn't go and see her. She was getting on and couldn't come and see him. He really missed her and I saw a picture of her that he had in his cell, so I offered to draw her for him. She was a nice old stick and it was a good photo. Besides, I badly needed a friend."

"What did he say?"

"He was very suspicious at first, me being "that bloody nancy boy". He knew what was happening, you see. Prison picks on some people and they had decided to pick on me. But he let me borrow the photograph to have a go at, and told me he'd tear me limb from limb if anything happened to it. So I did a full-sized drawing of his mum, and gave it to him. You should have seen it; this great big man and he had tears in his eyes."

"Aah," said Sandy, her eyes bright. "And did he stick up for you after that?"

"He put out the word that I was off limits, and smacked one or two people around when they didn't listen. I thought they'd just get him in a corner and set upon him, but you didn't pick a fight with Lewis unless you wanted to end up taking your food through a straw.

"He sounds nice in a funny way," Sandy said. "Caring about his mum like that. So nobody could touch Lewis, which meant that nobody could touch you?"

"That's about the size of it. I got on without any problem after that. In fact, I ended up drawing many of the blokes who'd been gunning for me originally. Once I was accepted by Lewis, the rest of them weren't really up for a fight.

"Then I got transferred to Ford prison down in Sussex. I think they'd decided I wasn't going to make trouble, and Ford is an open prison. Alfred was there, as it turned out. I was a bit worried because I didn't know what to expect, and Lewis stayed at the old place so I had to say goodbye to him."

"Did the forger bloke protect you in the new place, then?" Sandy asked.

Will laughed out loud.

"Two things," he said. "First of all, Alfred was sixty-five even then, so he wasn't up to offering protection to anyone at all. And the second thing is that open prison is completely different. You get your own cell instead of having to share one, and it's full of low-risk prisoners who don't want to make trouble. Crooked politicians and financial fraudsters. You can walk in and out if you want to, you see. It's what's called rehabilitating you into normal society. Everyone's keeping their nose clean so they can get out. I used to go to the local theatre and paint the scenery. Best damn scenery they ever had while I was there."

"But I don't get it," Sandy said. "What was so amazing about this Alfred?"

"We did have a bit in common," Will said, grinning sheepishly. "As I say, Alfred was a *real* forger, not like me; I was just bloody naive and got stitched up. He'd been doing it all his life and was very good at it, and only in the last few years did they notice the extraordinary number of old masters that were being discovered. He used to say that half the old master pictures in circulation are copies. He aimed for the ones that weren't so well known, and he knew all the tricks, believe me. I learned a lot from him."

She began to giggle suddenly.

"So he taught you how to forge pictures while you were in *prison*," she said.

He gave her a mock-serious look.

"They let us paint because it was considered to be therapy for our deranged minds," he said. "Alfred would paint all day and so would I, so we got to know each other. Except that he was *brilliant*. I've never seen anything like it. He could do Titian or Caravaggio or Monet, right out of his head and you'd swear it was the original. He knew all about ageing the pictures as well, so that you could only prove they were copies if you analysed them."

"I never understand half what you're on about," she said. "You mean he used to make copies of the old paintings? Don't they know straight away if you do that nowadays?"

Will grinned.

"You'd think they would but they don't. They test the well-known paintings, that's true; but they don't test them all. You can still make a tidy profit copying work from people most of us have never heard of. In fact, Alfred was doing very nicely until they managed to trace a sale back to him and raided his place."

Sandy slipped her feet back into her strappy heels and they set off again through the cloisters. The chapel clock chimed and Sandy suddenly realised that she was late meeting her boyfriend, so she made hurried apologies and departed in a rush. Will found himself walking back to the studio by himself, contemplating the last few hours spent with this intriguing, inquisitive young woman.

FOUR

Well, he would, wouldn't he?
MANDY RICE-DAVIES, as a witness at the trial of Stephen Ward on hearing that Lord Astor denied her allegations of impropriety

The Metropolitan Police's Art and Antiques Unit gathers information about art crime and targets criminals at the top of their profession. It is based in Wellington House in Buckingham Gate, right next to the passport office and not far from the tranquil lawns and green waters of St. James Park. It took Lucy twenty minutes to get there in a taxi, and a further ten to be logged in at reception and collected by Hugh Davies. They were pleased to see each other and he shepherded her up to his tiny office. As usual it was chaotic; covered with a disordered jumble of books and files and newspaper cuttings.

"Right then," he said, rather enjoying the drama and not noticing her distaste as she took in her surroundings. "Sit down, make yourself at home and I'll go and get the picture from the safe. Would you like one of our delightful cups of coffee or tea? We've got a special machine that mixes the two together, which is quite unusual really."

She declined this generous offer, sat on the hard visitor's chair and waited. In a few minutes Davies returned with a flat cardboard container.

"I popped it in here to keep the dirt off."

He put it on the desk and opened it up. The picture was fitted into a custom-made compartment between foam layers. Davies extracted the picture and leaned it on a low shelf against the wall.

"Good Lord," she said. "This is the Egyptian Juggler! I was expecting one of the less well-known ones. So it was found in an Islington lavatory. How was it lost?"

"It's normally in a private collection," Davies said. "But it was on loan to a London gallery and it disappeared in transit."

"Disappeared?"

"The perpetrators must have followed the art removals van that picked it up. When the driver and his mate stopped at a motorway service area, someone clipped them on the head. When they woke up the van was empty and various pictures were gone, including this one."

"What happened to the rest of them?"

"Some of them were sold anonymously way below the asking price, and have since turned up again. Some have never been recovered. This one you know about."

"So you don't actually know that they set out to steal *this* one," Lucy pointed out. "They might have been after one of the others and this one got taken."

"That's true, but the brown paper makes it look calculated. And this was the only piece that had real value."

"So they would have taken the others to cover up, or else just to make a bit of extra cash."

She took a close look at the picture. It was familiar to her from study but she had never before seen the original painting. It was signed and dated 1870. It showed an Egyptian clad in loin cloth and head dress, incongruously juggling eggs in front of seated observers. The figure was beautifully rendered as in all of Alma-Tadema's work, but the picture lacked the Victorian sentimentality that detracted from much of his *oeuvre*. It also showed the painter's mastery of perspective through a receding line of marble columns, and his attention to fine detail in the ceiling decoration. Though he was a Dutchman he had been a close friend of Lord Leighton, then the president of the Royal Academy. Their styles showed many similarities.

Lucy picked up the picture very carefully by the edges and turned it over. The canvas was exposed at the rear and was clearly old. Without analysis it was difficult to tell how old, but over a century seemed likely.

"Well, it looks all right on first inspection," she said. "What do you think?"

"It looks like the real one to me," Davies nodded cautiously. "North's had photographs of the back and sides taken as a security precaution, and they arrived by courier just before you. If you hang on I'll fetch them."

He left the room and returned after a few minutes with a large A3 envelope. He put the photographs on the desk and they put the original painting beside them, lying in its protective box so that the back was uppermost.

"Identical," Davies said after a minute or two. "Well that's a relief, anyway."

"Looks like it," Lucy said absently, studying the photographs and then transferring her gaze to the back of the picture. She took the picture out of the box again and held it up to the light, trying to peer through it. She could not. Impulsively she brought it to her nose and sniffed it.

She nodded. "It smells right," she said. "I reckon you're lucky, Hugh. Have you got a plastic spatula?"

"You mean a sampler," Davies said. "No bloody chance of that in Art and Antiques, girl. But I could do you one of those wooden coffee stirrers, if that would be any good?"

"Go on then, and we won't tell North's," she said, and he disappeared to the kitchen. When he returned triumphantly with a flat wooden stick, she took it from him and inserted it very carefully into the back of the stretcher, between wood and canvas. She moved it along and then brought it out at an angle, extracting a little dust that had been trapped there.

"Plenty of filth," she said. "Always a good sign; accumulated dirt. Did the picture ever go through full lab tests?"

"I'm afraid not," Davies said ruefully. "Nothing to compare it with."

"Well, you could still test it, just to be quite certain," Lucy said. "Though it looks all right to me."

"It looks fine, except for the coincidence. I feel there must be a racket going on somewhere which is staring me in the face."

"Well test it then," she said. "You can't go wrong if you test it."

"You say that," Davies said gloomily, "but North's have asked me to hold it until after the weekend. Their MD explicitly told me *not* to test it."

"Well he would, wouldn't he? He doesn't want you to test it, because what if it turned out to be a forgery? They'd be in a spot of bother then, wouldn't they? They'd be back to square one with no picture. They'd still have to pay out."

"Exactly what I'm thinking," Davies said in the same melancholy tone. "But I can't test it without them knowing because they use the same labs as we do. They'd find out I didn't just hold it for them. Then again if I do nothing and it turns out that there *is* a scam going on, I've let the buggers get away with it."

There was a long silence in which they didn't catch each other's eye, and then finally did so.

"We could take it to the lab that Hoffmans uses," she said at last. "It's Marcello's in Richmond. I know the chief technician there; John Ellis. He's a good man and he'd do it on the quiet if I asked him to. I've put a great deal of work their way so he owes me. You'd be the police escort and we'd have to make sure we didn't damage it. Of course it would be highly irresponsible…'

"…but we'd know for sure," Davies finished. "If it turned out to be Alma-Tadema's original work then we could stop worrying about that Frans Snyders of yours that so mysteriously turned up in Harrods."

She hesitated, then nodded slowly.

"It would be good to know."

Davies nodded with her and stood up decisively.

"Then let's do it."

FIVE

The time of year when the devil comes and spews art over London
JOHN CONSTABLE, about the Royal Academy's Summer Exhibition

Anna Levy dropped by the studio when Will had only been back a few minutes from his stroll through the cloisters with Sandy Lennox. She came up the stairs and appeared with a shopping bag and a whippet on a leash. Anna was a vet and one of his oldest friends. He had been to college with her husband George, who now ran a small design studio on the edge of the city.

"We said we'd pop round and make dinner tonight," Anna reminded him, giving him an affectionate kiss on the cheek. Will tended to forget to eat when he was painting, so his friends would come around and cook for him rather than have him subsist on fast food, and in turn their walls were covered with his pictures. "George is coming round later so I thought I'd pop in anyway as I'm finished at the surgery. Say hello to Molly. She stepped on a broken bottle and she's just been stitched up."

Will ruffled Molly's ears and she gave him a grateful lick.

"Isn't she Judith's dog? I've never understood why Judith has a whippet. She seems to me more like the King Charles spaniel type. In fact she *looks* like a spaniel with that lugubrious expression."

Anna laughed. Judith was a friend of hers whom Will disliked.

"Yes, Molly would normally be in the surgery for the night, but Judith's house is on the way back so I thought we'd drop her off. And Judith was very sweet to take Molly off me when someone brought her in as a stray, so don't be so horrid."

"As long as Molly's not unkind to Beauty and the Beast," Will said, looking around for the studio cats. They had come from Anna too. Will had protested weakly at the time, but had succumbed to the argument that mice and paintings are incompatible.

Molly was too sorry for herself to contemplate the pursuit of cats. She hopped around the studio for a while, holding her bandaged leg off the ground, and then settled down in the corner wearing a mournful expression.

Anna opened a bottle of wine and found glasses. They clinked and drank, and then she walked over to the easel.

"Oh I *say*; this one's coming along nicely. What happened to the other girl? This doesn't look like her at all."

"She's gone," Will said shortly. "She took umbrage at a chance remark I made, and walked out yesterday."

"You *were* always being rude to her," Anna said in the girl's defence. "You ought to be nicer to your models. They don't exactly grow on trees. So where did this beauty come from, then? Have you bedded her yet?"

He smiled.

"She walked in off the street this morning," he said. "Very sweet, very nosy, name of Sandy. And in answer to your question, I haven't touched her but I must admit I wouldn't fight her off. She's a perfect peach."

"Looks pretty flirty, too," Anna said, studying the picture, "unless that was just wishful thinking on behalf of the painter."

She went into the kitchen and started preparing salmon in a lobster and prawn sauce. Both she and George liked cooking and were good at it, whereas Will's culinary skills were more of the sausage and chips variety. He started cleaning his brushes, then saw one little bit that needed doing before he forgot. Before he knew it he was in front of the easel again, painting in background millinery. Anna called something from the kitchen and appeared in the doorway when he didn't answer. She looked at him, lost in painting, then smiled and went back to her cooking, leaving him be. George turned up after a bit, took one look at Will and went to find his wife. He sniffed around the kitchen, trying to interfere with the sauce until she shooed him away.

"George!" Will said when George came out again. "You're looking very dapper. When did you arrive?"

"Um, a while ago," George said vaguely. He was clever but his absent-mindedness sometimes gave a contrary impression. Anna's practical nature was exactly what he needed – they suited each other perfectly. Today George had been meeting clients, so he was smartly dressed in a white shirt and tie, with dark trousers and a blazer. Normally he wore threadbare shorts and an ancient blue sailor's smock, as both he and Anna were keen sailors and kept a boat on the Norfolk coast. He had curly brown hair, still thick but turning grey at the temples. He was tall and good-looking and had studied art with Will at college. Now he was a graphic designer, doing business with the rash of software companies in Cambridge Science Park.

He stood in front of Will's latest picture.

"This girl looks like a new one. Who's she?"

"She *is* a new one," Will explained again. "Sandy Lennox. Good looking girl and very chatty. We ended up going for a coffee at Blake's."

"He scared the other poor girl off," Anna said, coming in with cutlery and taking charge. "Will, I need you to stop now and lay the table. I daren't take my eyes off the sauce or it'll spoil and George will say he told me so and then I'll have to stab him." She brandished a knife to make her point.

They sat down to dinner, and George went into raptures over the lobster and prawn sauce, which turned the salmon into something very special. Will poured a bottle of Pinot Noir from the studio's stock of wine. Then they did nothing but eat and drink for a while, watched accusingly from the corner by a salivating whippet.

"We popped down to London last weekend," George said, wiping his chin with a napkin. He had finished first because he tended to bolt his food. He helped himself to more salad. "Did a gallery tour. Started at the Academy and saw the Summer Exhibition."

"Too many crusty old RA pictures at the Summer Exhibition," Will said. "I don't understand why they don't close it to the RAs and have completely unknown people. It makes me sick."

"Me too," George said. "And half of them can't paint. If you see something God awful you can bet it's an RA picture."

"Well that's a bit unfair," Anna said. "A lot of the RA work is brilliant."

"And a lot isn't," Will said. "But I'll concede that some of it is pretty good. So where else did you go?"

"Oh, all over the place," George said absently. "Where did we go, Anna?"

"Round the corner to the Fleming," Anna said.

"The Scottish painters?"

"Yes. One or two nice pieces, as always. Then we went over to the Angel Gallery, because George had managed to get an invite for a private view from one of his clients. Have you been lately?"

"I don't think I've ever been," Will said. "*Rupert* Angel, you mean? That huge glass-fronted place? I only ever met him once and talked to him about Vermeer. He was talking twaddle so I put him right. Everybody seems to worship Vermeer these days, and I'll grant you he was a great painter, but only about 35 paintings survive. Not exactly a lifetime's work."

"He probably painted loads more than that but they haven't survived," Anna pointed out. "And besides, one of them was Girl with a Pearl Earring." Will gave a conceding shrug and a small smile of acknowledgement.

"I suppose so. And how was Mr Pompous Stuffed-up Angel?"

"I thought he was all right, actually," George said. "Seemed decent enough. He was going on about their latest find; some young artist. I saw some of his work and it was pretty good. Angel doesn't go in for all these unmade beds and body parts in Perspex. He said to me: show me an unmade bed that's going to be there in five hundred years. He has a point."

"He certainly does," Will agreed fervently. "He was still talking a load of populist nonsense about Vermeer, though. That's what I despise about today's art world. It's not who you are and what you do; it's *when* you were around or how much you've been hyped. Anything which is Dutch is divine, even if it's some appalling old tat that has got through the years unscathed by some miracle. The sort of thing the painter would have *burned* if he'd thought for a moment it might survive."

"Well, he might be quite pleased," George said undiplomatically.

"Then he'd be a puffed up, self-opinionated idiot," Will said shortly.

"I wonder if there are artists like that around today?" Anna said, smiling with disarming sweetness.

Much later when Anna and George were long gone, Will lay awake. The night clouds were like an ice field breaking into ice flows, between which the inky sky showed like freezing water. Stars twinkled in the dark like the eyes of fabulous subterranean beasts. He didn't remember falling asleep, but he dreamed of prison and Alfred Smith. His brain remorselessly stepped him through each empty cell, hearing the clang of bars as he looked for an old man who was never there.

SIX

There is no harm in repeating a good thing
PLATO

Marcello's was a low single-storey building that was an ugly container for the beautiful paintings that passed through its doors. Built of cheap concrete blocks in the 1960s, it had been whitewashed in an effort to make it look better, but with little improvement. The corners were made of larger blocks still, so they stuck out like supporting buttresses. The guttering and drainpipes were black and the whole edifice was surrounded by a heavy-duty steel fence topped with razor wire. The tall gates at the front were electrically locked and further protected by a security guard during the day. It was a hot day and the air-conditioning inside Davies' unmarked police car was on maximum as he cruised slowly down the road towards the entrance.

"Sorry it's so bloody hot," Davies said to Lucy, as if he personally were responsible for the heat wave. He turned in at the gate and halted in front of the barrier. The gate man came out of his booth and Lucy opened her window and leaned out.

"Hello Bob, how are you doing?"

"Mrs Wrackham!" the gate man said. "It's always a pleasure to see you. Mr Ellis told me you were dropping in this afternoon." He gestured to the car. "And who is this gentleman?"

Davies showed him his identification and they were waved through. When the van was parked they extracted a large silver travelling case containing the painting. It was heavy and Davies puffed a little as he carried it in.

John Ellis met them on the steps. He had just a hint of a Yorkshire accent, watered down by forty years in London. He was in his late fifties, very tanned but with hair already as white as snow. He wore a white lab coat to match his hair and there was a pair of goggles in his top pocket. He greeted Lucy warmly and was introduced to Davies. They went inside, feeling the air-conditioning snatch away the heat. They were issued with guest passes and then followed Ellis past the reception. He waved his pass at the lab door and it glided open. Beyond it was another door, like an airlock. When they went through it the temperature cooled further and there was the subdued hum of machinery. The test laboratory was all white and steel, belying the primitive look of the outside of the building. There was a single decoration: a calendar from one of the London museums showing Van Gogh's "Café at Night".

"You were lucky to catch me here," Ellis was saying. "The wife and I have only just got back from holiday."

"How is Audrey?" Lucy asked.

"She's fine. We went down to Seville for a couple of weeks with the kids. Pretty warm." He directed Davies to a large white table and Davies laid the protective case carefully on it.

"Lovely place; have you ever been?" Ellis went on, pulling on a pair of surgeon's gloves. Lucy had been there but Davies hadn't. They chatted about Seville for a minute or two.

"So what have you got here then?" Ellis said at last. "I was rather intrigued by your telephone call, Lucy. "What's the big secret?"

She hesitated, deciding to be straight with him so that he could refuse to test the painting if he wanted to.

"It's an Alma-Tadema and we want to see if it's genuine," she began. "It *looks* as if it is but we want to make absolutely sure. The reason for the secrecy is because we're being a bit naughty. It isn't a Hoffman picture. Hugh here has it in custody for the weekend but it's with North's and not us. So we're not supposed to be testing it, and I'd quite understand if you'd rather not do so under the circumstances."

"North's?" Ellis said scornfully. "They use that shower in Uxbridge to test all their stuff. I went there once – the place wasn't clean and security was lax. Anyway, it won't hurt to take a quick look, now you've come all the way here."

Hugh avoided mentioning that his own office also used that shower in Uxbridge. Ellis snapped the four catches on the metal case and opened it very carefully. He lifted off the protective black foam; then a layer of anti-static acid-free paper; and after a few more layers exposed the Alma-Tadema. He contemplated it.

"Nice little painting, that," he said. "I've never tested any of this chap's work before. What's it called?"

They told him and he went over to a computer console, checking the painting on his database.

"Over 130 years old," he said pensively. He lifted the picture out of its protective case and inspected it very carefully, placing it on a green cloth. He leaned down and sniffed it, just as Lucy had done.

"Smells all right," he said, almost to himself. "Looks nice and bright; probably been cleaned. The surface of the paint is smooth except for a slight line along here, as if it's rested against something. It's caused slight paint cracking."

"You can see that on photographs," Davies volunteered. "Only with a high-resolution image, but it's there all right."

Ellis nodded. He turned it over and rested it on the padded cloth, supported by the front surface of the frame.

"Lucky the verso of the canvas is exposed," he said. "You can tell a lot from dust and dirt on the back when you know what you're looking for. There are a few wormholes in the frame and the stretchers, but just what you might expect. Let's have a look at the holes. They look like *Anobium punctatum* or *Lyctus brunneus*. The flight holes are too small and too round to be *Hylotrupes bajulus*. But you can usually tell by the colour of the bore dust formed by chewed wood mixed in with the beetle's excrement."

Davies caught Lucy's eye behind Ellis's back and licked his lips, so that she had to suppress a sudden desperate urge to giggle.

Ellis swung a microscope across the table on a spring-balanced arm, snapped on a bright light and lowered the lens carefully over the picture, taking great care not to let it touch. He leaned forward and put his eyes to the binocular viewing sights, lining the microscope up on a wormhole.

"Oh," he said.

"Oh?" Lucy asked.

"Let's try another one. That doesn't look like a frass gallery at all. In fact it looks more like a puncture made from the outside."

He adjusted the microscope, aligning it on a second hole, and studied it for a few seconds.

"Same thing," he said. "Let's pick another one over the other side."

The third one was identical.

"I smell a rat," Ellis said. "These look like punctures made with a sharp point, such as the point of a set of compasses. Do you have any photographs of the back?"

It is common practice to photograph the back and sides of a canvas as well as the front, because forgers often don't trouble to match them up with the original, concentrating only on the painted image.

"Right here," Davies said, taking a set of images out of a compartment in the lid of the silver case. "They looked fine, we thought."

Ellis took them out and laid them next to the picture. The wormholes were clearly visible and in the same place.

"Perhaps old Alma-Tadema took a dislike to it and used the back as a dartboard," he said. "Stranger things have happened, I can tell you. Let's take a photo of it."

He swung the microscope back out of the way and pulled forward a second arm bearing a vertically mounted camera. He switched it on and a large screen next to the table displayed an image of the back of the Alma-Tadema. He adjusted the range and the focus until the picture was perfectly aligned, and recorded the image. Then he slid the picture out of the way, still on its green cloth, and put the verso photograph in its place. He refocused the camera and took another shot. Then he sat down at the computer console again and downloaded both pictures into the machine. After a few minutes he had made each image semi-transparent and had superimposed one on the other.

"What do you reckon, then?" Ellis said with a broad smile on his face.

They looked at him and then at the screen.

"Well, it appears to be fine," Lucy said uncertainly. "Except that I know that smug look of yours, John! What are we looking at?"

John Ellis pointed at the bottom-right corner, where there were two tiny circles slightly overlapping each other.

"What about that, then?" he said. "All the wormholes align perfectly, except this little worm over here, which has moved to the left half a millimetre. He must be a bit of a fidget, eh?"

They looked at him incredulously.

"Can't it just be photographic distortion?" Davies said at last.

"It could be," Ellis said. "But it isn't, because everything else is in line."

He pointed to the perfectly aligned edges, and went on.

"I've seen this before. Puncture holes under the microscope look completely different from furniture-beetle bore holes. The inside of a genuine bore hole doesn't taper and it isn't necessarily straight. It's a bit darker, and you should be able to see some powder-like bore dust and cylindrical droppings."

He caught their expressions and grinned.

"A misspent life spent studying worm excrement," he smiled. "But that's why I checked the alignment. They often get one off centre. Very difficult to line them all up perfectly, you see."

"You mean it's a forgery?" Lucy said, still incredulous. "Are you absolutely sure it's not genuine?"

"It looks like a genuine fake," he said dryly. "Though to be precise, at this point we only know the frame is not the original. But I can't imagine they'd go to such trouble to make the frame and the back match the original, unless they'd swapped out the painting. Let's give it the full works, though. I'll tell you one thing – if I'm right, this is the most expert job I've seen for a long time. In fact, there's only one man I can think of with sufficient skill."

Davies leaned forward intently and fixed Ellis in the eye.

"And who is that?" he asked quietly.

Ellis gave him a cautious look.

"Let me take a look at it first, before I make a fool of myself. It pays to be thorough in this business. We'll have to use non-invasive tests but I think we have enough at our disposal."

Lucy looked at Davies sideways, her eyebrows raised, her mouth set in a grimace.

"If this turns out to be a fake then I'll have to get the Frans Snyders tested," she said glumly. "I mean, obviously we need to know the truth, but if the Frans Snyders turns out to be a copy as well then there's nothing for it – Hoffmans will have to pay out."

Davies gave the tiniest shrug with his head only.

"On the other hand we might catch the perps and find the loot," he pointed out.

She nodded slowly, looking thoughtful.

Ellis started with X-ray diffraction, but never even got as far as infrared microspectroscopy or ultraviolet light. When he brought up the X-ray image on the screen it was immediately clear that there was another painting underneath.

"Completely different style, of course," Ellis said. "It's some kind of Victorian portrait. You can see where the surface of the painting has been partly sanded off, but the X-rays are picking up the ghost images of the underlying layers. Was Mr Alma-Tadema in the habit of painting on another painter's canvas? According to my database he was not, but anyway, you can see what the forger has done. Standard practice really."

"Talk us through it," Davies said.

"Well, he probably started with any old Victorian canvas from an auction, then took it off the stretchers and sanded it down with pumice stone and water to get rid of any paint ridges. He didn't bother to erase the original image because he knew we'd find out anyway if we gave it the full set of tests."

"He must know his stuff," Lucy said.

Ellis nodded.

"No doubt about it. So then he would have dried it out and remounted it onto stretchers of the right size, having previously aged them. Then he painted the picture. And after all that, he aged the back, using the original as reference. But there's a catch. He would either need the original to work from, or these same photographs of the verso."

"We think perhaps he *did* have the original," Lucy said faintly.

"There we are then," Ellis said matter-of-factly. "Very professional piece of work. Just a misaligned wormhole that gave him away or we'd probably never have bothered to look any further. I can run a few more tests if you like but I'm certain it's not the original. You see too many of these in my profession. They reckon that 15% of art sold at auctions is fake. I think that's conservative, personally. Of course the dealers don't like word getting around about the number of forgeries. They're onto a cushy little number."

"I don't think we need any more tests," Davies said. "It'll have to be retested anyway, but it seems pretty conclusive."

"It takes a real craftsman to make something like this," John Ellis said, putting the painting back carefully into its carrying case. "You've got to admire it, really. The person who did this is a master restorer as well as a master painter. I know of only one man that could do it."

"You said that before," Lucy said, squeezing his arm. "Come on, John, spill the beans! Whose work is it, do you think?"

"Of course, I don't know for sure. It could be anyone's. I don't know every forger in the world, and there must be plenty of them out there if all these fakes are getting to auction."

"But if you were to hazard a guess," Lucy persisted. "Who would it be?"

Ellis snapped the case shut with its cargo safely secured within, and turned to face them, leaning against the table with his arms folded.

"A few years ago I came across a forgery of a Giacometti," he said. "Now that's nothing new. Giacometti is one of the most-forged painters of all time. We estimate maybe three out of five Giacometti's out there are fake. This was a forgery, but it fooled me. The equipment we had in the lab wasn't as sophisticated as it is today, mind. Anyway, this Giacometti was perfectly executed and the sides and verso were perfectly matched too, just like this one. I remember it because of the wormholes. It was a messy sketch of a small female nude and I passed it as the original, stamped the provenance and everything. Then I had second thoughts and ran some more tests with a new machine."

He grinned in recollection of one of the few times when he had been fooled, nodding slowly.

"It was a copy all right."

"Well who did it?" Lucy practically hissed in frustration.

"They didn't know to begin with," Ellis said, determined not to be hurried. "Took them a few weeks to trace it back, but trace it they did. It was a man named Smith."

"Smith?" Davies expostulated. "That's the most common bloody surname in the English language!"

"Yes, a brilliantly clever man – such a pity. They locked him up, so maybe he's still behind bars. A gentleman named Alfred Smith."

SEVEN

...the breathtaking view of King's College Chapel from across the river Cam, the rich intricacy of Gothic architecture, students cycling to lectures, and lazy summer punting on the River Cam.
WIKITRAVEL, Cambridge (England)

An hour later, Lucy and Davies had returned to Davies' office and the forged Alma-Tadema was safely back under lock and key. Davies was browsing the Police National Computer and Lucy was fretting because it seemed to her that he was taking forever. The air-conditioner in the ceiling had reluctantly stirred and was rattling. She stood by the window but the only view was a brick wall so she turned her eyes back into the room. There was no pattern in Davies' office disorder and that irritated her too. She picked up an art magazine and started to leaf through it in a desultory way.

At last Davies shifted position and looked at her.

"I've found Alfred Smith," he said, tapping his finger on the screen. "According to this he went down for six years and came out after three on a DCR, which he breached more or less straight away."

"What does a DCR actually mean?"

"A Discretionary Conditional Release," Davies said, disregarding her peremptory tone. "He buggered off. He left the care of Her Majesty and was supposed to report back on probation, but he stopped doing so. Mind you, I shouldn't think they're exactly burning the midnight oil looking for him. He wouldn't be seen as a threat."

"I don't see why if he's not reporting in when he should," Lucy said pointedly. "Either way, *we* need to find him."

Davies pursed his lips and nodded. He leaned back in his chair and knitted his fingers behind his head.

"It's what we call a measured response," he said glumly. "Which means that we don't have the manpower to blockade all the ports but if he actually walks into a police-station and gives himself up then we'll nick him. I've run the usual checks, but without any joy so I thought I'd try the prison governor. Mr Smith was in Ford open prison, which is at Arundel, down in Sussex. I went youth-hostelling there when I was a youngster, funnily enough. Not a bad spot and a bloody sight drier than Wales, though I don't recall a prison."

"Well they probably don't build them in the same street," Lucy said, and picked up the phone, handing it to him. "Go on then – give him a call!"

"Give *her* a call," Davies said, taking the phone and looking at Lucy blandly. "He's a she."

He was on the phone for a further fifteen minutes, talking to the unseen lady. Finally he hung up. Lucy stopped pacing up and down his office and sat down expectantly in his visitor's chair.

"Well?" she said.

"Quite interesting," Davies said. "The governor *does* remember Alfred Smith. He was a brilliant painter, she said. Painted half the inmates and one or two of the prison staff as well. She says that the probation office got hold of her when he'd been out for a few weeks, because he'd stopped checking in with them. He's supposed to contact them regularly you see, and live at a known address, until three-quarters of his sentence is up. So they sent one of our lads round to his house but it was all locked up. Fully furnished, but it didn't look as if it had been lived in for a while."

"No clues at all?"

"Evidently not. The local coppers didn't have anywhere else to look so they probably put it on the back burner."

"Well, that's pretty useless," snorted Lucy. "Why didn't they charge him with breach of probation or something? I expect he's busy turning out Alma-Tademas by the dozen."

"Probably," Davies agreed gloomily, holding out a piece of paper with Alfred's address scribbled on it. "We should have a look anyway, but I think we ought to check your Frans Snyders next and see if that one's real or not."

Lucy took the slip of paper and picked up her bag. Then she grimaced as she suddenly realized her predicament.

"I'm going to be popular: turning up a forgery so that we have to pay out on it after all. Still – it's the proper thing to do so that's that. I'll make arrangements when I get back to the office. We'll get the Snyders painting shipped over to John Ellis. The owners are not going to be very pleased if it *is* a fake, though. They were delighted to get it back."

"Before you rush off, there's another thing that the governor mentioned," Davies said. "Apparently Smith knew a younger man in prison, doing time for forgery just like him; name of Will Bentley. The difference is that he *did* check in during his probation period. The governor gave me his address as well."

He held a second piece of paper up in front of her.

"Now apparently Bentley came out of the nick after Smith. The governor said he wouldn't hurt a fly, so I was wondering if you might want to pop along and see him."

"*Me?*" Lucy said with a squeak of indignation. "Shouldn't *you* do it? He's an ex-con, after all. You surely aren't expecting *me* to make the initial advances."

Davies looked uncomfortable. "Normally of course it would be me," he said. "But it's too late to go today, and it's Carol's birthday tomorrow so we're planning to visit the family in Wales for a long weekend. If you want me to do it you'll have to wait until Monday."

Lucy looked doubtful.

"Well I'm not very happy going to meet with an ex con. Where does this Bentley live? In some frightful seedy tenement, I suppose."

"Ah yes, burning cars and needles in the gutter," Davies said. He handed her the second piece of paper. The address of Bentley's studio was in the middle of Cambridge, not renowned for its mean streets.

She sniffed.

"Well I suppose I could take a look from the outside and see what I think," she said. "But a woman has to be careful."

Davies looked at her innocently. "I thought if he gave you any hassle you'd vaporize him with a look."

"I have no idea what you're talking about," she said, but she was smiling as she gathered up her things to go.

"On a serious note, do be careful," Davies called after her. "Bentley is an ex-con, so he might not hurt a fly but he's certainly bent. Once a crook, always a crook."

EIGHT

Conscience is a man's compass.
VINCENT VAN GOGH

The next morning Lucy put on a white summer's dress, and then slipped into her favourite black linen jacket to cover up the straps – she didn't want this awful man to think that she was coming on to him. She also brushed her long blonde hair to tame it, but then pinned it up tightly and picked out some black and white bangles to tie the colours of the jacket and dress together. She wanted to look smart in Cambridge because she felt nervous about the intended visit, and being smart made her feel more confident. When she felt ready she got into her red MG Roadster and pointed it towards the ancient city.

She arrived at Bentley's address around noon, parked opposite and looked at the studio, feeling tense. A part of her wanted to run away but she was determined not to surrender to it.

Bentley's studio seemed big for a man who had been in prison. She supposed it must be founded on ill-gotten gains. The front of it comprised a shop window with the words "Will Bentley, Painter" etched on the glass. She crossed the road and her eye was inexorably drawn to the painting inside. It was a single large painting of an old road sweeper in a shapeless overall, leaning on his broom and looking at the viewer while the street around him swirled with rubbish. She studied it for a minute or two. It was extremely good. The eyes of the old man were weary, as if they'd seen too much. She tried to reconcile her preconceived view of an ex-convict with a man who painted like this, but it was difficult. She smoothed down her dress and looked up and down the street. Then she went to the black door and reached for the white bell push. Her hand stopped two inches from it as her brain adjusted. The bell push wasn't real, it was *trompe l'oeil* painted on the doorjamb, complete with shadow and a carefully painted 'metal' nameplate above it bearing the word "Bentley".

She smiled sheepishly and reached down for the brass doorknocker before she realised that the knocker too was just a painting. The man certainly had style. She gave the door an experimental push and it opened easily. Inside there was a vestibule lit with a shaft of light from a high tall window. The walls were painted white, as were the clean bare floorboards. A single spotlight was aimed at the door behind her, and when she turned around she found it had been painted with a view of the street outside, complete with pedestrians frozen in mid-step. This was beginning to feel slightly surreal.

She called hello but there was no answer. There was a corridor leading to a closed door, and beside it a staircase leading up. Then she noticed a painted sign with a hand pointing upwards and the word "Studio". A serpent was entwined around its outstretched finger. She went up the stairs.

At the top was a chair beside a closed door, and a small table bearing a stack of art magazines and catalogues.

"Hello?" she called again, uncertainly. Her mouth was dry.

"You'll have to wait," a voice called from a distance away. "There's no-one here."

She paused a few seconds to let this paradoxical statement sink in.

"You're here," she called back to the unseen voice.

"You'll have to come back later," the voice called, a little more insistently.

"Well I've driven all the way from London and I can't just go away. I need to talk to Will Bentley." She was moving rapidly from nervousness to irritation.

Footsteps echoed across floorboards and then the door was flung open and a man with long dark hair leaned out, a clutch of paint-loaded brushes in his hand.

"Can't you see I'm painting?" he bellowed in her face. He held out the brushes in front of her eyes. "It requires *concentration*. You'll have to *wait* or *come back later!*"

He enunciated the last words slowly and carefully as if speaking to a moron. Then without waiting for a reply he turned on his heel and disappeared the way he had come, slamming the door behind him.

"All right then, I'll wait," she yelled at the closed door, wondering how any man could bring her quite so instantly to boiling point as had this one. *I'll wait all day if necessary*, she muttered under her breath.

She waited an hour and a half; then again there were footsteps and the door swung open, but this time it was a vivacious young woman.

"Hi there," she said in a conciliatory tone. "My name's Sandy. I'm the model, but he's finished with me for today. The paint's got to dry or something, so you can go in." She smiled and shrugged at the same time. "He's just cleaning up."

She leaned closer.

"I know he's a rude sod," she said in a conspiratorial whisper, "but his bark's worse than his bite. He just cares about his work and he won't be disturbed when he's painting. He reckons if he gets interrupted then it ruins his flow."

"Thank you," Lucy said, her fury dissipated by the long wait. It was hard to be cross with someone as nice as this. "But he *was* very rude," she added, still a little piqued.

The girl nodded.

"I know; I'm surprised you waited, really. Most people storm off when he's like that. All I can tell you is that he's *all right* when you get to know him. Are you a customer?"

"No. I'm just visiting Mr Bentley on a business matter," Lucy found herself saying rather formally.

"Fair enough," the girl said incuriously. "Well, I've got to go home now. Just go right in."

She went down the stairs with a little wave and Lucy pushed the door open.

The studio was big, occupying a sizeable portion of the upper floor. As she advanced into the room she saw walls tightly packed with pictures, and canvases stacked several deep around the base of each wall. Towards the back of the studio was a working area with stacks of framing wood, and an elevated loft space with a ramp up to it. There were various doors; some open, some closed. Two large windows lighted the studio, and a professional easel was set up in front of one of them. The man with long dark hair stood next to it, cleaning brushes with his back to her. He had obviously forgotten that she was there, but turned to face her as she walked across the studio floor, her heels clicking on the boards.

"Mr Bentley?" she said.

"That's me. Welcome!"

He grinned disarmingly at her but made no apology for his earlier rudeness – in fact he seemed unaware of it. He was charming, but she reminded herself that he was an ex-forger: one of the men she constantly fought against in her work.

"My name is Lucy Wrackham, Mr Bentley," she said, adopting formality like a protective glove. She extended her hand. "I work for a company called Hoffman and Courtland, based in London. We insure fine art against theft, damage in transit: that sort of thing."

"Call me Will," he said, shaking her hand and looking at her. She had a firm, dry grasp. She was a beautiful woman and had natural blonde hair that he would like to paint, if she would only let it down instead of bundling it up.

"I don't really bother with insurance," he went on, deliberately casual in contrast to her formality. "Most of it gets painted and then sold, or sits here for a while until I exhibit it."

"I'm not here to sell you insurance," Lucy said, not knowing quite where to begin.

Then the sight of the painting on the easel distracted her. It was the second of a pair of paintings. The first stood on the table to the left of the easel: it depicted the model girl she had met outside, wearing a black bonnet and cast against a backdrop of Ascot. The painting on the easel was the same subject, but this time the girl was naked apart from her bonnet, and all the fine ladies and gentlemen in the crowd followed a similar pattern; top hats, beautiful millinery and bare skin. The girl had the same mischievous, provocative smile in both pictures, though she had shifted position. The second painting at a glance appeared finished, but Lucy's experienced eye could see that the detail was not yet developed.

Bentley watched her look at the painting.

"What do you think?" he asked. "I was going to take the hats off as well as their clothes, but I didn't think it would work like that – you'd lose the essential idea of what the picture is."

She looked at it intently and then went back to the first one.

"It's good," she acknowledged. "I like the way you've kept the same faces on the people in the crowd, but why take off their clothes?"

He looked at the two pictures and smiled.

"No special reason, it was just a whim. The original is a pretty picture of Ascot, but I also wanted to show that we all look the same under the finery. Clothes maketh the man. I need to think up catchy titles for them though."

She frowned as she looked at the pictures pensively.

"You could call one Beauty and the other Skin Deep," she said thoughtfully.

He finished cleaning the last brush and stuck it with the bristles pointing upwards into a jug containing twenty other brushes.

"I like that," he nodded, giving her a second appraising look. He emptied turpentine into a sink and rinsed it away, wiping out its container.

"So if you're not here to sell me insurance, what *are* you here for? Buying a picture, perhaps?" He waved his arm at the stacked canvases.

"Not today," Lucy said, deciding to plough right in. "I'm here because I'm looking for a man called Alfred Smith who used to be a friend of yours. I'm wondering if you've seen him."

He gave her a third penetrating look, but this time it was guarded.

"I haven't seen Alfred for a long time," he said. "We've lost touch. It sounds like you'd better tell me the whole story, but first tell me if you want tea or coffee." He went into the kitchen and opened the cupboard, taking down the coffee for himself. She chose Camomile tea, and when the drinks were made they sat down together at the table in the studio.

"It's a long story," she said, not quite knowing how to begin, or how much she should tell him. "Yesterday I saw a painting by Sir Lawrence Alma-Tadema. Do you know his work?"

She watched him closely for a flicker of guilt but there was none. Instead he looked into the middle distance and thought.

"Lots of Roman baths and dreamy women. Victorian."

"That's it exactly. Except that this particular painting turned out not to be by Alma-Tadema. We had it analysed and it's a fake. A very good one, but a fake nonetheless."

"So you thought you'd check out all the forgers," Will said with a hint of the swift anger she had already witnessed.

"Not exactly," Lucy said matter-of-factly. "I'm not here to accuse you. I presume that you're back on the straight and narrow."

"I always *was* on the straight and narrow," Will said bitterly. "It's just that this country's justice system is more in favour of the high and mighty than the common man."

"I'm sure that's not true," Lucy said before she could stop herself. "I mean that the law is biased, which is what you imply."

He didn't say anything; he just looked at her.

"Anyway," she continued hurriedly. "After the painting had been analysed we had a chat with one of the lab experts that does the analysis, and he had only ever seen copies of this quality once before. And on that occasion they had been painted by Mr Smith."

"So you thought...?" Will said.

"I thought I'd like to find Mr Smith and eliminate him from the investigation," Lucy said carefully.

Will looked stubborn.

"Then contact him and not me."

"We tried to do that, but he's no longer at his old address. It's closed up."

"He may just be away."

"But he stopped checking in with his probation officer," she said. "He moved away without telling anyone. And now forgeries of extraordinary quality are emerging onto the market. What am I *supposed* to think, Mr Bentley?"

"Alfred wouldn't start that up again," Will said, shaking his head but looking uncomfortable. "I talked to him about it when we were in the nick. I told him he didn't need to. With his ability I knew he could make a tidy living just making legitimate copies. All he needed was a good gallery. It's true he preferred copying old masters to doing original work of his own. He said he felt at ease with them. I know it sounds odd, but it's as if he were in the wrong century. I told him he could still pay the bills doing copies as long as he didn't pass them off as originals. People would pay plenty of money for work of his quality."

"So what happened?" Lucy said slowly. "Have you lost contact or can you tell me where I can find him?"

Will drank his coffee before replying, taking time to work out his answer.

"It's a funny thing," he admitted at last. "I came out after Alfred and I tried to contact him several times, but I never got any response. It was strange because we were good friends inside the nick – nobody else could paint so we used to spend a lot of time together, painting or just talking. We weren't allowed to sell our stuff because of what we were in for, but they were reasonable – they put all our work into store as our personal property, and we collected it when we came out. At least I did, and I presume they let Alfred have his stuff too."

"Did he paint any fakes while he was in there?" Lucy asked.

Will smiled.

"That would be ironic wouldn't it? But no, you can't do anything more than a decorative fake unless you have the right materials. You need an old canvas for a start, and you have to copy the back of the support and the sides as accurately as the front. It involves woodworking and chemistry and knowledge of how to stain woods."

"You seem to know a lot about it for a man who was wrongly accused," Lucy said tartly.

"Believe what you want," he said, suddenly bristling again. "I didn't do it. But I did spend six months in prison with Alfred Smith and we had to talk about something. It was a technical discussion between people who are interested in painting."

He looked at her but she didn't say anything. His anger blew itself out like a flame.

"It's fascinating," he went on, warming to his theme. "How to cut a quill from a bird's pinion feather, before you even *start* a drawing. How to mix the inks and make the glue. How to start with an antique canvas and paint a copy on top of it."

Lucy finished her tea, thinking about the old Victorian painting underneath the forged Alma-Tadema, and working out what she was going to say next. Bentley had already finished and he picked up the two mugs and carried them into the kitchen.

"But anyway, I can't help you," he called. "I haven't seen Alfred since he left prison. He was out before me and I never got back into contact with him."

She stood up and went to the door of the kitchen.

"There's another picture we're not sure of. You could help me identify if the work is his or not," she said. "Couldn't you? It may have been painted by someone else, but if by a bad stroke of luck he *is* back at his old tricks, then shouldn't we stop him?"

"As decent law-abiding citizens?" he asked wryly. "Perhaps being imprisoned has given me a jaundiced view. I think *you* should stop him if it turns out to be his work, because that's your job. But it isn't mine." He shook his head in emphasis. "It isn't mine, and I'd be grassing up an old friend."

"But you say he didn't do it," Lucy said persistently. "So you wouldn't be grassing him up, would you? You'd be helping to clear his name. The police would stop looking for him and start looking for somebody else."

"Then again perhaps they wouldn't," Will said darkly. "I don't share your confidence in them. Why would they play fair if they *did* find him?"

"I'm not going to let Mr Smith be falsely accused, I assure you," she said primly. "And I have often worked with the particular policeman who is handling this. He's in the Art and Antiques unit and he's a decent man – he wouldn't play games, I can assure you of that."

Will said nothing but shook his head as he went past her into the studio.

"Give me a few minutes," he said over his shoulder. "I've been painting all morning and I need to get some fresh air and think about what you're suggesting. This is all very unexpected, losing contact with Alfred for ages and then you suddenly pop out of the wide blue yonder."

In the darkest corner of the studio there was a narrow spiral staircase that she hadn't seen before. His shoes made a ringing note on the metal rungs as he went up it. There was the sound of a trapdoor opening and light spilled down the stairs. He must be on the roof.

She wanted to give him a few minutes to reflect, so she began looking at his paintings. Bentley painted *people* in all shapes and guises: there were no landscapes; no boats; no steam engines. It was as though he were trying to transmute the human soul into paint. Many of the paintings were of women, often nude and often erotic. None of them was of the girl Lucy had met on her way in. She supposed he had many different models – or many different lovers; he was the sort that would. As she looked at the pictures she felt as if she were peering inside his head. There were paintings of men as well as women; old or young, usually muscled, standing or seated or lying flat. Bentley paid great attention to shape and muscle tone.

He had an interest in paradox: a bus conductor seated in an empty bus with his head in his hands; a bishop in a bus shelter surrounded by jeering louts; a yellow hard-hatted man reading a book at a library table, with a mud-spattered road drill on the table beside him.

She wanted to look at all the canvases, including those stacked several deep against the walls, but she would have to do that another time, for now she judged she should speak with him again. She tore herself away and went up the spiral staircase after him.

The moment she stepped outside she understood what he meant about clearing his head. The light blazed after the gloom of the staircase. There was a blackbird seated on a chimney, its beady eye following her every move. Bentley was sitting at a black cast-iron table on the rooftop. Behind him was the peaked roof of the studio. The flat area was surrounded by a parapet wall, but the wall had been moulded and shaped into uneven ripples and curves with the use of concrete. Broken shards of ceramic tile had been set into the cement in a mosaic, so that the rooftop had been brought to life with extravagant bursts of colour. She recognized it immediately as she looked around.

"This reminds me of Barcelona," she said incredulously.

"The marketplace in Park Guell," Will said, standing up and spreading his arms. "At least, that's the effect I was after. I thought having Antonio Gaudi in the middle of Cambridge would link the city with a different culture. It's actually twinned with Heidelberg, which is a good match but more of the same. I think they should twin different styles, so I'm doing my bit."

She walked around, inspecting the mosaic patterns.

"This is amazing!" she said, the business of Alfred Smith temporarily forgotten. "It must have taken you ages."

"About two years. It would have been quicker but it's tricky to get hold of the ceramic tiles, and you can't use just any old thing. So I went to a factory in Spain that made them and explained what I wanted. They gave me a load of broken tiles for free. I shipped them back and this is the result. Of course it's only a fraction of the size of the original."

"Does anyone know it's here?" she asked.

"Oh yes. It's quite a famous landmark of Cambridge, now. The Guardian did an article on it, and The Times. A few tourists hear about it and stop by, though I don't advertise it. I always let them have a look unless I'm painting at the time."

"And if you're painting you yell at them," Lucy said with a wry smile.

"Something like that," he said with a grin. "I'm sorry I bellowed at you. It's when I'm locked in on a painting. Getting interrupted is the worst possible thing."

She went to the edge of the parapet and leaned out. The rooftops of Cambridge radiated into the distance, spiked with TV aerials and satellite dishes. She could hear occasional cars passing the front of the studio. There was the spire of a church in the distance and the towers of ancient college buildings. Next to the studio was a similar building, incongruously covered with washing lines full of exotic ladies' underwear. Will joined her.

"Racy neighbours," Lucy observed, looking at the array of thongs, cutaway bras and other exotica, all in pinks and reds and purples.

"Ah yes, you might not expect it of Cambridge but there's a knocking shop next door," he said with a short laugh. "I don't think the police have cottoned on yet because the madam is very discreet."

"Don't you mind having such a thing next to you?" Lucy asked, hearing how prudish she sounded as the words came out of her mouth.

"I don't mind at all, in fact I'm rather pleased," Will said with sudden relish. "A bunch of pretty girls who don't mind being painted naked. It makes me feel like Toulouse-Lautrec. Now and then they come over here and sit for me in the studio when business is slack, and I paint them. They can all get back in two minutes if there's a sudden rush. I pay them normal model rates when they come over, which isn't what they're used to but the work's nicer. They just sit and chat. Sometimes it gets so interesting that I forget to paint and have to tell them to shut up."

She turned around and leaned against the parapet wall, her back towards the building next door.

"Take care," he said. "The wall isn't as high as it should be."

She stood up.

"I should think you'd have to be drunk to fall off, though."

"I had some old college friends around here once," he said. "And we *did* all get rather drunk. One of them came up here thinking it was the lavatory. Then he saw next door's roof full of scanties and took it into his head to jump off."

"My God! Was he killed?"

"No, but it was a close call. He almost made it to next-door's roof but didn't quite cross their parapet wall." He pointed it out to her. "He ended up draped across the parapet and couldn't pull himself up. He yelled blue murder until one of us heard him and turned up. They had to call the fire brigade but they managed to get him down before he let go. He was stone-cold sober by the time they got him down. Frightened himself half to death. I think he couldn't believe his luck, though. He stayed behind with the girls next door and they looked after him. The mind boggles, but he was a modest sort of bloke. He refused to talk about it."

Despite her customary seriousness, Lucy smiled at this image. Then she noticed a black cat, curled up on a ledge that ran around the base of the chimney. She walked over to it and the cat opened one lazy eye, looking extremely comfortable. She tickled it under the chin and it purred.

"I have a cat," she said. "What's her name?"

"She's a he," Will said, coming over and running his hand along the cat's back. "He's called Beast and he's from a friend of mine who is a vet. She gets waifs and strays now and then and she offloaded a pair of them onto me. There's another one called Beauty around somewhere, except that Beauty has a bent ear, so Beast is really the good-looking one."

"You *are* beautiful," Lucy crooned at the cat, forgetting completely how alarmed she had been that morning at the prospect of meeting with an ex-con.

"I'm used to them now," Will nodded. "I always say I prefer dogs, but the roads are too busy around here so I gave in when Anna put the screws on me to have a couple of cats. It works out all right though. They keep the mice out of the paintings and they don't argue with me."

There was a silence which lengthened until Will Bentley finally returned to the subject of Alfred Smith.

"Tell me again," he said slowly, "why you think I should help you out."

"Mainly because it's the proper thing to do," she said. "But all right – let's go through it. If the paintings are being painted by Alfred Smith, then either he's passing them off as real, or someone else is doing so. If *he's* doing it then he's breaking the law and he needs to be stopped. But if it's not him, then he's probably being used like you were, and he'll end up being caught and locked up anyway, just as you were. Everyone will *assume* he's guilty; you said yourself that's how the system works. And if he's not painting these pictures, then I can go off and look for the real guilty party."

She paused for breath after this long speech. Will sat at the table, realising that one thing she'd said was right enough – someone might be using Alfred just as they had once used him. He felt he owed his old friend something and couldn't just abandon him. He also wanted to know what on earth had happened to Alfred, after they had sworn to remain in touch. He gave the tiniest of shrugs.

"Well, I'll tell you what I'll do," he said. "You mentioned you had another picture to look at, so I'll come and look at that one with you, just to see what I think."

She felt jubilant but kept her voice even.

"That's perfect," she said. "It's a Frans Snyders. When could you come and look at it? Hoffman and Courtland will pay your expenses, of course."

"How about this afternoon?" Will said.

She shook her head regretfully, remembering the invitation to the Limerston Gallery which she had now accepted.

"I can't do it today because I've got to go to a private view this evening. But anyway, I need to make arrangements with the owners first. I'll try for Sunday if that works for you – they told me last time I went there that Sunday is their best day for being in. By the way, the painting is on the Isle of Wight. I wanted them to ship it over but they refused."

"The *Isle of Wight?*" Will said, feeling slightly cross. "You kept *that* quiet until I said yes. How long does it take to get there?"

"It's not too bad," she said. "Though from here, you'll need to leave early if we're to do it in a day. Otherwise we'd need to stay over on Sunday night."

There was another silence.

"All right then," he said rather grudgingly. "I've said I will so I'll keep my word. I'll give you my number and you'll need to call me when you've made the arrangements."

Beast started to purr again. In the distance, a lone church bell began to toll plangently. Lucy thanked him and departed soon after. It was only after she had gone that Will Bentley had a moment of solitary reflection. He concluded that there were worse fates than a day out with someone as beautiful as Lucy Wrackham.

NINE

O what a tangled web we weave,
When first we practise to deceive!
SIR WALTER SCOTT

Detective Constable Billy Stokes brought the van to a stop just up the road from Will Bentley's studio, adjacent to a manhole that had been selected that morning. His colleague D.C. Emily Matheson was already in the back, keeping out of sight. He put on a yellow hard-hat and got out of the van. He was in plain clothes, and already had on a fluorescent yellow jacket. The van bore the legend "Cambridge Water" on the side panel, together with a blue logo. Billy went to the back and extracted a set of cones which he used to cordon off an area around the manhole, feeling a little as if he were on traffic duty. He removed the heavy manhole cover and dragged it to one side. Then he got a yellow pipe and trailed it into the hole, securing the end of the pipe into a portable pump. Finally he stood a large red and white metal warning sign beside the traffic cones, and put a sandbag on it to stop it from blowing over.

As he worked he looked around casually, but no one was taking the slightest bit of notice. Sometimes they suffered from inquisitive kids while they were setting up, but there didn't seem to be any in the vicinity, thank God.

He climbed back into the driver's seat of the van. When he was happy that he was unobserved, he crawled between the front seats, past a narrow doorway to a chemical toilet and into the back.

"All right?" Emily Matheson asked.

"We're all set up," Billy said, giving her a surreptitious look of approval. They had allocated a woman to work with him due to the nature of the job, and she knew how to use the equipment so there was no problem there. He reflected that she was certainly easier on the eye than D.C. Eric Small, his usual partner. She was wearing faded jeans and a tight blue shirt that emphasized her bust. She was a little short and her hair needed a decent cut, but Billy was giving her a nine nevertheless. Around her, the lights on the audio-visual equipment blinked and flickered.

"How's it going?" he asked.

She had worked surveillance before and was more experienced with the kit than he was, so she had set it up while he did the out-of-van work.

"I've got video but that takes hardly any time at all," she said, gesturing at a screen which showed a full colour picture of the black door a little way down the road. "I haven't sorted out sound yet. I need to line up the parabolic mike but I just want to get the recorder locked and loaded first."

He sat down in the chair next to her and started up the computer, smelling her scent as he passed close by her in the crowded space. He tried to catch her eye but she didn't look at him.

She knew she shouldn't have put on her best perfume. Her husband had given it to her for her birthday, and she was working today so she didn't need to smell nice. If she was honest, she was putting it on just to see what might happen, because she was bored with being ignored. But rarely are we so truthful with ourselves, so she wore the perfume with a vague sense of excitement, mingled with guilt.

TEN

Work is the curse of the drinking classes
OSCAR WILDE

It was Saturday lunchtime and Anna and George turned up at the studio to invite Will out to lunch. After a little rain in the night and a cloudy start, the sun was out in earnest again and had burned off the moisture. Will was painting Anna's freesias when they arrived, because the paint was still drying on the Skin Deep picture.

"Oh, how lovely!" Anna said, looking at the blooms taking shape on the canvas. "You've caught them beautifully. Now the question is, are you able to come out to lunch? George thinks we ought to go down to the Fort, because it's a sunny day and we haven't been for ages. And he's got a new client on the Milton Road that he promised to go and chat with at five, so it's all in the same neck of the woods."

"I also thought you might not have eaten anything," George said, and then peered at the painting on the easel. "Good picture, that." He looked back at Will. "What do you say? Lunch and a pint of Tribute? I hear the Fort has it back as one of their limited editions, and I haven't had a drop since last summer."

Will looked at the painting.

"I need half an hour to wrap this up," he said. "Then I'll join you."

They departed and he worked on. When he had finished the freesias and was removing cadmium yellow and titanium white from his brushes, the telephone rang. It was Lucy Wrackham, confirming the Isle of Wight trip for the next day.

"We can drive down from town in my car," she said, but it would speed things up if you could take a train as far as London."

They agreed that he would catch an early train from Cambridge and she would meet him in King's Cross Station at a quarter to nine.

When Will had finished the painting and cleaned up, he went to fetch a working man's brown vintage bowler that he had bought long ago in one of Cambridge's many eccentric shops. The bowler had started as a joke when one year he had worn it to the Fort St. George pub. He had explained that it was in honour of another George; George Seurat, who painted the huge 'Bathers' painting hanging in the National. It depicts working-class nineteenth-century Parisians spending the day at the riverside. The Fort St. George is also on the banks of the river; but it is the languid River Cam and not the dark thread of the Seine. Will's friends had teased him but he had ignored their taunts. Now he always wore it when he went to the Fort, and it had become an in-joke with his friends and with the regulars in the pub.

The Fort St George is on Midsummer Common, and it took Will about ten minutes to cycle there, criss-crossing through alleyways and along paths. On one occasion his hat almost blew off, but he preferred to cycle in Cambridge, as did many residents. The city was more accommodating to bicycles than to cars. In fact Will didn't even *own* a car, though he did have a Triumph motorcycle, which he had picked up second-hand as a swap for a pair of paintings. George was very jealous of it. It was a Bonneville T100 – a classic Hinckley air-cooled twin with off-road exhaust pipes and a more comfortable seat than the unyielding standard version. It was an extremely comfortable ride and Will loved it. He couldn't ride it that day though because he was drinking.

George and Anna had walked to the Fort because George said he couldn't pay tribute to the Tribute if he had to drive back afterwards. When Will arrived they were sitting out at the front beneath huge umbrellas. George had almost finished a pint of the Cornish brew which stood in front of him, and proclaimed it to be as good as ever. Will went in and ordered two more pints of the same. Anna was drinking a large glass of Pinot Grigio, which she topped up from the bottle in the ice bucket next to them. She and George were already tipsy and greeted him with much fanfare, bringing smiles to the faces of one or two other people at lunch.

"It's the *hat!*" George said, standing up and pointing. "The Fort St. George hat! I haven't seen it since last year."

"Of course you haven't," Will said gravely. "I keep it in a glass cabinet and I only bring it out when I come here. It's now an ancient tradition. One day I shall have twelve children and I shall buy each of them a brown bowler hat."

Anna grimaced in horror.

"Maybe I'll let you have Sarah, William and Charlotte for the day before you sign up for twelve," she said. Will sat down next to her and she poked him in the ribs. "What happened to you, then? We've been sitting here starving and getting drunk. You said half an hour and that was an hour ago."

"Sorry about that," Will said. "Mmm, you smell nice. What's that? Pass the menu here, George."

"Brazen flattery!" Anna said, "but I suppose I'll let you off. And the perfume is White Linen, in case you really do care. George got it for me last Christmas and he picked very well. Everyone says it suits me."

"It's because I have such good taste," George declared, "and a highly skilled olfactory organ, of course." He brought the pint of Tribute to his nose and inhaled blissfully before taking a draft.

Will and George both opted for the steak and kidney pudding, and Anna had linguini.

George as usual finished first despite devouring the contents of the breadbasket as well, and Anna chastised them for choosing unhealthy food.

"You'll both become fat and revolting," she said. "And I shall take some young toy boy as my lover and erase George's memory."

"Man cannot live by linguini alone," George said, mopping up the last of the gravy with a pad of bread and popping it into his mouth. "Now then Will, how's that gorgeous new model of yours?"

"She's definitely up for it," Anna said. "As a woman I know all the signs."

Will held up his hands protestingly.

"She is not `up for it'," he said firmly.

"She is."

"She isn't."

"She definitely is."

"Let's change the subject."

"Only because you know I'm right."

There was a pause while one of the bar staff hovered, ready to clear the plates, but then went away again because Anna and Will hadn't yet finished eating.

"I had an unexpected visitor yesterday," Will said, judiciously picking a new topic. "A ravishing blonde."

"Was she up for it?" Anna said.

"I'm not sure if I'm going to tell you since you're intent on winding me up."

A minute passed in which Anna convinced herself that she was not going to ask, and George finished a bit of linguini that she couldn't quite manage.

"Well come on, then," Anna said at last. "Who was this woman and what did she want?"

"Very interesting," Will said. "She works for a company that insures fine art. She wanted to ask me all about Alfred Smith. You remember? The man I was in prison with."

"How on earth did she know about him?" George asked, coming back to the present and focusing on what Will was saying. "Not many people do, do they?"

"Not many," Will admitted. "Anyway, it turns out that she's discovered that someone is forging paintings and she wants me to look at one, and tell her if I think Alfred did it."

"How exciting!" Anna said. "Nothing exciting ever happens to me, and you end up going to prison and then getting visited by mysterious investigators. It's not fair."

"I wouldn't call prison *exciting*," Will said. "Mostly it's just deadly boring, except when your life is threatened. I suppose that's exciting, but it's excitement I'd rather do without."

"So come on," George persisted. "The ravishing blonde arrived, cross-examined you about your wicked past, and then what?"

"She wants me to go to the Isle of Wight to look at this picture."

"Ha!" George said with a laugh. "And – let me guess – you told her where to go."

"On the contrary, I'm going tomorrow."

"He's up for it," Anna said.

ELEVEN

Dreams are true while they last, and do we not live in dreams?
ALFRED TENNYSON

When they had finished, they felt full of dinner and rather drunk, so they went and stretched out on the grass. George fell asleep and Will was dozing off himself when Anna spoke in a contented murmur.

"So is this blonde nice then? What's her name?"

"Lucy," he murmured back. "And she's a bit cold, but extremely pretty."

There was another long pause.

"Tell me about prison life, then," Anna said in the same dreamy voice. "You never do when I ask you. Tell me about this chap, Alfred. Did he like animals?"

This peculiar veterinary question woke Will up slightly.

"How should I know if he liked *animals*?" he retorted. "He never mentioned them. We talked about painting and we painted. They don't allow animals in prison."

"What did he tell you, then? Come on: teach me how to be a forger."

"Oh, you know…"

There was a silence which grew longer and longer. They had both fallen asleep, and running through Will's head was an image of Alfred...

Alfred had a peculiar habit of drinking hot tea from his saucer. He was slumped back on his bed, the tea steaming up his thick grey beard. Will studied him from the uncomfortable chair in which he was seated. Alfred had a fat stomach which was serving as a tea tray in this instance. He was round-faced, with his skin crinkled into a thousand fine wrinkles by the passing of sixty-five years. His lips had once been full and red but had now thinned with age. His grey hair was still surprisingly thick for an old man. He kept it unfashionably longer than a man of his age normally might, giving him a slightly rakish air. The best thing about Alfred's face, Will decided, was the way it so readily broke into a smile. His eyes were surprisingly sharp and keen beneath their steel-rimmed round spectacles, giving him the look of an aging Santa Claus. He wore standard prison-issue jeans, a T-shirt and a maroon sweatshirt, but despite this uniform he managed to maintain a certain distinguished air. Most important of all he was the cleverest painter that Will had ever met – and Will had met plenty.

Will looked around the cell. There was the easel with a half-finished portrait of one of the prisoners, borrowed from the art room on permanent loan. A photograph of the subject was pinned to the easel at the edge of the canvas. It was at eye height when standing, for Alfred only ever painted standing up, like Will. It was necessary to have fluidity of body movement – they were both in agreement on that. Will tried to stretch as he thought of this, but felt oddly unable to move in the chair, his legs in treacle. He knew the experience but couldn't quite put his finger on what it was. There was a painting of a saxophone hanging on the wall to dry, and Alfred's real saxophone was in the corner below it, standing on the flat end of its case. There were tubes of paint and the usual paraphernalia of painting. There were a number of magazines, too – Alfred had a monthly subscription to *Renaissance Artist*. Lastly there was a plain white enamel sink with a razor and a toothbrush propped on the shelf above it.

"Of course," Alfred began, with a glance at the door to make sure that there were no screws lurking about, "you only have to sign a painting if the master always did so. It can be more subtle not to sign it all."

"How's that?" Will said.

"It goes like this," Alfred said, settling himself more comfortably. "You paint a picture in the style of your chosen master. Now of course, you go to enormous trouble to make sure the painting looks genuine from every angle, front, back and sides. The best way is to pick up an old framed canvas from one of the auction houses. Choose something where the varnish has gone completely black and you'll get it for little more than the price of the frame, unless it has history. You do your research beforehand. You'll have picked your period and your painter. You have to know what sort of support he would have used, but it's easy to pick up old framed canvases, so the best bet is to get a job lot. You avoid wood unless you must have a panel, because it's likely to be rotten."

"And then you paint it," Will said.

"Not quite that simple, my boy," Alfred said. "If you're using oils then you may have to mix in a hard resin, to make it set fast and go slightly brittle. Then you need to know the colour palette that the artist would have used – terrible amateur mistake if you use a colour he wouldn't have had. And of course, it's best to avoid original ultramarines, because ground lapis lazuli is very pricey, and you can't get the same effect with bog-standard Ultramarine."

He sipped tea.

"So you have your old canvas and your proper colour palette and your mixers," Will prompted.

"Yes. You need the right brushes too, of course, but you can generally get the proper sort of thing by studying the original brushwork closely. Then you prepare the old canvas. Whip it out of the frame and lay the frame to one side to reapply later. Grind the surface of the painting with pumice stone if necessary, to strip off the top layer of paint. You have to support the back of the canvas or it will tear because the fibres on the canvas have usually gone. I generally scrape out all the dirt and keep it in a screw-cap jar. Then I cling-film the back and pack the painting down onto sand, so that it moulds to the back of the canvas."

Will nodded.

"Then what?"

"Then at last you paint the picture, dear boy. That's the easy part, really. You paint something in the style of the painter, and you might pick something out of the background and paint it at a different angle. If you were doing a Vermeer, for example, you'd pop that old antique map of his up on the wall somewhere. Of course you wouldn't do a Vermeer – van Meegeren mucked that opportunity up. Too much notoriety these days. Anyway, background objects can be anything appropriate. A fire screen is a favourite for a ladies portrait. They used them to stop the fire melting their wax make-up, you know."

Will nodded again.

"And then presumably you sign it?" he said. "Otherwise it wouldn't be a forgery."

"Ah, but that's where you're wrong!," Alfred said with a smile. "As I said in the beginning, much more subtle not to sign it with the master's name. No, I'll get to that in a minute. First you finish your masterpiece, and dry it for a few days in a low oven. Then you stick the dirt back in and return it to its frame."

"What about crackelure?" Will asked, referring to the myriad of fine cracks that generally covered the paint surface of old canvas oil paintings.

"Good point," Alfred said. "That's where the resin base comes in. It sets hard and brittle, so you find with a bit of thumb pressure from the back, you can make your own cracks where you want them, unless of course the painting already had a good crackelure, in which case you just encourage them to crack a little along the original lines."

"How do you know where to put the cracks?"

"Oh you know, ravages of time; wherever you want, really. But I generally aim for any impasto areas, especially if they are a different colour. A moon for example – lovely spot for a bit of crackelure, that."

"But you don't sign it?" Will said uncertainly.

"Ah, you don't sign it with the master's name," Alfred said with a chuckle. "Of course you might, if you've made a particularly splendid one and you can't resist it. But a neat trick is to leave it unsigned, and when you sell the picture to the unsuspecting dealer, you attribute it wrongly."

"I don't get it. You don't attribute it to the master whose style you've just taken all the trouble to copy?" Will said with a frown.

"You attribute it to a well known but minor artist of the same style, such as a famous student of the same studio," Alfred said. "You might even have knocked up a piece of provenance to prove that it has been attributed to that other minor artist."

"I still don't get it."

"Psychology, my boy. The dealer is convinced that he's cleverer than you are, for that is his profession. So when you offer him a painting attributed to a minor painter, and you ask an extortionate price for that minor painter, he looks at it and is about to turn it away. But then he notices that the painting bears an extraordinary resemblance to the work of Raphael or Blake or whoever's style it is that you actually copied. And he brings his expert eye to bear and notices details, like the background map or whatever. He begins to convince himself that what he has here is a genuine original which has been wrongly attributed at some point in the past. He has under his hand a lost masterpiece! He's so pleased that he *agrees to pay the extortionate price for the minor artist, as he can't bear the thought of losing the work."*

"What if he plays hard to get?"

"Then you look uncertain and begin to pack it away to take it back to your Aunt Mildred, to whom you made a solemn vow that you would get a good price."

"But doesn't he test it?"

"Not usually. Proper testing costs money. He's convinced himself that he's spotted a masterpiece because he's so clever, you see. He thinks you haven't a clue because you're an ignorant peasant. So he keeps it for a while, then he presents it to the art market as a wrongly attributed masterpiece. Other experts agree with him after careful study, and it gets sold at Christie's or Sotheby's for a large fortune to some unsuspecting punter."

"It sounds easy," Will said.

"And it is, my boy," Alfred said with a chuckle, heaving himself off his bunk and going over to the easel, his breath wheezing as it always did.

Will tried to move but it was as if his whole body was fixed in cement. He had a rising sense of panic. Then he began to hear a siren in the distance, and he shouted to Alfred to watch out, but the old man didn't seem to notice. Someone was shaking his arm and he looked around. It was Lewis – which was odd, because Lewis had been at his first prison, not this one. He could hear crackling and see smoke coming through the door now, and Lewis was tugging at his arm, shouting at him that he had to leave. But Will couldn't move, and Alfred wasn't listening, and the smoke was in his face, and the siren was getting louder...

TWELVE

If pleasures are greatest in anticipation, just remember that this is also true of troubles
ELBERT HUBBARD

Will sat up with a jerk, blinking in the sunlight. George's head was framed against the sun, giving him a halo like an angel in a fourteenth-century painting. An ambulance was speeding down Victoria Avenue across the Common, its blue lights flashing. George was shaking him by the arm and Anna was stirring beside him on the grass.

"It's half past four," George said. "Time I was getting over to this client, and I couldn't just leave you two sleeping like babies." He looked more closely at Will. "You all right, old chap?"

Will sat up, blinking and rubbing his eyes. "I was having the most extraordinary dream," he said. "Completely lucid."

Anna was sitting up now.

"Dream about what?" she said sleepily. "God, I drank too much. I need something which isn't alcoholic."

"Come back to the studio and I'll make you some tea," Will said. "I think I need some myself. I was dreaming about Alfred. There was a fire…I can't remember it clearly." He shook his head and pointed. "That siren was in it."

The offending siren slowly removed itself into the distance.

George departed to meet with his client. Will put his bowler hat back on and collected his bicycle from the railing to which it was secured, then he and Anna walked back to the studio, the bicycle cogs making a ticking sound as they walked.

"You were going to tell me about Alfred but I fell asleep," Anna prompted as they walked along. "You've never said much about prison."

"He was a nice old bloke," Will said. "He certainly knew how to paint, but it was *more* than that. He had studied technique so much that he had a highly developed instinct about the masters. It was almost as if he had been there right beside them, and watched them put the paint on the canvas. Like he'd got inside their skins. Not all of them, of course, but he knew a fair few of them intimately; their lives, their influences, their technique. He could demonstrate anyone's style. It must have been difficult in a prison cell, because he didn't have all the materials he needed. No red chalk for example, so he'd improvise with charcoal. But he got on pretty well. He was up to all the tricks, too. I remember once he told me he used to paint earlier versions beneath the final painting – they call them *pentamenti*. That way if they X-rayed it, the *pentamenti* would come up and the boffins would gather round and say `Yes, very characteristic of this painter'."

"It's amazing that they can see what's underneath."

"Yeah. Sometimes Alfred used to paint a completely different painting underneath, in the same artist's style, but he'd do a poor job of it."

She frowned for a moment and then her forehead cleared.

"So they'd think that the artist had painted the first picture, hadn't liked it and had painted over it?"

"Exactly. It's priceless, isn't it?"

"It sounds like it was some sort of game with him."

"I'm sure it was," he nodded. They crossed the road and turned into an alleyway that was a shortcut to his studio. "It wasn't just the painting, I'm certain of that. With Alfred it was a game of cat and mouse with the experts. I've read a bit about Van Meegeren and he was much the same. He forged Vermeers back in the forties. Sold one to Hermann Goering in exchange for a bunch of real impressionist paintings, if you please. At first they thought he was a Nazi collaborator, but he ended up as a national hero. My point is that he was playing games with the experts, too."

"I suppose I can see the attraction in it, hoodwinking all those stuffy people who think they know better," Anna said. "I mean, if you ever see them on art programmes, some of them really do take the biscuit. Eulogising about some pathetic installation."

"Most of them couldn't actually paint, so they went to college and learned to talk about it instead of doing it," Will said darkly. "I don't have any time for them. Mind you, they're very complimentary about my work, and you know why? I reckon it's the prison sentence they like; it fits in with their stereotype of artists being on the edge."

They crossed over the street next to some roadworks and a parked water board van. Anna let herself in the front door with her key while Will went down a narrow path to the back, where there was a small garage. He put the bicycle in the garage, looking speculatively at the gleaming black and silver Bonneville for a moment. He wondered whether he should take it to the Isle of Wight the next day, instead of taking the train. But then he decided that he'd rather drive down in the company of Lucy Wrackham. He felt unexpectedly interested in the prospect of meeting her again.

Anna was upstairs and the kettle was boiling when he went in.

"So do you trust this insurance woman?" she asked. "What's her name again?"

"Lucy Wrackham," Will said. "I *think* I do, but she's a hard one to read. It's early days yet and she had her barriers up. She was probably a bit upset because I yelled at her when she butted in while I was painting."

"Well, you *can* be perfectly horrible when you're painting," Anna said.

She made ordinary tea for him and Camomile for herself. When he smelled the pungent camomile he was reminded of Lucy once more, sitting on the same sofa in the same place as Anna, except that Anna had slipped off her shoes and gathered up her legs beneath her.

"Well, take care tomorrow," Anna said. "She's an insurance agent, you said? You don't want her lining you up for something you didn't do. It might be a ruse, all this stuff about Alfred."

"I'll be careful," he said. "But it would make me feel bad if I just walked away and did nothing. It would make me feel like I'd let him down."

RICHARD JOHN MITCHELL

THIRTEEN

A flow of words is a sure sign of duplicity
HONORÉ DE BALZAC

Lucy's younger brother telephoned just as she was about to leave for the private view at the Limerston Gallery. She and Dylan were close because her parents were dead and he was the only family she had left after David died. He played lead guitar in a band, earning little but enjoying every minute of it. When first their father and then their mother had died within a single year, she had been only nineteen and had felt lonely and broken-hearted, frightened and betrayed. Forced to grow up too early, she had watched her fifteen year-old brother go in the opposite direction and take to drugs and drink. Twelve years later he had moved on from self-destruction, but Lucy was still playing the part of mother. She had never been truly frivolous; never stayed up all night dancing; never been disapproved of. Even her marriage to David had been three rather conventional and uneventful years, until the tragic ending. Occasionally she resented her orderly existence, but in her most honest moments had to admit that mostly she was happy with it.

She spoke to Dylan for half an hour and heard about his love life and his latest musical exploits. He was in love with the girl who sang lead vocals, but she was in love with the drummer. Lucy listened for a while and tried to give advice, though she no longer felt qualified. Dylan tactfully avoided the subject of Millie and the disgraced Sam, though he knew all about it because she had called him on the day it had happened. He had always been very tactful – she knew he had never thought a great deal of David, for example, but when David was killed he had been the first one by her side and had stayed with her for days while she poured out her heart.

In exchange for his news she told him about the forged paintings and her visit to Cambridge. She knew Dylan would approve of Will Bentley but she hardly mentioned him except in general terms. Instead she came off the phone with her head full of talk about chords and lyrics and metre. She looked longingly at her own white baby grand, and touched one key lightly, sending a haunting A flat into the silence. Then she regretfully decided that she was late and had to leave. Besides, her cat Peaches was asleep on top of the piano and Lucy didn't want to wake her.

She ran out of the flat when her taxi arrived and dashed to the Kings Road in Chelsea, arriving for the seven-thirty appointment at almost nine. The taxi couldn't stop outside as she had expected because a Rolls Royce was in the way. As she walked back she tried to see through its darkened windows, but to no avail.

The door in the glass-fronted Limerston Gallery was closed, but there was already a hubbub inside and one or two people had spilled out onto the pavement, talking and smoking. She had been there twice before on business and the gallery always looked good. This time there was a new elongated bronze sculpture of a mother and child in the window, beside a vase of fresh peonies. A man at the door glanced at her invitation cursorily before she was allowed entrance.

Inside there were spotlights illuminating the individual paintings, which hung on understated cream walls to let their colours shine through. The private view was in full swing, the air loud with chatter and laughter. The art world uses private views chiefly for networking, though a sizeable retinue of dedicated aficionados wandered from room to room, earnestly studying the classical still lifes of Wayne East, the young artist on view. The gallery owner was Belinda Hodge, a posh forty-something who liked to be known as Lindy. She had salon-blonde hair, good looks and a polished charm through which she had established a foothold in London's art world. She also had an extraordinary ability to remember faces, which she put into practice now, making her excuses to a penniless punter and coming instead with outstretched arms to greet Lucy.

"*Lucy* sweetheart!" she said loudly, as if this were the highlight of her evening. She had a warm rich voice which seemed to befriend people and welcome them in. She gave Lucy a hug and kissed her on each cheek. "How *lovely* to see you, darling! And how is Hoffman and Courtland these days?"

She was wearing a small round red hat. It would have looked ridiculous on anyone else but she carried it off perfectly. She had matching carmine lips and dark eyes. She had a way of holding her head slightly tilted back, like an actress making a stage entrance.

Hoffman and Courtland insured Lindy's paintings while they were in her shop, and they had paid out a handsome sum for a burglary, at which point Lucy had become involved. She had been on the Limerston Gallery's mailing list ever since. Lindy grabbed a passing waiter and handed Lucy a glass of red wine. One could tell the wealth of a gallery according to the wine served at private views. This was a good red wine, so the Limerston was middle of the range.

As Lucy renewed her acquaintance with Lindy and made small talk, she gradually became aware of a man standing behind the gallery owner. As if instinctively aware of the intrusion, Lindy turned to the interloper and again became effusive when she saw who it was.

"Lucy darling, let me introduce you to my star guest!"

The man held out his hand. He was taller than Lucy though she was not short. He was a little older than her, with public-school charm. He was wearing a navy blue linen shirt and cream linen trousers. He was clean shaven and had light brown hair, left slightly long. He looked as if he had just come from tennis in the garden of some 1930s movie. When he smiled as he did now, he had a particularly handsome face.

"How do you do?" he said, in deep resonant tones as if he might be an opera singer who had momentarily wandered off the stage of the Albert Hall.

"Lucy Wrackham," she said, taking his hand. His grip was dry and firm and he had about him some unmistakable presence.

"Rupert Angel," he said. "I own the Angel Gallery; you may know of it? Lindy was kind enough to invite me to see Wayne East's work."

"Rupert is thinking of showing Wayne at the Angel," Lindy said, giving Rupert a look of adoration.

"I've only just arrived," Lucy said, smiling. "I must look at the work."

"Then you must let me conduct you, and tell me what you think of it," Angel said firmly, taking her elbow and steering her away from a slightly disappointed Belinda Hodge.

"She's very nice," he said conspiratorially to Lucy, "but she does talk a great deal. Oh I'm sorry, is that terribly rude? I hope you're not her best friend?"

"No," Lucy said, "and I know what you mean, but she's sweet in her way. She's also a good businesswoman and she's well connected."

"How do you know her?" Angel asked.

"I work for Hoffman and Courtland and we insure this gallery."

She wondered if this chance meeting might turn into a coup for her company – winning the contract for a top London gallery like the Angel would certainly be a feather in her cap.

"Really?" he said. "The premier art insurers of London, Amsterdam and The Hague. You know, I believe we may have been at the same event at some time in the past. You seem familiar. You might have caught my eye."

The wine was making her feel warm. "You didn't catch mine," she said, rebuffing him but sounding a little flirtatious nevertheless.

"Pity," he said, looking at her with challenge. "Perhaps I can do better this time round."

He held up his glass and they clinked.

"Now let me show you the best of this young man; Wayne East. Silly name but actually he's not bad at all. Do you know the work of Giuseppe Arcimboldo?"

"The vegetable man. Made faces out of vegetables."

"He's the one," Angel nodded, still guiding her by the elbow so that she glided through the doorway and into the second gallery room at the rear. He fielded a waiter on the way to replenish their glasses. Lucy drank some more

– it was very palatable wine, she decided. A young lady appeared with a tray of canapés, privately instructed by Lindy to ensure that Rupert Angel left the gallery well fed and watered. Lucy stood in front of a portrait of a woman's face, made up of pieces of fruit. Each piece of fruit had been sliced neatly in half, making the painting different – taking Arcimboldo's idea and yet somehow bringing it up to date. She studied it for a while, glad of the canapés. Truth to tell she was already feeling a little tipsy, drinking on an empty stomach. The painting was well executed and she said so, making Rupert Angel smile and nod.

Yes," he said. "I think this chap will get somewhere. It's formulaic, but it will sell like hot cakes to all the punters who know enough about art to recognise the allusions. This one pays homage to Arcimboldo, of course, but there are others in here paying homage to Fantin-Latour and Claesz and Ruysch. All still lifes."

"They'd be tough to copy," she said, unconsciously thinking of the forged Alma-Tadema.

He looked sideways at her.

"Decorative fakes, you mean? Oh I don't know. Plenty of people do them these days. I'm always getting emails from China. Cheap labour, you see."

She had almost finished her glass and he replenished it again. She realised she ought to slow down or else she was going to be sick on Lindy's carpet, which would not make her very popular. She giggled, and then realized she had giggled and he was looking at her quizzically.

"Not decorative fakes," she said, trying to re-establish her authority "Forgeries. I'm investigating a case of forgery at the moment."

"Are you really?" Rupert Angel said, now looking at her closely. "How exciting! You must tell me all about it, but first come in here and look at this one. He's painted a modern anamorphosis – a skull which works in perspective when viewed from a tight angle at the side, and other things to go with it: a torch, a gun and a mobile phone, I believe. Instead of a candle, a knife and a quill, perhaps."

She followed Angel and stepped to the side of the painting to view it. Where it had looked almost abstract from the front, now it formed the shape of the objects that Angel had listed. There was also a half-folded letter, on which one could recognise words but not read the actual writing. The title of the piece was "Murder".

"I agree, this one is very clever," she said. "After Holbein's `Ambassadors' in the National, of course. He can certainly paint, even if he does have a ridiculous name."

"He's here somewhere," Angel said with amusement, and she felt embarrassed that she had spoken loudly and looked guiltily around.

They moved around the room, looking at the other paintings on display. Somehow Lucy found that her glass never quite got empty before it was replenished, either by Rupert Angel or by the young lady with the canapés.

"So what's this about forgeries, then?" he asked after a while. "The world of insurance is obviously more interesting than I imagined."

"Just in the last few days I've uncovered a forged Alma-Tadema," Lucy said, aware that she probably shouldn't be divulging such things, but having a sudden ridiculous desire to impress Rupert Angel.

He looked suitably attentive and studied her keenly.

"Not too hard to copy, I suppose."

"I suppose not. It disappeared and then returned after a few months. 'The Juggler': do you know it?"

"I'm afraid not," Angel said after a pause. "Was the forgery easy to spot?"

"Funny you should say that. We were convinced it was genuine, but just to be certain we had it tested."

"Good for you," he said, and raised his glass to hers so that they clinked and drank.

"Anyway," she went on, "it looked exactly the same as the original, and all the photographs of the back and sides of the support matched perfectly."

"Then how ever did you know?" he asked. "Lab tests I suppose?"

"Yes, it was the funniest thing. The *wormholes* didn't look right. Apparently they didn't have…" she lowered her voice conspiratorially and leaned in close to him. "They didn't have worm excreta in them. Oh, and one of them wasn't in quite the right place."

He stood looking at her for a few moments without saying anything.

"Amazing what they can do in these labs," he said at last.

She nodded. "I must admit I was astonished. So now we're on the hunt for the perpetrator."

"Do you have any clues?"

"We think we do, yes. But I mustn't name any names in case we're mistaken. Now if you'll excuse me for just a moment, I need to find the bathroom."

He held her glass for her. She found a black spiral staircase at the back of the gallery that went downstairs. It reminded her of the staircase in the corner of Will Bentley's studio; where she had followed him up onto his beautiful Gaudi-inspired roof. She went down the steps, remembering suddenly that she was travelling with Will Bentley to the Isle of Wight tomorrow. She didn't regard Will as someone she could ever get close to; he was an ex-con and had a terrible temper, after all. But Rupert Angel on the other hand she found rather interesting. He was obviously clever and he knew about art. He was rich and he was good looking. She completed her make-up repairs in the Ladies and renewed her perfume from the small bottle of Parisienne she kept in her handbag. As she did so she concluded that Mr

Angel was definitely an item of interest. She decided to ring up Millie for a chat about it all, but then experienced the usual terrible sense of loss when she remembered they were not on speaking terms.

When Lucy returned, Angel was talking with an elegantly dressed blonde woman in her late fifties. A tall and pimply youth in an ill-fitting suit stood close by, looking disconsolate.

"Lucy!" Angel said, turning to her at once. "Let me introduce you to my personal assistant, Mrs Morris. We don't believe she has a first name."

Mrs Morris smiled. "Don't listen to Rupert, my dear," she said. "It's Julia. I hear you've been having a most exciting time, discovering forged works of art? Who would have thought it?"

Lucy smiled weakly. She had already realised that the wine had loosened her tongue, and now she grabbed a glass of orange juice from a passing tray. She felt uncomfortable that Rupert Angel had already discussed her story with his assistant. She must have looked put out, because Angel immediately said, "Lucy, I do apologise; I shouldn't have said anything about your private business. But let me reassure you that Mrs Morris is extremely discreet, and it's *so* fascinating."

"Your secret is safe with me," Mrs Morris said demurely, putting a perfectly manicured finger to her lips and looking Lucy straight in the eye. Though she was no longer young she had not entirely lost her looks, and her well-spoken silky-smooth voice gave her an air of calm and control. Her hair was the sort of uniform ash blonde only available from an expensive salon, and her lips were burgundy. A faint aura of Chanel Number Five surrounded her.

The young man standing near them cleared his throat.

"Oh and this is Lawrence, Mrs Morris's son," Angel said with considerably less warmth.

"Hi," Lawrence said, not making eye contact but fiddling with his cuff. He and Lucy shook hands, but he gripped her fingers too early so that they didn't clasp hands properly.

"Hello," she said, feeling a bit sorry for him. She had seen his type before in some of her brother Dylan's friends. He looked up and caught her eyes on him, blushed and looked away again.

"I'm afraid Lawrence hasn't quite developed his airs and graces," Mrs Morris said with pretended irony, and trilled a little laugh. Lucy caught a glint in the woman's eye that startled her for an instant, before she decided that she must have imagined it.

Lindy came over to their party and introduced the artist of the day, Wayne East. He was in his early twenties and waxed lyrical for a few minutes about his life and work, prompted in the right places by Lindy. Mrs Morris excused herself and made an exit, trailed by her gauche son, while Rupert Angel subjected Wayne East to a clinical examination of his knowledge and approach to art through a series of penetrating questions. The young man fielded them well and responded intelligently. He would do well enough, Lucy decided; he could talk the talk.

The crowd was thinning and Lucy began to think she should go. She had been drinking iced water for the last hour and thankfully her head had cleared. One of Eric Satie's *Gymnopedies* was being piped over the gallery's loudspeakers, and she became suddenly aware of it now that the hubbub had quietened. Someone found her coat and brought it for her, but then Rupert Angel was at her side.

"I'd like to see you again, Lucy," he said without preamble. "I have enjoyed the evening very much. Would you consider dinner? I have in mind a perfect restaurant in Mayfair. Should I go down on bended knee and beg you for your company?"

"I adore being begged," she laughed, and pretended to consider for a moment.

"All right then, that would be a pleasure. I've enjoyed meeting you, too."

She gave him her number and made her farewells, refusing his offer of a lift by saying that she lived in the depths of Richmond. Lindy saw her to the door and remarked that she certainly seemed to have hit it off with Rupert Angel. Lucy knew that it was Lindy's way of registering her part in the connection – in case it might later become a story she could dine out on. She thanked Lindy very prettily for her hospitality, and stepped into the cool night air of London. A light drizzle had started and the tyres of passing cars hissed on the Kings Road, their headlights dazzling. Three hundred and fifty years ago, Charles II had ridden along this same highway to visit his mistress Nell Gwyn in Fulham. Now it smelled of rain and diesel. The Rolls was still sitting outside as she hailed a taxi. She wondered if it was Rupert's and regretted her refusal of a lift, but then a cab drew in to the kerb and she stepped into it.

Still inside the gallery, standing back discreetly so as not to be seen, two figures watched as Lucy disappeared into the cab.

"Well!" said Mrs Morris to Rupert Angel. "I think you're going to have to get closer to *that* little cutie, Rupert."

Angel said nothing. Mrs Morris looked through the window glass again at the departing taxi.

"Don't get too fond of her," she said in an even tone.

FOURTEEN

Flirting is the art of keeping intimacy at a safe distance
SABINA SESSELMANN

As Rupert Angel and Mrs Morris stood at the window of the Limerston Gallery and watched Lucy's taxi disappear into the London traffic, Detective Constables Stokes and Matheson were holed up in their surveillance van 63 miles away, near Will's studio in Cambridge. They weren't watching Will; they were watching the brothel next door. Cambridge Constabulary had decided that it was going to prosecute the owner of the brothel and required evidence in support of its case. The Constabulary normally maintained a lenient attitude towards the sex industry, but recently a nasty case linked with foreign girls and drug abuse had been splashed across the tabloids, and word had come down from above that a crackdown would be politically expedient.

In the eight hours that Billy and Emily had been sitting in the van together they had so far only talked about work, noting people entering and leaving the suspect premises. They didn't have much to do because the camera watched the street without pause and recorded everyone entering and leaving. It had recorded Lucy Wrackham leaving the premises next door, although this was irrelevant to the investigation and hadn't been entered in the log. To reduce accusations of unreliable evidence, a separate handwritten log had to be kept of people entering and leaving the brothel, and it was very tedious. Even worse was the knowledge that they had to record several days of evidence, to provide plenty of information to support the case.

As the junior member of the detective team in Cambridge, Billy had drawn one of the short straws for this incredibly boring job. Emily Matheson had drawn the other, even though she had been in the team longer, because she was female and her boss, Detective Inspector Carter, had said that a female officer might need to be present. Neither of them had quite plucked up enough courage to ask why.

Billy looked at his watch. It was gone eleven and completely dark. There had been several visitors to the brothel in the last hour, all of whom were perfectly visible in the street lighting.

"Pubs are closing," he said. "Probably get a few more now."

"Desperate men," Emily said, with a giggle.

"I know how they feel," Billy said. "I mean, when you've had a few jars, it does get you in the mood, doesn't it?"

"I wouldn't know."

"Don't you get out much, then?" Billy said.

"Well I'm married, Billy Stokes, so you can leave it out."

Billy said nothing but decided sadly that she didn't seem to be interested. The only thing that still gave him hope was her style. Billy's dad was dead now, but he would have said there was something a bit saucy about DC Matheson. It was an old-fashioned word but it fitted.

He sat for a minute and became aware of her scent.

"You smell nice tonight," he said. "Is that new perfume?"

"Yes, it was a birthday present from my husband," she said, effectively putting a stop to that line of conversation.

She lapsed into silence and so did he. He picked up his newspaper and tried to address himself to the crossword, but he couldn't concentrate.

"First time Vic ever gave me something I actually wanted," she went on after a minute.

Billy felt a sense of jubilation which he tried to cover up. He looked sideways at her and she couldn't help noticing once again how young he was. And big, too – he must be a foot taller than her.

"If I was your husband I'd give you what you wanted all the time," he said.

"Cheeky devil."

There was an interlude in the conversation as a car crawled slowly past the brothel and parked. A punter went up to the door, knocked and was ushered in. They wrote it down in the log and entered the car's registration plate into the computer.

"You'd think they wouldn't park outside like that," Emily said.

"Probably doesn't occur to them that anyone's watching. I mean, normally we wouldn't be, would we?"

"No, but once Carter gets a bee in his bonnet you can't say no. He won't be happy until he's closed them down."

Billy did a passable imitation of DI Carter's clipped tones: "Get your arse down to the suspect premises and record everything that moves, Stokes. And no bloody monkey business with that DC Matheson."

She giggled again.

"He didn't say that!"

"He did."

"He did not. You're a liar, Billy Stokes."

"Must be wishful thinking, then."

"You should be so lucky."

FIFTEEN

Memento mori. Remember that you will die.
ROBERT O. LENKIEWICZ, 1941-2002. Painter

Lucy met Will off the train from Cambridge at nine on Sunday morning and they drove in her red MG down to Portsmouth, arriving just after eleven. They took the Wightlink Ferry over to Fishbourne, which was full of holidaymakers, and stopped for lunch in a pub. Lucy drank orange juice and explained to Will that she'd had a bit of a night of it. Then they drove the last forty minutes through rolling fields and hills to Brighstone Manor, home of Sir Philip and Lady Felicity Hall, and home also to a Frans Snyders painting.

"Two o'clock," Lucy remarked as they arrived. "Right on time." She turned into the stone-flagged drive.

"Quite a place they have here," Will said. "But I suppose if they own a Frans Snyders they must have a few pennies to rub together."

"Family money," Lucy said. "Except that each time someone dies they have to sell off one of the heirlooms to pay the taxes."

"So the Inland Revenue probably has its eye on the Frans Snyders," Will said. "Is it one of the big ones? The only one I ever saw was twelve feet wide and it would be tricky to forge that."

"It isn't huge but I know the ones you mean. This is more manageable."

"Lots of dead game, I seem to remember. He seems to have had an obsession about dead things."

"Hunting trophies," Lucy said. "Jan Fyt followed him, and the genre remained popular. The Dutch took a fancy to reflecting aristocratic sports, right through to the end of the century with Weenix, but Snyders liked to set his pictures up like a market stall. Trying to show a shift towards the common man, perhaps."

Will looked sideways at Lucy. She certainly knew her stuff. She sensed his examination and glanced back at him, giving him a friendly smile which broke her normal reserve. Then she looked away again.

The gateway was flanked by stone pillars topped with dragons, and wrought-iron black gates that didn't look as if they had been closed for years. There was an ancient carved stone plaque proclaiming the name of the manor, and a modern red and white sign next to it warning visitors to beware of horses.

"It's a gorgeous house," Lucy said. "You'll see in a minute."

The MG's tyres bumped over the uneven stone flags.

"The present manor is Jacobean, though I believe it's on the site of a much older building," she went on, sounding a bit like a tour guide. "Sir Philip once told me that it's mentioned in the Domesday Book. There, now – look at that."

The house swung into view around a bend in the drive, built of grey stone covered with yellow lichen. Two wings thrust forward on each side and the drive led up to a turning circle around a central fountain. Lucy drove slowly up to the front of the house and parked, turning off the engine. The car ticked as hot metal cooled, but apart from that the only sound was birdsong. Then there was the distant whinny of a horse.

"They have a riding stable behind the building," Lucy explained as they got out of the car. "It was started by Lady Felicity when she was a young woman, but I believe it's now maintained by her daughter, who has an odd name that escapes me."

Will stood by the car with his hands on his hips and inhaled deeply.

"I can smell the horses," he said.

A man of about sixty came around the corner of the house wearing green Wellington boots.

"Lucy!" he called when he was still ten yards away. "And this must be your young man."

Lucy and Will caught each other's eye for a moment and smiled. They were used to each other now; Lucy less aloof and Will less defensive.

"Sir Philip!" Lucy said. "Let me introduce Will Bentley. He's not my young man actually, he's a business colleague."

"Though I'm flattered," Will said gallantly.

Sir Philip had a firm handshake and a keen eye which he now used to appraise Will.

"Ah yes, an artist: Lucy did mention you. A bit of an expert come to look at our Frans Snyders, she said. Welcome to you both! Felicity's popped out but she shouldn't be long. She'll show you the picture when she gets back. Meanwhile I'll see if I can get Mrs Finnis to rustle up a pot of tea."

He opened the front door and an Airedale Terrier came bounding out, barking joyfully.

"Settle down now, Teddy!" Sir Philip roared. They followed him along the uneven floor of the hall into a beautiful study, its walls lined with books. The Airedale followed, sniffing at their legs. Will and Lucy were pointed to seats and their host disappeared to find his housekeeper.

"This place is remarkable," Will said. "It ought to be open to the public."

"I believe they have thought about it," Lucy said. "But the stable pays the bills. I know exactly what you mean, though. I stayed here a couple of nights when I was last over, because I was appraising several of their pieces. They put me up in a four-poster bed."

"Was there a ghost?"

"Probably several, but I was too asleep to notice. They say it is haunted, though. I expect all these old places are."

A grandfather clock ticked sedately in the corner. Lucy sat down and arranged herself neatly, folding her legs so that her mid-length skirt displayed a modest amount of elegant calf. Will wandered around the room, his feet creaking on the red-carpeted floorboards, looking at the various paintings on the walls. None of them was a Frans Snyders – they were all relatively small and seemed to be by local artists; Isle of Wight harbours and rolling landscapes for the most part. Several cricket scenes. As there was nothing much of interest there, Will turned his attention to the books, which comprised an oddly eclectic mix ranging from very old to brand new. He was thumbing through a biography of Rudyard Kipling when Sir Philip returned.

"I've spoken to Felicity on the mobile," his host said. "I'm afraid she'll be another half an hour. Would you like to visit the stables, or have a look through the main gallery, perhaps?"

Will raised his eyebrows. A gallery?

Sir Philip saw his look.

"We have all the best pictures in their own little gallery," he said. "Apart from the Frans Snyders: that's in its own special spot."

Lucy had seen the pictures but not the horses, so she went with Sir Philip on a tour. Will was more tempted by the gallery so he asked if he might be permitted to see it.

"Certainly you can," Sir Philip said. "I'll have to leave you to it though, or Lucy will get lost. Follow me, all." He marched down the wide hallway and deposited Will at a large closed door, his Wellington boots leaving occasional fragments of mud on the shining oak floorboards. The Airedale followed him adoringly, its paws scuffling for purchase on the floor.

"Pop in there and have a look around. There are some interesting pieces you normally wouldn't see outside an art catalogue. Light switch on the left."

The Airedale jumped up at Will, causing Sir Philip to roar at him again. Will caught Lucy's eye and winked.

When Sir Philip and Lucy had gone, Will turned the large brass doorknob and opened the heavy black oak door.

It was like entering a chapel. The gallery was long and narrow and dimly lit. Its windows were tall and narrow, formed at the top into cusped arches. An iron bar the thickness of a child's arm ran from top to bottom of each window, bisecting it in a discordant manner but necessarily protecting the contents within. Stained glass was set in the windows, depicting the Christ child on His mother's breast, with Mary clad in blue. There were also scenes of blue seas with fishes and an unidentified young damsel in the waves. Subdued light shafted into the gallery. There was a tall throne-like chair facing the middle window which cast a shadow on the stone-flagged floor.

Will found the light switch, which was actually a circuit breaker, and pulled it down. Spotlights sprang into life, illuminating each of the paintings in their own pools of light on the long wall opposite the windows. He walked slowly down the row, his boots echoing, conscious that he had half an hour so he could take his time. He found a varied mixture of paintings; some valuable and some by artists he did not know. They were interspersed with portraits of the Hall family; stern bewhiskered gentlemen, and ladies wearing extravagant dresses and earnest looks. There was a painting of Lady Felicity as an attractive young woman in a blue ball gown, and Sir Philip looking very smart in naval uniform.

About halfway along he found a painting by Sir John Everett Millais of a woman standing at a window. Her hair was wound into a plait and twisted over her shoulder, the colour of it echoed by her belt. She stood with her arms folded, looking out into an autumnal garden with a wistful expression on her face. Next to the Millais was a painting of badgers at the opening of a sett by Sir Edwin Landseer, with the skulls of small animals piled in the loose earth next to the opening of the burrow. In the middle of the gallery wall was a large religious painting; a very old picture of the Virgin and Child surrounded by angels. He stood in front of it for a moment and studied it, but suddenly became aware of someone behind him and spun around to find a young girl dressed in Goth style, about fifteen.

"My God, you startled me!" he said, feeling foolish.

"I was sitting in the throne," she said, indicating the large chair over her shoulder which he had seen as he came in. She looked like a pretty young witch, tall and skinny, clad all in black. Her hair was black to match her clothes, but the crucifix round her neck was silver, as were her skull rings and her spider earrings. It was such a sudden transformation from the past to the present that Will was rendered temporarily speechless.

"Who *are* you?" she asked with a frown. "You don't look like our normal visitors."

"I'm a painter," he said, finding his voice at last. "My name's Will Bentley and I've come here to look at a picture . Who are you?"

"I'm Acid Tears," she said.

Will managed to maintain a serious expression.

"I mean, what's your connection with Sir Philip and Lady Felicity?"

"I'm their granddaughter."

"Their granddaughter?" he echoed, hearing how stupid he sounded. "So, er… your mother runs the stables?"

"Yes."

He nodded slowly, examining her intently by force of habit, sizing up how she would look in a portrait. Quite good, he concluded – she was quirky.

"You're staring," she said accusingly.

"Sorry," he said, dropping his eyes. "I'm a portrait painter. I have a bad habit of sizing everyone up, and you'd be an interesting subject." He pointed behind him. "Like the Millais, but standing at a window all in black."

"Most people hate the way I look," she said.

"I don't see why," he said. "It's original, and that's a good thing. Why all the skulls and spiders? It's a bit miserable."

"The world is full of horrors," she said earnestly. "War and starvation. Death is something that should concern all of us, but it gets swept under the carpet. I don't believe it should be ignored."

"*Memento mori*," Will murmured as if almost to himself. "Remember that you will die."

She nodded and then shifted her gaze to look over his shoulder.

"You were looking at the painting behind you," she said, and he turned and contemplated the religious picture again. She stood next to him with her hands behind her back.

"It's very old, isn't it?" he said. "You must know it well if you've grown up here."

"I know every inch of it," she said, more natural and less dramatic now. She pointed to the virgin and child and indicated the cusped arch over their heads. "It's as if they're standing in a frame. What do you think of it?"

He looked more closely at the picture.

"The arch is a mandorla, or vesica piscis," he said. "Religious art of the time was full of symbols, and this is symbolic of the birth canal. It's formed by two overlapping circles. It's pagan, going back before Christianity, but the artist has used it as a symbol of fertility because of the birth of the Christ child." He spun on his heel and walked over to the windows, pointing to the top of one.

"Look!" he said. "The vesica piscis forms the top of a pointed arch like this, and if you look at the stained glass, it depicts the virgin and child again, and also the ocean." He touched a young woman with flowing tresses. "This is meant to be Aphrodite, I expect; or perhaps Venus. These windows are very old."

He looked back and she was staring at him. He returned to her.

"I never knew any of that," she said simply.

They contemplated the painting again for a moment.

"Do you notice anything unusual about the painting?" she asked. Her voice had an edge to it.

She touched one of the angels, set off to one side from the others, looking on at the nativity scene, and then answered her own question. "This one doesn't have a halo."

He looked at the other angels and had a sudden memory of George in his head, standing over him on Midsummer Common with the sun giving him a halo.

"You're right," he said, "And I think I can guess why. This angel is set off to one side, looking on at the scene as if he isn't part of it. Perhaps the artist meant him to be a demon, because demons were angels that had gone bad. Lucifer was an angel, for example, who challenged God. So the artist has added the demon, looking on jealously at the birth of Christ. That's why he doesn't have a halo."

"Yes but–," she began, and then the door opened before she could say any more and Sir Philip looked in.

"Ah, Mr Bentley," he said. "I see you've found Elizabeth. We've finished the tour of the stables and Felicity's just got back. Do you like the paintings?"

Elizabeth, also known as Acid Tears, walked towards the door and went straight out without acknowledging Sir Philip or saying anything more to Will.

Sir Philip looked embarrassed.

"My grand-daughter. Bit of a tricky stage she's going through at the moment as you probably noticed."

"On the contrary, we had a good conversation," Will said as he joined his host, and Sir Philip looked surprised and pleased.

"Really? Well, that's splendid. Now come along with me and we'll find Felicity."

SIXTEEN

Weristetone in Bowcombe Hundred, county of Hampshire. Records of the Exchequer, and its related bodies, with those of the Office of First Fruits and Tenths, and the Court of Augmentations
DOMESDAY BOOK, 1086

Will closed the heavy door and followed Sir Philip back to the study. They found Lucy there, talking to a small, bright-eyed woman.

Philip introduced Will to his wife, Lady Felicity, and she broke off from her conversation with Lucy and held out her hand. For a fleeting moment he wandered ridiculously whether he should shake it or kiss it, but he opted for the former. Her hand was surprisingly small in his.

"A painter!" Lady Felicity said with obvious interest. "What sort of thing do you paint, Mr Bentley?"

"Portraits, mostly," Will said. "Or anything with people in it. I'm trying to define the human character in paint."

"How interesting. And how large is your *oeuvre*?"

"About two or three thousand works. I've not counted, exactly."

"Good Heavens," she said, surprised. That's very prolific. And are these what I would call *proper* paintings?"

Will smiled.

"Some of them are rather *improper*, but they look like real people, if that's what you mean," he said slowly. "I'm not into squiggles."

"Good. One sees so much of that nonsense these days."

She turned to Lucy; the perfect hostess bringing her other guest back into the conversation.

"And how are you, my dear? It's only been a few months since we saw you, when you and that gentleman brought back the *Fruit*."

Will looked with raised eyebrows at Lucy.

"The Frans Snyders is called *Fruit in a Bowl on a Blue Cloth*," Lucy explained to him. "Painted in about 1630, we estimate. It's one of a pair of paintings. The other one is in the Hermitage in St. Petersburg and is on a red cloth, but rather similar apart from that. As I mentioned to you in the car, it was loaned to an exhibition of still lifes and disappeared. Then it turned up again a few months later, so I personally brought it back."

"And very good of you it was too," Sir Philip said. "I don't know when I've been more delighted. It's been in our family for generations, you know."

Mrs Finnis the housekeeper came in with a tray and laid out tea on the occasional table in front of two old brown leather sofas. She was a red-faced countrywoman who looked as if she had worked long hours every day of her life. She had a cheerful disposition and remembered Lucy from her previous visit. Lady Felicity poured out the tea when she had gone.

"It's a beautiful house," Will said. "Lucy was telling me that it was mentioned in the Domesday Book."

"Indeed," Sir Philip said. "It was in the Domesday Book as Weristetone Manor in 1086, but we believe the original building went back to 973. It's been destroyed by fire twice since then. The present building is Jacobean, built around 1622. Solid as a rock for nearly four hundred years."

"It must be quite a task to keep it up."

Sir Philip nodded.

"Sixteen rooms, eight acres and a modern stable at the back. The riding stables help to maintain the old place these days, of course. Best thing that Felicity ever did, setting up that business."

"One needs to be self sufficient," Lady Felicity said. "But Primmy keeps the stable going now."

She saw Will's raised eyebrows. "My daughter Primrose," she explained. "Except that I'm afraid we've settled into a ghastly habit of calling her Primmy. Primrose was her grandmother's name, you see."

They drank tea and munched biscuits. The Airedale sat at the end of the table and watched the plate of biscuits with a very intent expression until he was given one.

"So what's all this about our painting?" Sir Philip said. He was still wearing his green Wellingtons and looked slightly incongruous.

"As I said to you on the telephone," Lucy said, "another painting recently disappeared and then resurfaced after a time delay. When the painting was examined very closely we discovered that it was a forgery."

"Oh, there's no danger of that with the *Fruit*," Lady Felicity said. "At least I would be *extremely* surprised. We've had that painting in the family for generations, and I've known it for as long as I've known Philip."

"I've brought some photographs of the original, from when it was first insured by Hoffman and Courtland," Lucy said. "We'd like to do a comparison, if we may. Mr Bentley is somewhat of a specialist in forgery so I have asked him to use his skills."

"Not as a practitioner, I hope!" Sir Philip said, guffawing at his own joke.

"Oh, they've locked me up for it," Will said ingenuously, and Sir Philip laughed even more.

"Well, I don't see why we shouldn't let them have a look at it, Felicity," he said. "We'll look pretty silly if it turns out to be the wrong one, though."

"We'll look even sillier if it's not the original and we never spotted it," Lucy pointed out. Will noticed that Lady Felicity was looking extremely sceptical, though she didn't say anything.

When they had finished tea, Lucy went out to the MG and brought in a tube containing rolled up high-quality images of the original painting. Sir Philip led the way and they all trouped into the sitting room. It was a large room with a high ceiling, furnished with comfortable old leather furniture. It had a black Broadwood grand piano which Lucy eyed hungrily. She had played it the last time she had visited the house, but now was not the moment. It had a beautiful touch, she remembered.

The tube of photographs made a dull popping sound when opened. Lucy laid out its contents on a long table, and various paperweights were fetched to prevent the corners of the photos from curling up. Then they formed a group around the Frans Snyders and looked at it.

The painting featured two small bowls and a larger bowl in the centre. The large bowl contained oranges, figs, grapes, plums and greengages. The left bowl contained loganberries and the right bowl contained nuts. The three bowls stood on a deep blue cloth which provided a complementary background colour to the oranges. The painting was two feet high and three feet wide. Will's immediate instinct was that it was one of Alfred's, though he couldn't for the life of him have said why.

"Beautifully painted," he said, unwilling to declare it fake without evidence. He stared with great intensity at the picture. "How long have you had it in the family?"

"We have provenance back to 1761," Sir Philip said. "It has been in the family since around then but we're not entirely sure when it was acquired. It does appear in an inventory of goods of 1804, so we know it's been part of the family for at least 200 years. It was packed away during various wars of course, but has survived so far. That's why we were so upset when it was stolen and relieved when it was returned."

"I can imagine," Will said. "Could we take it down and put it next to the photographs? I need to do a close comparison."

"Of course, but give me a moment to switch the alarm off," Sir Philip said apologetically. "We've had a gadget fitted since all that unfortunate business. It made me realise how much that picture is part of the family, I suppose."

He disappeared for a minute.

"There we are," he said when he returned. "You can touch it now, but be very careful because it's fragile. Lift it carefully up and off the hook; it's not screwed down."

Will unhooked the picture very carefully from the wall and carried it down to the table, placing it next to the shiny photographic prints. After fifteen minutes of careful study, he still had not spotted any variation between the painting and the photograph. He turned the painting over and studied the back of the support. He didn't have any photographs this time, though it certainly appeared to be from the right era. But then, he thought gloomily, Alfred had spent hours telling him precisely how to age a painting.

"Well?" said Lucy at last, unable to contain herself any longer. "What do you think?"

"I can't see any definite signs that it *is* a forgery," Will said honestly. "I think if you want to find out for certain you'll have to send it off to the lab for tests."

"I don't believe we need any tests," Lady Felicity said with sudden firmness. "I am quite certain that this *is* our original. I have seen the back of the painting before as well as the front, and it looks just as it did when I was a young woman. Wouldn't you say, so, Philip?"

Sir Philip Hall looked at the painting and then at his wife. "Well dear, it looks the same to me, but as you know I'm not the most observant soul. And if Lucy thinks—"

"— I appreciate your concern, Lucy," Lady Felicity interrupted firmly. "But I think you're going to have to turn up some factual evidence before we let you take the painting off the island for testing. It was stolen when we let it out of our sight before, and we were most fortunate to get it back."

"That's what I'm worried about," Lucy said. "I understand how you feel, but it *was* lucky that you got it back. Perhaps it was too lucky."

"See if you can find another and then I'll entertain the idea that this is a fake," Lady Felicity said obstinately. "But until then, I do not want the painting to leave this house."

There was nothing that Lucy could do to persuade Lady Felicity otherwise, and Sir Philip was evidently unwilling to challenge his diminutive but determined wife. As a result, Lucy and Will found themselves driving away from the house feeling none the wiser. The Roadster's top was still down and the sun beat on them relentlessly, but the slipstream snatched its heat away.

"Are you *certain* you couldn't see anything to identify that painting as one of Alfred Smith's?" Lucy said suspiciously, once they were on the road and making their way back to the ferry.

"Actually when I first clapped eyes on it I immediately thought it was one of his," Will said blandly.

"*What?*" she said loudly in exasperation. "Well why on earth didn't you say so?"

He thought for a while about this and then shrugged.

"I spent ages looking at it very closely and I couldn't see anything wrong with it at all. The more I looked at it, the more it looked like a genuine old painting."

"Didn't Alfred have a distinguishing mark or something?" Lucy said, driving around corners with unnecessary haste.

"He didn't have a signature, he just used everyone else's," Will said, shaking his head. "There was nothing obvious. He didn't have a secret symbol if that's what you mean."

"Then how did you think you'd be able to identify it as one of his?" Lucy asked with sudden acidity.

Will looked at her, irritated by her tone.

"I never said I'd definitely be able to recognise it as one of Alfred's; I just said I'd look at it. And now I *have* looked at it so I've kept my side of the bargain."

"I'm sorry," she said immediately, throwing him an apologetic glance. "I'm just cross that we've come all this way and now they won't let me get it tested. It would only have taken a couple of days."

"Why don't you send someone to them," Will said.

She tilted her head at him and he grinned sheepishly.

"Oh I see; you just did. No, I mean one of your lab people. Can't you send one of them?"

"Not really," Lucy said, shaking her head. "I'm sure my lab tester John Ellis would love a day in the Isle of Wight, but you should see the size of the machines he uses. They're not portable, and somehow I don't think Lady Felicity would be very keen on me taking away a sample."

"No," Will said. "She was a bit steamed up at the idea of losing it, wasn't she? You could have said to her `Look Lady F, how about I take just one little grape, or a fig, perhaps. I'm sure she would have had a pair of scissors in the kitchen drawer."

Lucy laughed. Her blonde hair was constrained by a scarf but it was escaping. It whipped sideways and stung Will's cheek, and he stole a sideways glance at her, taking in her beauty.

"I'm going to have to draw you," he said, speaking louder over the slipstream. "You're a good-looking woman."

She turned to catch his eye for a moment and smiled enigmatically before she looked back at the road.

They caught the ferry without incident, and Lucy drove Will back to London. When she dropped him off she put her hand on his arm.

"Thank you for coming," she said. "It's been a frustrating day but I've an idea I was thinking about on the ferry. Alfred's last-known address is in Hastings. I would have gone today but it was too late, so I'm going to have a look tomorrow. If you come with me, we might find him and then all this mess and confusion can be settled once and for all. He might just have stopped bothering to sign in, and he may have been out when the policeman went around to his house."

Will looked as if he was going to say no.

"I'll let you draw me if you agree," she added enticingly.

He grinned.

"Naked of course?"

"Naked apart from several layers of clothing," she said sweetly. "We get to find Alfred, and you get to draw me, but I'm an old-fashioned girl so I'll be wearing clothes."

"You shouldn't trouble yourself on my account," Will said, giving her an earnest look. "You'd not believe the number of models I've seen naked."

"Not this one," Lucy said firmly, and looked him in the eye. "So will you come to Hastings?"

He met her eyes and knew that he definitely wanted to see her again. And of course he might find Alfred, though finding Alfred didn't seem to matter quite so much as it had.

"Just this once," he said.

SEVENTEEN

I was as virtuously given as a gentleman need to be; virtuous enough; swore little; diced not above seven times a week; went to a bawdy-house once in a quarter – of an hour; paid money that I borrowed, three of four times…
WILLIAM SHAKESPEARE, Falstaff, Henry IV, Part 1

"The painter's getting home late for a Sunday," DC Emily Matheson observed, watching the man unlocking the front door of the artist's shop next to the brothel.

"If that *is* the painter," Billy Stokes said.

"It must be; I saw him go in yesterday afternoon while you were making coffee. He had a bike and was with some woman. Anyway, he just took a key out of his pocket to get in with."

"Might be a burglar, you never know."

Billy imitated DI Carter again.

"Vigilance, Matheson. That's how we catch villains."

She giggled. Emily Matheson had a very nice giggle, he had decided. And she definitely wasn't uptight once you got to know her.

They remained silent for a minute or two, once Will had closed his front door and disappeared from view. The street was quiet and they were tired, having spent all day on duty due to a lack of resources to cover for them. They had to stay on duty until two in the morning and would be back at noon, on the basis that the brothel would do its main work in the night hours. Carter would have preferred round-the-clock surveillance, but even he conceded that they needed to eat and sleep.

The winking green figures of the digital clock in the van said 23:00. The street was empty; no-one was up to any hanky-panky that night. There had been a steady flow the previous night, but now there was nothing. Billy looked covertly at Emily Matheson. She wore a white shirt open at the neck, for it was hot inside the van. Her hair was tied back in a bunch, but not netted into a ball as favoured by uniformed women police officers.

"Your husband must be missing you," he said. "All these late nights."

There was a long silence after he had said this, so that he thought he had offended her and she was going to ignore him, or else flare up and have a go at him. But then she spoke softly, as if to herself.

"I don't know."

Another electric pause in which he could hear the ticking of the digital clock, the hiss of the fan inside the laptop, the almost-imperceptible hum of the video recording equipment and the soft sound of her breathing.

"Vic's all wrapped up in his business," she said. "He makes security alarms. It's going well but I never see him."

"That must be hard."

"I get by," she said with a shrug. "I wonder if I should have a kid but then I don't know if I want to. This job is all I have, really. It'd be a shame to give it up for a baby and then find out Vic doesn't want to be a dad. I'd be proper stuck, wouldn't I?"

"It might make him pay attention."

"Maybe it would," she nodded. "But he might pay attention to the kid and not to me, you know? Sometimes I wonder if he's got another woman."

"He'd be crazy to do that," Billy Stokes said.

She looked at him and he suddenly realised that her eyes were full of tears.

"Would he, Billy?"

She looked down. He took her hand and held it. A tear splashed onto the back of her hand and he rubbed it away and she laughed and cried at the same time.

"So stupid," she said. "I'm sorry."

She looked over his shoulder at the monitor, where an LED was blinking and a man had parked his car and was walking up the steps to the black door. She took her hand away.

"Another punter," she said.

EIGHTEEN

Venus and Mars, Tempera and Oil on Poplar, Made about 1485. Bought 1874. Mars, God of War, was one of the lovers of Venus, Goddess of Love. Here Mars is asleep and unarmed, while Venus is awake and alert. The meaning of the picture is that love conquers war, or love conquers all.
THE NATIONAL GALLERY, London, Room 58

Seven months ago

Alfred Smith had decided to paint himself an insurance policy. It was just after Christmas and freezing outside the large windows of the seaside house. He contemplated the painting on the easel before him. He knew the portrait was a good likeness though he had executed it from memory. There could be no doubt about the identity of the subject, though he had added the name and date to be certain. He picked up the antique canvas and felt its warmth from the oven where it had slowly baked for several days. He turned it through different angles, humming absent-mindedly under his breath; squinting at it to ensure that there were no ridges in the paint. The surface was smooth and he nodded to himself, pursing his lips. He sniffed it, front and back. There was no odour of paint, though the back had a sharp tang which made him wrinkle his nose, as if the ancient dust had locked within it the passing centuries. After a careful examination he was satisfied, and chuckled at the image before him. No-one would know about it, unless he needed them to; unless they denied all knowledge and tried to stitch him up. He replaced the canvas on the easel, opened a pot of primer, dipped a large flat brush in its virgin whiteness and began to paint smoothly and evenly over the portrait. When the white coat was completed he laid the painting aside to dry, and turned to his main project.

This was something else entirely – the most difficult thing he had ever attempted. When he had first learned of the "commission" he had laughed aloud. Could he make a perfect copy of Sandro Botticelli's *Venus and Mars*? This painting was created at the height of Botticelli's genius around 1485; the same decade that the great master's hand had produced his pagan masterpiece Primavera and the universally adored Birth of Venus. But when the proposed fee had been mentioned, Alfred had become thoughtful and had begun to consider whether it *could* be done. It would be the greatest challenge he would ever attempt, for he was getting older and knew he couldn't paint forever. In the last few cold months he had experienced arthritis in his fingers and he was afraid that it might spread, until like the aging Renoir he would only be able to paint with brushes strapped to his wrists. Before then he wanted to retire to his beloved Italy, there to live out his days in the Tuscan sun with enough money to enjoy life's pleasures. This painting would allow him to make that clean break, and it would also represent the zenith of his career; a fitting point at which to retire. So Alfred had accepted the proposal – and a new painting, as his friend Will Bentley had once joked, would soon be history.

By mid-February he had acquired a five hundred year-old painted chest. The painting on the front of it had been a worthless daub, but the chest was made of poplar wood and it was this that he wanted. Alfred had trawled through many auction rooms before eventually finding what he had been looking for; an early sixteenth-century Italian *cassone* – a wedding chest used to present the bride's dowry. He had started by looking for a painting on panel, but the *cassone* had served the purpose just as well. Many such panels of those times had been part of larger pieces of furniture, and the original *Venus and Mars* itself was thought to have been the backboard from just such a chest, so it couldn't be more appropriate.

It had taken him time and patience to find what he wanted. He needed it to be made of poplar wood, because the original was painted on a poplar panel – but many Italian *cassoni* of that period were made of chestnut. He did not want a beautifully ornate *cassone* from one of the great families, because this would cost a small fortune – he wanted a minor unadorned chest from an ordinary family, of the type that might have been used to store the newly wedded couple's household linen. The specimen that he had eventually found was perfect for his purposes. Once it had stood on four clawed feet, but three of them had broken off and disappeared, while the fourth was badly damaged. The lid was entirely missing, and the wood around the rear hinges was splintered badly, hinting perhaps at war or theft in antiquity. The painting decorating the front of the *cassone* had clearly been of a markedly inferior quality even when the unfortunate Renaissance artist had laid it down so long ago. But worse than that, bad technique had been employed by the hapless painter so that most of the paint had bubbled up and flaked away. The chest had never been restored. Given its missing lid and generally poor state, Alfred had managed to buy it for a modest sum.

Using handsaws and an old wooden block plane, he had cut away the front panel from the *cassone*. Then he had planed it down to size: 69 cm high and 173 cm wide. He had used the exact dimensions of the original Botticelli in the National, using data recorded accurately when the gallery had originally acquired the painting in 1874. He also had high-resolution photographic images of the back and sides of the original painting, which had been obtained for him via his partner. He had not asked how the photographs themselves had been acquired, but clearly someone in the employ of the National must have copied the museum's archived security copies. It was amazing what could be obtained in exchange for an envelope of cash.

He had worked on the back of the painting for several weeks – it was after Easter before he was satisfied, and the days were lengthening. The old wood had smelled of musk when the sharp blade of the plane bit into it. He had put his nose to the wood and inhaled the dry sap of wood half a millennium old, burned dark by time. Then he had smiled and nodded slowly, like a connoisseur tasting a good wine.

When cutting the panel to size he had exposed the edges of the ground on which the original painting had been based. Examination under a powerful magnifying glass had shown layers of size and gesso as normal, but he knew exactly why the paint had bloomed from the surface and flaked off, for he had seen it many times before in his days as a restorer. The original artist had painted the picture in oil rather than tempera, and had used weak size on the gesso, so the gesso had leached the oil out of the paint and both had become unstable. It didn't matter – he wasn't trying to preserve the original painting; all he wanted was the genuine sixteenth century panel on which it had been painted. All the chemical tests and X-rays in the world would reveal it to be genuinely old.

Using sandpaper to avoid any machine-made marks, Alfred had removed the unstable oil paint and its gesso base. When all the gesso was gone and the panel was smooth, he had roughened it a little to make sure that the new gesso would have a good tooth in which to grip, just as a plasterer does when preparing a new wall.

Next he had made the size which sealed the wood, using a recipe given in the Libbro dell' Arte by Cennini, a fifteenth-century Florentine painter. He had boiled up clippings of sheep parchments – the skin – until he had obtained a glue that would stick the palms of the hands together when tested. It had stunk to high heaven, as it always did. He had opened the rear patio doors and all the windows to let the stench blow out of the house, and smoked a cigar to mask the smell.

As soon as the gelatinous liquid had cooled he had strained it through muslin several times, then boiled half of it with water and applied it hot to the ancient panel. When it was dry he had applied a second coat of full-strength size. He wasn't certain that this was necessary, but he liked Cennini's original account:

"with the first size, not being so strong, it is just as if you were fasting, and ate a handful of sweetmeats, and drank a glass of good wine, which is an inducement for you to eat your dinner. So it is with this size: it is a means of giving the wood a taste for receiving the coats of size and gesso."

Once the size was dry he had applied a coat of coarse plaster, mixing it with size on a slab of plate glass. He had left it four days and then roughened it before applying eight successive coats of fine plaster.

All this had taken time, but by the end of April Alfred had created a perfect gesso surface, polished for smoothness with fine pumice, which shone with the brilliance needed to give the final painting the correct luminosity.

After that he had developed the under-drawing. He could not afford to do a grid-by-grid transfer in case the grid showed up under X-rays, but he needed the lines to be in exactly the right place, for a millimetre's difference would be discernible. Instead he had used a light projection of the image on the panel to get the lines perfectly in position. It wasn't his favourite method but he had taken great care and had turned the projector off once the main lines were in.

The National Gallery sold digital images of its paintings, and he had the largest copy of *Venus and Mars* available for purchase, mounted on the wall beside his large hand-cranked easel, plus a series of illicitly photographed high-resolution close-ups. He also had detailed colour notes that he had made from hours of studying the original, and most important of all he had a lifetime's experience. Despite all this he knew that he would need every ounce of skill he possessed. The folds of cloth on Venus's raiment alone were some of the most detailed that Botticelli had ever painted. But at least Alfred didn't have to design the composition – the master had already worked out the allegory and symbolism for him. Nevertheless, he felt that Botticelli would only have arrived at his final drawing after some corrections, so he had deliberately laid down the underlying drawing with *pentamenti*, moving the fingers of Venus's hands and giving a more cheerful set to her mouth than the serious and thoughtful expression she had in the final version. He would paint them wrong, and then paint over them identical to the original.

NINETEEN

My dear Whistler. It is a long time since we saw each other, it is a pity, because ideas change. Where is the time, my friend, when we were happy, and without other worries than those of art, do you remember Trouville and Jo who played the clown to amuse us? The evening she sang Irish songs so well, she had the spirit and the distinction of art...I still have the portrait of Jo which I will never sell.
GUSTAVE COURBET, excerpt from letter to James A.M. Whistler, 14 Feb 1877

The present day

Alfred was working on the final layer of *Venus and Mars*. It was an overcast Monday morning in July, and the rest of England was starting the week's work, or taking its summer holiday and regretting the lack of sunshine. There was the sound of seagulls outside the window but Alfred was unaware of them, for he was grinding pigment on a sheet of plate glass, and when he worked he forgot everything else. The large *cassone* panel was mounted on his easel, resting on cloth to protect its lower edge. The painting was already remarkable, and he was fine tuning it now.

He had a large worktable next to the panel, and it was on this that his jars of pigments were standing, with oil, water and eggs for binding. But as he contemplated which colour to start with that morning, he was interrupted by the crunch of tyres on gravel, and knew that he was about to receive a visit from his employer. This was the man who had persuaded him to paint one fake after another, steadily supplying in turn the hard cash that Alfred needed for retirement to his post-Renaissance Tuscan dream. He grimaced at the sound, but then acknowledged that a visit now was better than in two hours time when he would have mixed the fast-drying egg tempera paint and been in full flow.

"Hurry up then, old boy," he muttered under his breath to his unseen visitor, and wiped his hands on his apron. He went to the door when the knock came, and stepped to one side to let Rupert Angel in.

"Ah, Alfred," Angel said, almost shaking hands but then apparently thinking better of it at the last moment. He smiled and knitted his fingers together as if he had intended to do that all the time. "We purchased some victuals to save you the trouble. They're out in the car but Morton's bringing them in."

Angel was wearing a well-cut grey suit and a beautiful silk tie. Today he looked every inch the top executive. He walked through the hall and into the main room which was being used as Alfred's studio. He immediately spotted the panel on the easel and went over to inspect it.

"This is looking marvellous," he said with genuine admiration. "Have you had any difficulties with it?"

"None more than usual," Alfred said. He stood beside his employer and looked critically at the panel. "The ground is taking the paint well."

"Very good," Angel said, running a professional eye over the work. "Original materials for the ground?"

"Absolutely," Alfred said with a private wince at the thought that he might go to such trouble to acquire a sixteenth-century panel and then seal it with PVA.

"Excellent. Now when will you complete the actual painting? The Collector is particularly eager to receive this one. It will be the centrepiece of his gallery."

"It's virtually done."

"Excellent," Angel said again. "Now perhaps I could trouble you for a cup of coffee? Black, no sugar. I have brought fresh coffee in case it is needed."

Morton came in with his usual deadpan look. He nodded to Alfred but didn't say anything. Alfred scowled back at him – he had never liked Morton, who seemed to perform several jobs for Angel at once; chauffeur, security chief and odd-job man. He had red-blond hair and a square jaw which was concealed by a beard. His eyebrows met in a V-shaped cleft in the middle. He was from the North Kent town of Gravesend and had learned his toughness in the back streets of the town. He wore dark trousers, blue shirt and tie, and a black blazer which gripped his body tightly and emphasized the muscles on his upper arms. He was generally well dressed to avoid distressing Angel's clients, but the impression of gentility was an illusion – Alfred felt that Morton would tear off his head if Angel gave the word. It was an uncomfortable feeling that he could forget most of the time, except when Morton's muscles filled his kitchen as they did now. The man looked at him impassively, then dumped several bags of shopping in the kitchen and went out to get more.

Alfred began to make coffee.

"How's the other new piece coming along?" Angel called from the studio. "You said you would work on it in between the Botticelli."

"It's finished," Alfred called back, ignoring Morton, who had just come in with the remaining shopping bags. "It's wrapped in green baize behind the easel. It's dry, so have a look and see what you think. Put it on the spare easel." He began to hurry with the coffee preparations because he wanted to see what Angel thought of the painting.

When he came back in, Angel had set up the painting on the easel and was looking at it reverently.

It showed a woman in a white dress, seated on a rock on a beach. It was night and the sea behind her reflected only the merest glimmer to betray its presence. She was looking back over her shoulder at a bearded, long-haired man walking along the beach towards her. He smoked a pipe, betrayed only by a line and a speck of cadmium orange. She had a distant look in her eye. Her long brown hair was gathered up in a loose bun, as if done temporarily rather than neatly pinned. A white cloak was flung loosely about her shoulders, providing protection against the cool night breeze. Her feet were bare in the sand. A wisp of hair had escaped her bun and was flying in the wind. A plant grew next to the rock, painted with carefully separate leaves that gave the painting the slightest hint of a Japanese print. The entire picture was painted in a loose, impressionist way rather than with the tight precision of the Renaissance.

"Whistler," Alfred said, pointing to the signature barely visible against the black water. "Or in the style of. I've tried to create a cross between the symphony-in-white pictures and the later nocturnes. The moment when he moved from one period to another. What do you think of it?"

"I think it's a masterpiece," Angel said, and there was a catch in his voice that betrayed genuine emotion. This was one thing that Alfred liked about Rupert Angel; though the man was arrogant and selfish he had a true appreciation of art and a detailed knowledge of his field. Alfred knew that here was a man who understood what he had tried to do in combining the night-time beach and the girl in white, and could appreciate it. And on a more practical note, Angel could get a lot of money for it in the circles in which he moved, if it was presented as a genuine rediscovered Whistler.

"Now, isn't the girl his mistress? Or am I mistaken?"

"You are not," Alfred said, unable to keep a note of pride out of his voice. "Joanna Hiffernan. I borrowed her from other portraits that he did of her and changed her a bit but kept her dreamy look. Any Whistler scholar will know her instantly, of course. This one would need to have been painted around 1865, not three Saturdays ago, as was in fact the case. She would have been in Trouville with Whistler at that time, so I popped her on the beach and took it almost down to black so that she'd be silhouetted. Does it match the idea you suggested to me?"

Angel was still staring intently at the picture.

"It goes far beyond it," he said. "I feel sure we should be able to offload this one in a private sale. There'll be suspicion at an unknown Whistler, of course, so we'll have to cover our tracks carefully. But if it looks like a

Whistler and the story adds up, it's possible. Who's the man walking towards her; is that the great man himself?"

"They were in Trouville with Gustave Courbet," Alfred said with a chuckle. "So I've given a hint of Courbet in the approaching man. I thought Whistler might have been a bit piqued if he guessed she'd been unfaithful – who knows?"

Angel was nodding slowly and smiling. He lifted the painting carefully from the easel and rotated it, studying the dust-covered back of the old canvas.

"A masterpiece," he said again, giving Alfred a warm glow of satisfaction. "If I succeed in moving it into the market you shall have your usual fee."

Alfred nodded. It would add to his retirement fund considerably if Angel managed to pass the painting off as a genuine original, as he felt sure that he would. There was something about Angel's smooth urbanity and great knowledge that promoted confidence and respect.

"You can take it with you now," he said. "It's dry and has been baked to harden the paint. It passes the nail test."

The nail test was the simple process of trying to dent the paint with the edge of a nail, which would only work if it were fresh and not 140 years old.

He wrapped the painting back in green baize and packed it into a box for Angel to take with him. Morton carried it out to the car, having said nothing for the entire time he had been there, except to refuse coffee. Instead of coffee he had drunk a pint of iced water.

"I shall be bringing a new original for you soon," Angel said. "It will arrive at the Gallery shortly and I shall have a couple of Morton's men bring it straight here to you. In fact, they might stay for a few days."

"What for?" Alfred asked worriedly, raising his eyebrows and looking at his employer.

"Oh you know: security," Angel said vaguely. "They'll be instructed to make the food and clear up but otherwise keep out of your way, so don't worry. But don't you want to know which painting I've managed to obtain for you?"

"Go on then," Alfred said, feeling irritated at the thought of Morton's brainless dunderheads skulking around the house.

"The Hammershoi", Angel said with a smirk.

Alfred stared, forgetting about Morton's men.

"Good Lord," he said. "You've got the *Hammershoi*? The girl at the clavier?"

Angel nodded, smiling broadly now.

"Well that's first class, old boy. Hammershoi was influenced by Vermeer, of course, except that he favoured the monochrome colours. It will be interesting to have a go at that."

Morton tapped his watch and Angel nodded in acknowledgement before turning back to Alfred.

"I must be getting back. I have an evening appointment."

Alfred nodded vaguely, still thinking about the Hammershoi. He had been intending to announce his retirement after he had got in the money for the Botticelli, because he didn't think he was ever going to do better than that. However, the chance to have a go at the Hammershoi, working directly from the original, felt very tempting. Perhaps he would just do that one as well, and then stop. He hardly noticed Angel and Morton leave, and when the house was once more blissfully quiet, he cracked open an egg and began the process of mixing a perfect egg tempera colour needed for fine detail on the Botticelli.

TWENTY

Love is a smoke raised with the fume of sighs
WILLIAM SHAKESPEARE, Romeo and Juliet

Lucy and Will were driving south from London on the A21, heading for Alfred's last-known address. Yesterday's hot sunshine was gone, replaced by grey, brooding storm clouds that presaged rain. It was still warm so Lucy again had the top down on the car, but it wasn't as gloriously hot as the previous day, and they knew they might have to stop in a hurry and raise the top if the rain came down. The air was sultry, charged with electricity waiting to flash to earth in summer lightning. They were hungry and they considered stopping for an early lunch at the Royal Oak in Whatlington – "quenching thirsts since 1490" – but by that time they were nearly in Hastings and they were both, for different reasons, eager to find out if Alfred was at home. Will wanted to see his old friend and prove his innocence, or at least to warn Alfred quietly that the police were on his trail. Lucy wanted to solve the conundrum of the forged paintings, and she wanted either to exonerate Alfred or stop his nefarious activities. With these two radically different agendas they found themselves arriving in the seaside town.

"Smell that air," Will said appreciatively. "Fresh and salty. Fancy spending two days in a row at the seaside! Normally I don't see the sea for months at a time, living in Cambridge. It would be nice to do some paintings with a nautical theme. I know it sounds corny, but it's good to walk in the steps of greatness, and the sea is a favourite subject of the old masters; all those storm-lashed life rafts peopled by nubile maidens wearing beseeching looks and not a great deal else. Then there's Turner, of course: plenty of seascapes there. Not nearly as popular as Jesus, I'll grant you, though much of religious art was a good excuse for some gentle pornography in an age when they didn't have the Internet."

Lucy smiled. She liked the way he put everything into the context of painting. She often found herself doing the same thing, though she wasn't a painter. A private game of hers was to imagine how a scene would look painted in the style of a particular master.

"Have you ever lived by the sea?" she asked.

"No. I've always liked the notion of it but I never have. But we don't always do the things we dream of, do we?"

"We don't, though I'd like to live by the sea for a while. It would be like being permanently on holiday, but I expect the tourists would drive one mad."

"You think Cambridge doesn't have tourists?"

She shrugged, accepting his point.

"You get used to them after a while," Will said pensively. "Or if you don't, you move somewhere else and escape them. I like it though; I'm a figurative painter so I like a constant supply of people. I think it stops Cambridge from mouldering away in past glory. And of course you have the opportunity to live somewhere appealing, which is the whole reason why the tourists are there in the first place."

There was a companionable silence for a couple of streets. Gulls wheeled and swooped overhead. The houses were high; three-storied and terraced, like so many English seaside towns. They came to the seafront and watched a cavalcade of fish and chip shops and amusement arcades pass the window.

"Oh look!" Lucy said, pointing out of the window to the left. "A funicular railway up the cliff!"

They drove past slowly.

"I never go to the sea either," Lucy said after a while. "I spend too much time breathing London's traffic fumes. Sometimes I wonder whether I should escape the city and commute into town instead. You know; live in Buckinghamshire or Kent and get a bit of countryside. I never do, though. We spend too much time rushing about these days."

"I don't," Will said. "Although I used to before I went to prison. "I used to rush from commission to commission, and do one-man shows, and get into the galleries. That's how I got the studio in the first place, by working very hard. But it was all such a rush, and prison forced me to stop doing all that and reappraise my life."

"And what did you conclude?" Lucy said curiously, as she searched for a left turn that the SatNav wanted them to take.

"I concluded that I was going to rush my life away and die of a heart attack at fifty. So I decided to slow down and take things as they come."

"You've still got the studio, though," Lucy said. "So you've managed all right."

"That's the weird thing," Will said. "When I was speeding around all the time I did very well and paid off the studio, but when I calmed down I found that the work got better. Plus the media liked the whole tale of the wicked old Lord and the prison sentence, especially the way I told it. I perfectly fitted their idea of the eccentric artist, and they like to include the pictures in their articles because they don't have to write so much to fill up the space. So I found myself getting better known, and plenty of galleries are happy to hang my work these days. The notoriety of prison helped, and I'd done my time.

These days I get better prices than I ever got before prison, and I'm not dashing around trying to promote myself at all. It's ironic, isn't it?"

"It is, but I suppose it makes a sort of sense," Lucy said. "You relaxed, the work got better, and you built on your previous success. I'm not sure if people hold terrible grudges against ex-criminals unless they've done something frightful. Society doesn't vilify them the way it once did. They usually write their memoirs and make a fortune instead."

Then she looked at him and frowned.

"Well obviously I'm not *condoning* forgery, but it's not like rape or murder."

"Glad to hear it," Will said with a lopsided grin. He looked back at her and she held his eye for a moment.

"We ought to go down to the beach," she said, "when we've checked out your friend. Practice what we're preaching. I must admit that I don't really expect him to be there, but one has to check out every possibility."

"We should have fish and chips," Will said. "Though I don't know whether they've got real fish from fishermen. It's no good if it's all cardboard frozen fillets brought in on refrigerated lorries."

"I couldn't possibly eat fish and chips," Lucy said seriously. "It would make me instantly fat and disgusting."

Will laughed.

"Practice what we preach," he reminded her. "You don't have to eat chips every day, and you don't look to me like you're about to turn into a barrage balloon."

They stopped talking as they worked their way through the last bit of suburbia. Alfred's house was out towards Ore on the east side, just off the road to Rye, in a cul-de-sac containing older detached houses.

"According to my map," Will said, rustling the Internet print-out that Lucy had given him, "It's round the next bend."

As if agreeing with him, the SatNav announced that they were arriving at their destination.

"It makes me feel peculiar," he went on. "The possibility of seeing Alfred again after all this time. We were practically inseparable in prison, and then he left before I did and I never heard from him again. It's a bit upsetting, to tell you the truth."

"Maybe we'll find out why he disappeared," Lucy said, bringing the car round the corner.

"It's that one straight ahead at the bottom of the dip," Will pointed. "According to the map, anyway."

They checked house names and confirmed that they had found Alfred's house. They parked on the side of the road and walked through the gateway, their feet crunching on gravel. Tree foliage leaned down and snatched at their hair as they passed. A gull swerved down to inspect them for a moment, but decided that they were not a food source and angled away towards the

Channel. As they rounded the corner and saw the white wall of the house, they spotted a new BMW 7 parked on the gravel to the side of the building.

They looked at each other.

"Well *somebody's* here, anyway," Lucy said. "And he's not doing too badly for himself."

"For an ex-con," Will finished the sentence for her. "He must have made a fortune from his ill-gotten gains."

She looked at him.

"I didn't say that," she said, but privately she realised that was *exactly* what she'd been thinking, and exactly what she had thought when she had first seen Will's studio as well.

They went past the BMW and reached the house, but at that moment there was a loud crash from somewhere round the back and the earth shook beneath their feet. They heard the sound of splintering glass and shattering stone. An engine was roaring and as they came upon the house they realised that it was a ruin. The lower windows had been boarded up and the upper windows were gaping blackened holes. The house had been destroyed by fire; the roof was gaping open and the white walls were cracked and stained black in places. Wisteria grew over the front of the porch, incongruously untouched by the fire. Now that they looked more closely they realised that the garden was completely overgrown and that weeds were poking up through the gravel. The yellow tower of heavy plant machinery reached above the house to the rear, and then there was another crash and they realised that the building was being demolished as they watched.

They had intended simply to walk up to the front door and knock, but there was no front door. It had been blocked off with plywood boards, but these had in turn been prised away and the doorway gaped open. A solid line of barriers passed across the front of the building, set well away from the front face of it. A sign bore the name of a demolition company.

Another heavy, gut-wrenching thud shook the ground and there were more sounds of falling masonry. Then a man walked around the side of a building wearing a yellow hard hat, saw them immediately and made a double take. He was wearing a brown tweed suit and was in his fifties. He came straight up to them.

"I'm sorry," he said. "Can't have any onlookers. This is a private site and it's not safe. We're taking the building down."

Will looked as if he was going to argue, but Lucy quietly took his arm and spoke first.

"We're looking for Alfred Smith," she said. "He used to live here, apparently."

"Oh I see," the man said. He held out his hand. "Ken Dawkins from Browns. We're demolishing the building. It burned down about nine months ago, but it's taken this long to get all the legal paperwork sorted out. They couldn't find your Mr Smith, apparently. Do you have any forwarding address for him? The building society repossessed the property because it had burned down and he had stopped paying his mortgage. Now then, I'm sorry to insist but you do need to move right away from the building. I've come out to move my car, actually."

He motioned them back and they retreated with him.

"Is there anything left in it?" Lucy asked, rapidly seeing their only lead disappearing into thin air.

Dawkins chuckled. "Nothing at all I'm afraid," he said. "It was completely gutted, and I expect the local kids took anything else that survived. It was boarded up and repossessed, as I say. Now it's going to be replaced with two tasteful homes. That's not going to be done by Browns though; a local builder is doing the construction work, we're just knocking it down. It'll be gone in another hour or so and then the boys will be taking the masonry away in the lorry. We'll have the site completely clear in a few days."

"Does anyone around here know where Alfred Smith has gone?" Will asked.

Dawkins looked around and leaned in a little closer.

"Apparently he was a con," he said conspiratorially. "Been to prison, came out and then vanished. Something crooked going on, I reckon."

Again Lucy took Will's arm in a restraining fashion.

"How dreadful," she said. "But we do need to contact Mr Smith on an official matter. You're quite sure that there's no forwarding address for him?"

"I'm certain, Miss," Dawkins said. "At first they thought he must have been in the house when it burned down, but they can work all that sort of thing out these days, of course. No sign of a body," he added, giving them a macabre look.

They looked so disconsolate that he shrugged sympathetically at their predicament.

"I have to nip out, but I must ask you to leave as well," he said. "The lads won't know that you're here and you're likely to get a chunk of stone in your ear once they work round to the front."

Will and Lucy looked at each other and grimaced.

"Well," Lucy said to Will. "There doesn't seem a whole lot else that we can do. It's another dead end like the Isle of Wight."

They thanked Dawkins and he got into the BMW, while they walked back up the drive to Lucy's car.

"We need some fish and chips to help us think," Will said. "Fish is good for the brain. We need all the help we can get if we're ever going to find Alfred. I wonder where on earth he's gone. I'm a bit worried. He's a nice old boy, you know. You shouldn't think of him as a master criminal. I wouldn't be surprised if he's up to his old tricks, because it was ingrained in his soul, but he's not an evil man. I bet you'd like him if you met him and you didn't know that he was a forger."

"Maybe I would," Lucy said reflectively. "His work is extraordinary, if the fake Alma-Tadema really is his work. I've never seen anything so well executed."

Lucy drove back into the centre of Hastings and they parked on the seafront. It was quieter than normal because the day was overcast. A strong breeze came off the sea but it was fresh rather than cold. Will bought fish and chips for the two of them from a stall next to an arcade, and they sat on a wall looking out to sea.

"My God, these are gorgeous," Lucy said. "You're a very bad influence but they *are* delicious." She gave him a sideways look and grinned when she caught his eyes on her.

"What are we going to do now, then?" Will said, conscious that Lucy was about to move out of his life as swiftly as she had appeared in it. "Although part of me still doesn't want to find Alfred in case he's doing what you say."

"I understand that," Lucy said. "But I'm supposed to stop forgeries happening, and if Alfred is doing it then he needs to stop. I've never made a secret of that. That is if we ever find him, of course. He seems to have covered his tracks rather well."

"Can't your policeman friend find him? I thought these days they could find anyone they wanted."

"I don't know. I'll have to talk to him and find out," Lucy said. "It would be all right if Alfred had been using credit cards or drawing social security, but Davies said he hadn't, and if he's deliberately lying low we're going to have a job to locate him."

She popped the last piece of fish in her mouth, wiped her hands carefully with the paper and dropped it into a nearby litterbin. Then she took a packet of moist wipes from her handbag and extracted one, dealing with her hands and then her face. She took out a mirror and tidied up her make-up, while Will watched with amusement.

"You're very clean and tidy," he said.

"There's nothing wrong with being clean," she said, giving him a look. "Would *you* like to borrow a wipe?"

He held up his hands. "No, I'll pass," he said. "I want to savour the taste of fish and chips, and those things are altogether too lemony for me."

"I can't believe I had fish and chips," Lucy said absently as she repaired her makeup. "I shan't eat another thing today."

Then she suddenly sat bolt upright and her hand flew to her mouth.

"Oh my God, I'm supposed to be going out to dinner this evening!" she said suddenly. "I'd completely forgotten! What's the time?" She looked at her watch, found that it was four o'clock and started bundling things back into her bag hurriedly.

"We're going to have to go. I'll only just make it back in time and I need to change and – well, everything. Can we go?"

She stood up and looked impatient. Will felt irritated that she suddenly wanted to rush off.

"Is it a *vital* dinner appointment?" he asked pointedly.

"I can't miss it. A man I met on Friday at a private view," she said, oblivious to Will's look.

"Well I don't want to instantly rush off," Will said obstinately, feeling unreasonably jealous now as well as frustrated. "If you only met him on Friday, how come he's so very important all of a sudden?"

"He's a nice man," Lucy said, getting cross. "Come on!" She started to walk off down the esplanade and turned to wait for him.

Will remained seated.

"You go then," he said obstinately. "I'll take the train."

"Don't be ridiculous," she said with irritation. "I'll drive you back to King's Cross, obviously. I just need you to hurry up so that I'm not late. I *hate* being late."

"I bet you do," Will said rather meanly. "You go and I'll take the train. I don't spend every day at the seaside, so now that I'm here I want to walk along the beach and enjoy it. Just go, but do me a favour and don't ask me to help any more with looking for Alfred."

"Very well," she said stiffly. "If that's what you want. Send Hoffman and Courtland the bill for the train ticket."

She turned on her heel and went off at a smart clip towards her parked car, her blonde hair blowing in the breeze. Will sat on the wall angrily and watched her go. There was a distant ominous roll of thunder, and he knew from the look of the yellow-grey storm clouds that in another ten minutes it would be raining. He wondered how he could have moved so quickly from burgeoning friendship to total disconnection. Who was so important that she had to dash off like that? He didn't particularly want to walk along the beach, but he couldn't have tolerated a long drive back in the car, knowing that she was hurrying back for a date with someone else. He supposed that he should have asked her out, but by the time he had begun to entertain the idea she had gone. He hopped down off the wall and began to crunch along the pebbles, oblivious to the darkening sky. When the rain began to fall in huge globules that made him instantly wet, he ignored them and walked on, getting saturated, his hair hanging dank around his cheeks.

In her car and joining the flow of traffic out of Hastings, Lucy felt upset that she and Will had parted so swiftly. She tried to justify her actions to herself: she hated being late for any appointment, and it wasn't as if she were *going out* with Will – it was just a business relationship. But a truthful inner voice admitted that she liked him. Logic fought back and pointed out that he was completely inappropriate for her. Yet as she drove, she found that her head was filled with images of Will and not of Rupert Angel. She remembered his dark hair flying in the wind and his lopsided grin, and his impression of how "Lady F" would have hopped about like a distressed bird if they'd suggested taking a small snippet of her Frans Snyders.

And so, in this confused state, she drove up the A21 as fast as the Roadster and the speed cameras would permit.

RICHARD JOHN MITCHELL

TWENTY-ONE

Nothing weighs on us so heavily as a secret.
JEAN DE LA FONTAINE

The last thing Lucy wanted when she got home was to go out again. She still felt full of chips, and if anything she felt like waiting until later, making something green and healthy and eating it scrunched up on her sofa in front of a good film. She had spent yesterday in the Isle of Wight with Will Bentley, and today in Hastings. She had experienced the disappointment of not finding Alfred Smith, followed by the ridiculous row with the obstinate, strangely attractive Will. It seemed impossible that only three days ago she been at Lindy Hodge's private view at the Limerston, and had accepted Rupert Angel's invitation to dinner. However, that was the situation and she had arranged to meet Rupert at the restaurant at 8.30. Dinner was to be at *Le Gavroche*, the exclusive Mayfair restaurant of Michel and Albert Roux. She concluded from this that Rupert Angel had taste and must have money too. She also decided, perhaps in a private and unspoken snub to Will Bentley, that she was going to dress to kill for Rupert Angel.

She showered for ten minutes, turning slowly to let the water wash away the dust and dirt of the day's travelling. Then she stood in front of her bedroom mirror in fresh underwear, holding dresses against herself to see which suited her mood. She opted for a deep blue strapless tulip-shaped dress that fitted her perfectly. She complemented it with a crystal necklace, a blue leather clutch bag and a silver bangle wristwatch. She put on high heels which fastened with thin leather straps around the ankles and left her toes bare. Then she painted her nails silver and ordered a taxi for a quarter to eight. She finally left the flat at ten to the hour, fraught at being late, wrapping her white coat round her shoulders. She finished her make-up in the back of the cab. Rupert had offered to pick her up but she had opted to meet him at the restaurant in Upper Brook Street. By the time she arrived there she had calmed down and tucked away her make-up in her bag. She paid the driver and checked her watch – 8.32; not bad for a girl who had driven from Hastings that afternoon.

She straightened a few wild wisps of blonde hair and looked around her, taking stock before going in. The afternoon rain had moved on towards East Anglia, but the road still had a few puddles. *Le Gavroche* was decorated outside with flowers and ivy. It was well-positioned, just a short distance from the American Embassy and Grosvenor Square. The road was busy with one-way traffic which flowed from Park Lane into Mayfair like pieces on a Monopoly board.

She went in, feeling unaccountably nervous. After David had died so tragically she had experienced only the one relationship with Sam, and that had ended in tears. Now she was taking the relationship with Rupert one step further than a casual acquaintance, and she didn't seem to be able to get Will Bentley out of her head. It was all very confusing.

Her coat was taken by a young olive-skinned woman, who took her through to the bar where Rupert Angel was already waiting. He stood at once to greet her.

"Lucy!" he said, taking her hands for a moment and then just as quickly releasing them. "I'm so glad that you have come." He looked her up and down swiftly and added, "You look *very* beautiful."

"Thank you for inviting me," she said. "And to such an exclusive establishment – I am honoured!"

He leaned forward and held her shoulders lightly while they kissed on each cheek. His hands were warm and he smelled good; a subtle hint of something expensive. His teeth were straight and very white, with the tiny gap that she remembered from before. His skin was tanned and he wore a pale blue Versace suit, an unbuttoned white shirt and a loosely knotted marigold tie. He looked very good and she knew she did too from the way his eyes widened a little as he took in the blue cocktail dress. She sat down next to him on a tartan sofa and looked around, taking stock of the room.

The bar was shelved at the back in glass and sported regiments of bottles. A Rancilio coffee machine grumbled and hissed to itself on the bar top, and a short, greying man glided behind it. The walls were burgundy panels framed in green cloth and covered with pictures. There was a glass cockerel placed incongruously beside a pillar, and tall green leather bar stools which echoed the green of the wall panel frames. Across from where they were seated was a staircase that presumably led down to the main restaurant. Two or three other parties sat in the bar, and there was the low murmur of polite conversation that would later grow in volume and laughter as wine loosened the bindings of propriety. Lucy looked back at Rupert and found his eyes on her, a little smile on his lips.

"It has character," he said. "They manage to combine elegance and informality. Have you been to *Le Gavroche* before?"

She admitted that she hadn't, but said it was rumoured to be the best French food in town.

"Michel Roux would be pleased to hear you say so," Rupert said. He is the chef here. He took over from his father and uncle, who started the place. It was originally in Lower Sloane Street, I believe."

"You're well informed," she smiled. "Is this your first visit too, or do you come here often?"

He chuckled.

"Not as often as I'd like," he said. "I've been before, but I reserve it only for special guests."

"Then I'm very flattered," she said, but with a sudden odd concern inside, wondering if he was just a little bit *too* smooth. She suddenly knew David would have despised Rupert Angel.

"Let's get a drink," Rupert said. He looked up and the barman emerged as if by secret signal.

"*Monsieur, Madame*, welcome to *Le Gavroche*," he said. "Could I get you an aperitif before you go down to dinner?"

At Rupert's suggestion they opted for a glass each of Taittinger vintage champagne, and the little Frenchman disappeared to get it. There was a butler's tray table in front of them with the sides laid flat, and two red leather chairs. Lucy picked up a booklet from the tabletop and inspected it.

"Well, if we like the food it seems we can buy a cookbook," she announced, a little frown of concentration on her brow as she read through, then smiled. "And even souvenirs!"

"The cookbook sounds good," Rupert said, unable to take his eyes off her as she frowned and smiled her way through the text. She was so full of life, so animated, and so pretty. It was such a pity.

Their drinks arrived and they clinked glasses and drank. Lucy looked around the room, taking in more details. There were plants in corners, occasional bowls of fresh flowers and large lamps. As she sipped the champagne the bubbles tingled in her nose.

"What do you think of the pictures?" he asked her as she inspected her surroundings. The images around the room were mostly modern, some bright and childlike. There were vases of flowers like fireworks. There were children's faces. There was a couple standing by a window with green shutters, with the Eiffel Tower visible through the window like a name tag for the painted city. They were mostly limited edition prints or watercolours.

"Quite a mixture," she said. "Not really me, though. I prefer the classical, although I do quite like *that* one." She pointed with her finger across the room.

"The rearing horse?"

She nodded.

"Yes, it's well executed, and more classical in line," he said. "Although I don't entirely agree with you otherwise – I rather like these bright naive colours."

They sipped champagne in a comfortable silence for a minute or two, not needing to speak.

"This is a very special treat," Lucy said, turning to him after an interval. "Thank you! Now tell me something: where does the restaurant get its name? I keep thinking I've heard the word before, but I can't for the life of me think where."

"I went through the same process when I first came here," Rupert said, "So I cross-examined the waiter. Apparently a *Gavroche* is an urchin or ragamuffin, and you may have come across it before if you have ever seen Hugo's *Les Misérables*?"

"That's it!" she said. "Isn't Gavroche one of the main characters? I haven't seen it for years. I went with my parents when I was about fourteen and I haven't been since."

"Apparently Victor Hugo had a pet named Gavroche, so presumably that's where he took the name for his character. I have no idea whether Michel and Albert Roux were thinking of Hugo when they named this place, but probably not. Hugo simply made it a popular French symbol, like a Pierrot."

The Maitre D' arrived at their table and introduced himself. He was silver haired and spoke with a slight French accent. He was perfectly charming to them but Lucy imagined he would be formidable with tardy waiters. He chatted for a minute or two and remembered Rupert from his last visit, which she could see made Rupert rather pleased. They were asked if they would like to see the menus, but they chose to wait until they went downstairs. The Maitre D' moved on to the next table, and the barman appeared with a bottle of Taittinger to see if they would like a refill. Lucy declined gracefully, remembering that she had drunk too much last time she had been with Rupert in Lindy's gallery.

They finished their glasses and were conducted downstairs to the dining room by a waiter in black jacket, waistcoat and bow tie. The dining room was long and narrow like that of a ship. It had seating for sixty and was about two-thirds full. The style was similar to the bar above, except that here the walls were green and framed in gold and wood.

"Eating in such a place is a religious experience," Rupert said as they sat down. "And the snow-white tables are altars at which the faithful worship!"

She smiled at him, but wasn't entirely sure if he was joking or serious.

They were seated at a round table near the door, tucked into an alcove with a green curved seat that allowed them to face the table and yet be seated side by side. The white linen glittered with glass and silver, and each plate bore a distinctive Gavroche image. As a centrepiece it had a sculpture of a frog made entirely of twisted and moulded silver spoons. Other tables bore different animals, Lucy noticed: a pelican of fish knives; a pheasant; and was that a kingfisher?

The restaurant's atmosphere was warming up, the hubbub growing in volume so that it was difficult to distinguish individual conversations. There was laughter, especially from a noisy table of six on the opposite wall. She was conscious of being watched and looked up to find a grey-haired aristocratic-looking gentleman staring at her. He was alone at his table and looked down immediately. So did she, suppressing an inner smile at the success of the blue dress. The menus arrived and Lucy examined hers with interest. It was bound with a golden yellow cord and the cover bore a bright image of a chef intertwined with the ingredients of his profession. The smell of fine food in the air made Lucy's mouth water – it no longer seemed possible that she had eaten fish and chips on the beach only a few hours before. That was a different world.

She opened the menu and read the *Menu Exceptionnel* first; seven courses providing a little bit of everything. She was secretly pleased when Rupert insisted they go *à la Carte*.

"It is not a commonplace experience to dine here," he observed. "We must enjoy it to the full."

Lucy ran her eye down the *Hors d'Oeuvres* for the fifth time and decided to have the Soufflé Suissesse, because it sounded gorgeous and the Maitre D' had earlier accorded it special honours. Rupert opted for the Mousseline de Homard au Champagne; a lobster mousse with caviar in a champagne butter sauce. Lucy couldn't help noticing that it was the most expensive menu item – Rupert evidently had extravagant tastes. She wondered curiously how his gallery was so successful, and decided that it must be the location, directly in the centre of London, as well as the undoubted charms of the man himself. Perhaps he brought his top clients here to flatter them.

They elected to have a white Burgundy to accompany the fish and the soufflé, and Lucy was pleased that Rupert didn't show off but asked the waiter for his recommendation. A Puligny-Montrachet was duly selected and opened with great ceremony at the table.

When the waiter had departed they tinkled glasses again and looked into each other's eyes as they drank: she now a little tipsy and flirtatious; he devil-may-care.

"So, Mr Angel: I want you to tell me your philosophy for the Angel Gallery," she said.

"Is this a test?"

"It certainly is. If you make a dull answer or profess to admire something I despise, I shall know immediately that I hate you."

A smile curled his lips.

"Then I'd better not do so. By philosophy, do you mean some grand plan? Because if so, I confess to having none. Does that mean that I fall at the first gate?"

"Not necessarily," she mused. "But you must tell me what art you buy and sell."

"Anything and everything," Rupert said. "Of course I'll trade in famous names and follow fads. I'll also build people up if I think they're worth it. You ought to visit; I always have some super pieces in, though they're not necessarily all out on the gallery floor. Do you like Robert Lenkiewicz? I have a pair of portraits passing through."

"The Plymouth man?" she said. "A living Rembrandt, some called him. He's dead now of course, but I met him once and he was terribly sexy, I remember. He had a studio down on the waterfront. Very well; so far I approve. Could I come and see them?"

"You are invited at any time, of course, but I'd like to arrange a date so that I can conduct you personally."

"I'd like that," she said, and then, perhaps made reckless by the wine she said "So tell me: where does the gallery get its money?"

He looked into the middle distance. Today his chin was coated with stubble, and when he rubbed it thoughtfully it made a rasping sound which she found oddly erotic. He had brown eyes which were dark and compelling. He was undoubtedly intriguing and the sense of power he emanated was palpable.

"I make most of my money by acquiring works of art for private collectors," he said. "I have built a reputation for finding what they want, and they are prepared to pay for it handsomely. But I also try to keep the gallery at the leading edge by holding exhibitions of promising artists, such as young Wayne East."

"The young man at the Limerston? Yes, he *is* good," Lucy agreed. "That perspective painting was unusual."

"Yes. And my patrons are always looking for something different," Rupert said. "They have a lot of money so they seek the extraordinary. And it has to be said, they *are* trying to make money from art. They rarely need the money, but it's the challenge, you see. You would be surprised at the degree of rivalry among the great collectors."

"Actually I wouldn't," she said, thinking of her own similar experiences. "But do you think they care about the actual art?"

"Art for art's sake, you mean? Some of them do, I'm sure, but a lot of them buy art as a commodity. It's like playing the stock market, but more interesting; trying to pick a painter who is increasing in popularity, whether he died a hundred years ago or is alive and well and exhibiting in the Kings Road."

"It always strikes me as rather sad when art is reduced to a currency. It would be good if they bought it because they liked it."

"I'm sure some of them do," Rupert said, defending the honour of his clients.

"And what about *you*?" Lucy said, looking at him with a hint of challenge. "Do you buy for love or for money?"

He smiled.

"Oh I buy for money," he said. "And if I love it too, all the better!"

She wanted to be cross with him about his answer, but his smile was so charming that she couldn't bring herself to disapprove.

The *hors d'oeuvres* arrived and they were as delicious as they had sounded on the menu.

"Now that you know the dark secret of my hidden avarice," he said," you must tell me about *you*. How is it that such a gorgeous woman becomes an insurance expert? It sounds a little drab on the face of it." He disarmed the words with an innocent smile, but now it was her turn to be challenged.

"It does sound drab," she said. "But it isn't really. At least, not what *I* do."

"And what *is it* exactly that you do?" Rupert said. "I know you work for Hoffman and Courtland, but I'm not entirely sure in what capacity."

"I have rather an *odd* job," Lucy began, having first polished every crumb of the soufflé from its ramekin. "I started out with an MA in the history of art, but my father had always worried that I wouldn't be able to make a life for myself without what he called a *proper* degree. By which he meant "something in business". So to appease him I did a further degree in business studies, and then I looked around for something to catch my eye."

"And was that Hoffman and Courtland?" Rupert asked.

"Not at first. I worked for a gallery in Scotland for a while, and then I moved down to London and worked for the Royal Academy."

"*Did* you indeed? Impressive credentials!"

"Oh, not impressive at all, really. I was practically making the tea, to begin with. But it gave me a good grounding and I met an awful lot of people. One of them was my present boss, who suggested that I might be interested in art insurance. He told me all about it, and explained how I would work with some of the great masterpieces as they moved around from collection to collection. It sounded interesting."

"So you went with the flow?"

"Yes I did. It was odd at first to be working in an office rather than in a gallery, but I wasn't selling insurance; I was assessing works of art and agreeing the sum to be insured, which meant that I had to get out and see them."

"I suppose you needed your art history to assess them properly, and your business skills to cut a good deal."

She nodded.

"It was perfect. I was seeing works of art that weren't on public view, so I was honing my skills. Pictures do need to be insured, particularly while in transit between exhibitions when they are vulnerable to theft or damage. So I did lots of little galleries at first. Lindy was one of my first clients at the Limerston – that's how I know her. But then my job changed."

"Changed how?" Rupert prompted, looking at her attentively.

She paused.

"I met my husband David at Hoffman's; he was a partner and we just hit it off. He was the insurance investigator, so he had the job I have now. But then he was tragically killed."

"How awful," Rupert said, his face full of concern. "If it doesn't hurt too much to talk about it, how did it happen? He must have been very young."

It still made her feel choked up to talk about it.

"He – he was off out doing something or other, I'll never know," she said. "And he didn't call, so after a while I started to get worried and I called the police. Well, he was missing for three days and then they found his body in Boulters Lock in Maidenhead. It's on the Thames. His head was – well, terribly injured. They never knew exactly how although there was a theory that he'd got caught in the lock gates. The media had a field day and there was much speculation that someone had bumped him off, him being an insurance investigator."

"How terrible for you," Rupert said in a mechanical voice.

He remembered Morton's iron bar crushing the intruder's head. Rupert had got blood and brains spattered on his own shirt because he was standing so close. He had thrown up on the floor.

Rupert suddenly realised that he was looking disgusted and rearranged his features into a more suitable expression of concern.

"And when did all this happen?"

"About two, no, very nearly three years ago. I went a bit nutty for a while but I'm over it now."

"You're very brave," Rupert said, and held up his glass. "Let's drink to David."

They drank, Lucy gulping hers a little too quickly even though she knew she shouldn't.

"When David was gone there was no-one to do his job, and I knew how to do it because he used to tell me about it. So I began to specialise in finding works of art that had been stolen or had otherwise disappeared," she said. "And I discovered that I had a talent for it. After a while I became the official new art investigator, working with the police on art crime. It's very close to art insurance, if you think about it."

Rupert was looking at her with an enigmatic expression.

"And are you good at it?"

She laughed, though still feeling slightly brittle.

"I was born for it," she said. "I always get my man, so I hope *you're* honest and truthful, or I shall catch you in my web!"

He laughed too, and put two fingers to his forehead.

"Scout's honour," he said. "Though I must confess I never was a scout."

TWENTY-TWO

How cheerfully he seems to grin,
How neatly spreads his claws...
LEWIS CARROLL

The main courses arrived and there was a flurry of activity as their food was served. Lucy was having wild salmon and petits pois in the French style with bacon. Rupert was having grilled veal and the waiter carved it at the table. A half bottle of Pinot Noir was brought to accompany the veal, leaving Lucy to finish off the Puligny-Montrachet.

She leaned over her dish and inhaled deeply. "This is exceptional. I think I may have to develop expensive tastes and become a kept woman."

"You'll have plenty of offers in that case," Rupert said. "You're easily the prettiest girl in the restaurant."

She blushed a little.

By the time they had finished the main course, Lucy was feeling extremely comfortable and relaxed, though still a little tipsy despite the food.

"*Now* I understand what you were talking about the other evening," Rupert said once the plates had been removed. "You were terribly intriguing, you know. Nothing exciting ever happens to me, and yet here are you pursuing a forger. It makes me feel as if I am in an Agatha Christie plot."

Lucy looked at him demurely.

"Then of course you know that I can reveal nothing until the *denouement*."

He grinned his gap-toothed grin.

"Come on, I've been dying to know ever since you mentioned it. I promise I'll say anything to nobody. Is that what I mean? Nothing to anybody. I must be getting drunk."

But his eyes were clear and alert.

"You and me both," she said. "Well all right then, but you must promise to tell no one. Do you swear on your life?"

He said he did.

"I'll hold you to it," she said, putting her hand to his cheek for a moment and looking him in the eye. Then she grinned, breaking the solemn moment. "All right then – I *will* tell you. Do you remember how the story began? The police noticed that one or two paintings had disappeared and then mysteriously turned up again. So they called me in to review the evidence."

"By disappeared you mean stolen? I thought when that happens they often turn up again, because the thieves can't sell them."

"Be that as it may, it was a bit of a coincidence the way these pictures turned up. So we went and had a look at one of them. I mentioned it to you the other night, do you remember? It was an Alma-Tadema."

"Ah yes, the *wormholes*," Rupert said, leaning forward.

"Exactly; the wormholes. We have all our restorations and evaluations done by Marcello's, and as I told you, they tested it and found it was a copy."

"How extraordinary. And you think you know who did it?"

"We don't absolutely *know*," Lucy said, leaning forward conspiratorially. "But there's a master forger who apparently came out of prison a couple of years ago; a Mr Alfred Smith."

Rupert looked stunned.

"What's the matter?" she said, surprised at his expression. "Have you heard of him?"

"Well no, but I suppose I was, er – surprised that you have a name for the forger so quickly. How did you get on his trail?"

"Well, I hadn't heard of him, and neither had Hugh – that's my policeman friend," Lucy said. "But John Ellis at Marcello's is very reliable. He's been in the restoration trade for thirty years and he's seen everything. To cut a long story short, Ellis looked at the painting and said he'd only ever seen work of that calibre once before, and it had been done by this man Smith."

"Extraordinary," Rupert said faintly. "So what next?"

"They can't arrest him," she admitted, "because they can't find him. He appears to have vanished."

At that moment the cheese course came. Lucy was having goat's cheese in a herb salad and truffle dressing. Rupert was having the cheese platter, and when it came it was a board of thirty fine French cheeses, so it took a few minutes for him to choose.

Lucy looked idly around the restaurant, while Rupert and the waiter fussed over the cheeses as though it were a matter of life or death. Some of the paintings on the walls were similar to the ones upstairs, such as the Bewick ink and wash of melons and peppers. But there were renderings of Gavroche urchins too, and a good painting of one of the Roux brothers which had the same quality as the portrait of Pinter she remembered in the NPG.

The waiter went away and there was a pause before Rupert said through a mouthful of cheese," Well go on! You can't leave me in suspense like this. Can your policeman find him?"

"Hugh was off for the weekend. They don't really work around the clock, you know, unless it's murder. But I do have a possibility that I'm following up. I've been working with an old friend of Smith's, and he's turning out to be a pretty interesting character, though unbelievably stubborn."

Rupert stared at her blankly, but she didn't notice. He filled her glass with the last of the white Burgundy, and then took a gulp from his own glass.

"So who is this other old fellow?"

"I was very unsure at first," she said. "He's an ex-con who was in prison with this chap Smith. Another brilliant painter. He lives in Cambridge now. But he's not old; what makes you think he's old?" She gave him a teasing look. "Rather dashing, actually."

"Really?" Rupert said, wrinkling his brow. "Was he in for the same crime, then? Surely you're not using a forger to catch a forger?"

"It takes a thief…" Lucy said. "Though he says he didn't do it."

"Don't they all say that?"

"Yes, but in this case I think I believe him. He's arrogant and obstinate, but funnily enough I don't think he's a bad lot."

"You *say* that," Rupert said. "But if he's been to prison the court must have thought he was guilty. Maybe *he's* your forger!"

Lucy popped a last parcel of goat's cheese and salad into her mouth.

"Could be," she said. "But my instinct says not. Anyway, he's been helping me find Smith."

Rupert raised his eyebrows.

"Are you sure it's quite safe? He *is* an ex-con, after all."

Lucy smiled at a sudden fond memory of Will Bentley, and Rupert noticed it.

"Yes, I was a bit alarmed about that, too, but he's as safe as houses; wouldn't hurt a fly. He has a fiery temper, but he blows up and then he blows out, if you know what I mean. I rather *like* him. Mind you he was a perfect pig today."

"You met him *today*?" Rupert said, unable completely to conceal his shock. "But why is this man – what's his name? – why is he helping you to find his prison buddy?"

"His name is Will Bentley, and you're right – I had to do a great deal of persuading before he would help," Lucy said. "I pointed out that Smith was going to be under suspicion until he was cleared, and after all, he can't be exonerated if we can't find him."

"But you don't know where to look. Does this man Bentley have any idea?"

"No," Lucy said sadly. "We did go to Alfred's old house today to look for him, though."

Rupert didn't say anything, just looked at her.

"You're looking as if you saw a ghost again," she said with a little frown of puzzlement.

He arranged his mouth into the shape of a smile.

"Am I? I'm sorry. I suppose I'm *worried* that you are looking for this man, and I'm worried that you're working with an ex-con. Anything could happen."

"No it *couldn't*," Lucy laughed. "I assure you Will Bentley is harmless. And we haven't found Alfred Smith, but even if we do find him he's apparently getting on in years, so your guess was half right. I don't think he'd put up much of a fight."

The waiter returned, removed the remnants of the cheese and invited orders for dessert. Lucy said she was far too full to eat anything else, but she gave in without much resistance when Rupert insisted that she must have the whole Roux experience.

"So you were saying that you actually went to Smith's house *today?*" Rupert said as soon as the waiter had gone. "Where is it? Did you find anything?"

"It's in Hastings, but it was hopeless; a complete dead end. The trail has gone cold. Apparently the house burned down some months ago and they were in the act of knocking it down when we arrived. The demolition man wouldn't even let us in because it was unsafe. They were literally smashing the place down with a wrecking ball. We couldn't exactly go in and hunt for clues."

"So you found nothing?" Rupert said, as if trying to work out what line of investigation she could pursue next. "How very frustrating for you."

He poured more wine and sat back in his chair to drink it.

"Yes, it put me in a bad mood. And then we were tired and I realised I was late for this evening and we ended up having a row. It was all rather silly. I left Bentley there."

"Will you see him again?" Rupert asked, a little too quickly.

"I do believe you're jealous," She said with a disarming smile, raising her eyebrows and looking him in the eye.

"Of course I am. I'm jealous of anyone who spends the entire day with you."

"And yesterday, too!" she teased.

He looked concerned again, she thought. He was oddly over-protective considering that they had only just met. She couldn't quite read him.

"What happened yesterday?"

"Yesterday we went to the Isle of Wight to look at a second painting that I thought might be a forgery. It was another one of those that had vanished and then reappeared."

"Which one?" Rupert said. "I mean; what painting?"

"It was a Frans Snyders, but Bentley couldn't see any signs of forgery, and we weren't allowed by the owners to take it away, so that trail has gone cold too."

The desserts arrived before Rupert was able to respond to this. They each had a glass of Sauternes; its delicate flavour perfectly accompanying the sweets. Lucy had an apricot and Cointreau soufflé grandly named an Omelette Rothschild, and Rupert had a complicated mixture of puff pastry, strawberries and Mascarpone ice cream. He held out a clean fork so that she could try a mouthful, and she was glad she did – the evocative scent of the tiny wild strawberries was delicious. It reminded her suddenly of an incident long ago in her childhood, when she and her brother Dylan had been chased across a strawberry field by an irate farmer.

When they had finished she said she needed to freshen up.

"All right. When you come back we can relax on one of the sofas for some coffee if you like."

"It sounds lovely," she said. I'll join you in a few minutes."

She disappeared through the doors at the end of the dining room. When she came back she sat down very close to Rupert on a brown sofa, so that their knees touched. He took her hand and held it.

"I am shocked that you have been having all these adventures without me," he said. "But now I am fascinated. Tell me, do you think this man Bentley will manage to make any progress finding his friend? Does he have any leads?"

"I don't think so," Lucy said. "But you never know. I plan to go back and see him and make friends again. We did part rather abruptly. That is, if you won't be too jealous?"

"You're teasing me again," he smiled. "I can't help it if I want to protect you from dastardly criminals."

They had coffee and petit fours, and Lucy pronounced the meal to be the best she had ever eaten. After Rupert had settled the bill they made their way to the exit, shaking the Maitre D's hand and collecting their coats. Then they were delivered once more into the warm bosom of London. It was a balmy evening and occasional head-lamped cars whirred past. The clouds had thinned and there were stars almost hidden by the streetlights. Lucy stood on the pavement for a moment and breathed deeply, enjoying the night air made fresh and clean by the recent rain. The road was already dry and she had no need to don her coat.

A Rolls Royce purred up to the kerb and waited. It was the one Lucy had seen outside the Limerston.

She gestured with an inclination of her head back towards *Le Gavroche*.

"It's like a little bit of France," she said.

Rupert smiled and opened the rear door of the Rolls.

"I'm glad you enjoyed it. Can I offer you a lift?"

She found herself being whisked back to Richmond in the back of the Rolls, cuddled up to Rupert, laughing and chatting all the way about inconsequential things. She could barely see the back of the driver's head through the smoked glass, so she was only able to glean the impression that he was a big man. He did not turn around and when she pointed to him and whispered "Who's that?!" in Rupert's ear, he leaned close and whispered back that it was his man Morton, and that he was rather untalkative but very faithful. His breath tickled her ear and she rather liked it.

They were driven to her flat without incident.

"I've had a perfectly lovely evening," Lucy said. "It's been such a treat. Thank you."

"You have been my ideal partner," Rupert said. "When you walked into that dining room, heads turned. May I call you again?"

"You may, Rupert," she said coquettishly, and then she leaned forward and put her lips on his. When they broke apart after a minute or two, Rupert looked as flushed as she herself felt.

"You can ask me over to the Angel Gallery, if you like," she said. "I don't know if you're available next Thursday morning, but that's free on my diary so I could take it off."

He arranged to pick her up early on Thursday, and then for a lingering moment he just looked at her. Then he stepped out of the car, walked around and opened the door.

She got out and kissed him again, more briefly. He tasted different to Sam – older and richer, like a vintage port. She giggled without telling him why and then walked up the path while he stood by the car watching her.

"It won't be the Rolls on Thursday," he called after her departing figure. "Just me and a silver Mercedes."

She waved and then was gone, disappearing up the alley to her flat.

Rupert got in the car and slumped back into the soft leather seat, smelling a hint of Parisienne even though she was gone. He slid open the dividing window.

"That is quite a woman," he said to the driver, blowing out his cheeks. "Find out if Julia will be at the Gallery in the morning, Edward. And I'll need you too. I think we need a council of war."

TWENTY-THREE

Because we focused on the snake, we missed the scorpion.
EGYPTIAN PROVERB

The next day was a Tuesday, and at ten o'clock in the morning there were four people in Rupert's office in the Angel Gallery. Rupert himself was seated with Mrs Morris and Morton around a glass-topped conference table, while Mrs Morris's son Lawrence stood agitatedly at the window. Rupert had not invited Lawrence, but Lawrence generally turned up with Mrs Morris and Rupert had never quite been able to confess to Mrs Morris that this irritated him. His solution to the problem was to ignore Lawrence whenever possible, and to insult him for the rest of the time.

Today Rupert wore an open-necked white shirt, a pin-striped jacket over pale chino trousers and the white shoes he had worn the previous evening. He had a slight headache, perhaps because of the large brandy he had swallowed on returning home after dropping Lucy. The headache didn't do anything to improve his temper, which was very frayed around the edges following Lucy's disclosures of the night before.

The meeting had already been in progress for half an hour. In that time Rupert had described how Lucy Wrackham had not only learned that there were forgeries but even knew of the existence of Alfred Smith.

In the chair on Rupert's left sat Mrs Morris. No-one had ever seen Mrs Morris rattled, except a single time when some junior had asked her what had happened to *Mr* Morris, and she had told him to mind his own damned business. A day later his desk had been cleared and he had left the premises. No-one had ever asked again about her husband. Kinder employees of the Gallery said that something so terrible must have happened that she couldn't bear to speak about it, but one who had also fallen foul of Mrs Morris likened her to a scorpion, having a successful *Promenade à Deux* with the hapless Mr Morris and then gobbling him up.

But though she was disliked by many gallery staff, Mrs Morris had a particular benefit as far as Rupert was concerned: she could be relied upon to do whatever he asked with absolute discretion and without compunction, and more than once he had tested her limits and been surprised. She appeared to be truly wicked. She liked to win no matter what the odds, and she could not abide weakness in others. In her office next to his, Rupert would sometimes hear the strains of Brahms issuing forth as she sat at her desk and worked out solutions to his problems. He did not personally care for Brahms, but he considered it a small price to pay for the loyalty of this cold-blooded, highly effective woman.

Seated on Rupert's right was Edward Morton, but the other person in the room still stood at the window, as Rupert's cold stare made him uneasy. Lawrence Morris was 32 years old, tall and gangly, with pimples that had never entirely receded after adolescence. When he walked he had a loping gait that made him look ridiculous.   It was as if all the charm and sophistication had gone to his mother, leaving him with none.

Mrs Morris was painfully aware of Lawrence's gaucheness. He had been brought up by a nanny whom he had loved but who had been sent away by Mrs Morris for reasons unknown to Lawrence when he was ten and a half. The sudden absence of Mr Morris at the same time had been suspicious but Lawrence had never made any connection. He had been sent to boarding school and bullied there. He had not excelled academically, except in one area that partially redeemed him – he was remarkably good at languages. Lawrence appeared to be able to acquire foreign languages effortlessly, reading language primers from cover to cover and possessing an excellent ability in mimicry. He spoke French, German, Italian, Spanish, Danish, Arabic and Japanese as well as English – and was passably competent in half a dozen other tongues. Such fluency might have made a different man internationally minded, politically aware and culturally wise, but all this somehow seemed to have passed Lawrence by. He was left with neither girlfriend nor boyfriend, living with a mother who was embarrassed by him in the house of a man that he loathed. His mother was sarcastic about everything that he did, making him feel resentful and guilty in equal measure. Rupert Angel tolerated him because he came as part of the package with his mother, but Angel's smooth confidence and acid tongue made Lawrence feel clumsy and out of place.

Though Lawrence showed his alarm most obviously, there was no doubt that *everyone* in the room was worried. The fact was that Rupert Angel had neither invested wisely nor spent sensibly. When the Gallery had enjoyed huge successes, Rupert had poured his funds into stocks that had foundered, rather than investing in the art world that he knew best. As a result his expensive steel- and glass-walled gallery in the heart of London had lost a fortune rather than making one. Rupert had long since exhausted the generosity of the banks and his current creditor was becoming increasingly frank as to what misfortunes might befall Rupert if he didn't continue the high-interest repayments. Until a few years ago it had looked as if the Gallery would need to close, and that Rupert would have to flee the country to avoid the sharp sound of breaking bones. Morton was well aware of what might happen in these circumstances, and had broken his customary silence to elucidate Rupert's possible future with chilling clarity.

It was then that Rupert had come up with a solution to their difficulties. He had a rich and eccentric clientele of collectors who wanted original paintings by great masters. These were men – they *were* usually men – of almost unlimited means who could buy what they wanted, and a few of them felt themselves above the law. One in particular – the man they had taken to calling the Collector – was now their chief source of income. Once a work of art had been identified, Rupert would have it stolen and copied. The copy would be returned anonymously and the original sold to the Collector for an enormous sum. Since he had employed Alfred Smith as his copyist, the quality of work had increased and prices had increased with it. In this way Rupert Angel managed to keep his bones unbroken and chip away at his debt.

Mrs Morris sat with pursed lips, saying nothing but staring intently at Rupert, even though he had now completed his summary of the previous evening's events and had subsided into an uncharacteristically morose silence.

Morton spoke first, much to the surprise of the others because he normally gave a passable impression of a mute.

"Mr Harold won't be interested in excuses," he said simply, referring to Rupert's current source of finance. "If the whole scam collapses and you can't pay up, his people will pay us a visit and burn the place down with everyone in it. Mr Harold is a very nasty piece of work, Mr Angel, and he will always call in a debt. He has his reputation to think of."

Lawrence had opened the window as far as its three-inch restraint allowed and was inhaling outside air like a man close to suffocation. His long corduroy jacket brushed against an executive ball-bouncing toy, which fell on its side with a loud crash. Mrs Morris looked up with irritation.

"Oh for God's sake, Lawrence!" she said sharply. "Come and sit down or else leave the room. I'm trying to think."

"I'll go and get a drink of water," Lawrence said, puce with embarrassment. He tried to set the toy upright but it was entangled. He fiddled with it until Mrs Morris exploded.

"Lawrence!"

Rupert gave Lawrence a sneering look. Lawrence's mouth twitched with bottled-up emotion but he slunk wordlessly out of the room.

"Now then," Mrs Morris said when he had gone. "We need a plan and we need it fast. We mustn't panic because the going is getting tough."

"Agreed," said Rupert Angel. "But there is one thing I am going to stipulate right now, Julia. I will not have Lucy Wrackham harmed."

Mrs Morris looked at him for several moments. He was the closest thing to a Mr Morris she had these days, and Lucy Wrackham represented beauty and brains in equal degree, making her a dangerous interloper. Rupert obviously wanted to get in the girl's knickers, which meant that the poor widowed Mrs Wrackham could be their Achilles Heel. Her job was finding stolen art, for God's sake! In Mrs Morris's opinion, a more sensible approach to the problem would involve the immediate despatch of Lucy Wrackham to the bottom of the Thames, with a few heavy stones to keep her company.

"That's going to be very difficult," she said at last, looking him in the eye.

"Nevertheless it is my wish," Rupert said calmly, and she knew he would not be moved.

There was an uncomfortable silence.

"In that case," she said thoughtfully, "Perhaps we can send Mrs Wrackham plummeting off in the wrong direction. We do have the ex-con in the picture – what was *his* name again?"

"Will Bentley."

"Yes, Bentley. Perhaps the blame for the recent spate of forgeries could be directed at *him*, and Alfred could then continue his work undetected. We'd have to make sure Alfred doesn't discover we've implicated his old friend, but I feel sure we could work out the details."

"Bentley is definitely expendable," Rupert said, nodding slowly, and then went on after a moment: "I know you're annoyed that I will not tolerate violence with Lucy Wrackham, Julia, because I can see it in your face. But Lucy is like a work of art, and I will not see a work of art destroyed."

Mrs Morris sat stony-faced. If all he wanted was to screw the little bitch, she would have to wait until he had sown his seed. But she knew that if the Wrackham woman remained on the scene once the dust had settled, there would have to be an unfortunate accident. She smiled warmly at the thought and Rupert misinterpreted her smile as acceptance.

"Thank you for your understanding," he said, and she smiled a little more broadly at his words.

"The only question is: do we frame Bentley or merely frighten him witless?" she said sweetly.

At lunchtime Morton visited a hardware store, where he purchased an axe suitable for splitting logs. It had a stainless-steel blade with a razor-sharp edge and a non-slip rubber grip. He paid by cash and they packed it in cardboard. Then, with the long package securely under his arm, he melted back into the anonymity of the city.

TWENTY-FOUR

We are all mortal until the first kiss and the second glass of wine.
EDUARDO GALEANO

The digital figures on the clock inside the undercover police van skipped from 23:59 to 00:00, and it was Wednesday the 21st. Emily Matheson was watching the numbers as they skipped over. Billy Stokes was reading the sports pages.

"That's it," she said.

He looked at the monitor, saw nothing and then looked at her.

"What?"

"It's my birthday, look!" She pointed at the clock. "I'm a Cancer, on the cusp. I looked it up and it said I like to build a nest for my loved one. That's a laugh, that is."

She reached forward so that her breasts strained against the material of her white shirt. From behind the seat on the passenger side she extracted a carrier bag with something in it which clinked. She brought out a bottle of champagne and two glasses. She held up the bottle.

"Want to drink my health, Billy?"

Billy Stokes put down his paper and laughed.

"Well you're a bit of a surprise, Emily, and no mistake. I thought you were going to be stuffy, but now I think there's a wild one inside you that's trying to get out."

She put out her tongue at him and untwisted the wire while he held the glasses.

"For drinking while on duty," Billy intoned in Carter's voice, "you will be hung by the neck until you are dead."

She removed the cork very slowly and carefully so that not a drop of champagne was wasted. It made tiny squeaking sounds as she extracted it.

"Sod Carter," she said matter-of-factly. He held out the glasses and she filled them.

"Happy birthday," Billy said, holding up his glass to her. They clinked and drank.

When they had drained their glasses she topped them up again.

"It's our last night, anyway," she said. "We might as well celebrate not having to sit in this bloody van anymore."

"I've quite enjoyed it," Billy confessed. "Carrying out surveillance on you out of the corner of my eye."

She giggled and looked at him boldly.

"At least you take a bit of notice, which is more than I can say for Vic," she said.

There was a long pause while she waited to see whether she could pluck up courage to say what she wanted to say; what she had fantasized that she might say. When she finally said it, it came out in a slightly husky voice.

"So don't I get a birthday kiss?"

He looked at her for a moment without saying anything. Then he took her glass and his and put them on the workbench next to the logbook. He leaned over until his leg was touching hers and brushed her lips with his. Her lips were full and soft. She smelled wonderful.

"Happy birthday," he whispered, and she kept on looking at him, until they each leaned forward again and put their mouths together. They spent a long time just kissing. Then he put his hand behind her head and ran his fingers across the nape of her neck as their tongues played. He unbuttoned her white shirt with his free hand and slipped his fingers into it, cupping her breast in its sensible policewoman's bra.

"Just a minute," she said, and wriggled about until he could reach to unfasten the clip. He ran his fingers over her bare stomach and found a stud in her navel. He caressed her skin, moving his hand in slow circles as they kissed. Then he slid his fingers beneath the loosened brassiere and explored her nipples, feeling them swell at his touch. She shuddered and put her hands on him. After that they half fell onto the floor of the van and shoved the chairs to one side. She put her mouth to his ear. "Whatever you want," she whispered.

Her black skirt had a single button at the top but he ignored it and lifted the skirt, revealing pink underwear tied with little ribbon bows at the sides. The ribbons undid easily when pulled.

Later, a monitor light began to blink on the equipment behind them, but they were not paying it due care and attention.

TWENTY-FIVE

Good things of day begin to droop and drowse;
While night's black agents to their preys do rouse.
      WILLIAM SHAKESPEARE, Macbeth

It had taken Morton two hours to drive to Cambridge on Tuesday afternoon. Mrs Morris had found Bentley's address on the internet, but Morton parked in a multi-storey a mile or two short of his goal. It took him some time to locate the studio on foot, and he had to walk past it twice to make sure. After that he took himself off to a park to await the veil of darkness.

At one in the morning the building had been dark for some time. The city was as deserted as it ever gets at night and Morton gained entry to the studio with a swiftness which brought him professional satisfaction. Breaking and entering had always given him a perverse pleasure. His father had been a security guard and a violent bully, and each time Morton illegally entered a new establishment he felt like he was spitting in the old bastard's eye.

The lock on the front door was a sturdy Yale but it offered little resistance – he used a purpose-made tool and in twenty seconds had the door open. Now he was inside the darkened hallway, poised to take flight if an alarm went off – but there was silence and he stood still for a moment, getting his bearings and allowing his eyes to adjust to the darkness. He had been in many unfamiliar houses in the dead of night, so he knew just what to expect.

Anyone seeing him in the shadowy gloom would have found him a sinister figure. He wore a black hood to conceal his identity. His clothes were black and he wore thin black leather gloves. He was tall, fit, and muscled. Underneath his arm was a bulky object covered in cloth.

He went forward, using a small flashlight to see where he was going. He reached a dead end immediately; a locked door with no key. He went back to the hall and up the stairs, ignoring the occasional creak. There was some kind of a waiting room and a door which opened to his touch. The smell of paint and turpentine assailed his nostrils – the studio itself, presumably. He had known that smell many times before, most recently with Rupert when they had visited Alfred Smith. He went forward, using the tiny torch to shed enough light to avoid stumbling. There were paintings stacked against the walls. The torch sent a beam which glanced off the stacked shapes, caught studio mirrors and sent wild shadows careening around. He snapped it off and stood until his eyes adjusted to the moonlight coming through the large window. The walls were milky grey from the moon, which was almost full. He saw a high pitched roof with high cross-beams. The streetlamp outside cast a yellow strip onto one wall. Against the pale tones, paintings and easels and brushes stood out in black silhouette. He padded around on soft-soled shoes, making no sound except for an occasional protest from a disturbed floorboard. He tried doors. The first room was a bedroom containing just a bed and a chest of drawers, which looked as if it was used for guests. The second room was a study, lined with books and with a computer in the corner. The third was the kitchen and he was about to leave it when he realised that there was a corridor beyond it. He went forward slowly.

The corridor became a vestibule with two doors off it, both open. The right-hand door led to the bathroom. He could see a shower cubicle and a bath, with moonlight from a skylight glittering on the silver taps. The left-hand door led to a bedroom. He moved forward very slowly into the bedroom and became aware of the sound of breathing. The room was a good size and in the middle of it was a large four-poster bed. Morton shifted the heavy object under his arm in its cloth wrapping. He stood by the bed silently and looked down at the man asleep in it, his face expressionless.

The curtains were almost closed but a thin gap allowed sufficient light to see, albeit in shades of grey. Mrs Morris had found an image of Bentley on the internet. The sleeper before him was clearly the same person, though he looked a little different. In the internet picture he'd had short hair, but this man's hair was long and framed his face loosely. One of Bentley's pillows had been tossed to the side and had fallen to the floor. Morton looked at it speculatively. It would be so easy to fix the problem of Bentley.

He spent another ten minutes in the building and then slipped out as quietly as he had arrived. The only unavoidable loud sound was the click of the latch as it snapped home, and he took off swiftly, not running but taking long strides, stepping into an unlighted alleyway before removing the hood. It was easier to move swiftly now that he was no longer hampered by his heavy burden. He still held the cloth, furled into a roll. He peeled off the thin black gloves and stowed them in his pocket. It was some distance to his car but he walked fast, dumping the roll of cloth in a litter bin and making it back without incident. He was on the motorway within half an hour, roaring away from Cambridge along the twin cones of his headlight beams.

TWENTY-SIX

I never saw a man who looked
With such a wistful eye
Upon that little tent of blue
Which prisoners call the sky,
And at every drifting cloud that went
With sails of silver by.
OSCAR WILDE, The Ballad of Reading Gaol

Will awoke at eight on Wednesday morning when the alarm went off. He killed its squawking and lay for a while in the big bed, coming awake. He had been dreaming about Lucy Wrackham and now he tried hard to remember it, but it slipped away as dreams do. Instead he recalled the argument between the two of them a couple of days ago and felt rueful. He wanted to see her again but was too proud to ring her and say so, even though he had her card and could have called her there and then. As if that wasn't enough there was another problem. Just before falling asleep he had decided that it was wrong for him to be looking for Alfred. If his old friend *had* started up again in the trade then it certainly wasn't Will's business to catch him. And if Alfred was innocent he wouldn't thank Will one bit for connecting him with the whole business. Either way, helping Lucy Wrackham seemed a ridiculous thing to do, and therein lay the problem – looking for Alfred was the only reason he might see Lucy again, unless she had decided that her dinner date was so horrible that she must rush up to Cambridge and go out with an ex-con.

Feeling glum, he showered and dressed in jeans and a loose shirt, then put on his painting smock over the top and went through to the studio. He peered out of the window to inspect the sky, which was clear and blue. The street below was empty of traffic because it wasn't a thoroughfare to anywhere. The Water Board van that had been parked opposite had finally taken itself off.

He went over to his easel and looked at a part-finished nude of Sandy Lennox. It needed much more work, but yesterday he had done the underpainting, blocking in the main tones and colours on top of a charcoal sketch. He squinted at it. Not bad – the contrast was about right, but it was boring. It needed purple in the shadows to enliven it. He picked up a flat brush. It was hard to concentrate with all this other business going on – Lucy Wrackham had filled his mind up with other thoughts and memories. He put the brush down again and went into the kitchen, where he made tea and ate a bowl of cornflakes with a banana chopped into it.

Ian Simpson, his part-time framer, arrived at nine, and was as quiet as ever. Just about all that Will knew about Ian was that he had a passion for making and flying model aeroplanes, and that he was gay. He certainly knew how to make a good frame. Most of Will's frames were black, and once Ian knew what he wanted he would make a perfect frame in no time at all. From there the pictures would wait in the studio until exhibited, unless Will decided that he was short of cash and sent a batch of them to one of the galleries that showed his work.

Sandy arrived at half past nine and changed into a dressing gown while Will organised the mattress that she would be lying on. He was painting her as a reclining nude on a bed. He was inventing the bed frame, but he needed to have her on a mattress in order to reproduce the folds and shadows of the cloth on which she was stretched out. When he had everything in place according to the painting, Sandy took off the robe and lay down. They spent five minutes getting her into the correct position, moving the angle of a leg or the position of an elbow or the tilt of her head until she was exactly right. Then Will recharged the palette with fresh burnt umber – that was the only colour which had skinned over – and picked up a brush again. As usual he stared at her intently for a few minutes. Then he dipped the brush into the alizarin crimson, made a new island of fresh paint on the palette, added a dab of ultramarine and stirred the colour until it became a deep violet, almost black. He added white and watched the colour come to life; a strong purple. He adjusted it with more blue until he was satisfied. Then, after another period of staring intensely at Sandy, he began to dab paint into the shadows of the painting, causing the pale flesh tones to be heightened by the complementary colour.

Once he was painting he forgot all else. He knew he had been unusually distracted in the last few days – the Isle of Wight; the search for Alfred; his interest in Lucy. But once he began to paint he no longer fretted about it all. The world was just him, his paintbrush and the living canvas – and the voluptuous form of Sandy stretched out on the mattress, looking back at him with those big eyes of hers. If it hadn't been for Ian, working quietly away at the back of the studio, he might have allowed himself to be a little more distracted by Sandy. As he painted, a track in his mind examined precisely how distracted he might get with her.

There was the crash of heavy boots on the stairs. Will looked round with surprise and anger. The door of the studio was flung open abruptly and policemen began to pour into the room. It took a few moments for him to adjust to this extraordinary fact, and he had a sudden strong feeling of déjà vu. He stood there with the paintbrush frozen in his hand, his mouth comically open in disbelief. Ian took a few paces and then stopped uncertainly. Sandy leaped up with a shriek and grabbed her robe, putting it on and disappearing towards the spare bedroom where she had put her clothes. A policewoman tried to stop her but Sandy told her to sod off. As she was wearing only a flimsy robe and wasn't a suspect except by association, the policewoman thought better of it and let her go, though she stood in the doorway and blocked the gaze of one or two of the younger policemen who were grinning surreptitiously.

A man in plain clothes was leading the phalanx of uniformed policemen. He walked straight up to Will, holding some kind of ID card in his face. Will's tranquil mood was destroyed, leaving him as he usually felt when he was interrupted while painting – completely furious.

He took the ID card from the man and read it out.

"Hugh Davies, Detective Inspector, Art and Antiques. You're Lucy Wrackham's policeman friend. What on earth do you think you're doing barging in here?"

Davies looked him sternly in the eye.

"Are you Mr William Bentley, sir?"

"Of *course* I'm Bentley. It says so over the shop front and you just walked into my house without knocking. Who do you think I am, Rumplestiltskin? I'd love to hear what you have to say for yourself. This is police harassment. Does Lucy know you're here?" A fresh thought occurred to him, causing his confidence momentarily to falter. "*She* didn't send you did she?"

"This is nothing to do with Mrs Wrackham, Mr Bentley. We have received notification that there may be a valuable stolen artefact on the premises and I have an approved warrant signed this morning by a magistrate to carry out a search, during which time you and your assistants are required to remain present."

Will looked angry again.

"What bloody artefact? There's nothing stolen here. What are you talking about? Speak up, man."

Davies looked a little uncomfortable at the vehemence of the attack from Will, but he was firm and clearly intended to carry out the search.

"It is indicated on the warrant. I have a certified copy of it here which I am required to give you. As you will see on the attached schedule, we believe you have a painting concealed on the premises."

He handed a piece of paper to Will, who was now looking bemused.

Will took the warrant, shaking his head and muttering as he scanned it.

"A property stolen or taken under false pretences or embezzled, or found and fraudulently appropriated," he quoted.

He looked up.

"Unbelievable. You won't find a thing because there's nothing to find." He flipped over the page and read the attached schedule, which listed a single painting. His eyes widened and then he started to laugh.

"An original old master painting by Wilhelm Hammershoi entitled 'Interior with a Girl at the Clavier'. But this is a *famous* painting! It must be worth a bloody fortune. I used to have a paperback some Irish girl gave me and this was on the front cover." He folded the warrant in half and made to hand it back to the policeman.

"You can search the place from top to bottom," he said. "You'll find nothing here. What makes you think I've got it, anyway?"

"We had a very precise tip off," Davies said, refusing to take back the copy of the warrant. "And the painting disappeared a few days ago from a private collection. In view of your history we took the tip off very seriously."

Will looked at him disgustedly and used the paintbrush to point at the policeman accusingly.

"You jumped to conclusions because I've got previous," he said. "Some bloody nutcase has sent you a crackpot message and you've come steaming up here to catch the master criminal, which is all very well except that I *didn't* pinch the painting and I don't know who did. I'm very sorry it's been stolen because it's a pretty picture – but I – didn't – take it." He enunciated these last words with pauses in between and stared Davies directly in the eye.

Davies felt increasingly uncomfortable. Bentley's entire demeanour and body language was that of an innocent man.

"In that case we'll have a look round and if we find nothing, sir, then you will receive my full and personal apology."

He waved to the policemen and they began to search, starting with the studio since it was full of paintings. They were extremely systematic, moving the stacked paintings very carefully, looking for the image that the detective had showed them that morning before the raid.

After ten minutes one of them called out.

"Sir! I've found it. It's behind this stack."

Will leaped up from the chair where he had been sitting sullenly.

"What do you mean you've *found it*? You can't have found it," he yelled, marching over to the policeman.

"Step back please sir," Davies said in his ear, and took his elbow, moving him to one side firmly. Will watched as Davies put on surgical gloves and then reached in behind the stack of paintings. He brought out the Wilhelm Hammershoi and looked at it, turning it over to check the back and confirm that it was not merely a modern copy.

"This is it," he nodded, looking very satisfied. Then he looked at Will and all his politeness was gone.

"I must ask you to come with me," he said, then looked round at the only other policeman in plain clothes.

"Sergeant! I want this boxed up for transport, and no-one's to touch it, mind. Take it back to the AAU. I want our own forensics to take any prints off it and look for anything else at all, and I do mean *anything*." The detective sergeant was already wearing gloves, as were all the other policemen, and he took the painting carefully.

Will looked utterly deflated.

"Someone's stitching me up," he said, shaking his head. "I have no idea how that painting got there."

Davies looked at him dispassionately.

"We'll talk about it," he said. "I'm asking you and your colleagues to accompany me to Parkside police station to help us with our enquiries."

"Are you arresting me?"

"No I'm not," Davies said shortly. "I'm asking you to cooperate with our enquiries."

"Then I'm not coming with you," Will said, aware that once he was arrested the police would have to charge him within 24 hours.

Davies barely missed a beat.

"In that case I *am* arresting you, as I have reasonable grounds to suspect that you or your associates have stolen the valuable painting that we have this morning found on your premises."

He read him his rights, and after a few minutes more Will found himself being led downstairs and out of his studio by the policemen, together with Sandy and Ian, who had elected to accompany them rather than risk being arrested also. Ian looked shocked and subdued, but Sandy was loud and indignant. She explained in no uncertain terms just what she thought of a bunch of policemen who burst into a room when a girl didn't have any clothes on, much to the amusement of a few interested bystanders, who clapped as the three of them were put into the back of separate police cars and driven away.

TWENTY-SEVEN

*The strangest whim has seized me.... After all
I think I will not hang myself today.*
G.K. CHESTERTON, Ballade of Suicide

It was horribly familiar to Will. He had been sitting in the windowless interview room in Parkside for a couple of hours, with the spools of two tapes turning in the tape machine, one to be sealed for the court in the event of a dispute and the other to be used by the police as a working copy. He had been offered coffee, which he had accepted, and food, which he had refused. He had been told of his right to inform someone of his arrest, and he had asked them to tell George Levy. It wasn't that George would be much help – rather than by turning up and being outraged at the detainment of his friend – but George would tell Anna, and Anna was more practical and would put wheels in motion to try to extricate Will from the mess he had so unexpectedly found himself in.

He could have asked the Welsh policeman to tell Anna directly, but that would have hurt George's feelings. He had also wondered whether he should ask them to tell Lucy instead. But he remembered the terms on which he had parted from her and felt worried that she must have something to do with this, even though the policeman had denied it. He didn't suspect her of concealing the painting in his studio; he was sure she would do no such thing. He wondered for a moment if the police themselves had done it while ostensibly searching – they would have had the opportunity. But he knew they hadn't; he had been watching them all closely. His mind returned to Lucy. If she had been asked for the name of a possible culprit, would she have stood by him? He wasn't sure, but it hurt that she may have betrayed him.

In the room with him were DCI Davies, a stocky sergeant, and the duty solicitor they had called in; a double-chinned florid man of about forty with a rumpled suit and halitosis. The solicitor scribbled occasionally on a legal pad but otherwise appeared to be brain dead. Will didn't have a solicitor of his own because he had never thought he might need one. He suspected solicitors in general as being only half a step removed from the authority which had locked him up for a year on trumped up charges. But the moment the fat-faced man had walked into the room and looked him up and down, he knew it was a mistake and vowed to hire someone competent with all speed. He wasn't going to go like a lamb to the slaughter as he had last time.

The interview had so far been a frustrating one for Davies. He had received an anonymous tip off that morning that the Hammershoi was concealed within the premises of William Bentley. His department had been informed of the Hammershoi's theft from a private collection only a few days previously, but it was only by the merest chance that he happened to have seen the painting on a list of stolen items. Ironically he had seen its name while he was with Lucy in his office, using QUEST to search for Alfred Smith.

"Are you familiar with Wilhelm Hammershoi's painting entitled 'Interior with a Girl at the Clavier'?" he began.

"Of course," Will said. "It's a famous painting, and I am a painter. Anyway, you know I am because I told you I had a book with it on the front cover. Grace Notes."

"Grace Notes?"

"That was the name of the book. But I knew the painting anyway. Anyone connected with art knows it. You must know it, surely?"

"I know it, yes," Davies said.

"Maybe we're working together," Will said sarcastically.

Davies ignored this remark.

"We have established that you are familiar with the painting in question," he noted formally. "Please explain to me how it got into your studio."

"I have absolutely no idea."

"Someone must have put it there, I'm thinking."

"Well, it didn't walk in by itself."

"Then how did it get there?"

"I haven't a clue. I don't even know that it *is* the original. Have you examined it closely?"

"We have examined it very closely. It will undergo full tests but at this time we are almost certain that it is the original."

"How are you certain?"

"You'll find out in due course. You admit that the painting was concealed in your studio?"

"It was in my studio, yes. I was amazed when you found it, though. I have no idea how it got there, as I say."

"Why was it concealed?"

"Well it wasn't really. It was tucked behind some of my paintings, but it didn't take you more than ten minutes of looking before you found it. Not exactly a prime hiding place for an old master. Anyone could have tucked it behind there in a few seconds. I think if I was really trying to hide something I'd come up with a better place than that."

"Unless you thought that no-one would suspect it was there. Tell me then; why would someone steal a very valuable painting and then hide it in your studio?"

"I have no idea."

Davies consulted a pad of notes.

"When the painting was found, you said 'someone's stitching me up'. What did you mean by that remark?"

"Well, it's obvious, isn't it?" Will said. "I've been inside for forgery, although I always proclaimed my innocence and still do. If someone had nicked that picture and wanted to draw attention away from themselves, what better way than to hide it in my studio?"

"Who do you think would try to do that?"

"I have no idea."

"Do you have any past or present associates that might be involved?"

It was a question that made Will think that Lucy must be involved, and he felt bitter and sad at the same time. The policeman was watching him closely and felt instinctively that he had scored a point.

"Any other criminal that you may have been associated with or heard about recently?" Davies pressed.

"You mean Alfred Smith?" Will said. "Lucy Wrackham contacted me a few days ago and asked me to look for my old friend, Alfred Smith."

"How did you know Mr Smith?" Davies asked, although he knew the answer.

"In Ford Prison," Will said. "Although there was a difference between Alfred and me."

"What's that?"

"Alfred pleaded guilty," Will said. "He was a forger and he was proud of it. I on the other hand am not a forger and I never have been, although I was pretty naïve at the time. There's a difference."

"A difference not recognized by the court that found you guilty," Davies said. "I think you're at it again. I think you or your friends took this painting and you were going to make a copy of it, but you got found out before you could do so."

"You can think whatever you like," Will said. "It's conjecture. The fact is I'm innocent and I haven't done any such thing. I don't know how the painting came to be in my studio."

"When did you last see Alfred Smith?"

"I told you: ages ago in Ford Prison."

"Have you helped Lucy Wrackham to try to find him, as she requested?"

"Yes I have; she'll tell you so. Or at least I *hope* she will. We spent the weekend looking for Alfred but we couldn't find him. We went down to his house to seek him out but it's burned down, which is very convenient. Perhaps you should be investigating *that*."

Davies thought privately that he definitely should be investigating that, and decided that he must talk again with Lucy Wrackham at the earliest opportunity.

"So let's get this straight," Will said, counting points off on his fingers. "One: I'm asked to help look for forged paintings and I do my best to help. Two: someone calls you up and says there's a Hammershoi in my studio. They don't leave their name, which any normal law-abiding citizen would do. It was in the papers that I was in prison for forgery, so anyone could know. Three: you manage to get a search warrant anyway and turn up at my studio. Lo and behold, there's the picture, but you don't consider the possibility that I'm being framed. I expect if they'd left it at London Zoo then you would have arrested the zookeeper."

"Except that the zookeeper isn't a convicted forger," Davies said, feeling rattled.

There was a knock on the door and a police constable came in.

Davies looked at his watch, recorded the fact that the interview was being halted and stated the time, and then pressed the stop button on both tape recorders.

"Sir, could I have a word with you outside?" the constable said apologetically. He backed out of the room and Davies followed him, closing the soundproofed door behind him firmly.

"What is it?" he said rather testily. "I'm right in the middle of an interview."

"I realise that, sir, but a Mrs Wrackham is at the front desk and she's demanding to see you. She's making rather a fuss."

"Oh, bollocks," Davies said. "I'll have to go and see her. Ask the sergeant in there to have Bentley taken down to the cells if I'm more than fifteen minutes, would you?"

He went along the corridor towards the front desk with a feeling of foreboding. He had been so busy with legalities since the tip-off that he hadn't had a chance to talk to Lucy; and yet here she was. She was sitting on a hard chair waiting for him. And she was fuming, he could see that.

She stood up quickly when she saw him.

"What the hell is going on, Hugh?"

He caught sight of the duty sergeant on the desk looking down studiously and concealing a slight twitch of the lips while the London copper got dressed down by the posh blonde.

"Er, yes. Let's find somewhere quiet to have a chat," Davies said. He ushered her into an empty office and closed the door. "Things have been happening rather fast, you see. I'm sorry I didn't call you."

"Yes, for example while you were driving here, on your mobile which has got my number stored on it," Lucy said sarcastically.

"How did you hear what was going on?" he said rather sheepishly. He *should* have called her.

"I still don't actually know what's going on," she said. "Apparently the owner of our missing Hammershoi was informed by the police at lunch time that it had been recovered. He called Hoffman and Courtland, because we cover it. My boss told me because he knows what I'm currently investigating. So I made a routine call to Cambridge nick to find out what was going on, and they said a Mr Bentley had been arrested and I'd have to speak to the arresting officer, Hugh Davies."

"So you drove up here."

"Well the last time I saw you, *if* you remember, you were off to Wales on holiday and I was off to Cambridge to find Will Bentley. I spent two days with him looking for Alfred Smith and now I discover that you've arrested him."

"He had the painting in his possession," Davies said, and saw her waver. "The Hammershoi was hidden in his studio behind a stack of other paintings."

She frowned, and said nothing for several seconds.

"Let me speak to him," she said.

"No bloody way. I had to arrest him to get him to come in. I need to find out how a valuable painting that only just got nicked has suddenly turned up in his studio. Surely you must admit it's reasonable cause for suspicion."

She hesitated.

"Yes it is," she said, quietly now. "But I got to know him over the weekend. I don't think he did it. I'm not even sure he did it last time."

Lucy!" Davies said with exasperation. "It's not up to you or me to decide whether he's a forger or not. The court found him guilty last time and they banged him up for it. So what we have here is a previously convicted master forger who has a very valuable original painting in his possession."

There was a long silence.

"Let me speak to him," she said again.

"No. Not until I've spent all the time I need with him," Davies said. "I've only got 24 hours and then I've got to charge him or let him go. I might get an extension but not for long; you know how it works. No murder has been committed and he's denying everything. Says he has no idea how it got there."

"Probably because he hasn't," Lucy said bitterly. "So I've driven all this way and now you're not even going to let me talk to him?"

"I'm sorry, but I'm not."

"Wonderful. That's really great. All right then, well perhaps you would be kind enough to call me when you've made some progress?"

"Of course I will, but I can't let you talk to him now. It would be completely against procedure and I don't want to endanger any future decision of the court."

"Very well," she said icily, standing up. "Call me then. It's good to see that the spirit of cooperation is still alive – or at least has a pulse. Do let me know when you've finished with the prisoner, and I'll tell you in return the details of how he spent two days of his time helping me look for Alfred Smith."

She opened the door of the office and stalked out, her head held high. He watched her go down the steps without a second glance, and turned back gloomily to the job in question.

Davies interviewed Sandy Lennox and Ian Simpson and allowed them to go once he had taken their statements. They didn't have anything to add. The girl had nothing at all to say except that she was sure Will was innocent, and that didn't hold any water with Davies. The young man, Ian, seemed straightforward enough, and had one interesting fact to add, though it didn't help make the case *against* Bentley – quite the reverse. He said that only two days previously he had reorganised the stack of paintings where the Hammershoi had been found, and he would certainly have seen the painting if it had been there. He said he routinely dusted the canvasses as otherwise they accumulated cobwebs from the many spiders living in the nooks and crannies of the studio. He said that he would have noticed the Hammershoi's ornate gilt frame immediately, because all of Will's frames in that stack were matt black. Davies routinely checked both Ian Simpson and Sandy Lennox to see if either of them had a police record, but they were as clean as a whistle.

Parkside police station was having a quiet Wednesday, with only 12 people in custody. Will was one of them, in cell number 8. He was so quiet and depressed that they were concerned that he might be suicidal, so they took his clothes away for fear that he might harm himself with a belt buckle or a shoe, and dressed him in a boiler suit made out of paper. He didn't even protest about that – all the sting had gone out of him. He felt crushed by the system. Davies had reminded him that the parole board would take a dim view of recent events, so he could end up with a further year of his previous sentence to complete and a significant new sentence for the theft of the old master. Davies had further suggested that he could mitigate against these sentences if he gave the names of his accomplices, and described how the Hammershoi had come into his hands. But since Will had no idea how the painting had got there, he had nothing to confess and could see no way out. He lay awake for hours listening to the groans and coughs of men in adjacent cells, the incoherent mutterings of an addict, the discordant singing of a drunk and the occasional clang of metal doors as day prisoners were released or new prisoners were incarcerated. He eventually fell asleep at three in the morning when his body could take no more, and dreamed of endless days in prison cells, officious warders, the exercise yard, battles with violent inmates, and the whole dreary business of prison life.

TWENTY-EIGHT

Everyone suddenly burst out singing;
And I was filled with such delight
As prisoned birds must find in freedom
SIEGFRIED SASSOON, Everybody Sang

DCI Carter bore down on Davies while he was sitting in the Parkside canteen at 7.30 AM on Thursday morning, drinking a mug of tea and finishing a plate of bacon and eggs. He sat down in the chair opposite Davies. Carter was balding and had a slightly pointed cranium which was emphasized by his lack of hair. Davies didn't like him much from what he had seen so far – Carter had an unpleasant, rather supercilious air – but he was undoubtedly clever and knew his business.

"Morning, Carter."

"Good morning, Davies. I've got what you might call an interesting development with your case, in point of fact," Carter said. "Or a problem, depending on how you look at it."

"What's that then?" Davies said, his mouth full of bacon. "I could do with a bit of luck, to tell you the truth. I'm not sure if I've got him yet. On the plus side it definitely *is* the original painting; no doubt about that. I had it looked into as a priority, what with the media taking an interest. But Forensics has found no prints on it, though there were a couple of cloth fibres caught in the frame. No match for any cloth we could find in Bentley's studio, though."

"Anything from the interviews?" Carter asked. His people had assisted Davies with the arrest.

"His associates swear blind he would never do such a thing," Davies said, finishing the last mouthful of bacon. "One of them says the painting definitely wasn't there a couple of days ago. I've got two other friends of Bentley's who are upright citizens, and they're swearing his innocence too. Bentley denies all knowledge: he reckons someone knew he was banged up for forgery because it was in the papers, so they framed him. Really likely, that is: that they'd nick a famous picture and then give it back just to get Bentley. The trouble is, he could get off on reasonable doubt, I'm thinking."

"Bring your tea," Carter said. "I'd like to show you some new information."

Davies looked surprised, but he put his tray in the rack, grabbed his mug of tea and followed Carter. Carter took him along to his office and gestured to a seat. Then he took a video tape out of a heavy-duty green envelope and put it in a player.

"What's this?" Davies said with interest. Something on CCTV?"

"Not CCTV, but it so happens that the place next to Bentley's is a house of ill repute, and the Chief asked me to sort it out, so we've been filming. Take a look at this."

He pressed Play and the TV monitor came to life, showing the street where Will's studio was located, in full colour and reasonable picture quality due to the street lighting. The date shown was Tuesday the 20th and the time was 23:50:36. The seconds of the digital clock displayed on the screen constantly blinked upwards.

"We had a surveillance van out on the street for the last several days," Carter said, "disguised as a Water Board vehicle." He tapped the screen. "That's the doorway of the, er, house. But in the right hand side of the frame, you can see this other doorway."

"Bentley's studio," Davies said with great interest. He looked at Carter. "What have you got?"

Carter looked a little uncomfortable.

"Normally we would have noticed this immediately," he said. "The movement detector had two more registers that weren't on the log, and the two young DCs on the watch didn't notice."

"Probably having a natter, or a kip at that time of night. Was there a time stamp on it?"

"The movement detector isn't time stamped but we keep a separate paper log which has to match if it concerns the target scene. They had to wind forward through the tape to find the incidents so they could see if they needed to be logged. They didn't want to mention it to me, of course, because they knew I'd be unhappy with them for not doing the job properly in the first place."

"Okay then. So when was it? What did they find?"

"It's at 1.04 in the morning. I'll wind forward."

Carter fast-forwarded the tape to 1.00 AM and then let it run. At 1:04:25 AM on Wednesday 21st July, a tall hooded man built like a boxer and dressed in black appeared out of the right of the frame and stopped at Bentley's front door. He looked up and down the street but there was no-one to be seen – all the punters for the establishment next door had departed. He held a large flat bulky object wrapped in cloth. Carter hit the freeze frame.

"Could that be the painting in question, in point of fact?"

Davies stared at the screen and nodded, fascinated.

"It's about the right size. There's something bloody funny going on, I'm thinking. Let the tape run on."

Carter pressed Play and they watched while the dark-clad man unfolded a standard burglary tool that was recognised instantly by both policemen. They caught each other's eyes for a moment and then looked back. The man on the tape looked up and down the street again, opened Bentley's door using the tool and slipped inside, closing the door slowly behind him. The street was once again empty. It had taken him only half a minute to gain entry.

"Any idea who he is?" Davies asked.

"It's hard to tell with that hood," Carter said. "He doesn't look like one of our regulars. Besides, they don't usually cover up like that – too gormless. Could he be connected with your side of the business?"

"It seems likely, but as you say it's hard to tell. When does he come out again?"

"At a quarter past."

Carter wound the tape forward to a quarter past and they watched the silent empty street for a minute or two. Suddenly Bentley's door opened and the interloper stood framed in it for a moment, checking left and right. No-one in the street. He closed the door behind him as quietly as he could and then took off quickly, disappearing immediately out of frame to the right in the direction from which he had come.

"Wind it back a minute," Davies said. Carter did so and they watched again. "That's a pity – we can't see the face properly. But I see he hasn't got the package he was carrying anymore." He reached forward and pressed the freeze frame, tapping the screen. "He's carrying the cloth it was wrapped in, though. He's furled it up, look. He got rid of the painting but he didn't want to leave the cloth there in case Bentley found it in the morning and wondered where it had appeared from. I bet that cloth would match our fibre threads."

He looked at Carter.

"Anything else to be seen?"

"I had them go through the whole tape," Carter said with a shake of his head. "Just to remind them they should have been doing their job properly. If they'd been watching what was happening we could have had this man. I'm a bit surprised they weren't vigilant, to tell you the truth. Matheson and Stokes are normally very efficient. Anyway, it looks like someone visited the premises in the middle of the night and left the painting among Bentley's belongings, then tipped you off so you'd go there and find him in possession."

"It doesn't make sense," Davies said, shaking his head. "They framed him using a valuable painting that they'd only just stolen. And they knew enough to make sure Art & Antiques heard about it immediately. There are some very interesting implications here, but I need to think about them later. Right now I need to let Bentley go; I can't hold him in the light of this new evidence. I hope he's had a decent breakfast. It would be good to avoid an official complaint, what with the media swarming over the case to find out how we got the Hammershoi back so fast. I'd better go and eat an awful lot of humble pie."

Carter nodded in sympathy, and Davies began to think maybe he wasn't so bad after all. He had stood by his people when they'd made a bit of a cock up, and he had come forward with the new evidence as soon as he could.

Carter said, "It's pure luck we've got the whole thing on tape, but I'll tell you what: once you've sorted out Bentley, I'll help you try to find the hooded man. Cambridge is full of CCTV, and if we pull the tapes for some of the cameras in the area we might be able to see where he went."

"I'll take you up on that," Davies nodded grimly. "Someone's taking the piss and I don't like it."

Carter nodded and grimaced.

"One other thing," he said as he was going out. "We've got four journalists waiting to know what's happening. You'd better draft a statement that we've released the man who was helping us with our inquiries. They'll soon get bored if it looks like the story's turning out to be a dead end."

Davies nodded absently, his mind already on the forthcoming meeting with Bentley.

So it was that at 9.10 in the morning, having been given back his clothes and the contents of his pockets, Will found himself walking out of the main doors of Parkside police station in a dazed state. He had never in his life had such a handsome apology from a police officer. He hadn't believed it; he'd thought that Davies was winding him up until the final moment when he was actually allowed to walk out of the door.

He looked back and Davies was standing at the door, watching him go. He had offered Will a lift back to his studio but Will had declined, wanting to be out of the police's clutches as soon as possible. Davies had explained why they were letting him go. They had obtained new photographic evidence proving that an intruder had broken into Will's studio the night before his arrest. The policeman's words still burned in Will's ears. Someone had broken in and hidden the Hammershoi in the studio *while he had been sleeping in the next room.* Despite the rising heat of yet another sweltering July day, Will's blood ran cold at the thought of it. He wasn't used to this sort of thing.

He crossed the road and glanced once across his shoulder at the squat ugly police building. No posse of policeman seemed to be pursuing him. A feeling of the most extraordinary elation was bubbling up in him, such as he had not known for years. Suddenly he set off at a run across Parker's Piece, occasionally jumping into the air and whooping, much to the surprise of morning passers-by who walked the formal criss-crossing paths and eyed him curiously. He ran across the green and only stopped on the other side when he got to Regent Street, where he stood laughing and panting. He took his phone out and dialled George and Anna's home number.

George answered, sounding unusually grave.

"George! It's me! They've let me out!"

"Good God, Will!" He raised his voice and shouted in the background. "Anna! Don't go yet. It's Will on the phone. They've let him out!"

He came back to the phone.

"Why have they let you go? Where are you?"

"They got some bloke on a camera, breaking into the studio the night before I was arrested. He had the painting and obviously hid it there; they could see it on the film. So they let me go and they're after him instead. You should have *heard* the policeman that's been on my neck – talk about grovel! Anyway, I'm in Regent Street so I'll be back at the studio in twenty minutes."

Anna must have snatched the phone from George because she suddenly came on the line.

"Will? What's happening, they've let you out? That's fantastic! What's going on?"

So he walked up St. Andrews Street past Emmanuel College and explained it all again, laughing and talking so loudly and rapidly that pedestrians caught his eye and smiled back, infected by his happiness. As he explained the little he knew, one thought began to form itself solidly in his mind. Someone had been prepared to let him go to jail again to stop him interfering, but they hadn't succeeded. The irony was that he had only decided yesterday morning that he would stop looking for Alfred.

Now it was different. He didn't appreciate being manipulated by these people, whoever they were. He needed to discover what was going on so he had to find Alfred. At least Will knew he would get a straight answer from his old friend if he could find him.

He arrived at the studio and was unlocking it when everybody arrived at once. George and Anna turned up in Anna's Volvo. Will had phoned Sandy and she came round the corner too fast for the heels she was wearing, making all male heads turn in the vicinity at the brevity of her top. An anonymous-looking man even took a photograph. Ian the framer arrived on his bicycle, summoned by Sandy, and stood shyly to one side until he was ushered into the group. Once they had finished greeting each other like long-lost friends, they piled into the house and went up the stairs.

TWENTY-NINE

Nothing made by brute force lasts.
ROBERT LOUIS STEVENSON

Mrs Morris learned of Will Bentley's release in the one o'clock news bulletin:
"*A stolen painting by Danish artist Wilhelm Hammershoi has been recovered within days by police in Cambridge, acting on a tip off.*
The oil painting, Interior with a Girl at the Clavier, was painted in 1901 and is thought to have been inspired by the work of Dutch painter Johannes Vermeer of Delft. Wilhelm Hammershoi has seen a significant increase in popularity in recent years and this painting – about the size of a large tea tray – is his best-known work. Its theft last week from a private collection in Europe was considered a tragedy by art aficionados all over the world.
The painting was recovered by police yesterday during a raid on the studio of Cambridge painter Mr William Bentley, who has since been helping police with their enquiries. However, in a dramatic news conference at midday today, Detective Chief Inspector Hugh Davies of the Metropolitan Police Art and Antiques Unit said that Mr Bentley has been completely exonerated of any involvement and was released this morning. Davies said that irrefutable photographic evidence has proved that the painting was placed in Mr Bentley's premises by persons unknown. He added that police officers are pursuing a number of lines of enquiry but are unable to provide more details at this time."

Mrs Morris turned off the radio and walked across the hallway to Rupert Angel's office. He was picking up the phone but put it down when he saw the look on Mrs Morris's face.

"Our little plan has failed," she said, obviously rattled. "I've just heard on the news that they've let Bentley go. They have pictures of Edward putting the painting in Bentley's studio."

Rupert Angel swore.

"Edward checked for cameras but couldn't see any," he said. "But they're easily missed. I think I need to talk with Lucy Wrackham to see if I can find out what's been going on. I wonder if they have clear shots of Edward."

"If they have we'll find out soon enough," his assistant said grimly. "However, I talked to Edward about it after the drop and he said he was hooded for the entire time, so we may still be in the clear."

"Let's hope so, Julia. We're sailing a little too close to the wind on this one. What can we do about Mr Bentley, since the police have let him go?"

"I'm going to send Edward up to Cambridge to meet with William Bentley," she said, looking Rupert in the eye. "We may yet have to dispose of him, but there's still the question of the girl, Rupert. She knows too much and is unearthing facts we want kept silent. It would be better if she was out of the picture."

Rupert Angel glared at her.

"I don't feel we're at that stage yet. Lucy is proving useful to us as an unwitting voice on the inside. I suggest we encourage Bentley to discontinue his search for Alfred, and things should then calm down a little."

"I think you'll regret this emotional attachment," she said simply, and then turned on her heel and walked out. Rupert Angel knitted his fingers together in unconscious habit, and looked broodingly after her departing figure.

THIRTY

It is not nor it cannot come to good:
But break, my heart; for I must hold my tongue.
WILLIAM SHAKESPEARE, Hamlet

The Bonnie's engine sang; glad to be out of its garage on a sweltering summer afternoon. The sky was pale blue with occasional gossamer clouds. There was no wind and everyone with a convertible had their roof down. When Will looked into the distance the road shimmered with heat-haze, so that approaching cars seemed to swim out of nothingness. He wore black leathers, jeans, a black helmet and classic Wayfarer Ray-Bans. The slipstream had cooled him on the motorway but now he was becoming sticky. The motorcycle had eaten up the miles between Cambridge and London and now he was cruising through the streets of Richmond, zeroing in on Lucy Wrackham's home address with the aid of the SatNav. It was approaching two o'clock on Thursday afternoon and it already seemed impossible to believe that he had been let out of jail only that morning.

He had decided on a whim to revisit Alfred's last-known address. He wanted to see if he could find a clue to the old man's whereabouts, and there seemed nowhere else to start. As he was driving down he remembered the last time he had gone to Alfred's house. He had been with Lucy, and he imagined her face. It had been a good day, and it was a pity she had rushed off and spoiled it. A pity too that he had stubbornly refused to return with her. Instead he had been soaked by a summer shower and then had spent hours on delayed trains – all very frustrating.

Following his instincts he had decided to stop off and see Lucy on the way down to Hastings. He wanted to tell her that their enquiries had disturbed a hornet's nest. He wanted her to know that he wasn't going to be put off; that he was resuming the search for his old friend. And he wanted to see that blonde hair again.

She had scribbled her home address and number on a piece of paper, in case he turned up anything new about Alfred, and he had tucked it into his wallet and forgotten about it until he was on the road. She probably wouldn't even be at home, he realised ruefully; she would be at work. But he didn't have her business card with him – he knew exactly where it was, pinned to the notice board in the studio kitchen, but it wasn't much use there. He knew he could probably find Hoffman and Courtland in a telephone directory, but he was almost at her home address instead so he decided he would simply turn up.

The motorcycle manoeuvred effortlessly in and out of the London traffic, and he enjoyed the simple thrill of it, touching the throttle a little more than was needed when he wanted to make the engine growl at pretty girls.

He turned into Lucy's street and idled on the corner for a moment, confirming the road name. This was the one. His heart was beating a little faster and he marvelled silently as he became aware of the effect that she seemed to be having on him. He rode slowly down the street, with the chequered end-of-journey flag looming up on the SatNav. There was a silver Mercedes estate pulling out ahead, and the figure of a girl standing by the car on the driver's side. With a sudden rush of blood he realised it was her! He rode on to greet her, anonymous in his leathers and helmet and glasses, ready to give her a surprise. But she didn't look up; she was standing by the silver car and laughing at something its driver had said. As Will drew near she leaned in and kissed the man in the car, obscuring his face with her long hair. Will felt suddenly chilled, his happiness smashed out of him. He turned his head away and opened the throttle a touch so that the Bonnie surged past the silver car and the blonde girl. When he got to the end of the street he pulled in to the side and waited; for once irresolute. He felt punched in the face by reality. After a few moments the Mercedes approached and swept past him. He saw the man inside the car for only a second but it was enough. It was Rupert Angel – Will remembered him clearly from the only time that he had encountered the man. Lucy must have rushed back from their day in Hastings to meet with Angel. She'd said she was having dinner with someone she'd met at a private view, and Will knew that Angel was just the sort of man who would frequent such things. He was exactly the kind of good-looking public-school intellectual that Lucy *would* go for. She wouldn't be interested in an ex-con – Will laughed bitterly at the very idea. If he had disliked Angel before in a formless fashion, now he hated him tangibly and with feeling. He felt as if Angel had taken Lucy away from him, which was a ridiculous notion but he didn't care.

He looked back up the street and saw Lucy standing and waving. He experienced a moment of exhilaration before realising that she was waving at Angel and not him. She had no idea who the solitary motorcyclist was – she was probably looking straight through him, as he obstructed the view of her departing boyfriend. The Bonneville could take him back there in seconds, but now he had no wish to see her; no wish to watch the laughter in her eyes fade and be replaced by embarrassment.

As he rode away he realised he had been naive to dream of any attachment with the beautiful but remote Lucy, and he vowed to forget her. When he got back he would paint to cleanse his mind. He wanted to paint right now; to allow himself to be sucked into the canvas and absorbed in the pigment,

twisting in tourbillions of carmine and cadmium and cobalt. Not emerging for a while.
But he had a job to do first. He would search for Alfred Smith by himself.

THIRTY-ONE

This is not a letter. It is only my arms round you for a quick minute.
KATHERINE MANSFIELD, Letter to her husband Murry

Will peeled off the M25 at junction 5 and went down the A21, leaning in to the twists and turns of the road and taking care not to go too fast because he was upset. Other bikers passed him and he let them. The machine was like a young thoroughbred under his hands, light and precise to the touch but filled with naked power. He passed a field with posts and wires but no hops. There were converted oast-houses and then the rolling hills of Kent, transforming into Sussex soon enough.

He rarely went to the seaside so it was good to be returning so soon, especially on the bike so that he felt in control of his own destiny. No struggling with trains this time. He put Lucy out of his mind and reached Hastings by a quarter to four, stopping at a garage outside to pick up a street plan which covered Hastings, Bexhill, Battle and Rye. The SatNav would take him to the right spot, but he wanted to get a wider appraisal of the whole area. He had only been to Alfred's house three days previously, but it felt like an age because of everything that had happened in between. On the last visit he had been surreptitiously watching Lucy while she drove, and his mind replayed little snatches of their conversation as he turned into different streets. He found Alfred's house easily enough and motored up the drive at walking pace. In the intervening three days the demolition company had made rapid progress and Alfred's old house was no longer there; there was just a gap in the trees and a pile of rubble which was being loaded into a dumper truck by a man on a bulldozer. The foreman that they had met was not in sight, but Will felt there was nothing to be seen there anyway. He cruised out of the drive again and parked the bike on the empty residential street. He took his helmet off and shrugged out of the leather jacket, relieved to feel the air on his skin. He extracted a handkerchief and mopped his brow, which had accumulated a line of sweat where the helmet met his hair. He ran his fingers through his hair to loosen it, tossed his head and then flexed his body.

In the pannier of the bike he had a sketch of Alfred that he had drawn in prison. It was the only original image he had of his friend but it would have to suffice, so he went up the drive to the neighbour's house and rang the bell. A lady in her mid-fifties answered. She had short grey hair and a wart on her chin which he tried valiantly to ignore. He showed her the sketch and asked her if she had seen Mr Smith who used to live next door. She remembered him and she admired the sketch of him, which she said was a perfect likeness. But she hadn't seen Mr Smith for a long time and didn't know what had happened to him. His house had been repossessed and it was all very peculiar. She was clearly curious to know who Will was, but he managed to escape without telling her that he had got to know her neighbour in prison. He left her his card in case she thought of anything.

The house on the other side had no car outside and no-one answered the bell, so that was a dead end. The grass was unkempt so he surmised that they were on holiday. He tried the house opposite and this time got a young man of about fifteen who had no idea who the old man in the picture was and seemed very suspicious. Will asked where the nearest shops and post office were and the boy directed him sullenly.

Will slipped back into the leathers and started the Bonnie. The boy had come out of the house to watch, as if Will might be about to make off with a valuable garden gnome. He looked considerably more interested when he saw the black and chrome T100. Will started it with a roar and took off, accelerating very rapidly until he was out of sight, at which point he slowed down and grinned in acknowledgement of his childishness. Still a kid himself, really.

He found the post office in a local One Stop store, parked the bike and put the helmet and leathers away. Post offices didn't take kindly to men in helmets.

He brought out his sketch again and showed it around, getting the usual blank response. The lady at the till wasn't interested in the sketch but was quite interested in Will. She asked him if he'd come far, having seen the bike outside. They chatted for a minute or two but it was leading him no nearer to Alfred. He went to the Post Office counter but it was already closed. Will walked out of the shop cum post office and stood with his hands on his hips, looking up and down the small row of local shops. There was a Dachshund tied up outside the shop and Will patted its head. The dog was panting furiously in the hot sunshine but he licked Will's hand and wagged his tail with appreciation when Will made a fuss of him. Will noticed the headline boards outside the newsagents and thought he'd try there.

"I certainly do remember old Alfred," the lady behind the counter said, looking at the sketch. "He was a nice old chap. He lived in a house up the road but he used to pop in here for a paper every now and then. We used to have a bit of a talk. I haven't seen him for ages, though. I thought he must have moved away."

"At least you remember him," Will said. "I was beginning to think I must have dreamed him up. I don't suppose you have any idea where he might have gone?"

"None at all, love. He had a subscription to some magazine, I remember, but I don't have any details left now as it would have been in last year's books." She shrugged and smiled. "I'm sorry I can't help. Is he a friend of yours, then? You're an artist too, by the looks of it." She indicated the sketch.

"Yes, I'm a painter, and Alfred used to be a very good friend," Will said, "but we've lost touch. I thought I'd look him up but he's a hard man to find."

He gave her a card and turned to go.

"There's a hairdresser next door, love," the woman said. "You never know, he might have gone there."

Will didn't hold out much hope for this, remembering Alfred's straggly grey hair and bald patch, but he nodded politely and went out.

He went through the same ritual again in the hairdresser's shop. The girl sweeping up called a young woman in from the back. She was startlingly pretty and his bitter memory of Lucy with Angel faded just a little. He flashed the girl a smile, showed her the sketch and asked if she remembered Alfred.

She smiled back and then wrinkled her nose as she stared at the picture.

"You know, I *do* remember him," she said. "Or I remember that shocking head of hair, anyway. Is this your drawing or his? He was an artist, so he used to tell me."

"He *is* an artist, but the sketch is mine," Will acknowledged.

She nodded.

"I thought you looked arty. He painted a lot of people, you know. He had women posing in the nude, so he said. He wanted me to pose for him, the cheeky old bugger."

"I can see why he would."

She smiled, accepting the compliment.

"You're all the same, you artists," she said. "It's a good picture, though: you've definitely caught him. He used to tell me to cut his hair any old how, but as soon as I started he'd only let me trim it and wouldn't allow me to give him a decent cut. I used to be ashamed to have him walk out of the shop, to tell you the truth. He always looked half done but he wouldn't let me do it properly."

"I don't suppose you know where he might have gone?" Will asked. "I'm trying to get in touch with him again and I don't have a forwarding address."

"No idea," she said. "But I'll tell you something. He had a sister, name of Gillian. She lives in Hastings too, or used to. But she doesn't get her hair cut here."

Will's eyes gleamed.

"A sister – now I remember! He did mention her once. Gillian Smith, is it?"

"No, she was married, she was Gillian *Heath*. He didn't get on with her much; he was always moaning about her trying to boss him about. He used to call her the Blasted Heath, which is how I remember her surname. That's Shakespeare, that is. We did it in school."

"You're a genius!" Will said. "I don't suppose you happen to know where the Blasted Heath lives, do you?"

She shook her head.

"Have you got a phone book I can borrow for a minute?"

She went out to the back and returned with it. He sat down in one of the waiting chairs and went through the Heaths while the girls swept up around him and washed the brushes and combs. There were only five Heaths in Hastings and a few more in St. Leonards and Bexhill. The third had the initial G. He wrote down the addresses of all of them, in case the entry was listed under her husband's name. Then he handed back the book and thanked the girl.

"Come back any time and I'll trim those locks," she called after him with a hint of flirtation, and it was with a touch of reluctance that he continued his quest.

It took him ten minutes on the Bonnie to get across to Upper Park Road and locate the house of "G Heath". It was a tall three-storey detached building set back among rhododendron bushes, with a red brick wall at the front. He parked the bike just inside the drive. There was the sound of disjointed piano music coming from the open casement window to the left of the door. He rang the bell and the piano faltered but then continued.

"Keep going," said an unseen strident voice. There was the sound of footsteps.

A lady opened the door and said, "You're a little early – oh!"

Her hair was tightly drawn into a grey bun, and he could see Alfred in her features. She was taller than her brother, prim, and dressed in a loose white blouse and a blue skirt which ended below the knee. She wore reading glasses perched on her nose. She looked at him frostily over the tops of her glasses, as if imagining that he was selling dish cloths.

"I'm sorry, I thought you were my next pupil," she said. "Can I help you?"

He introduced himself and said, "I'm looking for an old friend of mine; Alfred Smith. Are you his sister?"

She looked a little sour-faced but then gathered herself together.

"A friend of Alfred's? Well, I haven't heard from him for a long time. He hasn't taken the trouble to tell *me* where he is, even though I'm his only living relative."

Will privately felt he could see why that might be.

"I'm sorry to hear that, but I haven't seen him either," he said. "I'd like to come in and have a chat about your brother if possible. I promise it won't take long."

"As you can see, I have pupils at the moment."

"I'm happy to wait," he said. "I'll be as quiet as a mouse."

He flashed her a big smile and she melted a little in its radiance.

"Very well, but you'll have to wait until seven. I've got my current pupil to finish and the next one follows straight on."

She stood back to let him in and he stepped into the hall. There was a 1920s hall stand that probably once belonged to her mother. It had a large plain mirror; coat hooks full of old coats; and umbrellas that hadn't seen much use, their points resting on tiles in the base of the stand. The hall floor was parquet and finished with burgundy Axminster rugs, somewhat threadbare as if they had seen better days. A staircase with burgundy carpet ascended from the hall. There was a smell of potatoes cooking for the evening meal and he could hear the distant rattling of a saucepan lid. Gillian Heath led him into a sitting room and returned immediately to her pupil. The piano hesitated again and then resumed with more confidence after a few moments. He examined his surroundings.

The room was peaceful and quiet, with just the ticking of an old wooden mantle clock to offset the sound of the piano from the other room. The floral-patterned chairs and sofa had antimacassars. There was a crucifix on the wall and a bookcase full of hymn books, gardening books, bibles and a large stock of organ music. There was a glass cabinet containing many little ornaments.

Against the side wall was a credenza with barley-twisted legs, two cupboards and a pair of drawers at the top. Will's own mother had owned a similar one, though without the attractive barley twists. The plain top of the credenza was cluttered with more ornaments. They were of the type which George would immediately have denounced as rubbish. There was a group of miniature teddy bears, some of them saluting, some with little red or blue coats, some hatted. There was a collection of dogs, including an Alsatian made out of coal and a pair of black and white collies with a food dish between them. There was a collection of paperweights, including one which had a crocus sealed inside and another with a snowstorm. He picked up the snowstorm paperweight and shook it, sending snowflakes whirling around the little figures inside.

The doorbell chimed and the pupils changed over. The new pupil was more assured and began playing Vivaldi's Four Seasons; the processional from the Autumn movement. Every now and then the student would pause and then start again, this time with a little more emphasis on the louder or quieter passages, or with a note sustained differently. A part of Will's mind was in there with them, listening to the music and hearing it slowly improve under the tuition of Gillian Heath.

He strolled around and looked at the walls. Usually at times like this he was happy to look at the pictures, but Gillian Heath had only one picture. It was a print of a horse and cart taking a stack of hay back to the farm, with children playing in the rutted road behind it and tired farm workers seated on the hay. Beside it was a windmill plate in blue and white, with a pony and a cottage in front of the windmill. There was a framed four-line poem entitled "Virtue", and he read a couple of the lines:

"Virtue is our safeguard and our guiding star,
That stirs up reason when our senses err."

Will pulled a face. He recalled that Alfred had been the most irreligious man he had ever known, so he was beginning to understand why his old friend hadn't got on too well with his pious sister.

Once Will had completed a detailed inspection of the room he had nothing to do, so he stood in front of the open window and looked out. He couldn't see far because of the rhododendrons, but if he looked past his motorbike through the open gateway he could see the road, and beyond it glimpses of the park through the trees.

At last the piano music stopped and the front door opened and closed. A young woman stepped swiftly away down the drive. She was perhaps sixteen, her brown hair tied in a bunch, wearing a white blouse and a tartan skirt. When she came to the motorbike she stopped for a moment and looked at it, then spun on her heel and looked back at the house, seeing his outline framed for a moment in the opened casement window before she turned away. Gillian Heath came in to see him after a few moments, and apologised graciously enough for keeping him waiting. She offered him tea. While she went to make it he sat down in the chair beside the bookcase and studied the titles of the books. The lighting was dim but somehow in keeping with the room. When she came back a Sheltie dog bounded in behind her, barking and wagging its tail in equal measure.

"I'm on my own these days," Gillian Heath said when she had settled down on the sofa. "Brian passed away a year ago, so he's in the Lord's hands now. But I keep busy – I'm the organist at the local church and I spend one day a week doing the church accounts. And then of course there are my students. Brian left me very comfortable, but I like to feel I'm still doing my bit. How do you know Alfred? I should warn you that we never really got on while Brian was alive."

"Alfred and I are artists," Will said. "I got to know him through the art connection. I have a studio in Cambridge."

"Oh I see," she said. "And do you live by your art?"

"Yes, I sell most of my work," he said.

"Yes, Alfred does too," she said. "He went off on a long trip abroad a year or so ago. Morocco or some such. He collects ideas and sketches and then comes back and paints them. He showed me one of his Morocco pictures when he came back, and I liked it. I have one of his pictures in the hall."

He didn't tell her he went to prison, Will realised suddenly.

"Why don't you get on with him?" he said.

She looked a little prim.

"Alfred has always been rather intolerant of my faith. Not to mention that over the years he has mixed with some questionable characters, Mr Bentley. And I must admit that Brian and Alfred never got on."

She paused and looked into the middle distance over her steaming cup of tea. "Brian used to feel that Alfred was racy," she said, voicing her thoughts. "My Brian was a very steady man – he hated anything out of the ordinary, and Alfred was so wayward, especially when he was younger. Then there were the women, of course."

Will raised his eyebrows, trying to come to terms with a sudden image of Alfred surrounded by concubines.

"The *women*?"

"Well, *models*, he called them." She harrumphed. "You could walk in on him and find some young lady completely *naked*, Mr Bentley. I know it's all supposed to be art, but I was shocked and I know Brian was disgusted."

Will suppressed a burning desire to tell Gillian Heath to lighten up.

"I am rather hoping to get into contact with your brother again," he said. "He's a great painter and I want to have a chat with him and exchange views."

"I do understand, but I don't know where he is. He's gone off on one of his painting trips, I'm afraid. I haven't heard from him for months, and he has left me no forwarding information. It's very frustrating, because a terrible thing has happened in the meantime – his house was destroyed by fire, and the authorities came to me because they couldn't contact Alfred. At first they were worried that he might have burned to death, but the house was empty, thank the good Lord."

"I went to his house when I started looking for him," Will said. "They were demolishing it."

"I know," she said. "It's perfectly horrible. Alfred and I may not always have seen eye to eye but I can't bear the thought of my poor brother coming home after his trip and finding all his belongings gone. The mortgage wasn't paid up, apparently – he had borrowed against it and had some debts, and so the house was repossessed. It's a great worry to me."

"When did you last see him?" Will asked.

"Perhaps a year ago. He dropped one of his Moroccan pictures around to me one day," she said, reflecting. "I was very touched. Once Brian was gone we saw a little more of each other, and I liked him better. If you've finished your tea I'll show you the picture if you like."

He put down his cup and followed her. The Sheltie followed them both and he patted the dog.

The Moroccan picture was the one he remembered. Alfred had painted it in his cell from a picture out of the National Geographic. Will presumed that he hadn't wanted to tell his sister about his incarceration, especially as they were just becoming closer after the departure of Brian. He felt heartily relieved that he had not put his foot in it earlier. He admired the picture, which showed a crowded bazaar with men in fezzes repairing an upended bicycle.

"It's not the sort of thing I would normally pick out myself," she said, "but I have never followed the art world. Brian used to say they were all mad. I have contented myself with music and the church."

"It's a *very* skilled painting," Will said.

"Yes," she said, and he noticed a sudden flash of pride that he liked. "I can't tell you how many visitors have admired it. The mother of one of my pupils runs an art gallery, and she told me it's extremely good and might be worth – well, I shouldn't say, but ever such a lot of money. Of course I shall never sell it. It's my present from Alfred."

She looked at him in sudden worry.

"I do hope you find him, Mr Bentley. I am very worried that he has not contacted me for such a long time. And then there is the matter of the loss of his paintings in the fire. It's awful."

She looked suddenly very frail and old and as if she was going to cry. Will suddenly felt sorry for her.

"I'm sure he'll turn up as fine as can be, wondering what all the fuss is about," he said. "The main thing is that he wasn't caught in the fire. Pictures can be painted again, remember."

"I suppose so," she said, and then suddenly stood up. "I just remembered something! I had a *letter* from him a few months ago. Let me see if I can put my hand on it. I'm getting rather forgetful these days."

She bustled about upstairs for a few minutes while he waited. The distant lid no longer rattled so she must have turned off the potatoes. He looked at the Moroccan picture and had a sudden memory of Alfred sitting there in front of his easel, painting it.

She came down the stairs again, holding out an envelope.

"Here it is," she said. "You can read it if you like. It's private, but I *would* be pleased if you could find where he's gone. He's always driven me mad, but with Brian gone, I find myself wanting to preserve the remains of the family."

"You don't have any children?" Will asked.

"A daughter, but she's married and living in Australia," she said. "Brian didn't–".

She broke off. He sensed the pain in her voice and didn't enquire further. It was beginning to sound as if Brian had passed on none too soon.

He sat down on the stairs and took a single sheet of writing paper out of the envelope. It had a date about six months previously, but no address.

Dear Gilly,

Over the past years I regretted us growing apart. I know you cherish Brian's memory but I think he had something to do with our estrangement, because since the funeral you and I had more contact than in the last ten years. You know I'm not a religious man, but I did enjoy the recital you invited me to. It's a nice old church and they were very welcoming.

You haven't seen me for a while but I haven't forgotten you. I have had to go away on one of my painting trips and I'm not sure how long I'll be. I am in our own British Isles for a change, and at the seaside as well, though very different from Hastings. I know you liked the Moroccan picture so I am doing you one of the sea. I'll be back in a few months and hopefully I will have sorted myself out a bit so that I can pay off the last of the house. As I said to you, I am beginning to think about retirement. You may have to teach me some of your admirable gardening skills. I was impressed with your roses, though you lost me a bit with all that talk about acid soil.

Best wishes to you,

Love Alf xx

Will turned the sheet over but there was no other ink. He was putting the letter back in the envelope when he noticed the postmark. It was partly obliterated but some letters were still visible. It started with a "B". He carried the envelope over to the window and angled it so that it caught the sun. He took the letter out of the envelope again, and held the envelope up. "B"… "U"… "R".

"Somewhere starting with BUR, beside the sea," he said. "It's a start. Do you have any idea where he might have holed up?"

"I've been racking my brains," she said, shrugging with her hands and shaking her head. "I can't think of anywhere, but then of course, I didn't really *know* Alfred."

"I've never heard him call himself Alf before."

"It was a childhood name," she said with a nostalgic look. "He was Alf and I was Gilly."

There was nothing else to be learned. She wanted to keep the letter so he did the next best thing and captured a picture of the envelope and the letter with his phone. Then he thanked her kindly and left, with a parting promise that he would contact her if he managed to find her brother.

THIRTY-TWO

I will never be by violence constrained to do anything.
ELIZABETH I

It took him a while to get back to Cambridge, and by the time he got home it was dark and he was bone weary. He cruised up the side path to the garage, killed the lights and halted the thud-thud of the engine. The silence rang in his ears and the darkness enclosed him. He took off the helmet and shook his hair loose. Then he climbed off stiffly and pushed the bike into the garage, where he chained it up and secured the helmet and leathers. It took him a few minutes to get everything locked away, working quietly and whistling through his teeth. When he emerged from the garage it was a second before he realised that there were men around him in the near darkness. With a sudden feeling of stupidity he realized that he should have been on his guard. He was seized roughly by many hands and took a sharp blow in the face which stunned him and made him dizzy, knocking him to his knees. He could feel blood running down his chin and dripping onto his shirt. He was forced down until he was kneeling forward awkwardly.

A man's voice grated in his ear with a London accent.

"Is your name Will Bentley?"

He thought about denying it and waited a little too long before replying. Something hard and unyielding hit him in the small of his back and pain exploded there. He gasped and swore.

"I'm Bentley. What do you want?"

A sharp blow on the side of his head rattled his teeth. He blinked, trying to focus.

"Are you right handed or left handed?"

Will felt confusion through the pain.

"I'm right handed," he said, "but what –?"

His right hand was grabbed roughly and pinned down on a block of wood. There was the glint of something and with a sudden gut wrench he realised the man was holding a chopper; an axe for chopping wood. A rush of adrenalin thrummed the blood in his ears and he tried to struggle, but they held him still. The man who had spoken was wearing a hood and there were two other men around him, holding Will in an immovable grip. The man raised the axe as if he was going to use it, then lowered the blade slowly to

Will's wrist and held it there on the skin. The steel was cold. The man drew it along and it opened the skin.

"You are going to stop looking for Alfred Smith," the voice in his ear said. "Because if you don't, I'm going to come back here one dark night and chop your painting hand off. Do you clearly understand what I'm saying?"

The man's breath was hot on his ear. Will nodded violently.

"Yes."

"Say it then."

"You're going to cut my hand off if I don't stop looking for Alfred."

"That's right. And I don't want to see the old bill around here, you hear?"

Will nodded.

"Okay then."

The man stood up and moved the blade away from Will's wrist. Then something hit Will on the back of his head. He pitched forward and everything ceased.

He awoke slowly to the sound of his own bubbling breath. He was slumped on his front, his face against the grass patch that ran down the middle of the path. Blood was congealing at the side of his mouth. He got his elbows underneath him and heaved himself upwards. His head was thumping. He wiped his mouth and felt the back of his skull gingerly, finding an egg-shaped bump. He looked around but there was no-one there. He stumbled down the path towards the street and then threw up on the grass. When he emerged from the path the streetlamps were dazzlingly bright and he screwed up his eyes. He fumbled in his pocket for his key and got the studio door open. Closed it and locked it and put the catch on. Went up the stairs and through the kitchen, pressing the kettle switch on his way. Into the bathroom and clicked on the pull-string light. Turned on the water in the sink, putting in the plug. Filled it with water from both taps; the water warming slowly. He turned off the taps and washed his face, leaning on one elbow across the back of the sink. He washed his hands and bathed the thin sharp cut on his wrist, drying it and sticking a plaster on it. He looked at himself in the mirror and found a wild man in the glass. Mothers would lock up their daughters. His nose was bruised and swollen but didn't seem to be broken. He had a dark bruise on the side of his face and his hair was awry. His pale shirt was covered with crimson. He grinned to himself slowly in the mirror and winked at his reflection.

"Close," he said aloud. "A little too close."

He felt better when he was sitting at the table where he always sat, wearing a clean shirt and with a cup of strong coffee and some toast before him. He had put a large splash of scotch in the coffee.

One thing was certain: these people could threaten him all they liked but they weren't going to stop him looking for his old friend now. Alfred had obviously managed to get himself mixed up with some very nasty people, and Will didn't feel he could simply abandon him. He thought about what his attackers had said they would do, and wondered if he were being stupid, but then shook his head. He wasn't going to stop. However, he did think soberly about the possible consequences, and he shivered. He needed to get some protection, but where did you go for that? He yawned and put the thought to one side for the moment, deciding to think some more about the problem in the morning.

It was a quarter past midnight and he wondered if he should call someone. What about talking to the police? He had been warned not to, though he didn't care about that; but he didn't *trust* the police. They might turn up at the studio despite him asking them not to, especially after the recent raid when they had acted like they owned the place. What about calling George and Anna? No, they would insist on coming out to see him when he just wanted to sleep. He felt very tired. Should he go to the hospital? No, they would make a fuss but then keep him in casualty for hours when they discovered that all he had was a bump on the head and a bloody nose.

Suddenly he realised exactly who he should call. He should speak to Lucy Wrackham and tell *her* what had just happened. He should also let her know what he had discovered about Alfred after his day of investigation. Even if she was going out with Rupert Angel, she still needed to know what had just happened to him, in case it happened to her too. She was the one leading the hunt for Alfred Smith, after all.

He didn't pick up the phone immediately, but munched toast and mulled over the idea of calling her. He sipped the coffee and felt it warming his stomach and calming him. The question was: could he trust Lucy? Suppose these people were connected with her? That was ridiculous, though. The fact was that he *did* trust her. It might have upset him when he had seen her with Rupert Angel, but she had not deceived him. She had never mentioned Angel by name, but there was no reason why she should; she had simply said that she was having dinner with a man.

Will felt for his wallet with her number in it but the wallet was gone. With rising alarm he felt through all his pockets but it wasn't there. He went out on the landing and downstairs, his eyes on the treads. He unlocked the front door a crack and opened it, but the street was empty. He stepped outside and there it was, right on the ground beside the door. He must have dropped it as he took out his key, when his head was still whirling. He picked it up and went back inside, looking up and down the street before locking the door. Then he sat down at the table again and finished his coffee. It was twenty to one: too late to call? Normally yes, but she might be in danger. He picked up the phone and dialled the number handwritten by Lucy. There was a ringing tone and he willed her to pick up, but the answer-phone kicked in and he heard Lucy's calm and well-modulated voice telling callers to leave a message after the tone.

"Lucy, it's Will Bentley," he said into the mouthpiece. "Pick up if you can hear this because a lot's been happening and I need to talk to you. There are some very nasty people who want me to stop looking for Alfred. I've been threatened and I'm worried you're in danger too, so *please* call me when you get this message no matter what time it is, even if it's the middle of the night."

He left his number just in case and for five minutes after disconnecting he stared at the phone in a sort of trance, as if it might ring simply because he was willing it to do so. Then he carried it with him into the bedroom and put it by the bed. There was a phone there already but he wasn't thinking straight. A great weariness came over him and he lay down on the bed, pulling the cover roughly over himself. He fell asleep without undressing.

Earlier that afternoon Lucy had been on the phone in her flat. She had taken the morning off and looked around the Angel Gallery with Rupert, and he had dropped her back home. When he had driven away she had gone inside without ever realising for a moment that the lone motorcyclist on the street had been Will Bentley. Once inside she had plugged in her computer and picked up an email from Davies pleading for forgiveness. At first she had felt angry all over again over his treatment of her in Cambridge. But the email was very charming and mentioned further developments, so after a minute of residual peevishness she picked up the phone and dialled his number. The first part of the conversation was taken up by Davies being very apologetic and mumbling about police procedure, and Lucy letting him squirm a little.

"What's all this about new developments?" she said at last.

"Ah well, it's getting very interesting," Davies said with a discernible note of relief in his voice. "It turns out you were dead right about Will Bentley. The lads in the Cambridge nick discovered that they had video footage of a man breaking into Bentley's house the night before we were tipped off. He had something under a bit of cloth which was the size and shape of the stolen painting. It looked all of a sudden as if Bentley was telling the truth and someone really *was* trying to frame him."

"So what happened about Will?" Lucy asked, feeling exultant.

"I let him go first thing this morning, and I was bloody nice to him, I can tell you. I felt bad, to tell you the truth. He was right really; I did jump to conclusions. I spent all yesterday afternoon giving him a right grilling, only to find out that someone else was leading me up the garden path."

Lucy felt so relieved that she didn't even say she had told him so.

"So he's back at home then? That's excellent. Have you got any leads on the man who broke in?"

"Not yet but we're working on it. The local DCI in Cambridge has sent out a couple of the lads to collect CCTV tapes, to see if we can work out where our night visitor went after he'd dropped off the painting."

"Or how he got there *before* breaking in," Lucy added.

"That as well, yes."

"Did you get a good look at him on the video?"

"Not really. He was wearing a hood, but he might have taken it off once he was away from the scene. He wouldn't have wanted to get stopped by a patrol car."

"Shall I help you look through the tapes? I might recognise him if he's connected with the art world."

"I was wondering if you would mind," Davies said awkwardly. "But you'll have to pop over to my office."

"I can do that," Lucy said, feeling happy. "The good news is that we've stirred something up. They've confirmed that there *is* something going on and we're on the right track."

"Very thoughtful, I call it," Davies said. "And they gave us back the Hammershoi into the bargain. They should have left well alone and we would have run out of ideas. When can you come over? The tapes will be arriving shortly."

"How about later this afternoon?" she said, taking a quick look at her calendar.

When she had put the phone down, Lucy found Will's number. She paused for a moment to work out what she was going to say, because the last time she had seen him in Hastings they had ended up having that ridiculous row. When her thoughts were in order she dialled, feeling oddly excited to be speaking to him again. But it was not to be – after ten rings the call went into voicemail. She hesitated for a split second but then disconnected the call, unwilling to leave a message when she wanted to speak with him directly. Instead she fetched her bag, put on a light jacket and set off for Buckingham Gate.

She reached the offices of the Art and Antiques Unit later than she had intended, and Davies escorted her up to his dingy office. They still had to wait twenty minutes for the CCTV tapes to arrive from Cambridge, during which period he filled her in on the details of Will's arrest and subsequent release. When the tapes arrived there were a lot of them. They put the stack beside the player that Davies had requisitioned from technical support.

"This is going to take a while," he said, inserting a video. "Before we get going I thought you'd like to see the tape which started it all off."

He lined up the tape and she watched as the film showed a hooded man working on Will's door for a moment with a metal tool before he succeeded in opening it and slipped inside.

"That's very clever," she said, looking intently at the screen. "It didn't take him long to get in."

Davies then showed her the later section of tape where the hooded man had made his escape. When she knew as much as he did, he picked the first of the new tapes off the top of the pile and fed it into the machine. It was marked with a full address which included the postcode, so they were able to find its normal location by bringing up a map on Davies' computer.

"There's the edge of Will's studio," Lucy said, tapping the screen. "And here is the vantage point of this particular tape, so if the intruder approached along this road then we've got him."

But there was no sign of anyone on the street around the appointed time. They tried the next tape and this time they picked up the intruder walking away from the studio.

"Got the bastard!" Davies said excitedly. They watched the dark figure striding confidently down the street, reproduced in a series of jerky freeze frames. When the man was almost out of the camera's range he reached up and slipped down his hood.

Davies pressed the pause button and they stepped back and looked.

It was disappointing. They couldn't see what the man looked like because he was too distant; the only thing evident was that he had light-coloured hair. After they had made notes and recorded the sequence onto a second tape, Davies removed the tape and put in another one. The next seven tapes in a row drew a blank, though it took them a long time to be sure. Three of them were instantly rejected because the location was wrong, but four had to be searched through. It was a wearying and frustrating business.

The eighth tape picked the intruder up again, moving swiftly. This time they could see his face reasonably well, though from a distance. He had a beard and short hair and he moved like a boxer, light and strong. Neither of them recognized him. He paused at a rubbish bin for a moment, fiddled and then carried on.

"Hold on a minute," Lucy said at once. "Go back a bit."

Davies rewound the tape and they studied it carefully.

"He gets something out of his jacket," Lucy said, frowning. "And he throws it away. It looks like an umbrella or something."

"It must be the cloth," Davies said suddenly. "He had the painting wrapped in cloth and now he's chucking it away. We need to work out where that litter bin is."

It took them twenty minutes to get the map coordinates, using satellite photographs and then street view to find the bin. Then Davies phoned Parkside police station and spoke to the duty officer. He put down the phone looking satisfied.

"They're going to send a car out right now to see if it's still in the bin," he said with satisfaction. "If we can find the cloth and it matches the fibres found on the painting, then we'll have hard proof that this man dropped off the painting at Bentley's studio. We might even get DNA off the cloth."

They made more tape copies and notes, and continued the search over three more tapes before they lost their quarry without trace. He disappeared into an alley and they had no tapes left for that part of Cambridge.

Davies sat back in his chair and looked at his watch. "Christ, it's eleven o'clock," he said in alarm. "Carol's going to bloody kill me. I think tomorrow I'm going to have a good look for Alfred Smith on the computer. I don't feel as if I've exhausted every avenue to find him yet. And I'll talk to Carter as well – he's the Cambridge copper – and tell him about our progress with the video. With a bit of luck he might be able to get us a few more tapes."

"I can't wait," Lucy said, rubbing her eyes.

As she drove home she began to develop a headache, her head full of the jerky images of the man they had been tracking. She began to think she *had* seen him somewhere, but she couldn't think where. He seemed familiar from the back. She yawned all the way home and arrived after midnight. Peaches had run out of food and was meowing around her legs when she came in. She fed the cat and then stumbled upstairs to bed, her head throbbing. The phone rang sometime later, but by the time she was conscious it had stopped its clamour. She turned over and went back to sleep, unaware of Will's urgent message that she might be in danger.

RICHARD JOHN MITCHELL

THIRTY-THREE

Stiffen the sinews, summon up the blood,
Disguise fair nature with hard-favour'd rage;
WILLIAM SHAKESPEARE, Henry V

When Will awoke on Friday he wasn't frightened but angry, though it was an icily controlled fury. His head ached and his nose throbbed. The cut on his wrist was sore and represented a stark reminder of the inhumanity of these people. They weren't just a bunch of mindless bruisers intent on warning him off — somewhere behind them was a cold-blooded intelligence that had devised a way to threaten the most important thing to him; his ability to paint. His guts churned at the thought of the axe blade on his skin and the man's voice croaking in his ear. He shook his head as he shuffled out of his dirty clothes, as if physically trying to shake the wickedness out of his brain. He had known men like that in prison, who could commit sick acts of violence without emotion. It wasn't good if they knew where you lived.

Unfortunately he couldn't simply run away. He was established in Cambridge and making a successful living. Galleries were falling over each other to display his work. Word was spreading to London and the prices for his paintings were increasing steadily. Just the other day he had seen a market stall selling prints of one of his pictures. He couldn't simply walk away from all this without a fight.

He took a shower and dressed, then walked up the spiral staircase onto the roof. It was after nine, later than he usually started the day. It was a clear sunny morning in Cambridge and the sky featured perfectly white clouds of the type that children imagine into shapes. In the distance was a bank of grey cloud which heralded an end to the fine weather, but it was still far away. He leaned on the curving Gaudi-like balustrade and looked out across the rooftops. A silver jet droned far above, leaving a white trail like a speedboat on a blue ocean.

He went through in his mind what he knew. He knew that someone didn't want him to find Alfred Smith, which suggested that if he could do so then the puzzle might be revealed. Lucy had told him about the Alma-Tadema, so he knew that *someone* was forging paintings. It had to be Alfred since Will was being warned to stop looking for him. So if Alfred was doing the art work, others would be converting the paintings into money and would not want Will to upset the whole venture.

They had already made two attempts to stop him; getting him jailed for the presumed theft of the Hammershoi, and then making a direct attack on him when that plan had miscarried. What would they do if he didn't desist? Presumably they would carry out their threat, but *would* they? Putting to one side the horror of the situation, such an act of barbarism would trigger a nationwide hunt for the perpetrators, spurred on by the promise of forgeries and the millions of pounds that could potentially be recovered. And unless they followed him every minute of the day, how would they know whether he was looking for Alfred or not?

He thought about Alfred himself. Alfred had written to his sister and told her that he was going away for a while. He knew that Alfred was at the seaside somewhere in 'our own British Isles', and that it wasn't Hastings, but started with 'BUR'. Or at least, he knew that it had been *posted* in a place starting with those letters. He went downstairs and picked up a map book from the bookshelf, then went up to the roof again and opened the map out on the table. The wind riffled the pages and the sun felt good on his back. He felt as if he needed to be outside, if only to show that he was unafraid of the new day.

He found Hastings on the south coast and then went either side of it along the coastline looking for place names beginning with BUR which were on or near the sea. Immediately it felt like an impossible task. Looking at a map made him realize just how many places there are in England alone. He found Burmarsh first, inland from Dymchurch on Romney Marsh. There was nowhere else that jumped off the page as he followed the coastline. He had difficulty with the Thames because he didn't know how far to look inwards – at what point was it too far up the estuary to be the 'seaside'? He decided that Tilbury docks was far enough and carried on up the coast. There was nothing so he started again at Hastings and this time worked to the left, along the south coast through Bexhill, Eastbourne, Brighton and Worthing. On the outskirts of Southampton he found Bursledon, then Burton near Christchurch, then Burton Bradstock just past the Abbotsbury Swannery and Chesil Bank. He remembered Chesil Beach, where he had once spent an enjoyable day with a paintbrush, an easel and a pretty girl who had done a good job at distracting him from his determination to paint.

By the time he had reached the Lizard and was moving his eyes up the north coast of Cornwall, he realized that he was no longer seeing the place names; his eyes were scanning over them but he wasn't taking them in. He tried looking up 'BUR' in the index but there was a whole column of places starting with those initial letters. Even if he narrowed the list down to those on or near the sea he would end up with ten or twenty places, and it was too many to visit each one without further information. He would be travelling all over the country. He could spend the whole summer hoping to bump into Alfred that way, and sooner or later his attackers would return with the axe.

He shivered despite the rising heat of the morning, looking up from the map and staring out sightlessly across the city.

He went downstairs to make tea and discovered that the milk had gone sour, so he needed to visit the corner store. Images of the previous evening's attack flooded unbidden into his head. Coming out of his front door he felt alone and unprotected in the glare. He looked cautiously up and down the street, then walked to the side of the building and looked up the path to the garage. He realised he had not closed the garage door the previous night, so he walked up the path and looked in it. There was nothing to indicate anything untoward. The Bonnie was just as he had left it, so he closed and locked the garage door, looking constantly over his shoulder. The path was empty and he felt foolish. The laburnum in next door's garden hung over his fence and smelled sweet and fresh. He walked back to the street and looked up and down. He couldn't *see* anyone watching him, though they could easily be there somewhere. There were five parked cars and he examined each one to see if anybody were sitting inside, feeling faintly ridiculous. He went to buy the milk and when he came back he noticed that a crude outline of a hand had been drawn on his door, with a line through the wrist. He looked around wildly and realised that he didn't know if it had been done just then, or if they had done it the night before. He went upstairs and got a cloth and some cleaning fluid, scrubbing at the outline until it was gone. He closed the door and leaned against it, breathing hard and wondering what he was going to do next.

He needed some protection. He wasn't a man of violence and he couldn't stand up to several men who were. No-one could be expected to do that, except – and it was then that a sudden image of *Lewis* popped into his mind, and for the first time that morning he grinned. The man who had saved him from many prison beatings. Lewis would be a good man to have on his side if he were going to continue the search for Alfred. He went upstairs and looked through his address book. He had an address in Brixton and a phone number for Lewis's wife, and he guessed that by now Lewis should be out of prison. Will phoned the number but got no reply, so he decided spontaneously that he would go there. He was in no mood to waste time so he drank a glass of water, picked up his wallet and phone and left the house. He rolled the Bonnie out of the garage, feeling his confidence grow as the throaty backbeat kicked into life. It was a sound that very clearly said *fuck you* to any psychopathic maniacs in the vicinity.

THIRTY-FOUR

*Candy is dandy
But liquor is quicker.*
OGDEN NASH

It took him 90 minutes to get to Brixton and he was able to park the bike outside the terraced house which was Lewis's last-known address. The woman who opened the door had the chain on, but she obviously decided that Will didn't pose a threat because she closed it and then opened it fully. She had dark hair and a slight double chin. She was wearing a black V-neck tee-shirt that emphasized her cleavage, and jeans. The black top had a wide neck so that it hung off one shoulder, exposing a black bra strap. She wore her hair in a pony tail and there was a stud in her nose.

"I'm looking for Lewis," Will said.

"Well you won't find him here," she replied. "Who are you then?"

"My name's Will Bentley. I met him in prison and I'm a painter."

"Oh yes, he mentioned you," she said frostily. "The *artist*. What do you want?"

He raised his eyebrows. "Are you *Mrs* Lewis?"

"I *was*, but not anymore. I'm not sticking with a man who's been in and out of the bloody nick, if you'll pardon my French. The divorce has just come through, thanks very much."

"Fair enough," Will said, unabashed. "But I do need to get hold of him. Do you have a forwarding address?"

A man came to the door behind the ex-Mrs Lewis. His chin was unshaven and he looked as if he had just got up. He was wearing grubby boxer shorts and his scalp was shaved around the edges and shiny in the centre.

"All right, love?" he said to her.

She nodded.

"Man here looking for Lewis," she said.

"He ain't here," the bald man said.

"I can see that," Will said, struggling to remain polite. "Any idea how I can get hold of him?"

"I don't have an address," she said. "We fell out, like. But I s'pose you could try the Hallam. That's where he last worked. No-one wanted him once he got banged up. They thought he might do it again."

"How come they knew?"

"Word gets around, I s'pose."

He waited but she didn't say anything else, just watched him as if he might be about to take her purse. The man caught her look and glowered at Will.

"We can't help you, mate." He stepped back and made as if to shut the door.

"Hold on," Will said. "Just tell me what the Hallam is."

"It's a nightclub down near the Academy," she said. "It's a total dump actually, but I s'pose he takes what he can get. He's on the door."

"You mean the Brixton Academy?"

"Yeah."

He started to thank them but the man closed the door in his face. He shrugged, climbed back onto the Bonnie and motored down the road to the Brixton Academy on Stockwell Road, remembering its curious dome-shaped frontage. He had visited it several times in his youth but hadn't been back for years. It was closed but he stopped the bike anyway out of nostalgia and went up the step to read the forthcoming attractions. It had the same old mixture of well-known sold-out bands and new musicians he had never heard of. These days it changed its name according to whoever was sponsoring it, but it would always be the Brixton Academy to him and millions of others. He turned and watched a young man go past carrying a bible, wearing a yellow tee-shirt and tracksuit bottoms. He was telling bemused passers-by in a hectoring tone that there was a Higher Power. Will stopped a different pedestrian and found out where the Hallam was. It was up a side street beyond Brixton Market; a small and seedy looking place with a black-painted front and a heavily reinforced door. He parked the bike and walked back to the place. The door was open and there was neither Lewis nor anyone else stationed at it. There were pictures of naked girls on posters inside, with stars covering their nipples. He went in and came to a small office accessible through a glass window hatch which was further protected by steel bars. A sign on the hatch said `Closed'. Inside the tiny office was a man in a dark shirt and white braces, who was reading a newspaper and smoking a cigar that was almost spent. He was fat and balding. He had a jewelled stud in his left ear.

"We're closed," he said without looking up.

"So I see," Will said. "I'm looking for Lewis."

The man looked up, narrowing his eyes.

"Who wants him?" he asked.

"My name's Will. He's an old friend of mine."

"Lewis is on the juice, mate," the man said. "The gaffer fired him yesterday for being pissed on duty."

"That's bad news," Will said with a frown. "Have you got his address? I still need to find him."

"Yeah, well, we don't give out staff addresses," the man said self-righteously.

Will leaned close to the glass.

"How am I supposed to get hold of him then? I've got a job for him."

"Sooner you than me, mate." The man said. He stood up and looked through the window and down the stairway. "Tell you what, though," he said in a low voice. "I'm out of cigars."

Will looked at him blankly for a moment but then realised what the man was getting at. He took out his wallet and extracted a banknote which he held in front of the window glass."

"I'm a heavy smoker," said the man pitifully.

"You'll get cancer," Will said. "Take it or leave it."

The man looked down the stairwell again and then opened a small card index on the desk behind him. He found the card that he wanted and tore it out of the index.

"There you go," he said, taking the money with his other hand and swiftly pocketing it. "You can have that card; we won't be needing it again."

Will nodded and walked out as the man settled down once more with his newspaper.

This time he killed the Bonneville's engine outside a block of council flats, some of which were boarded up, all of which were dilapidated and in great contrast to the spacious Victorian houses down the road. Here there was rubbish everywhere and needles at the bottom of the concrete stairwell. A boy came down the stairs and looked at Will incuriously as he passed.

"Where will I find flat 217?"

The boy paused for barely a second.

"Second floor up, turn left and keep walking," he said, and was gone.

Will trudged up the staircase, which stank of urine, turned left at the second floor and located Lewis's door, which was coated in pale blue peeling paint, identical to every other door in the block.

There was no bell so he knocked on the door, wondering if this was a very stupid course of action to be taking. There was no answer and he decided that he must be condemned to wander around the country for the rest of his life looking for people who had either gone away or were out when he called. He knocked again and peered through the window into a dingy kitchen.

Then the door opened and Lewis stood there. He stared at Will blankly for a few seconds before his face broke into a big smile.

"Will Bentley!" he said in obvious pleasure, and held out his hand. "Fancy you looking me up. Come on in!"

He disappeared and Will followed him into the flat, noticing a lingering smell of stale alcohol. He sat down on a sofa and eyed the array of empty bottles on a table beside the television. Lewis made coffee and came in with two mugs. He was as big as ever, but he hadn't shaved for a couple of days and he looked as if he needed a shower. He was wearing jeans and a black shirt. He shifted bottles and put the mugs down on the table.

"I'm afraid there's no milk," he said apologetically. "I've been a bit distracted. Lost me job yesterday and it's hit me hard. I don't know how I'm going to pay the bills."

"I spoke to your ex-wife," Will said, "and then I went to the Hallam and they gave me this address. What's going on? Things seem to have gone downhill for you."

Lewis looked down moodily into his mug of black coffee.

"It's never been the same since I came out of the nick," he said. "Word got around that I wasn't to be trusted, y'see. The club owners knew about the GBH and they didn't want to risk another one. Bad for business. I told 'em I'd learned me lesson but they closed ranks. So I wasn't getting into the normal clubs that I used to work for, and I ended up working for dumps like the Hallam."

"And your wife left you?" Will prompted gently.

"Yeah," he said bitterly. "Didn't fancy living with a jailbird, Josie said. But the truth is she took up with another bloke while I was in the slammer. Did you see him when you went round there?"

"No hair?" Will said.

Lewis nodded grimly. "That's the one. So I walked out on her, Will, and the next thing I know is I got a load of divorce papers and that was bleedin' that."

"Was there any trouble?" Will asked.

Lewis looked at him, surprised.

"Eh? Well, not with Josie; she's a lady, after all. And she's got a point, hasn't she? I'm not much of a catch these days."

"You don't need to be a bouncer for the rest of your life," Will said. "You've got lots of muscle. There are plenty of things you could do. You could get into something similar, like security. Or you could be a builder. I bet you could shift a lot of bricks if you had a mind."

"I suppose so," he said, drinking more coffee. "I thought about going back into the boxing game again, but I'm 38 now. Too old to start again; I'd get me bleedin' lights punched out."

"They told me why you got fired from the Hallam," Will said. "What's your side of the story?"

Lewis looked uneasy again. "Yeah, well, if they told you I'd had a few too many jars, that would be about right," he said.

Will didn't say anything; just waited until Lewis started talking again.

"You see, I came out of the slammer and I was on top of the world. *You* know the feeling, right? I got home all ready to give Josie a surprise, like, and I found her in bed with the bald coot. So we had a few words and I walked out of that situation pretty fast before I got meself into trouble. I'd never touch a woman, but I was tempted to lay that bloke out flat. I didn't, though – I knew if I laid a finger on him I'd be straight back in the nick and he'd have the last laugh. Anyway, next thing I tried to get a job and that was the worst thing of all. I went through a load of lousy jobs and ended up in the Hallam."

He stared into space.

"So I ended up in this fleapit, and having a little drink or two seemed to take the edge off things. Five or six drinks and it felt better still, and here I am today." He waved his arm at the empty bottles and shook his head in disgust.

There was a silence while Will contemplated the situation.

"I can offer you a job for a few days," he said at last, and mentioned a wage. "I've been doing all right in the art business, but I'm looking for an old artist friend of mine. He's an old lag too, name of Alfred Smith."

"A job would be great," Lewis said. "But what do you need me for?"

"I've run into some nasty people looking for Alfred," Will said," and I'm worried that they're going to knock him off when they've finished using him. He doesn't deserve that – he's a nice old bloke."

He held up his wrist to show the sticking plaster.

"They threatened to cut my hand off."

"What's going on?" Lewis said, his face deadpan.

So Will told him everything he knew, right up to the attack the previous night that had made him realise he needed protection.

"The only thing is, you need to get off the booze," Will said at the end. "Can you do that, do you think? I'll be straight with you; I'm not having you around the place pissed. I won't be able to work and you won't be able to stop these people. And believe me, they aren't the sort you'd want to be dealing with if you were pissed."

Lewis looked at him seriously, and held out his hand.

"I need to get out of this place," he said. "There's nothing for me here. So I'll give it a go and I'll keep off the booze. You've got my word on it."

Will shook the proffered hand.

They agreed that Lewis would make his way up to Cambridge the next day on the train, because he needed first to go to the Hallam and collect his final pay packet. Will gave him the studio address and money for the trip, thinking privately that if Lewis didn't make it and got drunk on the money instead, that would decide it.

"One thing I want to show you before you go," Lewis said, and led Will into a surprisingly clean bedroom. He gestured to the wall and Will immediately recognised the drawing that he had done of Lewis's mother, now behind glass.

"I had her framed properly," Lewis said with a touch of pride. "Looks smart, doesn't she?"

"They did a good job," Will said, looking closely at the drawing and having that strange frisson of delight that an artist feels when he sees a previous work after a long interval. "How is your mum these days?"

"She's all right," Lewis said. "I took the picture up to Felixstowe and showed her. Proper chuffed she was. And I showed me sisters an' all."

"I can't remember how many sisters you've got," Will said, frowning.

"Four," Lewis said with affection. "All too clever by half. They're still in Felixstowe. I'm the only one that ever moved, and much bleedin' good it did me."

"You never know," Will said. "Sometimes you have hard times and then things get better. Maybe this is a turning point."

Lewis looked at him and nodded seriously.

"I feel like I've hit rock bottom," he said. "Carry on like this and I'll be on the street, so I reckon it's time for a change. I'll be there tomorrow; you can count on it."

THIRTY-FIVE

Opera is when a guy gets stabbed in the back and, instead of bleeding, he sings.
ED GARDNER, American radio comedian

When Will got back to the studio there was no sign of anyone watching and no hand outline on the door. As he put away the Bonneville it was still light, but he looked swiftly over his shoulder to make sure that no-one was behind him.

Once inside the studio, there was a message on the answer-phone from Lucy.

"Will, it's Lucy. I'm sorry we parted in such a horrid way on Monday. I heard about you being arrested, and I can tell you that Hugh Davies was very embarrassed when he found out you were telling the truth, especially since I'd had a row with him and told him you wouldn't have done it. Anyway, we've been finding a few things out about the man who left the Hammershoi in your studio and I thought you'd be interested. Give me a ring when you pick this message up."

He listened to it twice. She had such a lovely voice. But she hadn't mentioned the message that he had left for her, which made him worry that she hadn't heard it. She had given him her work number so he called it, but was told by her secretary that Lucy had gone out. He asked her to get Lucy to call him as soon as she could, and said to tell Lucy that he was still looking for Alfred Smith. He rang her home number after that, but there was no reply so he left another message, more urgent than the first. He went into the kitchen and fixed himself a coffee, then paced up and down the studio. Lucy didn't ring.

When he had eaten, he wondered into the studio and looked at the nude Sandy on the easel. He needed to call *her* too, and schedule some more modelling sessions. He didn't want to stop working because he needed something to keep him sane. Painting was the single thing that made him forget everything else. After a few minutes he picked up his palette and renewed the colours that had skinned over; burnt umber, French ultramarine and cadmium yellow. He picked up a paintbrush, dipped it, stirred colours for a few moments, added white to lighten, added the complementary to dull the colour, and applied paint. The brush made the faintest of rasping sounds as he applied pigment to the canvas.

Lucy didn't ring.

While Will had been locating Lewis in Brixton, Lucy went in to work that Friday morning. She addressed herself to all the mundane tasks that had built up while she had been looking for Alfred Smith and Will Bentley's nocturnal visitor. She was excited because Rupert had said that he was taking her out for a surprise in the evening, and that she should wear a long dress and look glamorous. She was asked to be hungry and ready at home for a very early pick-up at five o'clock. She therefore worked solidly all morning on email and post and spent a considerable amount of time on the phone. She remembered to call Will but was again frustrated to find him not at home: or at least, not answering the phone. She left him a message that she was sorry about the row on Monday, and that she wanted to speak to him. After lunch she had to visit an irate client who had been trying to contact her for several days and had worked himself up into a lather, and when she had finished with him she went straight home, phoning Vicky on the way from the car.

"A man called for you," Vicky said. "A Mr Will Bentley. I told him you were out but he sounded as if he needed to get hold of you urgently. He said to tell you that he's still looking for someone called Alfred Smith." She paused. "He sounded rather dishy, actually."

"I don't know how you can work out he's dishy on the phone," Lucy said tartly, but then after a moment added, "Though I suppose he is, as it happens."

"Would he be the same Will Bentley who was on the news for stealing the Hammershoi and then released without charge?" Vicky asked in her most guileless voice.

Lucy smiled at the phone in its hands-free mount as if able to look straight through it and see her secretary's expression of wide-eyed innocence.

"Yes, *Victoria*! He would be the very same. And were there any other calls?"

"Hugh Davies called from the Met but I told him you were dealing with a stroppy client. He said could you call him when you've got a moment?"

"Okay, will do."

"And Rupert Angel called, so you were very popular this afternoon," Vicky went on. "Are you *going out* with him? He seemed to act as if you were and said he's confirming that he's picking you up at five o'clock sharp from home."

"Yes I am," she said. "I met him last week at the Limerston, and he's charming. He's taking me out somewhere tonight for a surprise."

"You could do a lot worse," Vicky said. "He's that chap who was a judge at the Portrait Awards, isn't he?"

"That's the one. Very erudite."

"And *very* good looking," Vicky added with a throaty chuckle that made Lucy laugh in turn.

Rupert arrived at five to five in the silver Mercedes.

"So what's the surprise?" she said when she opened the door of her flat to him. "I've been itching to know!"

"I'm not sure I'm going to tell you yet," Rupert said. He was looking very dashing in a dark suit, a cream shirt with a button-down collar and a mottled green bow tie.

"Please," she said. "I might be wearing completely the wrong thing."

He looked her up and down with appreciation. She was wearing a long red dress and carrying a matching red clutch bag. She had a heart-shaped necklace to emphasize her décolletage, and a long cream jacket around her shoulders.

"You look perfect," he said. "But all right then: let me put you out of your misery."

He reached into his pocket and withdrew an envelope, taking from it two tickets and handing them to her for inspection.

"Oh my God, the opera!" she said. "And Stalls seats! I've only ever been when I was a kid and then I sat up in the gods. *Thank* you!" She put her arms around him and kissed him.

"Or we could just stay here!" he said with a grin when she had parted from him.

She punched him lightly on the arm and closed her door.

"If you're well behaved you can come back for coffee," she said, "but right now, I want to go to the opera and see…" she consulted the tickets, "…Tosca. But that's about a *painter*. How clever you are!"

Despite the Friday traffic they managed to get to the Royal Opera House in Covent Garden by six.

"I hope you haven't eaten?" Rupert said anxiously. I've booked a table in the Vilar Floral Hall restaurant, which is right here in the theatre."

"I'm famished," Lucy said truthfully.

"Good," he said, taking her arm. "We have starters and main courses now and desserts and coffee in the first interval. "The actual opera doesn't start until half past seven so we have plenty of time, but I wanted to get us here so that we wouldn't have to worry. The main hall was the old flower market, you know. We'll be eating next to it."

They sat down and took in the scene: other diners seating themselves at nearby tables; a domed glass roof over their heads; silver and white interspersed with splashes of colour from the flowers on the tables and the ladies' dresses. There was a rising volume of conversation and laughter, both from the restaurant they were in and from the bar. Rupert ordered a bottle of the best Perrier-Jouët Belle Époque champagne, making Lucy's eyes widen when she saw the price, even if she was becoming used to Rupert's extravagant ways. They had to choose quickly because they had not preordered – Rupert said it would have spoiled the surprise. The specials were an avocado and prawn cocktail, which seemed too ordinary, and a roast vegetable cannelloni, which seemed too virtuous, so they elected to choose from the main menu instead. She ordered asparagus with an olive tapenade on bruschetta, followed by salmon with grilled asparagus and minted new potatoes.

"I adore asparagus," she said. "I can't get enough of it."

He opted for a smoked trout starter followed by a poached lobster and crayfish Caesar salad.

The waiter came and poured their champagne with a flourish, for it was the best in the house. They clinked their glasses together and looked into each others' eyes as they drank.

"Mmm," Lucy said. "You're setting a high standard by spoiling me so much this early in our relationship."

"I always start with champagne," Rupert said. "It'll be fish and chips in a month or so."

She smiled at him, but into her mind came a momentary image of herself and Will Bentley sitting on a seat on the seafront at Hastings, eating fish and chips and smelling of vinegar. Her smile became a little crooked but Rupert didn't notice; he was expounding on the floral notes of violets and iris in the champagne. But it was very kind of him to take her out for such an extravagant evening. She realised she was being unfair and tried to put Will out of her mind.

It wasn't long before Rupert asked for the latest news on her 'life of art espionage'.

"The policeman I'm working with is going to do some further computer checks for this Alfred Smith character, because he hasn't turned up anything yet," she said.

"What sort of checks is he doing?"

"Oh I don't know; all sorts of things. Apparently it's very difficult to disappear completely in England. There have been some interesting developments, though. Have you been reading the news?"

"No," Rupert said untruthfully.

"You remember I told you about a painter I was working with to find Alfred Smith: a chap called Will Bentley? He was arrested for stealing a Hammershoi."

"Well I did express some concerns," Rupert said. "You mean the picture that was stolen last week?"

"Yes, Interior with a Girl at the Clavier," she confirmed. "And I agree you did warn me, but there's more to the story."

The waiter arrived and refilled their glasses, so they drank some more champagne. The starters came and they ate for a while.

"It turns out he didn't do it," she went on between mouthfuls. "It's an amazing tale. Somebody hid the painting in his studio and then tipped off the police that he had it."

He looked at her, and she detected the same stillness she had noticed once or twice in Le Gavroche. It was an odd mannerism.

"Extraordinary," he said eventually. "And how did the police discover that? They are becoming so ingenious these days."

"They certainly are," she agreed, "but this time they were just lucky. They had CCTV of this chap breaking in."

Rupert drank his glass of water and topped it up from the jug.

"I saw the tape. He was all clad in black just like David Niven in one of those old jewel-thief films, and he had the painting under his arm."

"Did you see his face?"

She finished her last mouthful of bruschetta, with three snipped-off asparagus heads arranged neatly on it, before she answered.

"No, he was wearing a hood," she said. "But we are making progress."

"Really, in what way?" Rupert asked immediately.

She was reminded of the Limerston when she had realised that she was talking too much.

"I probably shouldn't say," she said. "Anyway, I'm glad that Will Bentley wasn't locked up for long. He spoke to my secretary today because I wasn't there. Says he wants me to call him and that he's still looking for Smith, so being arrested hasn't put him off."

"He's a determined man," Rupert said.

"Yes, I suppose he is. You'd think he would just walk away, but he and Smith were really close friends. I'm beginning to realize that he's not going to give up until he finds him."

Rupert smiled a bleached-white smile.

"Then we must wish you both the very best of luck," he said and raised his glass. They clinked and drank. The salmon and the lobster came then and they ate without discussing Will Bentley or Alfred Smith again. After that was the opera itself.

THIRTY-SIX

The whole wood seemed running now, running hard, hunting, chasing, closing in round something or - somebody? In panic, he began to run too, aimlessly, he knew not whither.
KENNETH GRAHAME

"Tosca is an amazing story," Lucy said when they emerged for the first interval. "I'm always surprised about how much I understand these things when they're not even in English."

They sat down to their desserts. She had strawberries and raspberries with sorbet, and he had British cheeses, which he pronounced not quite as good as Le Gavroche but a very fine second. The rest of Tosca passed in a whirlwind and before Lucy knew it she was arriving back at her flat in Rupert's Mercedes. She had drunk more than Rupert because she wasn't driving.

"You should have got that chauffeur of yours to drive us so that you could have had a bit more to drink," she said. "But I'm glad you didn't. Having him around is a bit like having a chaperone." She stepped through her door and then looked back around it with big eyes.

"Now I believe I promised you coffee," she said, and reached out a hand, which he took and followed her through her front door.

The door opened directly into a large and beautiful room. The style was uncluttered but not minimalist – there were white shelves with subdued lighting and interesting artefacts; a silver clock with twisted silver wires spiralling out from it; a brightly coloured bowl filled with huge fir cones; a camel's skull; a pair of brightly glazed china cockatoos. The walls were painted in two tones; deep red and ivory, and they were crowded with paintings and prints. The floor was tiled in black and white like a Vermeer drawing room, but softened by a large red rug between a pair of white sofas. There was a drinks cabinet in the form of a lunar globe, split open to reveal bottles. Glass shelves on the wall behind bore crystal glasses in different shapes and sizes and colours. To one side there was a small dining area which was very plain; just a white ash table and four black and white chairs.

There were two bookcases in the main room and they were overflowing with art books, music manuscripts, and an assortment of fiction and non-fiction, with a strong emphasis on the classics. A white baby grand piano stood against the further wall. There were burgundy uplighters in the corners and ceiling spotlights to illuminate the paintings. In the corner was an antique bureau which extended to a wooden cupboard on top, its doors open to reveal a mixture of things; a stack of envelopes and writing paper on one side; a teapot and a genie's lamp on another. A computer sat on the bureau writing table. A framed picture of a young man of perhaps twenty-five stood next to the computer, and Rupert strolled over to look at it. Then he froze as he caught sight of the picture next to it.

"My husband David," Lucy said, seeing him looking at it and picking it up. "You remember? He died in an accident."

Rupert nodded, his throat suddenly dry.

"Yes," he said. "I remember you telling me about it in Le Gavroche. Such a tragedy, I'm so sorry."

They never knew how David Wrackham had got onto them but he had come to a Summer Music Concert at the Collector's house. He had followed Rupert and seen everything.

Rupert glanced at Lucy but she hadn't noticed his sudden distraction. He summoned up something normal to say.

"What a – what a beautiful apartment."

"Thank you," she said, and then raised her voice.

"Peaches? Where are you, sweetheart?" A large fluffy white cat stalked haughtily into the room, went up to her mistress and rubbed herself against Lucy's legs.

"Make yourself at home," Lucy said, and went into the kitchen. While she was making coffee he came up behind her and took her by the waist, pulling her to him, forgetting the photograph of the dead man. She turned around, wrapped her arms around his neck and kissed him.

"Would you like to stay?" she said a little breathlessly. "Then I can fix you a proper drink."

"I'd like that," he said, and they kissed again.

In that case I need some time to change out of my glamour wear," she said, uncurling herself from him. She led him back into the main room, waving her hand at the drinks cabinet, "Fix yourself a drink while I freshen up."

They kissed again and then she disappeared into her bedroom and closed the door. He inspected the drinks cabinet and mixed himself a gin and tonic. She even had a lemon on standby, and a knife, and a small wooden chopping board. He located ice from the freezer. When he had mixed the drink he sat down on the sofa next to a small round table and put his drink on it. There was a copy of A.S. Byatt's `Still Life' on the table with a bookmark in it. He was about to pick it up when he noticed that a small red light on the telephone was winking. He looked at the bedroom door and it was closed. He leaned over and looked at the telephone. It had a scrolling display which read `You have 2 Messages'. He suddenly felt hot and uncomfortable. It could be something perfectly innocuous, or it could be messages from the accursed Will Bentley. He stood up and padded to the bedroom door and was immediately rewarded by the sound of the shower being turned on. He waited for another minute or two and then went across to the phone and examined it. It was possible to see who had called, and both numbers started with 01223. It wasn't a London number but he didn't know what code it was. His eyes fell on Lucy's computer and he hurried over to it, casting a look over his shoulder at Lucy's door. It was the work of a moment to enter "01223 UK dialling code" into the search engine, and the computer immediately came back with Cambridge numbers. He cursed under his breath as he cleared the computer screen and went back to Lucy's closed door with perspiration beading on his brow. The shower was still running and he could smell the sweet damp scent of shower gel from underneath the door. At any other time he would have been tempted to go in and join her, but not now. He picked up the phone and pressed the playback button.

"Message received Today at twelve, fifty-one, A.M.

Lucy, it's Will Bentley. Pick up if you can hear this because a lot's been happening and I need to talk to you. There are some very nasty people who want me to stop looking for Alfred. I've been threatened and I'm worried you're in danger too, so please call me when you get this message no matter what time it is, even if it's the middle of the night."

Rupert cradled the phone for a moment, wondering what to do. Bentley must be going to tell her about the attack from Edward and his people. She would probably connect it with the man she had seen on the videotapes.

He pressed the button to listen to the second message.

"Message received Today at eight, fourteen, P.M.

Lucy, it's Will again. I just got your message and I'm sorry too about Monday. I'm glad the policeman is embarrassed, and by the way thanks for sticking up for me. What I wanted to tell you is that I was beaten up last night, and I'm worried you might be in danger too. They want me to stop looking for Alfred, but no way am I stopping now. Don't talk to anyone about this because I'm not sure how they got onto us, but the fact is that they have. Anyway, as I said before, call me when you get this no matter what time it is. I'm in the studio and I'm planning to be here all tomorrow."

Rupert silently thanked God that he had taken Lucy off to the opera. He debated for only an instant what to do, and then he deleted both messages. After that he drank half of the gin and tonic in one gulp. He realised that he was getting too damn close to being caught. It was time to take urgent action.

When Lucy emerged from her bedroom she was wearing a dressing gown and looked gorgeous, but she found Rupert pacing up and down and talking into his mobile phone in an annoyed voice about some shipment of art that had gone wrong. He was becoming increasingly exasperated, but finally said "Oh very well," and disconnected the call.

He came over to her and put his hands on her shoulders. Whatever the call had been about had obviously shocked him because he looked quite pale; not his usual calm and collected self.

"Is everything all right?" she said anxiously.

"Major problems," Rupert said. "That was Mrs Morris. Apparently a whole shipment of paintings has been embargoed by customs because they require my personal signature. I'm dreadfully sorry."

"But..." Lucy said, dismayed as the mood of the evening suddenly evaporated. "You don't mean *now*?"

Rupert licked his lips, his mouth in a frozen grimace.

"'I'm afraid I do," he said. "I feel awful, but I need to go and sort this out. They are for an exhibition, you see, and if they remain embargoed then the exhibition is not going to happen and we will surely be sued. I'm most dreadfully sorry."

He was gathering up his jacket, putting it on.

She began to move from dismay to irritation.

"Can't it wait until tomorrow morning?"

"I'm afraid not," he said, shaking his head.

"What a pity no-one else can do it."

"It's ridiculous," Rupert said. "Customs require my signature and mine alone. Can I call you once I have sorted it out?"

"Well I *suppose* so," she said, feeling very cross. He kissed her briefly without passion and then was gone. She looked out of the window, hurt and puzzled, pursing her lips and holding her dressing gown tightly together in a protective gesture. She watched him hurry down the path between the apartments and get into his car. The lights of the Mercedes flared and then he was gone.

THIRTY-SEVEN

I never forget a face but in your case I will make an exception.
GROUCHO MARX

Lucy had never experienced such a thing before. It was as if Rupert had been panicked by something. She found his whole story impossible to believe about customs embargoes in the middle of the night. She herself had experience with shipping paintings, and customs simply didn't demand signatures late in the evening. They wanted all the paperwork up front, and if they didn't have it, they notified you after a day or so, and during normal work hours.

On the other hand she couldn't understand why he would make such a thing up – and even more alarming, if he *had* made it up, then he had been *pretending* to talk on the phone to a non-existent person, which was decidedly weird and deceptive.

Perhaps she had been too forward with him? She didn't think so – he had been fine when she had disappeared to freshen up, but looked like he had seen a ghost when she came back. She picked up his half-drunk glass of gin and tonic and drained it herself, feeling very cross. She had been dropped like that once or twice straight *after* sex, but never, *ever* before. It made her wonder if there was something wrong with her. She wondered around the room disconsolately. David entered her mind guiltily and she picked up his photograph again from beside Dylan's.

"Perhaps you were right," she said to the picture, recalling how she thought David would have felt about Rupert Angel.

She checked the phone but there were no messages – she had thought that Will Bentley might have called her after the message she had left him, and she felt irritated with him that he hadn't. Didn't he ever pick up his phone? Why were all men such a pain?

She mixed herself a vodka and tonic and put it on top of the white baby grand, but then moved it instead to the shelf at the left edge of the keyboard and opened the top lid. She leaned her elbows on the top of the piano and cradled her chin in her hands, staring moodily into the instrument at its impeccable array of strings and dampers and felt pads and wood. She dipped her head down inside and inhaled her favourite smell deeply – the musky wooden interior of the piano. Peaches was curled up on the piano stool and Lucy picked her up and snuggled the cat to her breast, tickling her under the chin so that a soft purr of contentment began to reverberate from the fluffed-up white body.

"*You* wouldn't walk out on me, would you darling?" Lucy crooned.

She put the cat on the sofa and sat down at the piano, taking a mouthful of her drink and then staring unseeingly into space. She stamped hard on the sustain pedal and held her foot down so that the strings reverberated, making a sonorous echo that slowly receded into silence. Peaches sat up and looked at Lucy warily, then began cleaning her paws. Lucy rippling her hands over the keyboard, then began to play Consolation Number 3 by Liszt, because she felt sorry for herself and oddly comforted by its melancholy mood. Liszt was a stretch for her fingers and this piece was no exception, so she forgot all else until she allowed the last couplets to die away, *ritenuto perdendosi*. Then she sipped her drink and found herself suddenly wondering if Hugh had made any progress with his investigation into Will Bentley's intruder. She was supposed to have called him back. She suddenly remembered that her mobile was still turned off after the opera so she got up and padded across the apartment barefoot, looking for her bag.

She was glad she had thought of it when she turned the phone back on, because there *was* a message from Hugh, telling her that he had spent all day looking at tapes in Cambridge and had isolated their mystery man to a car park. He ended up by suggesting that she should call him, so she dialled his mobile number.

His voice was very sleepy.

"'Lo?"

"Hugh, it's Lucy. Oh God, are you asleep? I've just realised how late it is."

"Just dozing off. Don't you ever go to bed, girl?"

"That *was* the plan," she said with irony that only she was aware of. "Shall I call back tomorrow?"

"No, I'm awake now. Just let me find the light. I'm in a hotel room and I can't quite get my bearings."

There was a long pause and then his voice came back on the line, stronger now.

"You got my message, then?"

"About our mystery man, yes. Where are you then – still in Cambridge?"

"Yes, in a very nice hotel across from the nick. Carol's mad at me because it's Friday night and she's stuck with the kids while I'm swanking about in Cambridge, as she puts it."

"Poor Carol; I know how she feels. All men are monsters. So you've traced our man to a car-park?"

"Yes, but I still don't have a better head shot. The one you and I got is pretty indistinct. The car-park offers hope though – we might get a registration plate with a bit of luck. Then we'll have the bastard."

"Unless he stole the car."

"There's a good chance he didn't. And there's another bit of news. Carter's lads found the furled up cloth in the rubbish bin. Remember, we saw him put it in there on the tape."

"Oh, that's good!" Lucy said. "Have you tested it yet?"

"No doubt about it, really, but forensics are doing their stuff to make sure. I've had a preliminary report from one of their blokes. They're analysing the fibres to see if they match the ones caught in the frame of the Hammershoi, but they reckon they're identical from a quick look. But it gets better than that: they've found a human hair inside the furled-up cloth."

"A hair! Can they get a DNA profile from a single hair?"

"Easily, so they say. And if he's in the database, up he'll pop."

Lucy smiled down the phone, forgetting the irritation that she had been feeling earlier about Rupert.

"That's fantastic, Hugh. Well done you! When will you get the car-park tapes?"

"Tomorrow for certain, Carter says. He got a bit of a bollocking from his boss for sending the first lot of tapes down to the Met, so that's why I had to come up here to look at them. A bit of internal politics going on, apparently. I was wondering if you might be free to come up and have a gander at them tomorrow."

Lucy thought about it, but only for a moment.

"I don't see why not," she said. "I feel like I'd like to be in at the finish, if there is one, since I spent a whole evening staring at the first lot of tapes. I might pop in and see Will Bentley while I'm up there. Last time I saw him we had a silly row and I was a bit grumpy with him, so I'd quite like to make friends. And I want to hear his story, of course."

"Sounds like a good plan," Davies said. "I might accompany you, if that would be all right."

"Oh I don't know," Lucy said gravely. "After his recent experience of police brutality I don't want to turn up with you and put the fear of God into him."

"Very funny. Well, let's play it by ear then, but I'll look forward to seeing you up at Parkside nick in the morning. About ten, Carter said, no point in being earlier or we'll be there but the tapes won't be."

They ended the call and Lucy felt better now that she had an objective. She picked up her copy of Still Life and carried it with her drink into her bedroom, where she peeled off her dressing gown and hung it up, then ruefully removed her pretty underwear and slipped into bed.

Peaches came into the room and looked at her, but knew better than to attempt to get up on the bed. Instead she came over to the side of the bed with her tail in the air and meowed for attention. Lucy reached down and tickled her under the chin again, making the cat purr in ecstasy. Then she opened her book, put her bookmark to one side and took a mouthful of vodka and tonic. The ice cubes were melting but they still tinkled. She tried to concentrate on Frederica and Vincent Van Gogh, but though it would have suited her earlier, now it was a little too dark for her mood. She closed the book and picked up a magazine. She liked to read before sleeping, but after a while she clicked off the light and snuggled down, feeling the cool linen on her toes. She lay and watched a pale orange oblong on the ceiling which was cast by the streetlamps, and white flashes from the crystal in the window that would be riven into rainbows by the morning light. She thought about Vincent for a while and tried to imagine how it might have been different if he had lived to a ripe old age like Monet, rather than going out into a field and shooting himself. *La tristesse durera toujours*.

After a while she found herself thinking about a different painter. She felt unexpectedly pleased at the thought of seeing Will Bentley again.

THIRTY-EIGHT

One should forgive one's enemies, but not before they are hanged.
HEINRICH HEINE

Rupert Angel stopped the Mercedes with a vicious jerk so that it skidded on the gravel in front of his Chelsea house. He saw the curtain in the study window lift at one side so that a yellow triangle of light framed Morton's outline. Morton lived in the back and Mrs Morris and her son occupied a self-contained flat on the top floor, in what had once been servants' quarters.

Angel climbed out and forced himself to stop and stretch, taking a deep breath and then exhaling loudly. His nerves were jangling. It was a hot night and the air felt charged, prickling his face. There was a distant rumble of thunder. He had driven much too fast; he knew that. He grabbed his jacket from the back seat and locked the car remotely as he went into the house. Morton came out of the study into the hall. He was clad in black – black chinos and a black long-sleeved shirt with three buttons at the wrist. He said nothing, just looked.

"As you can see I'm back unexpectedly," Angel snapped, "and we need to have a talk. Where's Julia?"

"I think she's gone to bed, Mr Angel. Can it wait until morning?"

"Get her up," was the reply, and Angel stalked into the study, where Morton could hear the sound of clinking bottles as he made himself a drink. The evening's entertainment had apparently gone badly: perhaps the blonde hadn't responded to his advances; maybe they'd had a row. Whatever it was, Morton knew that when Rupert Angel was in this mood you didn't argue – you simply did what you were asked. He picked up the phone and dialled Mrs Morris' internal extension. There was a long pause before she finally came on the line.

"He wants you down here," Morton said.

"What, *now?*" she said incredulously. "But it's *half past twelve*. Perhaps the little bitch turned him down."

"I did wonder," Morton said, and lowered his voice. "He's definitely not in a good mood. You might want to get down here and see what he wants. He's in the study."

"All right," she said in an exasperated tone. "Give me ten minutes."

They sat in the study. Two floral sofas faced each other, and the walls were lined with books. French windows faced the rear garden, concealed now by curtains. Mrs Morris had appeared with Lawrence in tow as usual. She was wearing a rose-embroidered ivory dressing gown and ivory silk slippers, with silk pyjamas that were exposed beneath the gown when she moved. Lawrence was dressed in jeans and a white shirt despite the hour.

Angel was standing at the desk, talking on the phone. He was still wearing his dark suit trousers and cream shirt, but he had hung his jacket over the back of the desk chair and undone his bow tie and collar button.

"You are quite certain that you have not used any credit cards of any kind?" Angel was saying into the phone. There was a pause as the other party responded.

"And no other official documents? No communications whatsoever?"

There was another pause and then came Angel's answer, a little more conciliatory now.

"Yes, I understand you're upset and I know it's very late, Alfred. I'm sorry to cross-examine you but you must understand that this is very important. The police are hot on our trail and if they discover you then this entire project is going to go to hell. You must *not* attempt to make any phone calls or contact anyone; is that quite clear? All right, put Robbie on again."

Morton and Mrs Morris caught each other's eyes for a moment but said nothing. She switched her gaze back to Angel but Morton continued to observe her surreptitiously. Normally immaculate, a wisp of hair had now escaped her perfect coiffure, and the dressing gown exposed the ageing skin at her throat. During the day she would be adorned with subtle hints of gold, but now she looked oddly denuded, like a dog without a collar. Lawrence sat beside her but didn't catch Morton's eye. He wasn't looking at anyone – he appeared frozen into a catatonic state.

Angel was still talking, this time to one of the two men that he had sent up to baby-sit Alfred Smith.

"Robbie? I want you to make sure that he does *not* leave the house and cannot get access to the phone. You do the shopping, even if he wants tobacco or booze. I don't want him idly chatting with anyone and I don't want anyone that might recognize him. We're at a sensitive stage and we have to have more time."

He spoke some more and then finally put down the phone, sitting on the edge of the sofa but looking too angry to settle comfortably into it. Mrs Morris handed him his drink.

"Well at least Alfred appears to have made no contact with the outside world," he conceded grudgingly. "I was worried because Lucy revealed that the police are now actively seeking him."

"Do they have any leads?" Mrs Morris asked quickly.

"Not so far, but if Bentley helps them he may turn something up we haven't thought of. Which brings me to the subject of this discussion: I thought we agreed that he was to be severely warned off?"

There was a note of sarcasm in his voice that irritated Mrs Morris.

"He *has* been warned off," she said coldly. "Morton and his crew did it. I believe he was suitably frightened, wasn't he Edward?"

"He was scared to death," Morton said. "We got him in the dark outside his house and smacked him around a bit. I told him we'd be back to chop his hand off if he kept on looking for Alfred Smith."

"His *painting* hand," Mrs Morris said, smug because it had been her idea.

"And he definitely believed you?" Angel asked silkily.

"No question," Morton said. "I had a chopper and I cut him a little with it. He swore blind he was going to forget all about Smith."

"Then perhaps you'd like to explain why he left not one but *two* messages today for Lucy Wrackham," Angel said, "saying that he is *still* searching for Alfred, and wanting to give her the low-down about being attacked."

There was an awkward silence. Morton sat very still, genuinely surprised. Mrs Morris's self-satisfied look had sagged. Lawrence sat frozen except for his leg, which had started going up and down as if operating a sewing machine.

His mother suddenly became aware of the jiggling leg.

"Keep *still*, Lawrence," she snapped. Her son stood up as if someone had taken a shot at him and went and stood by the bookcase.

"I don't know what he's always doing here anyway," Angel said testily, breaking the unvoiced protocol that Lawrence's uninvited presence was never remarked upon.

Mrs Morris looked shocked.

Lawrence then did an extraordinary thing. He came over and stood by them, his lower lip quivering slightly.

"This whole thing is falling apart," he said in a brittle voice. "We've lost control and we should stop. We should stop the whole thing right now."

There was a deathly silence after he had proffered his opinion. Morton for once looked down at his shoes, wondering if Lawrence was actually right. Things *were* getting out of order and Morton had not maintained an unblemished record by taking stupid risks.

"Lawrence?" his mother said, and there was a note of incredulous surprise in it – no, it was *pride*, Morton suddenly realised. She was proud that her son had for once spoken up.

But Rupert Angel had broken the protocol and there was no going back.

"Get out!" he ordered Lawrence. "No-one is interested in what you think, least of all me."

Lawrence looked defiant for a moment, but then all the heat went out of him. He unclenched his fists, which were balled up by his sides, and lowered his eyes. He slunk across the room and closed the door quietly behind him. Morton continued to look at the floor, wondering if Mrs Morris would lose her temper with Angel.

"We are *not* stopping," Angel said quietly, pronouncing his words very succinctly. "We are not stopping because we *can't* stop. We are almost clear on the debt and if we complete the deal on the Botticelli we'll have more than enough cash to stop the whole enterprise, or at least put it on hold. But right now we can't stop, otherwise you'll recall Edward's words – Mr Harold will break our limbs."

Morton looked up and caught his eye and nodded.

"And worse," he said simply.

Angel looked at Mrs Morris, and she looked back at him. Then she nodded slowly.

"Very well then," Angel said, having re-established his authority over the group. "As far as I am aware, our artist friend has not yet spilled the beans to Lucy. I think the time has come for us to stop messing about with Mr Bentley. If we start mutilating the man then it'll be a police matter and he'll talk his head off. I think we need a more permanent solution to the problem."

Mrs Morris was still nodding slowly.

"We'll have to make it look like an accident," she said.

"We haven't got time for that," Morton said. "It'll have to be in the morning or we might as well not bother if he speaks to the Wrackham woman first."

Mrs Morris was looking into space with a little smile beginning on her lips.

"I wonder if you could feign a suicide, Edward?" she said thoughtfully. "The ex-con, unable to integrate back into normal society. It's hard to imagine the police looking too hard for killers if they have a viable suicide and the victim is an old lag."

Morton thought about this, visualising the interior of the studio in his mind's eye.

"It's short notice," he said, "but we could have a go. "We've got a tow rope and Bentley's studio has high beams; I saw them when I was there the other night. We could string him up."

"String him up and watch him kick," Mrs Morris said sweetly. "What about the note, though? He should leave a note."

Morton thought for a moment.

"He's got a computer," he said after a bit. "I could type it on that. If I wear gloves, only his prints will be on the keys."

Rupert Angel got up and walked over to the French windows, where he stood with hands clasped behind his back and looked out. The storm had broken and huge raindrops were striking the glass panes. He was calmer now, his anger receding.

"Don't leave traces," he said without looking back at them.

THIRTY-NINE

Violence against women is an appalling human rights violation. But it is not inevitable. We can put a stop to this.
NICOLE KIDMAN

Sandy was due at the studio on Saturday morning, but she arrived late and in a furious temper. It was raining heavily outside and the noise of it thundered on the roof. Will had already set out his palette with gobbets of bright pigment, and mounted a fresh canvas on the easel. He was scumbling a pale purple wash roughly across the canvas with a cloth as she arrived, lowering the white glare.

"Hello," he said, "what happened to you then?"

She stalked across the room and flung down her bag and umbrella on the chair. Then he noticed the bruise on her cheek and put down the cloth.

"Oh. What *did* happen to you?"

"My bleedin' boyfriend socked me one," she spat. "Turned out one of them newspapers got a picture of us all outside the studio when you got out of the nick, and he only bleedin' saw it in the paper, didn't he?"

"Sit down," Will said, guiding her rapidly into a dining chair next to the table. "I'll make you some coffee and you can tell me about it."

But she was up again in a moment.

"I can't sit down, I'm that mad," she said.

She paced up and down, her high heels clicking on the bare floorboards of the studio. Then she followed him into the kitchen and went through into the bathroom, where she stood and inspected the growing bruise in the mirror.

"Bastard," he could hear her muttering under her breath.

"So what does he object to then?" Will said when she came back into the kitchen. "The fact that I'm an ex-con, I suppose?"

"Oh no, not that," she said. "The fact that I'm modelling for you."

Will looked blank.

"Taking me clothes off," she said. "That's what he doesn't like. He went into a rage about it. Said no fucking woman of his was going to strip off for some poofter artist, if you'll excuse my language."

"I've a good mind to go and punch *his* head," Will said.

"No, you wouldn't want to do that, he's an evil sod and he'd make mincemeat of you and enjoy doing it."

"So he didn't know you've been modelling then?"

She shook her head, taking the cup of steaming coffee from him.

"I didn't dare tell him because I knew he'd lose his rag, but I never thought he'd actually bleedin' hit me."

"So what happens now then?"

"I'm moving back in with me mum for a bit," she said, "and I told him he can sod off because it's all over."

"Good for you. So I don't suppose you feel like being painted today, then?"

"It depends," Sandy said. "I *want* you to paint me because I don't want him to have his way, but I don't suppose you can paint me with this bleedin' shiner."

Will walked over to her and put his hands on her shoulders, looking at her face intently.

"On the contrary," he said. "It could be rather interesting. Did you bring a red dress as I mentioned?"

"In my bag," she said. "And it's very slinky, just what the doctor ordered. Dark red with spaghetti straps and a bit of cleavage." A ghost of a smile crossed her face. "Looks like it's been sprayed on when I'm wearing it."

"Okay then," he said with a nod. "Finish your coffee and go and get into it. I'll paint you standing by the window looking back into the room, perhaps with your hand up as if warding off a blow. The bruise on your eye will show up nicely if I get the light right, and we'll put the painting in the window downstairs in case your boyfriend walks by. I'll write the title on a white card. We'll call it `Jealousy'."

"He'll break the glass!" she said, giggling.

"No he won't. It got broken by some yobs once so I had toughened glass put in. He'd have a job breaking it; he'll just have to look at it."

He was still holding her shoulders and looking at her appraisingly.

"I think I might make you look even more sexy than usual."

She leaned forward and kissed him on the mouth. Her lips were full and wet and tasted slightly of mint.

"You're lovely, you are," she said.

He painted like a man possessed, giving her minimal intervals to move about between poses, cradling the palette on his arm and holding five or six brushes in his left hand, using them like weapons to develop the picture. He had planned to paint Sandy languidly stretched out on the chaise-longue beside the window, but due to the change in circumstances he had instead reoriented the canvas vertically and was painting her full size. It was a better composition to suit the conditions, because the light from the window was dulled by the rain. He started with a brief charcoal outline but almost immediately switched to paint, blocking in the colours of the dress with two large brushes, one loaded with alizarin crimson moved towards violet with ultramarine, and the other loaded with almost pure cadmium red for the highlights. When he had roughed in the dress he started immediately on her skin, adding pigment to her arms and the outline of her head, then switching to smaller flat brushes and blocking in the main angles of her face. Traces of red tried to leak into the flesh tones, and he controlled them as best as he could. He took a clean brush and filled in her long legs below the dress, emphasizing the curve of her hips and the swell of her breasts and the vulnerability of her naked feet. After a pause he switched to finer brushes and started to develop the face, working the bruise into her slowly emerging features with perfect colour integration, echoing its violet and green colours into the shadows of her hair and the dips of her collarbones and puffing up her cheek beneath the blemish. He spent a considerable amount of time on the fingers of her hand, held up to ward off the unseen aggressor, painting them much larger as her hand was outstretched towards the viewer. As he worked he painted in the shadow of an unseen figure falling across her.

When it was lunchtime he put his wet brushes in an empty waiting jug, put down the palette and slowly returned to earth.

"All right," he said. "It needs to dry off for a day or so now, then I'll tighten it up some more. It'll work."

He stood back to look at the picture from a distance, as he did so often during the act of painting. She relaxed and stretched her arms and came and stood beside him, looking at herself on the wet canvas.

"Blimey," she said, staring at the picture. She looked at him. He had a dab of crimson paint on the side of his nose.

"Not that I'm an expert," she said, "but that's one of the best you've ever done."

"It's because I'm angry with your ex," he said. "I paint better when I'm worked up."

She went and changed back into her ordinary clothes.

"I need to nip out to the shops," she said when she returned. "Hope I'm not going to get soaked. Do you want me back this afternoon?"

He said he did, if she wasn't feeling too sore.

"I'll have to start another canvas while this one dries for a day or so, but that's all right. I can stretch up another while you're out to lunch – pity I didn't get Ian to come in or he could have done it. Come back at two o'clock and I'll be ready to start again."

She offered to buy him a sandwich, and Will suddenly realised that he was ravenous.

"That would be wonderful. Though I might have some toast anyway to keep body and soul together."

"It's not fair that you men can eat what you like and not put a pound on," she said, grabbing her bag and umbrella and heading for the door. "By the way, what's happened about that mate of yours that you were looking for? The old geezer. Have you given up?"

He shook his head.

"I haven't given up," he said. "But I've run out of ideas where to look. I want to speak to Lucy Wrackham again – the blonde girl, remember? – but I can't get hold of her. I keep leaving messages but I never get a reply."

"Giving you the cold shoulder, is she?"

"I don't *think* so," he said pensively. "Well, maybe. We did end up yelling at each other the last time we were together."

Sandy opened the door to the stairs and then leaned back.

"Give her another ring. The worst that can happen is she tells you to get stuffed."

He pursed his mouth and nodded. Sandy gave him a little wave and disappeared, her heels staccato on the stairs.

FORTY

Truth will come to light; murder cannot be hid long;
WILLIAM SHAKESPEARE, The Merchant of Venice

Will stepped over to the window and watched her walk down the street, remembering the kiss. Then he grinned and went back to his brushes and started cleaning off the oil paint. The paint was still wet but by tomorrow it would have started to dry on the brushes and they would be ruined if he didn't clean them now. He would leave the palette to one side to remind him of the colour mixes, but he was going to start again with clean brushes. He heard more footsteps on the stairs, but it wasn't Sandy – he would know the click of those heels anywhere.

The door crashed open and four large men piled into the studio, wet from the rain. For a moment he stood looking at them in comical surprise, but then he was reminded of two nights ago, when he had returned from Hastings on the Bonnie and had been set upon in the darkness. He knew instinctively that these the same people. One of his attackers had been bearded, and one of *these* men had a blond beard. Next to him was a thickset man, and beside him an older man with a battered face like a boxer. The fourth one was dark-skinned and big, with dreadlocks and a striped woollen hat. Adrenaline flooded into Will's body like a physical blow and at once he was twisting away towards the back of the studio. They crossed the floor after him in great bounds, determined not to let him get away.

He yelled for help too late, then they were upon him and the bearded man was holding an open razor to his throat, stilling his resistance. When he swallowed he felt the cold touch of the blade.

"Any more yelling and I'll cut you," the bearded man said, and then Will knew without doubt that this was the man with the axe. He started to twist and struggle but was firmly held by several pairs of heavy hands. He subsided as the razor blade remained unwaveringly at his throat. His imagination careened off in wild directions: what if he leaped backwards through the window – would he survive the fall to the pavement? What if the razor slashed open his throat and sent crimson arcing across the studio?

They taped his mouth with duct tape, joined his hands behind his back and fastened his legs together. In only a minute he was lying on the floor unable to get up.

The bearded man was clearly the leader.

"We need to be quick," he said to the others. "Before the girl comes back. She already kept us waiting too long."

He opened a black holdall and took out a rope. Will was terrified and yet grateful that the man had not brought out the axe. He remembered the axe as if its image had been etched onto his eyeballs with acid. As he was bound he couldn't at first see what they intended, but then he saw the end of the rope, which had been fashioned into a noose. At the sight of it he began to buck and kick violently, drumming his heels on the floor.

"Shut him up," the leader said. "But don't mark him."

The thickset man and the boxer sat on him to hold him still, winding him with their weight. He tried to scream but was unable to make a sound. He continued to struggle but couldn't make any headway. He had a terrible sense of helplessness and impending doom, like a man drowning. He watched as the leader tossed the rope over the high beam in the middle of the studio's angled roof. He made it first time, then fetched a dining room chair and placed it under the noose.

"Bring him over," he said. "We'll do the note afterwards. "All three of you hold him very tight; he'll try to get away."

He was completely matter of fact about the whole process, which in a way was most terrifying of all. The two men sitting on Will took their weight off him and were joined by the man in dreadlocks.

"Get a move on!" the leader said.

The three men carried Will's twisting body over to the chair and got him upright. He was struggling so much that the leader had to hold him as well, but the four of them were more than a match for Will. They got their victim upright on the chair and slipped the noose over his neck. The leader pulled the rope to take up the slack and Will could feel it tighten uncomfortably. He stopped struggling, realising that he was in danger of falling off the chair and hanging himself before they did it for him. The leader was looking for somewhere to secure the rope. Then he found it – a metal stanchion at the end of the beam crossed in a diagonal to a large metal plate on the wall. It was part of the roof support and Will knew that it was easily strong enough to bear his weight. The leader tied the rope to the stanchion and tugged it to make sure it was secure. When he did that the noose yanked at Will's throat and made him gag.

There was a pause as the four men looked at their victim. Will stood on the chair and glared back at them grimly and defiantly. He supposed that his life should be flashing before him but it wasn't. Instead his mind felt numb, like an erased blackboard. He wondered if there were life after death. He wondered if there was a God and he felt tears prick his eyes at a sudden discordant memory of himself as a child in church, holding his mother's hand. His senses were very acute. He could hear each creak of the men's shoes on the floorboards and feel each fibre of the rope tickling his skin, each tiny tug of the tape on the hairs of his ankles. He could smell his own sweat and the cheap cologne of the boxer, and taste blood in his mouth where he had bitten his lip in the struggle.

The leader walked across to him and the others stood back, unwilling to perform the actual execution. The man took the back of Will's supporting chair in his hands, but before he could pull it away there was the sound of the door opening downstairs. All four men froze. Will couldn't do anything other than make gagged sounds and he couldn't struggle because he would fall off the chair.

"The girl's coming back," the leader said in a low voice. "We'll have to cut her up so they think he did her in and then topped himself."

He handed the razor to the boxer.

"Do her as she comes in."

The boxer took the weapon and ran across the studio floor, his brown trainers making hardly any sound.

There were footsteps on the stairs. Will started to shake his head violently from side to side.

The footsteps stopped and the boxer was in position, concealed to one side of the door, razor at the ready. There was a hesitant knock, three raps and then silence.

The bearded man looked across the room at the boxer. He pointed at the door wordlessly and made cutting motions. The boxer gestured with his hands and raised his blade ready to strike.

The door opened and Lewis stood in its frame.

FORTY-ONE

My business is hurting people.
SUGAR RAY ROBINSON

Lewis had a bag in one hand, and his hair and jacket were wet. There was a frozen tableau as Lewis was confronted with the sight of Will standing on the chair with a rope around his neck. Then the unseen man with the razor catapulted around the door and slashed at Lewis.

But Lewis was no longer there. Despite his enormous size he swayed back out of harm's way. The boxer was still looking surprised that it wasn't the girl when Lewis's steely fingers clamped over his wrist and slammed it against the door jamb. The razor clattered to the floor. Then Lewis yanked the man towards him and at the last instant hit him in the face with a massive fist. The man staggered back with blood erupting from a crushed nose.

The other three men left Will and rushed across the room, while Lewis smoothly extracted a baseball bat from his bag. He swung the bat at the head of the boxer, knocking the man's defending fist sideways and connecting with his jaw in an audible crunch of breaking bone. The man slalomed backwards with the force of the blow, falling at the feet of his three associates and stopping them in their tracks. He didn't get up.

Lewis stepped into the room and gained space. He whirled the bat lazily round his head in an arc. It made a hissing sound. The three remaining men looked at him and appraised the situation, professional fighters acknowledging a serious adversary, but certain they would defeat him.

Lewis moved to one side, exposing the door as a means for them to escape.

"You can go," he said emotionlessly, and two of the men started to move towards the door.

"No," the leader said. "We leave Vinnie here and they'll find us. We need to finish it and complete the job."

The thickset man and the dreadlocked one stopped and eyed Lewis warily. Lewis looked right back at them, veteran of a hundred prison fights with men more vicious than these.

He smiled encouragingly at the man in dreads.

"Come on then my son," he said. "Let's see if your mum recognises you with *no fucking teeth.*" He swung the bat and charged forward, but at the last moment he changed direction and lashed out a boot sideways, connecting with the thickset man's kneecap. The thickset man lost his footing and started to fall, reaching his hand out for balance. Lewis grabbed his outstretched hand and smashed down on the man's elbow with the bat. The broken arm flapped and the thickset man started to scream. The man with dreadlocks came back in close and Lewis whirled the bat at arm's length, missing the man's head but clipping his nose so that it exploded in a crimson burst. Meanwhile the bearded leader was trying to make his way back to the chair on which Will stood precariously balanced. Lewis moved to block him.

The bearded man picked up a heavy stool and hurled it at Lewis, catching him by surprise on the shoulder and making him grunt and stagger back for a moment. Then he got his hands on Will's chair and tried to shift it, but Will's weight was still on it and the chair resisted. Before the leader could get his strength into it, Lewis arrived and he had to jump out of the way. Immediately the leader and the dreadlocks man made a rush at Lewis and he was badly cut on the arm with an open razor before he could swing the bat and force them back out of range. The bearded man brought out a knife and dreadlocks picked up his stool to ward off the baseball bat. They advanced on Lewis in a pincer movement. Dreadlocks seemed to be having trouble seeing, as blood streamed down his face and over his clothes. Lewis had a cut lip which had occurred sometime during the impact with the thrown stool, giving him a ghoulish appearance. The cloth of his jacket was flapping on his left arm and a red stain was growing from the cut he had sustained, but he was still able to use his other arm. He gripped the bat firmly and watched his attackers, weakening but not yet out of action. The fight was no longer going well for him but he wasn't about to surrender.

As the two men circled him and looked for an advantage, the studio door unexpectedly swung open across the room and Lucy Wrackham stood there open mouthed beside Hugh Davies. No-one had heard them come up the stairs in the fury of the fight. The bearded man again reached Will's chair and this time aimed a kick at it, so that it rocked and Will scrabbled desperately for purchase. Now he found himself balancing with his feet on the tilted chair back, one foot in front and one behind, pinning the back and rocking to keep it upright, using the noose around his neck to steady himself, desperately trying to keep from losing his balance.

Survival of a hanging is unlikely. The probability of avoiding serious damage is very low after even a few seconds on the end of a rope. The neck conducts blood to the brain, air to the lungs and bears the all-important spinal column, whose neural pathways control every critical organ in the body. Disconnect any of these vital pathways and the organ in question simply switches off. If the first drop doesn't break your neck, the impact of a full adult body weight is sufficient to stretch the vertebrae in the neck up to two inches, which does not do a great deal of good to the spinal column, the airway, or the passage of blood. Loss of consciousness typically occurs within

20 seconds. Damage to the airway usually requires an emergency tracheotomy with whatever comes to hand, such as a stab in the windpipe with a pen. Will didn't know any of this, but he did know that falling off that chair was going to be a very bad thing, so while the battle raged around him, he concentrated ferociously on one thing only – remaining on the tilted chair.

Davies surged forward, holding up his badge and yelling "Police officer, put down your weapons!"

Lewis was swaying a little, getting light-headed from loss of blood. The bearded man lunged forward and stabbed him in the gut with his knife; a swift cut, in and straight out. Lewis looked down at the wound almost comically. Lucy ran forward but the man with the stool swung it heavily, catching her on the shoulder and knocking her to the ground. Then Davies was upon the leader and they were fighting furiously, tumbling back and forth among the furniture. The knife went flying, but then dreadlocks swung the stool at Davies and caught him on the shoulders and the back of the head. The policeman fell to his knees with a look of surprise on his face.

The bearded man – Morton – looked around, shook his head grimly and then picked up the man with the broken arm and hefted him over his shoulder.

"Out of here right now," he said to dreadlocks. "Bring Vinnie."

The other man needed no prompting. He dropped the stool as if it had suddenly become hot and sped across the room, picking up the unconscious man with the broken jaw and the bloody face. Then the two of them made their way crab-like through the door and could be heard stumbling down the stairs.

Lucy gathered herself up and ran forward to Will, who was still scrabbling for purchase as the chair tilted and rocked beneath his feet. She snatched up a discarded razor from the floor and sawed wildly at the rope, just as Will finally lost his balance and the chair went from under him. But instead of being brought up short on the end of the rope, his weight parted the slashed fibres and he tumbled down onto her, knocking her flat on her back. He landed on top of her and she grunted with pain, the air expelled forcefully from her lungs. She tore at the rope around his neck, loosening its deathly grip.

"I'm *so* sorry," she was whispering repeatedly, shaking her head. Her blonde hair fanned out around her head on the floor as she tried to shift him. He rolled sideways off her and she sat up. She found the razor again and cut the tape binding his hands and feet. Will sat up slowly and peeled the tape off his mouth. Then they just looked at each other for a moment, until he smiled slowly and reached forward and put his arms around her. For a few seconds they hugged, rocking slowly, and then they parted and inspected each other.

"Good of you to pop round," he said.

For a moment she thought he was going to kiss her, but then he caught sight of Lewis over her shoulder and shook his head.

"We need to help Lewis," he said, and got to his feet.

Davies had picked himself up too and was rubbing his head. He was looking around the room in confusion and his eyes stopped at the enormous bulk of Lewis with uncertainty. Lewis had sunk to his knees, red stains spreading on his arm and his abdomen.

"I'm with Mr Bentley," Lewis croaked, his face twisted now into a grimace of pain. "I walked in on that lot trying to do him in."

Will and Lucy appeared from behind Lewis and steadied him. He looked at them gratefully.

"Bloody good job you came when you did, I'm thinking," Davies said, reaching for his phone and pressing buttons. "I'll have you an ambulance in a jiffy."

He ran a professional eye over Lewis's injuries and his brow wrinkled. There were tears in Lewis's eyes at the pain from the knife wound in his gut.

"Hang on now, old son," Davies said kindly. "You can't be a hero and then go and snuff it."

He began to speak urgently into his mobile.

FORTY-TWO

Tea is drunk to forget the din of the world.
T'IEN YIHENG

Ambulances and police cars arrived after six minutes in a cacophony of sirens. Sandy returned from her lunch break as they were arriving and took in the bloody scene in amazement. Almost immediately she came across Lewis, who was the hero of the hour, and Will told her who he was and what he had done. Lewis was sitting on the floor and gave a crooked smile but was obviously in great pain. Will reminded Sandy that he had described his friend to her on the first day they had met – when they went for a walk in the college cloisters and she had somehow extracted his entire life story from him. When she realised how brave Lewis had been she took him firmly under her wing and would accept no argument. The paramedics set up a mobile infusion and he was swiftly lifted onto a stretcher. They put a pressure bandage around his arm over the razor slash. His shirt was cut open at the front and a second pressure bandage covered the wound in his gut, though it was rapidly darkening as he haemorrhaged. Sandy insisted on accompanying Lewis in the ambulance to the hospital, saying that she wanted to do something useful.

DI Carter and a number of uniformed policemen arrived, interviewing Davies and Lucy and Will. One of them went in the ambulance with Lewis at Carter's order. It was clear to both Lucy and Davies that the bearded leader of the attack was the same man who had broken into the studio a few nights previously. They had recognized him immediately from the hours of CCTV tapes that they had poured over. Will also told them about the attack on him with the axe.

A team of boiler-suited forensic men arrived and were keen to usher everyone out so that they could gather fingerprints and DNA without the scene being further corrupted. Their work took them some time, and when the various officers had finally finished bagging up the evidence and interviewing, Davies accompanied them back to Parkside to muster their forces and assess the new developments.

Will had a painfully sore neck but apart from that he was all right. He declined to go to hospital but instead disappeared into his bedroom and lay down on his bed. The paramedics were frustrated by his intransigence but he ignored them, and Lucy said that she would stay and keep an eye on him.

It was odd for her when everyone had finally clumped down the stairs and she found herself alone in the studio, acutely aware of Will settling down in the other room. She followed the last of the policemen downstairs and bolted the front door behind them at the insistence of Carter. When she came upstairs again, the floor was filthy with all the feet that had tramped in and out from the rain. There were splotches of blood. She couldn't bear the mess so she picked up fallen stools and put them upside-down on the table. There were brushes scattered everywhere on the floor around the easel, so she gathered them up and stacked them in a jug. Some of them were covered in paint and she cleaned them before stacking them with the others, and wiped oil paint off the floor where the brushes had fallen at the start of the attack. She paused and looked at the astonishing picture of Sandy on the easel. Somehow he had perfectly created an expression of fear on the girl's face.

She located a mop and cleaned the floor, replaced the water and cleaned it again. After that she put down the stools and wiped the table, then scrubbed every surface, mainly as a therapy for herself. It took her an hour and a half, but when she was finished the studio was spotless and looked tidier than it had done in months. She washed the mop and bucket and put them away, then suddenly felt very weary and sat down at the table. The intense activity had displaced her shock, but now she felt tearful and exhausted. She stood up and went into the kitchen, where she found more mess and spent another half an hour cleaning. Then she took down a bottle of whisky from a glass-fronted cupboard and poured herself a generous measure, which she drank all at once. It made her feel better. She washed and dried the glass and found herself with nothing to do.

She looked in on Will but he had dozed off, as if his brain had decided to disconnect for a period of recovery. She leaned in close to inspect him, remembering the dire warnings of the paramedics, but he was breathing evenly and she kneeled down and stared at him for a minute or so. He looked a bit of a rogue even when sleeping. There was a mark on his neck where the rope had rubbed his skin. She liked the way he had dismissed his own experience but had been so worried about his friend Lewis. He shifted a little in his sleep when her face was only inches from his, so she stood up hurriedly and backed out of the bedroom, sensing the embarrassment if he should suddenly open his eyes. She felt a little woozy after the whisky on an empty stomach, so she made Camomile tea and sat down with it in the studio to try to read a magazine. The tea filled the air with its heady vapour and sent tendrils of steam curling upwards. She found herself thinking about the man asleep in the other room. He made her take herself a little less seriously. He was in complete contrast to the urbane Rupert, but Rupert was too smooth, and she had not forgiven him for deserting her after the opera with such an unlikely excuse.

She wondered how Davies was getting on with the investigation and tried to phone the policeman, but heard only a voicemail response and left no message. Her eyes felt heavy. After a while, she dozed off in the armchair.

FORTY-THREE

Was it a vision, or a waking dream?
Fled is that music:—do I wake or sleep?
JOHN KEATS, Ode to a Nightingale

Lucy awoke because someone was shaking her arm gently. She stretched sleepily and opened her eyes slowly to see Will, wide awake and kneeling beside her chair.

"Oh," she said, smiling feebly and squeezing her eyes tight shut for a moment to dispel her sleepiness. She looked at her watch and saw that it was mid-afternoon. "Sorry, I'm supposed to be keeping an eye on you but I must have fallen asleep."

She suddenly realised that she was slumped indecorously in the chair, so she sat up and pulled down her dress, then groaned and rubbed her aching bruises.

"It's okay," Will said. "the fairies seem to have been while you slept and scrubbed the whole place spotless. It looks marvellous! And anyway, I fell asleep myself. I only meant to lie down and clear my head."

"Are you feeling better? It's not every day you almost get hanged."

"I'm all right," he said, pulling up a chair and sitting down. "I want to thank you for staying. I was a bit disoriented when I woke up, but I stumbled in here and found you. It was a lovely surprise."

"It was the least I could do," she said. "How's the neck?"

"A bit tender but no more than that."

"It looks sore."

He shrugged and she looked at him, not quite knowing what to say next.

"Are we friends?" she asked at last. "Last time we were together we were yelling at each other."

He felt rueful because he had seen her more recently than that, kissing Rupert Angel outside her house, but he decided not to mention it.

"Let's forget about Hastings," he answered. "I'd had a good time so I was pretty disappointed when you had to rush off."

"We *both* had a good time. I'm very sorry about rushing off. I'm obsessive about being on time for things."

"It's ancient history now, and anyway I've got something more pressing on my mind. Are you *hungry*? I haven't much in the house to eat but Sandy apparently bought me a club sandwich, so if the coppers didn't take it away as evidence then we could have half each."

"Is there any coffee to go with it?" she said. "I need something to wake me up."

He didn't answer, and when she looked at him she found he was staring intently at her, until eventually she pulled a face at him and laughed with embarrassment.

"*What?*"

"I just remembered you owe me a sketch of you," he said. "You promised faithfully."

"You can't possibly want to draw me *now*," she protested weakly. "I look a complete mess."

"You don't, you look perfectly fine and I need something to get these nightmares out of my head. What do you say?"

"Do I get coffee?"

He got up in one swift movement.

"You do, but only if you promise not to move."

He came back with two mugs, the sandwich and a cafetière of pungent coffee.

"Do you want anything in it?" he said. "Only I've got some scotch. It's a bit early in the day, but given that I've nearly been hanged and you've been whacked with a stool I think that qualifies as special circumstances."

"I found it earlier and had a bit," she admitted," but what the hell."

They shared the sandwich and sipped coffee and whisky for a while in companionable silence. Will finished his first, put down his empty mug and fetched a sketch pad and a tin box covered in pink flamingos that turned out to be full of charcoal.

"I can't believe you want to draw me when I've only just woken up," she said protestingly, tossing her head and attempting to smooth down her hair.

"Well I do, but you must stop tidying yourself up. Spontaneous pictures are the best, so just sit and look in this direction and drink your coffee."

So she acquiesced and sat with the mug of coffee cradled on her front, slumped anyhow in the chair, the whisky relaxing her. The rain still came down outside, drumming on the roof, tapping on the window pane and gurgling in the gutters, but the studio was warm and cosy. She looked at Will over the top of the coffee mug. He stared at her for a full minute before opening the flamingo tin, then took out a stick of charcoal and started to make bold strokes on the pad, looking at her every few seconds. She couldn't see the drawing as it developed because he kept the pad almost upright to avoid perspective distortion. He drew her for half an hour and she drank the rest of her coffee but still held the empty mug in order not to change the picture.

Then he stopped and looked at the picture thoughtfully.

"Okay, you can relax."

She stretched and then craned her neck.

"Come on then," she said curiously, "let me see!"

He held the drawing up so that she could see it. She was a tangle of limbs on the chair, her dress riding up a little to expose her legs, her fingers knitted around the mug. Her hair framed her face and was tucked behind an elfin ear to one side. She was looking out of the picture with a smile just turning up the corners of her mouth and a little frown crinkling her forehead slightly. She looked quizzical. It captured her exactly and she felt suddenly moved.

"You've made me look beautiful," she said with a slight catch in her voice.

"Well, that's the benefit of art over photography," he said with a grin. "No matter how ugly the model, you can tidy it up and–"

She threw a cushion at him, then got out of the chair and stretched her legs. She picked up the picture and looked at it.

"You really like it?" he asked.

"Of course I do," she said. "I love it."

"Then you must have it," he said. "But give it back to me for a bit first. It's a standard size so I've probably got something to frame it in."

It took him fifteen minutes but in that time he had the drawing framed in a standard pre-cut mount and fixed into a frame, complete with glass. The air was filled with the petroleum odour of fixer. Will put the picture on a spare easel and she stood back and admired it.

"It's lovely," she said and squeezed his hand spontaneously. "Thank you very, very much."

"Will you sit for another?"

She pretended to consider for a moment.

"All right then," she said. "I suppose it's not fair for you to draw me and then not even keep the drawing. But let's go out after that and I'll buy you some dinner to say a proper thank you for this. Sandy's sandwich was a good start but I could do with something more substantial."

For the second pose she took a magazine from the corner bookcase and sat back in her chair, crossing her legs over the arm. At his request she kicked off her shoes and pulled her hair back from her face. Then she leafed through the magazine while he drew her.

She loved the second drawing too – her face was in three-quarters profile with the magazine spread open before her, but she was looking up into the middle distance as if in a daydream. The magazine seemed to have caught the light from some invisible source and reflected it into her face.

"You're very good," she said. She swung her legs down onto the floor and he noticed that even her legs were beautiful. The magazine slipped off her knees and she picked it up and handed it to him.

"There we are," she said, reading out the tagline beneath the title in an affected tone. "You too can be a Renaissance Artist."

He put it back on the bookshelf but then retrieved it and looked at it thoughtfully. He had a sudden picture in his head of the woman in the Hastings newsagents, telling him that Alfred had subscribed to a magazine.

"I just had a sudden thought," he said. "Alfred used to read this, but it's a bit specialist so you can only get it on subscription. It's a kind of techie journal for professional artists."

She padded over in her bare feet, took the magazine from him and read the cover again.

"Do you think he still subscribes to it?"

"He may do."

"So," she said, reading his mind. "If we could get the subscription list we *might* find Alfred's name and address on it."

"We might," Will said. "*If* he still takes it and *if* he's updated his address so that we don't end up in dear old Hastings. Lots of ifs but it's worth a try."

"At least it's a lead," she said. "And we're short on leads right now, unless Hugh Davies comes up trumps."

"I vote we follow it up, then. I've had about enough of these people, and they might be successful next time. We don't know that today was the last of it."

Lucy leafed through the magazine to find the Contents.

"There's the address of the publisher here," she said. "They're in Bedford and it says they're open until six on Saturdays. Where *is* Bedford? I know it's up here somewhere but I can't think where."

"About an hour to the west," Will said. "Which is lucky because it could have been at the other end of the country."

"Let's go there," Lucy said impulsively, looking at him over the open magazine. "They're not going to tell us anything over the phone."

"A woman after my own heart," he nodded in agreement. "But do you have your car here? Because otherwise we'll have to go on my motorbike and get a little damp."

FORTY-FOUR

It is a capital mistake to theorize before one has data.
SIR ARTHUR CONAN DOYLE

Even with Lucy driving as fast as she dared it took them over an hour, for they were not helped by the rain, which caused lorries to throw up curtains of blinding spray. They arrived at five to six. The magazine publisher was located in a dingy road in the back of an industrial area. They parked under trees in a little car park just up the road and hurried down to the unprepossessing office building, sharing a white umbrella of Lucy's, keeping very close to avoid the rain and trying not to splash in the puddles. Will was acutely aware of her proximity, and she was aware of his, but neither said anything. At some point she had managed to apply perfume and she smelled delicious. The whole world seemed to be filled with water; disappearing down drain holes, bubbling out of drain pipes and falling in diagonals out of the sky like Rousseau's painting of a tiger in a jungle. A man was loading a bundle of plastic-wrapped newspapers into a white van as they arrived.

"Bloody horrible weather," he observed.

"Is there anybody still in?" Lucy asked him.

"Are you placing an advert? There's one bloke left in the office but he's a miserable sod. You'll have to come back on Monday I reckon."

"We'll try anyway," Lucy said firmly. They hadn't come all this way to be repelled at the last moment.

The paint around the double doors was chipped and a pane of glass had a crack in it that had been taped up. They went in and Lucy shook the umbrella out of the open doorway. They looked around but there was no-one at the reception desk. There were a few closed doors and an open stairway wound upwards out of sight. They ascended the stairs, calling out as they went. At the top was another set of double doors, this time made of wood. They knocked and went through them.

"Hello?" Will called. "Anyone about?"

The office to the left was locked and the lights were extinguished, but the one in front of them still glowed yellow so they knocked and went in. A man was standing in front of a computer, putting files into a briefcase. He was about fifty, very short and balding, with steel-rimmed glasses and a small pointed beard. He wore a cheap pale green shirt and an unmatching blue tie which had seen better years. He took a dark blue coat off a hook and put it on, buttoning it up halfway.

"You're not allowed in here," he said in an irritating voice. We're closed now, open again on Monday morning at eight sharp. You've missed the deadline for the Echo anyway."

Lucy stepped forward.

"We're not here to place an advert," she said, her voice soft and suddenly flirtatious. Will looked at her in surprise. "We're enquiring about a subscriber to your Renaissance Artist magazine. We've come all the way over from Cambridge. I'm terribly sorry we're so late but we got stuck in traffic because of this awful rain."

Unfortunately the little man seemed impervious to her charms.

"As I say, we're closed," he said primly. "Anyway, I've just shut down the computer." He pointed to the machine in front of him in case neither of them knew what a computer looked like.

"We really can't come back on Monday," Lucy said sweetly. "We're going back down to London."

"All we need is the address of our friend," Will added. "It's his birthday and we've lost his details. It won't take a minute and we'd be most grateful."

The man snickered.

"Oh *dear me*," he said, sounding smug. "Even if you come back every day next week I'll be unable to give out the names of subscribers. That's *confidential information*, that is." He enunciated his words very precisely as if speaking to morons.

Lucy reached into her handbag and took out her purse.

"What if I were to give you fifty pounds to thank you for your trouble," she said, abandoning charm and appealing instead to avarice.

The little man clicked his briefcase closed and folded his arms across his chest.

"You ought to know better than to offer me bribes, madam," he said pompously. "I must ask you to leave immediately or I'll call the police."

Will suddenly snorted with impatience and Lucy cast him a glare.

"You might as well forget it," Will said, shaking his head. "You're wasting your time with this silly little prick. I'll wait for you by the car." He went to the door, tugged it wide open and went out so that it slammed heavily behind him, rattling on its hinges.

Lucy watched him go incredulously, unable to believe her ears. With difficulty she kept control of her own temper.

"What about a hundred?" she said faintly, extracting a bunch of twenty-pound notes and flourishing them at the man.

"Out!" he shrilled. He picked up the phone and stood looking at her with a belligerence that denied his size.

"Very well then," Lucy said coldly. "I'll be back here on Monday morning and I'll bring the police with me. Then we'll see if you are prepared to give the information to *them* when they ask for it."

The man looked unabashed at this new threat.

"I thought you just wanted to send a *birthday card*," he said sarcastically. "Suddenly it's worth a hundred pounds, is it? I can't see the police being much interested in sending *birthday greetings*. Now if you don't follow your friend this moment then *I'll* call the police and report you for trespass."

He went to the door and opened it, leaving her no option but to walk out grimly. Will hadn't even waited for her so she opened her umbrella and stalked up the road, feeling maliciously glad that he must by now be completely soaked. Her heels tapped and splashed on the wet pavement. She wished furiously that Will wasn't so ridiculously hot-tempered. When she reached the car he wasn't even standing by it as promised and she raised her eyes heavenwards in exasperation. He really was the most *infuriating* person. She unlocked the car and got into it, shaking the umbrella out of the door and having a good mind to start up and drive away without him. She knew that he would soak her spotless seats when he finally deigned to turn up. She decided to give him five minutes and if he hadn't returned by then she would drive away and serve him right. She was too cross to put the radio on so she sat with her fingers drumming on the steering wheel and feeling as if the irritating little printer man's behaviour was somehow Will's fault.

As if on cue the irritating little man himself came out of the office building and locked it behind him while Lucy watched. He held a black umbrella over his head, which whipped about in the gusts of wind that were getting up. Suddenly his umbrella turned inside out and he dropped his briefcase, dancing around in the puddles until he had the umbrella back in its normal shape again.

"Silly little prick," she muttered under her breath, unconsciously echoing Will's description.

The man quickly looked up and down the road to see if he had been spotted, but didn't see her beneath the trees. He crossed the forecourt of the building, got into a small blue car and drove away. Lucy's phone rang in its hands-free holder, flashing "Will Bentley".

She punched the green button.

"Well thanks very much for *your* help," she said sarcastically. "What the bloody hell happened to you?"

"You were never going to win against that guy," Will's voice said. "Though I didn't think he'd be able to resist your charms when you first spoke to him. I would have lain down on the ground and woofed."

She snorted, still furious.

"Very funny. It might have worked if you hadn't insulted him and then slammed out. And where the hell are you? I've a good mind to drive off and leave you here."

She craned her neck behind her into the leafy depths at the back of the car park, but he was not visible.

"And me only recently set upon by murderers," Will said pitifully.

"*Will!*" Lucy said with exasperation. "I'm not in the mood. Are you coming or not? You must be getting soaked out there. I can't even *see* you."

"I can see *you*," he said. "I'm waving."

She looked all around and then stared. Will was standing in the open door of the publisher's. He fluttered his fingers at her and grinned. Her mouth fell open comically and she shut it with a snap so that her teeth clicked. As if in a daze she ended the call and got out of the car again. She put up her umbrella and walked back down the road. Will held the door open for her and she looked up and down the street.

"I hid in the toilet," he said when she got up to him. "He wasn't going to give us what we wanted in a million years."

"But this is completely *illegal*," she spluttered.

"Who cares?" Will said. "I went to the toilet and when I emerged, to my shock and surprise the man had locked the offices and left the premises. But actually we do need to get a move on in case there's a silent alarm. It usually takes them fifteen minutes, so I'm told by Bungalow George. It's amazing what useful things you learn in prison."

He disappeared up the stairs swiftly. She looked up and down the empty street again, gulped and then followed him. When she got to the top of the stairs and came back into the dingy office, he was already sitting down at the computer and starting it up. Fear of discovery was making her heart beat like a drum and she felt like a naughty schoolgirl, delighted with being back inside but horrified at how they came to be there.

They emerged from the offices after seventeen minutes. There were no sirens in the distance and the rain beat down relentlessly, keeping people off the streets. They had located the database of names and addresses and saved it in its entirety onto the flash memory stick that Lucy kept on her key ring. This had saved vital minutes waiting for the printer to crank itself into life. Will ushered Lucy out and then locked the doors on the inside by doing up the top and bottom bolts again and knitting the doors together so that the deadlock latch fitted snugly back into its socket. He joined her in the car five minutes later.

"I let myself out of the toilet window," he said. "The window's not latched but it's closed and they'll think they left it undone. Shall we go?"

She started the car and drove. By the time they were out of Bedford and joining the A421 she was laughing and talking more than she ever usually talked.

"You're absolutely crazy!" she said. "I can't believe what we just did! I never do *anything* illegal. God, I was so furious with you when you walked out like that."

"I thought you would be," Will said. "But that made it all the more believable. I'm glad you didn't drive off, though. I couldn't call you until he'd gone in case he heard me. The poor little chap would probably have puffed up so much with rage he would have exploded."

"You've turned me into a criminal," she said with a frown, but then spoiled the effect by starting to giggle.

He rolled his eyes at her.

It was approaching nine when they arrived back so they stopped at a little restaurant on the outskirts of Cambridge and ate.

"It'll still be there when we've eaten," Lucy said, waving the little memory stick in the air. "My God, I hope it's copied all right. Now I'm getting paranoid."

"Well if it didn't, the publisher's window is still unlatched so we can pop back."

As soon as they had ordered, their minds went back to the recent attack on Will and they started to revisit every detail of it. Lucy was in the middle of telling Will about the search of the CCTV tapes and how she had immediately recognized the man with the beard when she saw him in the studio, when they both remembered guiltily about Lewis. Will phoned Sandy to find out if she knew how he was, and discovered that she had waited for him to come out of theatre and had then talked with him when he woke up. She was able to reassure them both that he was all right. She had finally left him sleeping peacefully at the hospital.

"He's a very nice man actually," she said enthusiastically. "I talked to the nurses and they said he'd lost a load of blood but the knife didn't do anything the doctors couldn't fix up, so he was really lucky. They said he wouldn't have done so well but he's really fit. He's had loads of stitches, including them ones that dissolve inside you, and two pints of blood. And he might have to stay in for a few days but I've promised to go and see him. When he woke up he was a bit groggy to start with, but we ended up having a right old chat."

"Thank you for looking after him," Will said with relief. "We'll go and see him in the morning." He got directions from her before disconnecting

"I think Sandy's taken a bit of a shine to Lewis," he remarked with a grin. "It's probably all those muscles. She told me the other day she likes tough guys, and I teased her about it at the time."

RICHARD JOHN MITCHELL

FORTY-FIVE

You have witchcraft in your lips
WILLIAM SHAKESPEARE, Henry V

When they went up the stairs into the studio, it seemed oddly normal. Will looked troubled and went in slowly, remembering the battle. He didn't voice his fears but Lucy caught his expression and divined his thoughts.

"Come on," she said quietly and squeezed his arm.

The drawings of her were on the table and she picked up the one he had framed for her.

"You *are* a clever boy," she said, and he smiled, recognizing her misdirection.

"And you are very sweet," he said.

By unspoken consent they searched the house.

"That's all right then," Will said when they were sure they were alone. "Would you like a glass of wine?"

Lucy said she couldn't drink any more as she had to drive back to London that night, so he offered her the use of Lewis's bed.

"He never even got a chance to sleep in it, so it's pristine."

To his surprise, Lucy suppressed a yawn and accepted his invitation.

While Will opened a bottle of Rioja, Lucy went into the study next to the spare bedroom. Its walls were lined with books, giving it a comfortable, lived in feel. It had a thick sheepskin rug covering the polished floorboards. In a corner next to the window was an old leather armchair beside a low table with a reading lamp on it. She switched on the reading lamp and turned on the computer, then looked out of the window with her hands on her hips while it started up. The window looked out onto somebody else's back garden. Will wasn't much of an expert with computers but George had helped him choose this one, because George's design studio work entailed sitting in front of such a machine all day. When it had started up, Lucy sat down and plugged her memory stick into it and transferred the database onto the machine. Will came back with her glass of wine and she raised it in a solemn toast.

"To crime," she said, and they clinked glasses.

"And now," Lucy said, pressing a key to open the database, "let's see what we've got."

They started to scroll through the list of names in the database and one thing quickly became obvious – the list was enormous. This was a database for subscribers to *every* publication the little publishing house put out. They went to the "Smith" section and there were dozens of them, but not a single Alfred.

"We need to find the meaning of all these publication codes," Lucy said with a frown. "One of them must be for `Renaissance Artist' but I haven't a clue which. Wait a minute; let me see if you're in there. You subscribe to it, after all."

They found him immediately and looked at each other.

"Maybe Alfred's stopped subscribing to it," Will said gloomily.

"Maybe," Lucy said, fiddling with the filter settings. "I'm just selecting the list of people with the same publication code as you." The screen filled with a new list, much shorter this time. There was still no sign of Alfred Smith.

Will fetched the wine bottle from the table next to the armchair.

"We'll just have to get drunk instead," he said. "Anything under `Hastings'?"

"I'm looking. Half a minute."

He was restless. He went into the kitchen and found some olives in a jar. He put them in a dish and poured a little olive oil on them. His eyes fell upon his mobile phone and he went back to join Lucy, taking the phone and the olives. She was leaning towards the screen in concentration, scanning the text and scrolling slowly, her left hand pulling gently at her earlobe, toying with the earring in it. He noticed that her hair was combed now in long, straight folds, but he didn't remember when she had done it. At the restaurant, perhaps, when she had disappeared for a while and had come back smelling of Parisienne again.

"I've an idea," he said, holding up the phone. "When I visited Alfred's sister in Hastings she showed me a letter from him. I took a picture of it with this."

He fiddled with the phone until he found the pictures he had taken in Gillian Heath's house, but they were too small to examine so they had to upload them to the computer.

"Golly," Lucy said when they had the letter displayed on the screen. "Alfred Smith is starting to be real. This is the first proof that he actually exists, and it gives me a funny feeling."

Dear Gilly,

Over the past years I regretted us growing apart. I know you cherish Brian's memory but I think he had something to do with our estrangement, because since the funeral you and I had more contact than in the last ten years. You know I'm not a religious man, but I did enjoy the recital you invited me to. It's a nice old church and they were very welcoming.

You haven't seen me for a while but I haven't forgotten you. I have had to go away on one of my painting trips and I'm not sure how long I'll be. I am in our own British Isles for a change, and at the seaside as well, though very different from Hastings. I know you liked the Moroccan picture so I am doing you one of the sea. I'll be back in a few months

and hopefully I will have sorted myself out a bit so that I can pay off the last of the house. As I said to you, I am beginning to think about retirement. You may have to teach me some of your admirable gardening skills. I was impressed with your roses, though you lost me a bit with all that talk about acid soil.
    Best wishes to you,
    Love Alf xx
"So we know he's by the seaside," said Lucy. "That's useful information. What was the Moroccan picture?"

"A brilliant painting. His sister didn't even know he had been in prison but he painted it for her while he was banged up. I watched him do it."

The next image was the envelope.

"There we are," he said, pointing. "You can see the postmark. It looks like `BUR'. Can you find place names that start with that?"

She did so. Now there was a shorter list of perhaps a hundred or so names. According to the database there were exactly thirty places starting with `BUR'.

She scrolled immediately to Burnham-on-Sea.

"Nobody named Smith or even with the same initials," she said in frustration. "We need to work out which of these places is close to the sea."

Will took down a map book from the shelf and started working through the index, finding each place, and Lucy one-by one excluded the inland locations from the search. When they had finished they had reduced the list to only eight subscribers. Will leaned in close and read slowly down the list, as if hoping that by some miracle Alfred's name would suddenly pop out. Then he smiled slowly and tapped the screen.

"I think this might be him. `A. di Mariano.'

"Alfred di Mariano. Did he have an Italian mother or something?"

"Not Alfred, *Alessandro* di Mariano."

She wrinkled her brow and lifted her eyes, staring unseeingly out of the window, lips pursed.

"That rings a loud bell but I can't think why."

Then her face cleared and she looked at him with surprise.

"You mean, Sandro Botticelli! *Sandro* di Mariano, not Alessandro, and that's his real name rather than his nickname. But I don't understand why you think Alfred would take Botticelli's name. It seems a very peculiar thing to do."

"I don't know for sure, but I think he wants that magazine and he's covering up his tracks," Will said. "And Botticelli was Alfred's hero; he was obsessed. He used to go on about him, not just his skill with a brush but the fact that he was a pioneer of perspective and composition, his amazing imagination, his pagan art, his skill with portraits and figures. He was a man ahead of his time and then he was forgotten because of Leonardo."

"So he liked Botticelli," Lucy said, frowning, "but it's a bit of a leap to say he would take his name. It could be anyone just messing around."

"Let me tell you a story to convince you. Alfred did a 'Botticelli' when we were in the nick, just for a laugh. It all started, funnily enough, because there was an article in *Renaissance Artist* about Botticelli's muse, Simonetta Vespucci."

"The face he used for his Venuses."

"Yes, and probably a few Madonnas as well. Apparently he was besotted with 'La Bella Simonetta'. He used her for the Birth of Venus, for example."

"The clam shell and the extraordinarily long neck."

"That's the one. Except that Alfred said it was surprising because she died five or ten years before he painted it, so Botticelli must have done it from memory. Anyway, when Alfred saw Botticelli's picture of her in the magazine, he went all peculiar and said he had to have a go at it. It was a sort of homage to the master, I think. He had that picture done in a few days and when he signed it he put 'A. di Mariano'. I asked him what *that* was all about and he told me all this stuff about him."

"Remarkable," Lucy said slowly. "But why put that instead of 'Botticelli', or else his own name?"

"It's just the sort of thing he *would* do. It would amuse him to use the original name of his favourite painter rather than his adopted nickname. It would be a way of signing it Botticelli, but not like a crude forgery when clearly it was knocked up from a magazine photograph on modern canvas. He wouldn't sign it with his own name because it was a copy of the masterwork. He liked to give subtle little clues. He told me once he would make tiny deliberate changes in a forgery, and no-one ever noticed. I suppose that's what I was looking for on the Hammershoi, but I couldn't see anything."

"Why didn't you tell me about this before?" she said.

"Since you saved my life today I have decided to trust you," he said simply.

She blushed, and then felt the blush and was embarrassed. She looked back at the screen but knew he had noticed.

"Well in that case," she said, busily scrolling along to the right, "we need to go and find Mr A di Mariano. According to this list, his address is *Nelson's Rest, Gong Rise, Burnham-Overy-Staithe, Norfolk*. Wherever *that* is. I've never heard of it."

Lucy had a small travelling bag with her in the boot of the car, and Will came out with her to get it. The rain was still coming down but it had slowed. They both felt exposed and vulnerable as soon as they stepped outside, especially as it was night and the shadows were more threatening. They looked up and down the street and saw a few parked cars but no other signs of life, so they hurriedly collected Lucy's bag from the car and regained the studio without incident, stepping carefully over the gurgling gutter. Once inside they locked and bolted the door, and scuttled upstairs like frightened mice, laughing at themselves. Will reorganized his work area while she used the bathroom. She had put things back very tidily while he had slept, but in the wrong places, so he organized the brushes and paints and put various additives back where they should be.

When she emerged from the bathroom she came over to him. He wanted to take her in his arms.

"Do you fancy a Sunday jaunt to Norfolk tomorrow?" she inquired.

"A day on the Broads! I think we have to, though we'll need to be careful what we turn up."

"All right then. Well, I'm going to go to bed."

She hesitated a moment, again feeling awkward, and then reached forward and kissed him on the cheek.

"In a very peculiar way I've enjoyed today," she said, and he grinned. He put his hand under her chin and lifted her face, then kissed her on the lips.

"In a very peculiar way, I have too."

In the street below, Mrs Morris's car was parked three up from Lucy's, with all the lights extinguished and rain streaming down the windows. She had been there for hours, watching and waiting. Morton couldn't show his face so she had decided to do a little field reconnaissance herself. When she saw the kiss through the brightly lighted studio window, her face cracked into a grim smile of satisfaction.

FORTY-SIX

Let us have a dagger between our teeth, a bomb in our hands and an infinite scorn in our hearts.
BENITO MUSSOLINI

In the morning, Mrs Morris asked to see Rupert Angel early in his study. They were both tired; he because he had lain awake worrying, and she after the previous late night in Cambridge. The maid had prepared them fresh Colombian coffee, which filled the air with its heady aroma. Rupert sat in an armchair, sipping the steaming liquid with an increasingly grim look on his face as he absorbed further bad news.

"Mrs Wrackham stayed the night with Bentley," Mrs Morris was saying. "I was outside watching. It was late at night and they suddenly emerged together. They were very friendly and she fetched an overnight valise from her car and then they fairly *skipped* back in. They were holding hands and she was giggling. A short while later I saw them kissing in the studio window."

Rupert stopped drinking his coffee as the dart struck home.

"You saw them *kissing*? You mean a passionate kiss?"

"Well, it was raining hard so I didn't have a perfect view, but they were *locked* together and then the lights went out," Mrs Morris said coyly. "I waited another half an hour but they obviously weren't coming out again."

There was an aggrieved silence.

"I'd expected more loyalty of Lucy," Rupert said at last.

Mrs Morris shrugged, as if defending Lucy.

"Well, you did leave her suddenly the other night, and I must admit that Bentley is a *very* good looking man." She looked at him calculatingly. "I'm not surprised that she has succumbed to his charms."

Rupert stood at the window, looking out at the new day with pursed lips, folded arms and a frown of discontent. The weather outside was at last showing signs of brightening, although the entire landscape was waterlogged and every surface bore a cargo of jewels. A blackbird settled on top of the wall outside and looked around, its head moving in suspicious jerks.

"Bentley will have told her everything he knows by now," Rupert said, his voice still betraying a note of irritation. "She may even suspect *me*."

Mrs Morris shook her head decisively.

"I don't think he knows that much. He certainly has no inkling you are involved – how could he? He'll have told her about the first attack, and

Edward has told us about the fiasco of the second attempt, when she and the policeman actually walked in on the whole thing. Bentley may have told her that he suspects there's an information leak, but there's no particular reason why she should associate it with you. It could just as easily be the police, or some associate of Bentley's, or a competent journalist. Mrs Wrackham herself may have told others. She does appear to have a loose tongue."

Rupert looked unconvinced. He drank the rest of his coffee.

"So what do you suggest?" he said at last.

She folded her legs, treating him to a view of immaculately sheathed knee. Her legs were still good and she knew it. She weighed her words carefully before she spoke.

"Bentley continues to be our biggest security risk, Rupert. And I'm afraid that Mrs Wrackham is our second biggest problem, now that she appears to be sleeping with him. *She* wants a win for herself and her company, and *he* wants to find his friend, so together they are a very dangerous pair. We need to address the problem sooner rather than later, or we'll be facing them across a courtroom."

Rupert contemplated this uncomfortably real possibility.

"We can't use Edward," he said. "His face is known to the police now." He went over and closed the door quietly and turned to face her with his back to the door. "In fact, Julia," he continued *sotto voce*, "I am beginning to think that Edward himself..."

"...has become a liability," she finished, observing his shrug. "I'm glad you think so, Rupert. I have come to the same conclusion. But I do have a plan that I worked out last night while I was driving back down that long empty motorway."

Rupert sat down at the desk and took a cigar from an ornate mother-of-pearl box, even though it was only seven thirty in the morning. He smoked cigars rarely, and then only after dinner, but he felt sufficiently rattled at that moment to have one. He lifted the brandy decanter and waved it interrogatively at Mrs Morris. She held out her cup in mute consent and he added brandy to her coffee, then poured himself a separate one in a crystal glass. He lit a cigar and the smoke tasted bitter in his mouth, but it woke him up.

"Tell me," he said.

She smiled her sweetest smile.

"First of all we need to change Edward's appearance. He can shave his beard and cut his hair. He can put on a pair of sunglasses and a hat. He'll look different enough for our purposes. Then we send him up to Cambridge to deal with Bentley. Bentley has been lucky, but he can't be lucky forever. And this time I'll go up with him to make sure there aren't any more mistakes."

Rupert rolled the brandy around the glass with his hand cupped around it, warming the liquid within. He raised it to his nose and inhaled the sweet scent, then took a pull of brandy and felt its subtle fire in his throat.

"What method are you thinking of? It needs to be foolproof this time."

"Do you remember Lecombier? Morton's specialist made two of those devices but only used one. We still have the other in the safe. I see no reason why it shouldn't still work if we charge it up."

Rupert did remember Lecombier. Two years ago, Lecombier had been a prospective rival bidder in a very important deal. How could he forget the irritating little Frenchman, with his pretentious little moustache and his arrogance; his bald pate and his sly cleverness? But Lecombier's car had exploded on a French autoroute and he had shuffled off his mortal coil.

"You want to *blow Bentley up?*"

Mrs Morris smiled.

"We've tried threatening him, Rupert, and we've even tried hanging him, but the man has an irritating habit of surviving. A bomb would certainly *shut his mouth.*"

She spaced out the last three words for emphasis.

Rupert pondered in silence for a full minute, drawing on his cigar and taking another pull of brandy.

"The police would *really* take notice if he got blown up," he observed at last.

"Yes, but their star witness would be in several pieces. And he's the man who can find Alfred Smith if anyone can."

There was another long pause and then Rupert nodded very slightly and she knew she had him.

"All right," he said, then added, "the painter, but not the girl, Julia."

"If you say so," Mrs Morris said smoothly. "We'll deal with Bentley and then you can decide what you want to do about the girl. She'll be less trouble without him helping her."

And if the little bitch accidentally gets blown to bits, what a pity.

Rupert nodded again, more definitely now.

"And Edward?"

"Edward Morton cannot show his face around the Angel Gallery ever again," said Mrs Morris quietly. "It would only be a matter of time before someone made the connection. The police may post his face or find him on CCTV somewhere. Anything could happen. When he has despatched our painter friend," she said, shaking her head sadly, "I think he'll need a little Special K."

She patted her Louis Vuitton handbag affectionately, in which Rupert knew she carried a small syringe and two phials of Ketamine; a veterinary anaesthetic.

Rupert contemplated Mrs Morris for a moment, and she looked right back at him, sipping her coffee and brandy. She had a way of simply doing what needed to be done. He had no precise idea what was going to happen to Morton after she had injected Ketamine into his veins, but he knew that he would need a new security man, because Morton would never be seen again.

"It makes sense," he nodded. "There's one other problem, and that's Alfred himself. I'm worried that he may try to run off if we don't keep a close eye on him. He's angry that Robbie and Peter are there in the house and he isn't allowed out. While you are dealing with Bentley, I think it might be wise for me to bring Alfred down here in one of the vans."

"You'll definitely need to go yourself," she nodded. "We certainly can't trust those two morons to pack up the pictures. "Perhaps it would be sensible, as you say. But where would we keep him?"

Rupert made a wide sweeping motion with his arm.

"Right here in this house. We can keep him on the middle floor and lock him in. Give him some cigars and an occasional woman to keep him happy. There are more amenities in London. He's all but finished the Botticelli. After that we won't need him anymore, especially since we had to part with the Hammershoi."

At that moment the study door handle twisted and the door swung open. Morton came in, looking surprised to see them in conference but saying nothing.

"Good morning, Edward," Rupert said blandly. "Julia has been keeping an eye on Bentley for us, and she has a new plan."

Morton observed the brandy glass and the cigar smoke but still said nothing.

Let me tell you all about it, Edward," Mrs Morris said guilelessly, "while I cut your hair."

FORTY-SEVEN

*Whenever I prepare for a journey I prepare as though for death.
Should I never return, all is in order.*
KATHERINE MANSFIELD

Sixty-five miles to the North, Will and Lucy were getting up, unaware that their demise was being plotted. Lucy was an early riser and was showered and dressed by the time Will emerged sleepily from his bedroom.

"Is it a vision, or a waking dream?" she teased.

Will smiled crookedly and disappeared into the bathroom, closing the door firmly. He appeared later in jeans and a yellow shirt, encountering the smell of coffee and bagels; Lucy had been to the corner shop and purchased breakfast and newspapers.

"Would you believe it?" she said crossly when he emerged. "I only popped out to find croissants and some beastly little photographer snapped pictures of me coming out of the studio."

Will didn't say anything immediately. He hadn't yet reached the speaking stage. He sat down at the table and poured fresh coffee from the cafetière into a mug saying 'Bollocks to Picasso' on the side. He picked up the paper and saw a picture of the studio on the front page, and started reading the article.

"*Police were called to the incident...Renowned Cambridge artist Will Bentley narrowly escaped execution...thugs escaped...police appealing for witnesses...*"

He looked up.

"It mentions you further down," he said. "If they got a picture of you this morning, you'll be my lover by the time it hits the tabloids tomorrow morning."

"In your dreams," she said. "Shall we attempt to give the gentlemen of the press the slip and go to Norfolk for the day? After yesterday I'm getting a taste for adventure."

"Yes, but we should go and see Lewis first. I didn't mention being stabbed when I asked him to come up and watch my back. I feel terrible about it."

The rain had stopped but its aftermath was everywhere: the hissing of car tyres on wet tarmac; the pedestrian pace of the traffic; puddles in the dips and a small flood from a blocked drain in the Hills Road. They made their way to Addenbrooke's Hospital, located Lewis without too much difficulty and spent forty-five minutes by his bedside. When he began to tire they were shooed away by a vigilant nurse. On their way out they bumped into Sandy in the car-park.

"I'm just popping in to see Joe," she said, bright-eyed, and then perceived their blank expressions.

"Lewis," she added.

Will raised his eyebrows.

"I didn't even know he *had* a first name," he said. "I spent months in prison with the man and he never mentioned it, but you've got it out of him in five minutes."

She looked pleased.

"Joe and me are getting on really well," she said. "He's cute."

"Cute isn't the word I would immediately associate with Lewis," Will said dryly.

"No, he *is*," she contradicted him. "And very brave," she added proudly.

"He certainly is that," Will agreed. "Anyway, I'm sure he'll be pleased to have another visitor. He's quite tired, though; we were sent away by the nurse."

"I'll wait," Sandy said simply. "Shall I see you tomorrow for modelling at the same time as usual?"

He nodded and Sandy gave them both a little wave before disappearing through the doors.

"You're right," Lucy said, watching her go. "That girl is completely smitten with Lewis."

They returned to the studio, planning to have an early lunch and then set off for Norfolk. They were wary when they returned but there didn't appear to be any photographers skulking in alleyways, or knife-wielding killers, so they parked quickly, dodged the puddles and hurried inside.

Five cars down from the studio entrance, Mrs Morris and Morton sat in her black BMW, slumped down in the seats. Morton had a shaved face and was conscious of how cool his skin felt, exposed to the air for the first time in years. His hair was cut short and he wore a baseball cap. A pair of steel-rimmed spectacles completed the new look.

"Go on then, Edward," Mrs Morris urged. "They've gone inside but they might come out again in a moment. "Get on with it."

He looked at her and picked up the cardboard box on the floor. From it he took a plastic box with a mobile phone strapped to the side, and wires leading from it into the box. He handled it very gingerly.

"Do you want to give it one last try before arming it?" she said. "We can't afford to make a mistake again."

He didn't think it was necessary but knew better than to argue with Mrs Morris, so he cradled the device on his lap and carefully checked that the device was in its passive state.

"It's disarmed," he said, and she nodded.

He pressed the speed dial on the phone in the dashboard cradle and after a few moments the phone strapped to the device lit up as it received the call. He felt a tingle of fear in his groin even though he knew that it was disarmed. After a moment or two a red light illuminated on the box.

"Bang," he said. He pressed a small black pushbutton on the box and the red light turned to green.

He turned to the woman beside him and raised his eyebrows, characteristically saying nothing.

"Off you go then," she said matter-of-factly, as if suggesting he go and buy a newspaper.

She had not told Morton of Rupert's specific insistence that only the painter should be eliminated and not the girl. If Morton blew them both up and she subsequently dispatched Morton, she could blame Morton's incompetence.

The street was empty of people so Morton slid out of the car and walked swiftly towards Lucy's red MG. He looked quickly up and down the street and towards the studio; all clear. He got down on his knees and reached in under the car, clipping the box securely onto the exhaust pipe. When he was certain it was stable he armed the bomb via a slider switch, with his heart in his mouth in case it went off. The device didn't explode but blinked a green LED three times to indicate that it was correctly armed. Morton straightened up and walked hurriedly away, getting back into the BMW and closing the door before he brushed down his damp trousers and turned to Mrs Morris.

"I hate those damn things," he said.

"Well done, Edward," she said, patting his knee. "Now we'll wait for them to come out again."

Will and Lucy emerged from the studio at twelve-thirty, looked up and down the street but saw no-one, and got into the red MG. Lucy pulled out and pointed the car towards the main exit routes out of Cambridge. Almost immediately she noticed the innocuous black car that fell in behind them and kept a discreet distance back. She indicated her rear view mirror.

"The press are trailing us," she said conversationally.

Will leaned sideways and looked in the wing mirror.

"The black beamer? Can you give them the slip in this?"

"I can try, but not until we get out of town. Let's see if they stick with us."

The day was brightening up. The roads were still wet and the car sloshed through puddles as they made their way to the A14. They felt excited and filled with anticipation. As she drove he talked about the North Norfolk coast, which was 'Cambridge on Sea'; a retreat for boating enthusiasts and full of second homes for the rich. Behind but still in sight, Mrs Morris watched the empty road and the red car on the horizon. Then she glanced once at Morton, reached forward and pressed the speed dial on her phone.

FORTY-EIGHT

It is grievous to be caught.
HORACE

Earlier that morning Rupert Angel had taken the same road. Just as Will and Lucy were arriving back at Will's studio after visiting Lewis, Rupert was driving up Gong Rise, going carefully because of the narrow winding road. His large grey Ford van twisted its way up the gentle hill, past a children's playground, past suburban bungalows, and finally crunched onto the gravel of Nelson's Rest. He turned off the engine and sat for a moment, hidden behind the darkened window glass. The door of the bungalow opened and Pete came out. Rupert had called to say that he was coming, but he had not explained why for fear that Alfred might get wind of it and flee across the fields while Rupert was in transit.

He opened the door and stepped down from the van, stretching.

"I need a cup of coffee, and then we need to move out," he said. "Everything out, as soon as we can. There's a chance the police might be on to us."

He went inside, leaving the man to open the rear doors of the van. Pete had simply accepted his statement and done his bidding – not so with Alfred Smith.

The old man was in front of his easel, with a rigger brush and a mahl stick in his hand, making fine adjustments to the huge Venus and Mars painting in front of him. He was angry and incredulous when Angel said they had to move out immediately.

"I'm at a very delicate stage," he said. "The work is still wet in places. I can't possibly move it now. It's out of the question."

"Do you want to be here when the police turn up?" Rupert Angel asked him bluntly. "Because I don't think it will be long now. They're all over us and sooner or later they'll pick up a clue and they'll be swarming over this place. Do you want to be sitting here at your easel with a Botticelli copy in front of you when the blue lights turn up? You'll get another five years plus suspension of parole. You could die in prison."

Alfred Smith glared at him.

"How do you know they're so close?" he asked. "They have nothing to guide them here."

"They're working with an old friend of yours," Rupert said with a nasty tone in his voice. "Remember Will Bentley? The insurance people are using him to find you, and they're in league with the police."

Alfred looked shocked and said nothing at all for half a minute.

"I don't believe Will *would* work with the police," he said at last. "Not of his own volition, anyway. He didn't think much of them for putting him away."

"Believe what you like," Angel said brusquely, as he went into the kitchen and clicked the switch on the kettle. "But I need you back in the London house. You can paint there and keep out of sight. There's a room with plenty of light and space on the first floor."

"And I suppose I'll be kept a virtual prisoner, as I have been for the last week," Alfred said bitterly. "Not even allowed to go out for a pint. It's like being back inside."

He put down his palette in exasperation and cleaned his brush vigorously in an old baked bean tin containing white spirit.

"Anyway, I can't move this," he said, gesturing at the painting. "It's my best work."

Rupert walked over and looked at the painting, then stared closely at it, nodding slowly.

"It's a masterpiece," he said, deliberately adopting a more conciliatory tone despite his inner irritation. "But if you are caught with it when the police come, this painting will most likely be destroyed. They'll break it up or burn it. Do you want that?"

"That would be sacrilege," Alfred said, looking very alarmed. "Perhaps you're right then, but we'll need to be very careful. What kind of transport do you have?"

"Don't worry," Angel said quickly; "I've brought one of the work vans. It's big enough to fit this in, and all your painting materials and other canvases as well. It has proper straps and brackets so we can safely secure it. The only thing we won't be able to get in is the oven."

Alfred looked over to the far side of the large room at a large industrial oven. It was used for slowly baking paintings to harden the paint.

"We'll need that," he said regretfully. "We'll need it to dry the paint on this one. I've used a mixture of egg tempera and oil, as on the original. The oil will need baking."

"As I say," Angel said, maintaining his most reasonable tone, "we can't fit it in so we'll have to make do without it. If necessary I'll buy another one, but it's certain that we aren't going to be able to fit it in the van today."

"Can you come back for it?"

"That's an idea," Angel said with a nod, having absolutely no intention of doing so. "But if they find this place, coming back for it would expose us all. These people are too damn clever these days. They've got computers which can find a license plate in the twinkling of an eye, and television cameras on every junction."

"At least it'll be pleasant to get out of this place," Alfred said, still resentful. "As I said, I've felt like a prisoner recently. It's not what we agreed, Rupert."

"All I can say is that it was necessary," Angel said darkly.

Pete and Robbie came in and started gathering up the materials of Alfred's trade, while Alfred directed operations and fussed around them. The Venus and Mars picture took the most time and care. Rupert Angel was at least as protective as Alfred about it. They put cloth at the edges and carried it out slowly to the van, with Rupert in front of them, warning them of steps they already knew about. Alfred trailed behind them, fussing like an old hen, imploring them to take care and not to touch the surfaces. The painting was secured upright in the van in mounted spring-loaded gimbals designed for transporting delicate items. Normally it would have been packed in protective foam and crated up, but they couldn't do that because the paint was still wet. However, the base of the panel was supported on foam blocks and the top was similarly held in place. Nothing was allowed to touch the painted surface. A hood of plastic sheeting was pulled over the top of the painting and stretched down on each side, to prevent floating dust from settling on the surface during transit.

After the Venus and Mars painting had been safely secured in the van, Alfred relaxed a little. The rest of the canvases and spotlights and painting materials went in more quickly, and in turn the three men's bags were packed up and bundled into the capacious boot of Robbie's ageing Jaguar.

"I can't think how Will has got involved," Alfred said as if to himself, shaking his head

He was silent after that, thinking. Once or twice he looked thoughtfully at Rupert Angel. He supervised the packing up of the last oddments and followed Angel out to the van. Then he stopped at the door and went back in again.

"I can't travel all the way to London without going to the toilet," he said in an embarrassed tone. "I'm not as young as I was, old boy. Bit of trouble with the old waterworks these days."

After a few more minutes he emerged and got into the van next to Angel.

"Why the darkened glass?" he said.

"Keeps the light off the paintings," Angel said absently. The van also had no logos or identifying marks, to reduce the likelihood of it being accosted in transit by thieves. Angel started the engine of the van but then wound down the window, gesturing towards the house and addressing Robbie.

"Take a last look around to make sure we haven't left anything," he said. "I'll wait for you."

He double-checked the back of the van while he was waiting, securing any items that might move about and making sure that the Botticelli copy was well strapped in. Robbie came out after ten minutes and waved to him.

"All clear," he called, climbing into the driving seat of the Jaguar.

Rupert backed the van out into the empty road and they set off – first the van, picking its way slowly down the narrow road with its precious load, then the Jaguar in its wake. As they rounded the last sharp corner before the pub they almost collided with a red MG that came speeding around the bend and swerved to avoid them.

Alfred had a sudden glimpse of the beautiful blonde girl driving it, and then with pleasure he saw the man beside her –Will Bentley! His young friend's hair was longer but it was unquestionably him. Neither Will nor the pretty girl saw him through the darkened windows of the van. Beside him Rupert gave a tiny intake of breath as he reacted to the sight of Lucy with Will seated beside her, almost at the bungalow. They had literally escaped in the nick of time, and he was so shocked that he exited the road junction at the bottom without looking, causing a passing car to hoot angrily as the driver had to stand on his brakes.

Neither Alfred nor Rupert mentioned the red MG to the other.

FORTY-NINE

Whatever women do they must do twice as well as men to be thought half as good. Luckily, this is not difficult.
CHARLOTTE WHITTON

"It should have activated by now," Mrs Morris said with irritation. It's been over two minutes. "Doesn't anything ever simply *work*? Surely we can't be out of range?"

"Not possible," Morton said, shaking his head. "It's a mobile phone call. Perhaps it's a bad signal in this area."

She tried again but the distant red dot refused to explode into flame and dust. In fact the bomb *had* received the call, but surface rainwater had penetrated its casing and stopped it triggering. A large globule of trapped liquid was rolling around inside the box, shorting out the electronics. All that stood between Lucy and Will and oblivion was a little water.

Lucy drove on, oblivious to the danger they were in, and chatted with Will. When she noticed the black car still behind it seemed like a rude intrusion; as if someone were listening to their private conversation.

"I can't believe these people," she muttered, pointing with her thumb over her shoulder. "I don't think we want to take a bunch of journalists where we're going today."

She watched the SatNav map for a minute or two, then after the next bend she told Will to hang on tightly and braked so hard that she practically stood the car on its nose, taking a sharp left into an overgrown country lane and veering immediately right onto a rough track beneath dense trees. The car bounced over ruts and she halted it when they were out of sight of the road and switched off the ignition. After the white-noise hiss of the wind and the subdued roar of the road surface, the silence was eerie. As the sound of the engine died away into silence, the wood held its breath indignantly for a moment at the unexpected intrusion, before the sounds of birdsong slowly started up again.

They looked at each other and burst out laughing.

"Round about now they'll be realizing they can't see us," Will said.

"Then they'll think we speeded up and they'll hurry to catch us."

"Have you got a proper map? We need to work out an unlikely detour."

They calculated that they could stick to small roads and rejoin the highway twenty miles further on. As Will pointed out, if they went back to the main road too soon, the BMW might simply pick them up again at an intersection – the red MG was easy enough to spot.

Accordingly they drove on, slowly relaxing and enjoying the brightening day. The sun was burning away the clouds and the roads were drying out. The radio spoke of heightening temperatures and long dry spells, and pollen count was mentioned for the first time in a few days. They stopped in the market town of Swaffham for coffee, then drove on towards the north Norfolk coast, turning left at Fakenham and arriving first at Burnham Market, then over the fields to Burnham Overy Staithe. They located Gong Rise and went up it. Lucy was impatient to be there and almost collided with a large van coming the other way.

"Oops, sorry. It's like Piccadilly Circus around here," she remarked when the van and the Jaguar following it had disappeared. "Now then, we're looking for Nelson's Rest, and the SatNav thinks we're here already because I didn't have a house number."

They couldn't see it, but were directed by an old lady walking a Scottish terrier. Within a few more minutes they found the gateway. It was heavily overgrown with a spiky yellow-flowered shrub, but it did have a sign once you knew where to look.

"What do you think – should we simply go in?" Lucy said, suddenly anxious. "What if he's there with a bunch of hoodlums and they decide to do us in?"

"Let's park further up and sneak back," Will said, as they drove slowly past the gateway. He craned his neck down the drive. "There are no cars parked outside."

Lucy stopped the car and they clambered out of the low-slung seats. The sun was hot now, beating down on them, making the metal of the car warm to the touch.

"My God, smell that air!" Lucy said, raising her arms dramatically wide as if conducting a concert. "And the sun is drying everything out."

"Wonderful place to paint," Will said. "Come on then. I don't suppose they issue insurance agents with Kalashnikovs for moments like this?"

"Not even a peashooter," she said, shaking her head. "The recommended procedure in the event of trouble is to run like hell."

It didn't take very long to establish that there was no one in Nelson's Rest. They crept up the gravel drive trying to make no sound and peered through the windows one by one. There were no signs of personal belongings and no-one in sight.

"We need a criminal to break in," Lucy said. "Can't you pick the lock or something?"

"I keep telling you: I was *innocent*," Will said in exasperation. "Besides, I don't have a lock pick."

He peered through the heavy plate glass to each side of the door.

"There's a key on the mat inside," he said, pointing. "He must have dropped it through the letterbox. I've got a bad feeling that the bird has flown."

"Oh for God's sake," she said with her nose against the glass. "*Now* what shall we do?"

"We can't come all this way and not get a look inside," Will said. "We'll *have* to break in." He looked around for a heavy stone.

"Just a minute," Lucy said in alarm. "Let's look around first. There might be an open window."

All the windows and doors were locked. However, the rear door of the garage opened with a firm push. There was a lawnmower, a roller, some garden canes, some moss killer and an assortment of garden tools. They searched the garage in vain for conveniently placed spare keys on high nails or ledges, but none was apparent.

"I'll have a look around the back," Will said. "According to my friends in low places, people often leave a spare key under a stone."

He went round to the rear of Nelson's Rest, humming to himself. The sun was burning away the last of the clouds and was now so bright that it made him squint and was hot on his back. There was a rather forlorn rockery beside the rear patio, so he started to look under each stone, muttering to himself that any one of the stones would easily get him into the house if it was well aimed. But in the midst of his search the patio door slid open and Lucy stepped out of the house, looking very pleased with herself.

He dropped the rock he was holding and got up from his knees rather sheepishly.

"Leave it to a woman if you want things done," she said airily.

FIFTY

Friends, though absent, are still present.
MARCUS TULLIUS CICERO

"You found a key then?"

"I certainly did not. I used one of those garden canes from the garage and stuck it through the letterbox and threaded it through the string of the key on the mat. It only took half a minute."

"If you ever get sick of insurance you have the makings of a good thief," Will said, following her inside the house.

The house had a large floor plan, and as soon as he went into the main room it was obvious that someone had been painting in there.

"You can smell turps," he said with a sniff. "And cigars too. Alfred's been here all right – but cleared out, by the looks of it. And not long ago either, or the turps smell would have dissipated. You can see where he had his easel, look. Just here by the patio doors where he would get the best natural light."

He pointed to a mark on the tiles and a spot of yellow ochre.

The room had a large fireplace standing free from the wall, with a cowled black chimney hood and a thick black flue running up through the ceiling. The kitchen was open plan, separated by a breakfast bar. In front of the breakfast bar was what appeared to be a huge commercial pizza oven. There were a couple of sofas and a television on one side, but the whole place had the look of a rented property. Beyond the big open-plan area was the hall through which Lucy had entered, plus a bathroom and three small bedrooms.

As there was nobody in the house they set about searching it to see if they could work out where Alfred had gone. After two hours they had found only two things of interest, both in the kitchen waste bin. There were the contents of an ashtray, with a number of cigarette ends in it and a single cigar stub. The cigar was a miniature, bearing the name *Cohiba* – a brand from the Dominican Republic that was Alfred's favourite. There was also a small empty tin which had contained Flake White oil paint. The remaining paint was still sticky when Will touched it.

"The lid's off so it's exposed to the air," he said. "You use Flake White on older pictures, because they hadn't invented Titanium White. It's toxic, so they only supply it in tins rather than squeezable tubes these days. You have to be very careful to avoid getting it on your skin because of the lead in it."

He dabbed his wet finger on the end of his nose, making it white in turn, and gave her a serious look.

Her normally serious demeanour evaporated and she giggled.

"Now you look like a clown. How old do you think the paint is?"

He wiped the paint off his nose and inspected the tin critically.

"It's hard to say, but probably not more than a day or so at most. It *could* be only a few hours old; the paint hasn't skinned over, and Flake White dries faster than Titanium."

"Very well," she said, "let's summarise what we know. We believe Alfred was here because someone with his adopted name had a magazine subscription sent here, and besides – he was smoking his favourite cigars. We know it wasn't more than a day or two ago because otherwise the paint scrapings in the tin would have dried out."

"And we know he cleared out for some reason, " Will added. "But we have no idea where or why."

"He might have got wind of the fact that someone's on his trail," she mused. "Perhaps he moved out rather than risk getting caught."

"Or he might have *been moved*," Will said. "We know he's involved with some very nasty people. Perhaps they somehow guessed we were getting close."

"The trouble is, only *we* know we're very close," she said with a frown. "Yesterday we had no idea where to look until we suddenly thought of the magazine, and I don't see how they could know about that because we haven't told a soul."

"Maybe they don't actually *know*," Will said, pacing around. "Maybe they're just getting jumpy."

He walked over to the pizza oven and opened its wide drop-down door. "I was wondering what *this* is for, but I think I've worked it out. Apparently you have to bake the pictures very slowly to get the paint to harden. This would be perfect for the job. It's wide enough to get a large picture in, and you could keep the thermostat barely on so that it would warm things through rather than cooking them."

They looked at it together. Inside the oven they found a thin line of dried paint down one side; evidently where a wet canvas or panel had touched the edge. That pretty much confirmed its purpose.

"Well, we can't simply *leave*," Lucy said in exasperation. "Let's take one last look around, really carefully this time. We should move the furniture and see if there's anything underneath, feel down the back of the sofa; do everything we can think of. It's going to be beastly if the trail simply goes cold again."

There were a few coins down the back of the sofa but nothing else. There was nothing underneath the beds. They rolled back the rugs but found only dust. They again went painstakingly through every kitchen cupboard and drawer, finding nothing other than a motley collection of cutlery and crockery and kitchen implements. There was an inventory of all the kitchen equipment in one of the drawers, proving without doubt that they were in a rented holiday cottage. Unfortunately they found no other clues.

"We're going to have to give up," Will said, standing and looking with distracted irritation at a poster of Monet's Poppy Field at Argenteuil. Then he leaned closer and chuckled.

"Fancy that! Someone has signed it 'Renoir'"

She stood beside him and examined it. Monet's faded signature was on the left, but someone had written 'Renoir' in the bottom right hand corner, apparently in thick pencil. She took it down and turned it over but there was no other mark.

"I don't get the joke – why's that funny?"

"You don't know the history. It's as if Alfred is telling me that he was here."

"How's that?" she said, looking at him intently.

"Well, you used to see the Poppies all over the place, but everyone's got a bit sick of it now so you don't see it so much. But there was one on the wall in the prison, and one of the screws thought it was by Renoir. After that Alfred and I used to rather smugly refer to it as The Renoir."

"He'd surely be mad to copy a *Renoir*," Lucy said thoughtfully.

"You don't know Alfred," Will said. "He's pretty good, and Renoir's not that hard. Better than Titian any day. But it means you'll have to find out if any Renoirs have recently been nicked and then returned."

"I can do that easily enough," she said, tacking the poster back on the wall. "But I think I would already know. After all, it's what I *do* every day. I'd be sure to know if a Renoir had gone missing."

"Wait a moment!" he said thoughtfully. "We haven't checked all the *pictures*."

So he went through the bedrooms one by one while Lucy examined the three pictures in the main room. He came back holding a cheap framed print in his hands, showing a nude young woman of ample proportions having her hair combed.

"Whoever rents out this place must be mad about the Impressionists," he said. "I just found a Renoir in the toilet."

"And of course it's somebody's little joke," she said, coming over and glancing at it. "Because this one is actually called 'La Toilette'."

"Take a look at the back."

She turned it over and felt her heart quicken. There was a brief message written in graphite, scrawled in big, ballooning letters.

The Triumph of Good over Evil – Procaccini

"I think this is what we sleuths call a first-class clue," she said, looking at him with bright eyes.

"It certainly looks like it. Oh and by the way, this is definitely Alfred's handwriting. It's quite distinctive, as you can see. I don't remember Procaccini, though."

"There were a couple of artists called Procaccini, as far as I remember, but I don't know which one did the Triumph of Good Over Evil. It's all around the time of the Renaissance, though I have a feeling that Procaccini was in Milan rather than Florence. I'll look it up as soon as we get back."

"I wonder where Alfred has taken himself off to now," Will said, his voice a little wistful.

Something in his tone made her lay her hand on his arm in a sudden intimate gesture, and he twisted a smile onto his face as if doing battle with it.

"My old friend is out there somewhere but I keep on missing him," he said. "It's as if he just stepped out for a moment."

She was nodding slowly.

"It's different for you," she said. "You've known him but I never have. It's more personal for you, but it's odd for me too. Even though I'm trying to catch him I'm warming to him as we go along, and I don't usually feel that. I wonder why on earth he would write this message on the *back* of a picture?"

There was a pause while they both silently sought an explanation. Will spoke first.

"It's as if he left us a cryptic clue," Will said slowly, "so perhaps he *knows* we're looking for him. Perhaps he's trying to help us find him."

"A forwarding address would have been more useful," Lucy observed in the tart way that she sometimes had.

"Maybe he didn't dare. The guy with the beard certainly put the fear of God into me, and he might have done the same to Alfred. Maybe Alfred wants to get out of the whole business and they won't let him."

"It sounds a bit far-fetched," she objected. "He's been up to it for months – we know that from the paintings that have been stolen and the copies that then turned up."

"Well then I have no idea," Will said in exasperation. "I'm just trying to build a plausible explanation based on no information."

"I know you are," she said pacifyingly. "I didn't mean to stop you. Keep going."

"Okay then, so let's imagine that they turn up here and tell him he's got to leave in a rush; stop what he's doing and go. If that were me I'd be furious if I was in the middle of a picture."

"Right. So he's angry and he's forced to leave. Why does he leave a cryptic message on the back of a little print in the toilet?"

There was a silence for perhaps half a minute. Then Will said, "It only really works if he knows that it's *me* looking for him, *and* he wants me to find him. If he knows it's me, then he leaves me the message on the Poppies poster, to tell me that I've found him. The poster points to the clue, but no-one else would have looked at this Renoir picture."

"So he goes to the toilet, locks himself in, scribbles the message and then adds an extra signature to the Poppies poster on his way out."

"It makes a kind of sense. If we're right then this is *our* special clue – we just need to decipher it."

They spent another ten minutes checking the other pictures but found nothing else, so they left the house. They copied down the message from the picture before replacing it on the wall, and took with them the contents of the waste bin, since it was the only other tangible evidence that they had discovered.

The bodywork of the car was hot and they put down the roof before setting off. The engine turned over and started smoothly, its oil still pleasantly warm. They turned around and drove away, making their way back down Gong Rise. Beneath the MG, the bomb was still in position, still armed, still triggered, and still disabled by the water. Except that the water had evaporated to only half its original amount in the heat of the July afternoon. As they returned to Cambridge, it shrank a little more with each mile of their passage.

FIFTY-ONE

Every dog must have his day.
JONATHAN SWIFT

Will and Lucy arrived without incident at six thirty, parked outside the studio and locked up. There was an old white-bearded man with a boisterous cocker spaniel on a bit of rope, and two teenagers arguing as they walked, but no groups of armed and dangerous men. It was a beautiful evening: the rain had washed every surface clean and freshened the air, while the sun had dried everything out and was a delight after the wet weather. The light was turning everything to gold and the shadows were lengthening. Will and Lucy went quickly into the studio and locked the door behind them. When they got upstairs and had flung down their things, Will disappeared into the kitchen to make coffee and Camomile tea. At this rate, he reflected, he was going to have to buy more of Anna's horrible tea-bags. When the drinks were made, Lucy slumped down in the armchair to drink her tea, tired after the long day of driving. Will preferred movement after the confinement of the sports car so he paced around, cradling his cup.

    He stood in front of the easel for a while, contemplating the picture of the bruised but beautiful Sandy in her red dress, and knew it was a good one, because it gave him a little proud feeling of certainty in his chest. No ordinary person would want this on their wall, but he knew he would sell it, nevertheless. One of the galleries would snap it up, and it was a good feeling. The only blot on the landscape was the whole problem of Alfred, and everything associated with that. At least he had got to know Lucy, though he wasn't sure if she had any feelings for him. He turned round to look at her, but she was asleep and her tea was balanced precariously on the chair arm. He removed it to the sanctuary of the table top. He looked at her with a frank and open artist's stare, stealing her image while she slept. Her blonde hair was tumbled loose, as it had been previously when he had drawn her. Her face was very serious, with perfect closed eyelids, full lips and a straight nose. Today she was wearing a green skirt and a white blouse, with knee-length brown high-heeled boots. Her breasts seemed to be hardly contained by the flimsy material of the blouse. Around her neck she wore a thin gold chain that she never appeared to remove. There were no rings on her fingers. In her ears she wore sensible pearl studs. She shifted a little and he immediately retreated to the easel in case she should awake and find his eyes upon her.

He looked out of the studio window, sipping his coffee. Two pregnant ladies stood chatting next to Lucy's car, their bellies enormous, one clad in a flowing dress and the other in a stretch-fitting top.

His eyes went back to the painting again, examining it critically for flaws. Should he tighten the contrast on the jaw line a little? Should he increase the shadow of the collarbones? Good collarbones were sexy, there was no doubt about that, and this picture was definitely charged with passion.

He glanced out of the window and saw a man on his knees behind Lucy's car, fiddling with it. There was something very familiar about him.

"Hey!" he shouted, though the man could not hear him with the window shut. Lucy began to stir at his shout. Will looked around wildly and his eyes fell upon Lewis's baseball bat. He snatched it up, ran across the studio, dived through the door without a second thought and went down the stairs two at a time.

Mrs Morris and Morton watched the red MG arrive and tuck itself into the same parking space that it had left six hours previously. They were parked several cars back in the black BMW, deliberately keeping out of sight of the studio windows.

"Well, the stupid machine has failed utterly," Mrs Morris said in cold fury. "We'll wait until they've gone inside and then you must retrieve it, Edward. We'll have to find another way since it appears to have packed up. This is really most embarrassing."

Morton looked at her.

"*I'm* not going to retrieve it," he said with unaccustomed bluntness. "It's an armed bomb, for Christ's sake."

"Oh don't be so ridiculous. It's not armed or it would have gone off. We can't just leave it there or else they'll find it and the police will analyse it and trace back its components. We can't risk that, so you have to get it back. Surely you're not planning to leave that job to a woman?"

He looked at her sourly, knowing how easily she was able to get him to do just what she wanted.

They watched and waited. Two pregnant women were gossiping beside the Wrackham girl's car, but after a while they moved off and for the moment there was no-one in the street as everybody made their way home to dinner.

"Now," Mrs Morris hissed at Morton. "Do it now while there's no-one about, Edward. It will only take a minute and you can press the disarm button before you even touch it."

Morton paused for another second and then got out of the car without saying anything, leaving her with a smouldering look. He strode down the street to the red MG, looking about as he went. There was still no-one in sight and he got down on his hands and knees behind the red car and looked underneath. The bomb was still there, clamped to the exhaust pipe. It was a little muddy now. He could see the tiny black button that he had to press to disarm it, and beside it, a glowing red LED. A shiver of fear went up his spine. He reached forward, pressed the button and the tiny LED turned green to show that it was safe. He exhaled, realizing that he had been holding his breath, and unclamped the device. Then he straightened up with exaggerated care.

Mrs Morris watched him from the car. It was a significant complication, the bomb not going off – now Morton could talk to Rupert and reveal that her instructions had been to dispose of Lucy as well as Will. The syringe in her bag was ready and loaded, and she wondered whether she should use it when he got back into the car, and deal with the situation herself. After all – he was a liability now that his face was known.

But then the front door of the painter's studio was unexpectedly flung open and Bentley appeared framed in the doorway with a baseball bat in his hand.

"Hey *you!*" he yelled at Morton.

Morton was turning back towards the BMW, trying to conceal the device behind him, but at that moment a dog sped around the corner, trailing a short length of rope. It was surprised by Morton and cavorted around him, barking furiously. Morton aimed a kick at the dog and somehow the box in his hand slipped and fell, clattering to the tarmac. He froze, staring at it, but it seemed to be all right. The dog gave a yelp and disappeared the way it had come. Morton reached down and snatched up the box, aware of Will Bentley's imminent approach. It was at that moment that some obstruction cleared itself in the damaged mechanism, and he felt a dull click as the relay activated, followed a split-second later by oblivion.

FIFTY-TWO

We wish to suggest a structure for the salt of deoxyribose nucleic acid (DNA). This structure has novel features which are of considerable biological interest.
JAMES WATSON AND FRANCIS CRICK, 1953

Will was angling around a parked car when the bomb detonated. The force of the blast lifted him like a feather and threw him back through his open studio door, narrowly missing the heavy wooden frame. He landed on his back in the hall, sliding along the polished parquet flooring; winded and temporarily deafened but otherwise undamaged.

Edward Morton simply disappeared. He had been holding the device at the time and the detonation blew him to pieces. The windows of the surrounding houses were shattered and the white balcony tables of the adjoining flats were polka-dotted with blood. Only the toughened glass of the studio window remained stubbornly intact, further protected by a parked car which took much of the blast.

Lucy's red MG was thrown onto its side and the petrol tank burst open. Flames quickly enveloped the vehicle. Car alarms started to sound all down the street, adding to the cacophony. A scantily clad woman was leaning out of a window next to the studio and screaming. People were appearing and running towards the burning car. A man was speaking urgently into a mobile phone. Mrs Morris started the BMW, her face a little paler than usual. She did a U-turn and drove away from the scene of mayhem. People were running past her as she drove away, and she forced herself to drive sedately. By the time she was a mile away, the banshee wail of emergency sirens could already be heard ululating in the distance.

In the studio, Lucy had been stretching sleepily but was immediately jerked awake by the blast and showered with broken glass as the upper window blew in. She ran to the window and stood there in shock, her boots crunching on the shards, looking down at a burning car and then realising in utter disbelief that it was hers. When she found that Will wasn't in the studio she ran into his bedroom but he wasn't there either. She sped out of the door and down the stairs with a sick feeling in her stomach. The front door was open and for a moment she thought he was out there, but then she saw him inside, flat on his back in the hallway with a baseball bat still clutched in his hand, picking himself up and shaking his head. She gave a little sob of relief.

"Are you all right?" she found herself shouting, kneeling beside him and taking his hands. He had minor cuts on his face. He was blinking to try to get dust out of his eyes and he looked at her in confusion.

"There was a man at the back of your car," he said. "Then I don't know what happened."

She stood up and went to the door and looked out, her knees feeling weak at the scene of devastation. She didn't seem to be able to think. Her mind had stopped working entirely at this critical moment and she stepped out and looked vaguely up and down the street. People were running from all directions but they took no notice of her, forming an awed circle around the burning remains of her car. Somebody had found a severed leg on the ground and was being sick. She stumbled slightly and grabbed the doorframe, which felt wet. She looked at her fingers and realised that they were scarlet with blood. The bile rose in her own throat and she swallowed, her head feeling dizzy. She went back through the door and over to Will, squatting down in front of him but then seating herself on the floor, where she took his hands.

"I think it was a bomb," she said, her voice high and taut. She squeezed his fingers, getting blood on him, and managed a more normal voice. "You nearly got yourself blown up, silly."

He smiled crookedly, remembering.

"I'll tell you something," he said. "The man at the car was the one that tried to hang me – he had shaved off the beard but I still recognised him."

Emergency vehicles began arriving. There was a knock on the open door and they turned to find DI Carter leaning in through the opening and looking at them.

"You seem to be Mr Popular, laddie," he observed sardonically, looking at Will. "Carry on at this rate and Hollywood is going to want the film rights."

Two hours passed. Outside the studio, a forensic team was scraping up pieces of the unknown bomber for DNA analysis. Officers were searching the surrounding area for evidence of any kind. There were bloody fragments of the bomber's viscera on the sides of parked cars facing the blast, and broken glass which crunched underfoot. No-one else had been injured, apart from a lady who had sustained a cut from flying glass, but the twisted and burned-out wreck of Lucy's car gave a stark and sobering message of violence, especially now that the fire-fighters' foam was dripping off it in gobbets, like flesh from a charred skeleton. There was a strong smell of explosive and burned rubber. Other surrounding cars had also received a battering and some had lost their windows, but their owners were not yet allowed to cross the yellow barrier tapes to inspect the damage – the road was cordoned off and reporters and television crews were gathering on the far side, seeking eye-witness reports from the crowd of onlookers. The wreck of

Lucy's car had already been captured by telephoto lenses and its image was winging its way around the world to feed content-hungry news channels.

Lucy felt amazed at how close they had come to death. She felt a savage pleasure that the bomber had been killed, but revulsion at the manner of his death. All in all she felt emotionally battered, as if she needed to step out of the frame for a while.

She had a long telephone conversation with her brother Dylan, who had seen the devastation on the evening news and had telephoned her to make sure she was still alive. Then she had a surprise that cheered her up a little – her best friend Millie rang. They had a tearful reunion on the phone and Lucy wanted to see her friend and give her a hug and say that it was *all right* – because suddenly it was: she hadn't thought about Sam once in the past few weeks, and now it transpired that Millie hadn't seen him either. She felt better after the call with Millie. She and Will were interviewed by Carter, together with various people from the security services who were charming and affable but never gave their names. She decided she needed to go home and recover from the excruciating pace of events. She made an excuse to Will and said she needed to use Hoffman and Courtland's databases to get to the root of Alfred's cryptic message. Her words sounded false even to her own ears, and they left each other a little awkwardly. She was not good at telling white lies, and Will's normal eloquence somehow deserted him where Lucy was concerned. She squeezed his hands, kissed him on the cheek and then was gone.

When she was no longer in the room he felt exhausted. He wished everyone would leave him alone. As soon as he could he closed the door on the floodlit street and the men in white boiler suits. He stapled raw canvas over the gaping studio window as a temporary means of closing it to the elements – a glazier would be along tomorrow to sort it out. Then he shut his curtains, stripped off his clothes and slid naked into the cool comfort of his bed. The phone rang immediately and it was George and Anna. He laughed when they asked if they should come and see him, explaining about the media circus and the cordoned-off street. He reassured them that he was all right but needed sleep. Then Sandy rang, and he reassured her too but told her he would call her tomorrow if he needed her. Then a national newspaper rang, at which point he put down the phone and unplugged it. He lay in bed for a while, eyes open, looking at the almost-dark room and hearing the sounds of voices and vehicles outside as the investigation continued. He wished he had a tumble of blonde hair on the pillow beside him.

Lucy sat in a brightly lighted carriage as the train clanked its way out of Cambridge, feeling guilty and ashamed of running away. But the ancient university city felt suddenly dangerous, and smoky old London seemed a safe haven. There was nobody there, so she pressed her nose to the glass and watched the back gardens slide by until they surrendered to open fields. On the seat beside her she carried the framed drawing that Will had made of her, wrapped in cardboard and tape. When she arrived back at her apartment it was late and she felt very tired, so she went straight to bed and was almost instantly asleep.

FIFTY-THREE

"Will you walk into my parlour?" said the Spider to the Fly.
MARY HOWITT, 1829

It was Monday morning, the day after the blast. Lucy was on the phone in her office and feeling back in control of her world.

"I'll need an art-transportation courier within the hour, so please get one on standby and charge it to our account."

There was a voice on the other end of the phone and she replied and then hung up. Vicky arrived in the doorway with a cup of Camomile tea, noting this change to the woman who normally drank only iced mineral water.

"Vicky," Lucy said, taking the tea. "Be a dear and find me a hammer and a hook, would you? I want to put this picture up."

She pointed at the frame resting on the floor. It was a drawing of Lucy sitting in a chair – a beautiful drawing, Vicky realised, picking it up. She looked at the signature in the top left-hand corner.

"Wow, so this is by the man himself," she said.

"What do you mean?" Lucy said, turning a little pink.

"The artist," Vicky said archly. "The one that nearly got blown up. The papers are saying that you and he are…you know."

Lucy looked at her with just the trace of a smile on her lips.

"That's what we might call a premature articulation, Victoria."

Hoffman and Courtland's client database quickly revealed the source of Alfred's clue. The "Triumph of Good over Evil" was a painting of the Madonna and Child, surrounded by angels glowing with light. It was by Procaccini, and the second Lucy saw an image of the painting she recognised it. She had stood in front of this painting once before, in a long, cold stone gallery, in Sir Philip and Lady Felicity Hall's house on the Isle of Wight. She felt embarrassed that she had not known immediately which painting it was, but in her defence it was difficult to remember every one of the thousands of paintings that were insured by the company. And of course, her entire focus on their last visit had been the Hammershoi.

It was interesting that the Halls had apparently been victims of *two* forgeries, not just the one that she and Will had gone to investigate. She picked up the phone to ring Will and tell him, but then put it down again and tapped her nose with the side of her pencil as she stared into space. She wanted to think about Will a bit. She was beginning to like him very much.

It was odd the way things happened. When Hugh had first mentioned Will Bentley she had imagined some half-crazed ex-convict; a large, shaven-headed, dull-witted violent beast. She had been reluctant to visit him without an escort. She laughed aloud at her recollection of this fact, just as Vicky returned with a hammer and looked at her strangely.

"Do you want me to put it up for you?"

Lucy shook her head, still smiling.

"I'll do it, don't worry. How's the argument with Facilities over the replacement car?"

Vicky consulted her notebook.

"They could do you a nice white van," she said.

"Lovely!"

"But I did check the list of cars in the car pool and there's a BMW Z4 which belonged to that frightful sales director woman who got chucked out after six months. It's only eleven months old, silver grey and has all the latest bits and bobs."

"Is it in a reasonable state?"

"I had a quick look in the garage, and it's gorgeous. You'd be the bee's knees and the cat's pyjamas."

"It sounds wonderful. Do you reckon you can wheedle it out of them, though? It's a grade up from the MG, surely?"

"I checked with them and they said you can have it. Technically it *is* a grade up, but it's second hand and they don't want it sitting in the garage gathering dust. I'll go and sort out the paperwork, but apparently you can't have it until tomorrow because the insurance will start from midnight tonight. I should think you'll have to sign a load of forms to say you promise not to, you know..."

"...blow it up," Lucy finished with a wry grin.

She telephoned the Isle of Wight and spoke to Lady Felicity. It was a difficult conversation but in the end Lucy convinced her that the painting needed to be analyzed immediately if they were to catch the art thieves, as it was strongly suspected of being a brilliant forgery. At first Lady Felicity resisted, but when Lucy told her that Hoffman and Courtland would not sustain insurance cover on a suspected forgery, she relented. Lucy told her the name of the courier, the agreed password and the estimated time of arrival, thanked Lady Felicity profusely and disconnected. Then she called Vicky and got her to organize the transport of the painting to Marcello's for testing. Finally she phoned John Ellis and begged him to stay on late – the painting was likely to arrive at about seven in the evening, but she felt too impatient to wait until the next day to start the analysis.

With the courier arranged and in transit to the Isle of Wight, there was nothing to do but to sit back and wait, so she worked on her email, which had stacked up to alarming proportions. She also phoned Davies and got through to him directly.

"You've been bloody busy, woman," he said. "Are you all right? I saw the pictures of your car on the news. You were lucky, I'm thinking. Then I spoke to Carter and he told me that Bentley identified the bomber as the chap with the beard."

"Yes he did," Lucy confirmed. "He'd shaved his beard off but Will was certain it was the same man."

"Well he was right," Davies said. "Carter said they already did a DNA test on the remains, and they match up perfectly with the hair on the cloth that was wrapped around the Hammershoi, and one or two traces found in the studio after the hanging."

"I'm not surprised," Lucy said. "Will was pretty certain, even though he only saw the man for a few seconds. He's probably good at remembering faces, being a portrait painter. Have you managed to find out who it was?"

"Not so far," Davies said, his voice regretful. "He's not on any police database as far as we can tell, or at least we don't have a previous record of his DNA."

"It's a shame," Lucy said. "If we could only find out who he was it would probably clear the whole thing up."

Davies could not attend the testing at Marcello's that evening, but he made her promise to call him after the test and say what the result had been. She swore faithfully to do so and they ended the call. She clicked open the next email, but before she could attend to it the phone rang again.

She picked it up.

"Did you forget something?" she said.

"Yes, I think I forgot *you*," a voice said, and she felt a sudden shock of recognition.

"Rupert!" she said. "I didn't think I was ever going to hear from you again after you bolted off the other night. In fact," she added, recovering fast, "I'm not sure I was very keen to."

"Yes, I'm terribly sorry about that," Rupert said. "I felt awful, but I simply had to go and sort out the consignment. I did call you but I always seemed to miss you."

"You do have my mobile number," Lucy said, continuing to be distant. Her heart was beating very fast. "You could have got me at any time on that."

"Yes, I know," Rupert said contritely, and she found herself melting a little at the sound of his voice. "You see, I didn't want to speak to you on your mobile when you might be in the middle of lunch with somebody. I wanted to speak to you privately."

"You could have left me a message," she persisted, but with a slight note of hesitation in her voice that he was quick to notice.

"I know," he said. "But messages never say fully what they mean, do they? I wanted to speak to you in person, and now here you are at last."

"Here I am at last," she said. "Have you seen the news?"

"Of course I have," he said. "That's why I decided I had to speak to you, no matter what, and called you in your office on the off chance that you might be in. Are you all right? I've been terribly worried."

"I'm fine, thank you. I just don't have a car, but I'm perfectly fine apart from that."

"Thank *God*," he said warmly. "And have they managed to find out who this madman is that tried to blow you up?"

Not so far," she said. "But I was speaking to the police just now, and they've identified him as the man who tried to hang Will."

"Ah yes, the painter", Rupert said. "The papers seem to think that you and he are, er..."

"Well, you know the media," she said sweetly, neither confirming nor denying the charge.

"Yes, well, it seems I was wrong about him," Rupert said unexpectedly. "He's turning out to be rather a hero."

"Everything a girl could want," she said, smiling into the telephone at Rupert's evident discomfort. It was somehow extremely satisfying to find a crack in the man's smooth façade.

"Yes, well I hope he's not that," Rupert said uncomfortably. "I was hoping you and I might meet up for a chat; have a cup of coffee or something."

She paused for a long time, thinking about it.

"I'm not sure, Rupert," she said. In some mental weighing machine she found herself comparing Rupert against Will Bentley – the last time she had done that, Rupert had come up trumps, but this time she felt that Will was in the lead. In fact, until this telephone call had thrown her into confusion, she had almost forgotten Rupert. It was unexpected to have him suddenly turn up like this.

"But we did have a lovely time," he said persuasively. "That wonderful meal at Le Gavroche, and then the opera – *that* was a night to remember."

"Ye-es," she said, feeling guilty after all he had done to entertain her in grand style.

"Well how about tonight?" Rupert said, pressing home his advantage while she was feeling cornered. "Just a cup of coffee and a chat. I'd like to hear how you've been, and to apologise in person for dashing off and leaving you like that. It was unforgivable."

"Yes it *was* unforgivable, Rupert," she said, seizing upon the word. "And I am not sure I *am* going to forgive you. I was very embarrassed and hurt. I felt like a jilted schoolgirl."

"I'm *very* sorry," he said, sounding genuinely contrite. "If you'll let me buy you more than coffee, I'll treat you to dinner if you like. I'd love to hear about your adventures first hand. Are you still on the track of that old chap you were looking for? What was his name, now?"

"Smith," she said. "Alfred Smith. And the investigation is going very well, thank you, but I can't talk about it. I shouldn't have told you anything about it before, really. I can't imagine why I did."

"Don't worry," Rupert said, "I swear I haven't told a soul."

"I should hope not," she said. "Anyway, I can't come out anywhere tonight because I'm having a painting tested at Marcello's. I want to get it resolved as fast as ever I can, because these people, whoever they are, are so violent."

There was a silence for a moment.

"I realize it may be too late for you and me," Rupert said. "But at least I'd like to meet up just once and say I'm sorry in person. Surely that isn't too much to ask?"

"It's too much to ask tonight," Lucy said.

"How are you getting to the test lab?" he asked suddenly.

This threw her. Until that moment she had not thought about it, but now she realised she couldn't just drive to Marcello's as she wouldn't be getting her replacement car until tomorrow.

"I can take a taxi," she said uncertainly.

"That's it, then," he said triumphantly. "How about I give you a lift in the Rolls? We can have a chat in the back. It's my driver's night off but I'm sure Mrs Morris wouldn't mind driving us so that we can talk properly. I shall shut the window on her so that she can't be nosey."

"Well," Lucy hesitated.

"Please?"

She contemplated the prospect of trying to get a taxi to return to Marcello's and pick her up after the testing was complete, versus the Rolls. She also felt she owed Rupert one last chance to explain himself, though she wasn't quite sure why. And it was hard to say no to him.

"All right then," she said. "As I don't have any transport I'll agree to it. But please don't jump to any conclusions. Things aren't the same as far as I'm concerned."

"I wouldn't dream of it," Rupert assured her. "When should I pick you up so that I get you to your laboratory on time?"

"About six," she said, and made sure that he had her office address.

She put down the phone, feeling exasperated and not a little apprehensive to be meeting up with Rupert again. She didn't trust him the way she had before. She certainly wasn't going to tell him anything more about what she and Will had been doing. She was already beginning to regret giving in to him.

Rupert put down the phone in his office and looked at Mrs Morris, who had sat motionless and mute across the desk throughout the entire conversation.

"Tonight," he said, "we are taking Lucy Wrackham to Marcello's, which as you probably know is a test lab where they evaluate paintings. She says she is testing a painting that may have bearing on the investigation."

"Which painting is it?" Mrs Morris said, leaning forward slightly.

"She didn't say, and I didn't dare ask," Rupert said. "She was very touchy, Julia. It took all my powers of persuasion to get her to agree to see me at all."

"I told you," Mrs Morris said rather tartly, "she's sleeping with the painter so she doesn't care for you anymore."

"It probably didn't help her mood to be almost blown to bits by you and Morton when I had given you explicit instructions only to dispose of Bentley," Rupert replied with equal acidity.

"Rupert," Mrs Morris said guilelessly. "I already told you that I made it perfectly clear to Edward that only the painter was to be terminated. I don't know why he did it. I know he didn't like the girl, after she made a fool of him at Bentley's studio, but I didn't think he'd do that. He didn't tell me that he had put the bomb on the car until he had actually done it, and then it was too late. He said he must have made a mistake and misheard what I said, which was complete nonsense. He was quite brutal about it – he was going to take her out too. At least he had the decency to blow himself up and save us the trouble of getting rid of him." She sighed. "Poor Edward."

"Poor Edward," Rupert echoed sourly. "Unfortunately, poor Edward couldn't have chosen a much more public way to do it. Now we'll have the security services looking for us as well as the police. We probably have the same classification as terrorists. I think we need to get out while the going is good."

"I agree with you absolutely, Rupert" she said. "But first I suggest we complete the last stage of the plan and get the money. We *must* swap the painting now. Then we can pay off our debt to Mr Harold, keep the balance and disappear for a while."

"The painting isn't finished," Rupert said. "The paint hasn't been hardened, which will take a week and we don't even yet have an oven."

"I understand that, but I'm not sure if we *can* wait," Mrs Morris said. "But never mind about that now; we need to deal with our latest problem. It all depends what the painting is that Mrs Wrackham plans to have tested."

Lucy tried to call Will at four and again at a quarter to six, partly because she was excited and wanted to bring him up to date with what she had discovered about the Procaccini, and partly because she wanted to hear his voice. She wanted to tell him that she had been persuaded by Rupert to endure a lift with him, and now she was regretting it but didn't see how she could get out of it. But she couldn't do any of this because Will didn't answer the phone on either occasion, so she put it down without leaving a message.

Will, meanwhile, had tried to paint a little during the day, but had sent Sandy home when he found that nothing was going on the canvas the way he wanted. He simply couldn't concentrate. He wondered how Lucy was getting on with the investigation, but George and Anna arrived just as he was picking up the phone to call her.

"Hello old chap," George said, coming into the studio and shaking him by the hand. We thought we'd better come and see you quickly before they succeed in bumping you off."

"Oh shut up, George," Anna said, giving Will a hug and then holding him at arm's length to look at him. "Are you all right?"

He assured them that he was perfectly all right.

"In that case, I think we need a little libation at the Fort," George said firmly. "After what you've been through I should think you need a pint of Tribute."

"And anyway, I want to hear all about Lucy Wrackham," Anna said. "I saw her picture in the paper. You didn't mention that she's absolutely stunning. Oh my God, isn't this her?" She picked up the second sketch that Will had done of Lucy.

"Yes, that's her," Will said rather proudly. "She *is* turning out to be a rather interesting girl, actually. All right then, let's go to the pub. I can't paint today; my mind's not on it."

FIFTY-FOUR

Show me a liar, and I will show thee a thief.
GEORGE HERBERT, Jacula Prudentum

A rather interesting girl emerged from her office at a deliberately late ten past six, but saw the Rolls purring at the curb, waiting for her. Mrs Morris looked a little incongruous behind the wheel and Lucy wondered what had happened to Rupert's driver. Something was on the edge of her memory about the driver, but she couldn't think what. Rupert stepped out of the car to greet her and she permitted herself to be hugged briefly before sliding into the back seat. Mrs Morris had the driver's connecting glass open and she positively gushed about how lovely it was to see Lucy again – none of which Lucy believed; Mrs Morris struck her as a hard woman who said what she thought you wanted to hear. Rupert was as gorgeous as ever, at once grave and courteous, managing to convey a perfect mix of abject apology tinged with rakish charm. Characteristically he had a bottle of champagne on ice and his first action was to pop it open and pour Lucy an effervescent glassful.

"Perhaps later on I can get you that cup of coffee I promised," he said, handing her the glass of champagne, "but for now, you'll have to make do with this."

She found herself charmed in spite of her determination to be cold and distant, and the champagne took the edge off her anger and put her in a more congenial frame of mind.

"I was expecting you to have a large painting tucked under your arm," Rupert said. "I was hoping to see what all the fuss is about."

"The painting has already been shipped to Marcello's," Lucy said, sipping champagne as the Rolls transported them ghostlike through London, detaching them from the rush of traffic as if they were in a parallel universe.

"Oh what a pity, I would like to have seen it," he said. "Although I expect it was all packaged up anyway so you could hardly have fished it out in the back of the car. Who did you say it was by?"

"I don't believe I mentioned it," Lucy said sweetly, but then felt she was being more churlish than even Rupert deserved. "But I'll tell you, I suppose. It's a Procaccini."

"Oh really?" He frowned in thought. "I only vaguely know the name. Italian Renaissance?"

"Early seventeenth century. I didn't know much about him either so I looked him up."

Rupert didn't say much for a few minutes. He remembered Alfred's rendering of the Procaccini only too well – they had borrowed it for three weeks while it was at an exhibition, and the owners had never even missed it. He racked his brains to think why Lucy would be investigating the Procaccini, and wondered whether it could possibly survive full-scale professional tests in a laboratory such as Marcello's. He doubted it.

"You'll have to drop me off outside," Lucy said. "There's only one chap opening up for me as a favour, and he said he can only let *me* in. Marcello's is very tight on security and he's only doing it for me because he knows me."

"No problem, we can wait outside," Rupert said easily. "I don't want to leave you stuck in the suburbs of London as it gets late."

Privately she felt relieved that he was going to stay and give her a lift, though she was still cross with herself that she had given in so weakly.

They arrived outside the unprepossessing gates of Marcello's, and Lucy thanked Rupert for the lift. She had already called John Ellis on her mobile, and now his familiar figure came into view.

"It's very kind of him," Lucy said. "Everyone else has gone home."

Ellis came up to the tall gates and pressed the security button so that the small side gate clicked and unlatched. He pushed the door open so that she could come through, waved towards the Rolls and allowed the door to click shut again.

"Hello Lucy," he said, looking at the Rolls with raised eyebrows and the little mischievous smile that she so liked. "I'm obviously mixing with the wrong people. Normally I wouldn't work late, but I did see the news and it sounds like you've been through the wars a bit, so if there's anything I can do to help then I'll be pleased to do it."

"Hello John," she said. "I had to get a lift because of what happened to my car."

"I saw the pictures on television," he said soberly. "Was anyone hurt?"

"Some poor lady cut her head," Lucy said. "Oh and the bomber was killed, of course. They had to pick him up in a bucket. It made me feel sick."

John Ellis nodded, unlocking the front door of Marcello's with his pass. "Serves him right. A thing like that could have killed a dozen people, easily. Have you any idea who he was?"

Lucy shook her head, following him down the corridor.

"Not yet," she said, reluctant to go into the whole story of the attempted hanging of Will and the connection that had emerged. "You said the Procaccini has arrived. When did it get here?"

"The courier was pretty quick, considering that they had to fetch it from the Isle of Wight," Ellis said. "Must have been about five thirty, just after reception had closed up for the evening. I haven't opened the box yet, though. I thought I'd wait for you."

There was a large aluminium case in the lab, leaning up against a wall with other similar cases. He lifted it up with Lucy's help and they put it flat on an inspection table. He clicked open the snap-locks around the edges, and with great care lifted off the lid. The painting itself was protected by further layers, but after a few minutes he had exposed it and removed it from its packaging.

She looked at the picture again; the Madonna and Child surrounded by various angels. It was a beautiful old painting and she found it difficult to believe that it could possibly be anything other than real. However, the last time she had been in this lab she had been thinking the same about the Alma Tadema, and that had turned out to be a forgery, albeit from a more recent era. In an odd way she hoped that this one would be a copy too. For one thing she needed a further clue and fervently wished this to be it. And for another, it would be embarrassing to have to return the painting to Lady Felicity and explain that it had all been a false alarm.

"What shall we start with?" John Ellis said, but she knew from long familiarity that with him this was a rhetorical question. He had a habit of talking to himself as he worked, as if stepping himself through the various tests. She used to answer these questions but now she had learned to keep quiet.

He inspected the paint surface carefully and sniffed the picture in several different places. He turned it over and looked at the verso. The picture was painted on canvas and had at some time or other been put onto a new canvas backing, though the backing itself had now become extremely darkened with age.

"No verso photographs?" he said.

She shook her head.

"All right then. Straight onto the X-ray, I think."

He carried the painting over to another flat table, switched on an X-ray fluorescence machine and fiddled with its settings. Then he spent some time aligning the machine perfectly over the painting.

"It's on a remote trigger," he said apologetically. "Like the dentist. We have to retire beyond the screen."

When they were at a safe distance he pressed the button and the machine buzzed slightly for a second.

"That's it", Ellis said. "Not very dramatic but it does the job."

They walked back to it. Lucy looked at the negative image on the screen and then stared at it with a frown. The Madonna and Child were there all right, but underneath the "Procaccini" there was a monochrome portrait – the head of a man.

"That's weird, it almost looks like…can you show it as a positive, John?"

"I think I can do that for you," Ellis said. He leaned forward to the screen and touched an icon so that the picture flipped from negative to positive.

Lucy gasped.

"But I don't understand," she blurted out. "What's *he* doing there?"

"Most extraordinary," Ellis said, looking keenly at the image. "There are words written underneath, and a *date*, look! Not early seventeenth century, though. It was painted about six months ago. Remarkable work."

He leaned forward and squinted, manipulating the image and zooming on the lower section.

"It looks like `Expert Angel' but it's partially obscured."

He touched the Print icon and a screen copy spooled out of a nearby printer. He glanced at Lucy.

"Are you all right? You've gone quite white!"

"It doesn't say `Expert', it says `Rupert'," Lucy said in an oddly brittle voice, looking at the perfect likeness of the portrait and feeling a terrible sense of betrayal growing inside her. "*Rupert* Angel. That's Alfred's clue. Rupert is involved in this whole thing."

Suddenly a wave of white-hot anger burst out of her.

"He's been stringing me along all this time, the complete *bastard*."

She snatched up the print-out and before Ellis could stop her she was running out of the lab.

"Let's see how he explains *this*," she yelled over her shoulder, plunging through the double swing doors so that they crashed back on their hinges and swung violently closed behind her.

"*Lucy*!" Ellis called in surprise and exasperation after her departing figure. He couldn't think of any circumstances to justify her behaving in such a fashion, for he had no idea that the man in the X-Ray portrait was at this moment sitting in the Rolls outside. He went to the lab doors and peered through their glass windows, but Lucy was already out of sight.

"For God's sake," he muttered to himself, shaking his head. He went back to the XRF machine and looked at the image on the screen with a frown. He supposed that she would return in a minute when she had calmed down. Meanwhile, the image could be a lot better than that. He reached forward and made adjustments, concentrating on his work.

Rupert was talking in low tones with Mrs Morris when the front door of Marcello's suddenly banged open and Lucy Wrackham emerged from it, flourishing a sheet of paper.

"She looks rather upset about something," Mrs Morris observed dryly as Lucy marched across the car park towards them and punched her hand on the gate release button. She looked livid. Mrs Morris and Rupert both got out of the Rolls as Lucy reached them, and Mrs Morris picked up her bag.

"Whatever is it, Lucy?" Rupert said with real concern in his voice.

"*This!*" Lucy hissed, practically spitting as she brandished the paper in his face. "How do you explain *this*? It's an X-ray of the Procaccini."

He was confused. He took the picture out of her shaking hand and looked at it. The blood slowly drained out of his face. He was looking at a picture of himself. It was perfectly executed; in fact, an excellent likeness. As if that was not enough evidence, Alfred had actually painted *his name* beneath the portrait, and added the date so that there could be no mistake."

"I, er…"

For once Rupert could think of nothing whatsoever to say. Lucy raised her hand and slapped him hard in the face, and he took the blow without resisting, his cheek reddening.

"I can explain," he found himself saying, but realized at the same moment that he *couldn't* explain. While he stood at a loss for words Mrs Morris moved behind Lucy. Now she swept her victim's hair aside in one swift movement and thrust a needle into Lucy's neck. Lucy felt the sting and started to turn around angrily, but then Ketamine flooded into her brain and all thought ceased.

John Ellis heard the urgent beeping of the gate speakerphone and supposed that Lucy had locked herself out in her sudden mad dash. He went out and crossed the car-park towards the noise, grim faced. He was going to give her a piece of his mind – he had, after all, opened up the whole building as a special favour because she had begged him, and in return she had behaved in a completely unprofessional manner. He was mystified to see a smartly dressed lady at the gate. She was looking very worried.

"I'm terribly sorry," the smart lady said, "but Lucy seems to have had some kind of a fit. It's quite awful; she's frothing at the mouth. My driver's looking after her but I think we need to take her to the nearest hospital. Could I be very rude and pop in for a moment to use your telephone?"

"Of course," Ellis said, immediately concerned and feeling guilty that he had been so cross. He had *thought* Lucy had acted very strangely. He didn't know what was going on but no doubt he would find out soon enough.

"Oh, thank you so much!" Mrs Morris said, giving him a grateful smile.

He opened the gate and they hurried back to the building. He opened the reception office and switched on the lights, holding the door open for her.

"You can make the call in here," he said. "Use that telephone and just dial 9 first to get an outside line."

"Oh *thank* you," she said, and then looked flustered. "Could you just dial for me?" she said. "It sounds ridiculous but I'm all shaken up."

"No problem," he said staunchly. "Do you want me to get the number of the hospital from directory enquiries?"

"Oh, that would be very kind," she said, and he nodded and picked up the telephone. But as he was selecting an outside line he felt a tremendous blow on the back of his head and everything blurred. He pitched forward and fell across a chair at an odd angle, knocking over a small table so that the printer on it went flying and scattered paper everywhere. Mrs Morris stood over his inert shape for a moment, still holding the glass paperweight that she had picked up. She had not even had to use the second syringe. She picked up the fallen receiver and listened to it. It was a dead line – he had not managed to dial, though it had been a close-run thing. She tucked the unused syringe back into the little case in her handbag, next to its empty partner, then leaned over and looked at John Ellis. Blood was staining his shock of white hair but he was still breathing. She lifted her arm and crashed the paperweight down onto his skull several more times, until there was a clearly evident dent. Then she took out a tissue and wiped the paperweight with it. There was blood in the engraved "Marcello's" logo. When it was clean she replaced it on the secretary's desk and wiped the phone. Her finger snagged and when she looked at it she discovered that she had broken a nail. She frowned, put on her gloves and then left her victim, ignoring his stertorous breathing.

Forty-five minutes later a fire in the laboratory began to spread very rapidly throughout the whole of Marcello's. Three oxygen canisters exploded, destroying eight sixteenth century oil paintings which were in for restoration. By the time the fire brigade reached Marcello's, flames had burst uncontrollably through the roof and were shooting up into the sky. It took three fire crews the rest of the night to put it out, and nearby houses had to be evacuated because of the heat and the danger of explosion from the burning chemicals used in art conservation. When the light coagulated into an uneasy dawn, the flames were extinguished but a pall of black smoke hung in the windless sky like a giant's fist.

FIFTY-FIVE

There was a laughing Devil in his sneer,
That raised emotions both of rage and fear ;
And where his frown of hatred darkly fell,
Hope withering fled — and Mercy sighed farewell!
LORD BYRON, The Corsair

Will was dropped off by George and Anna at a quarter to midnight, somewhat the worse for wear. As he was opening his door, one of the girls who worked next door went past him, wearing a skirt with a hemline at the crease of her buttocks.

"Special rates for local residents," she said with a grin.

He smiled and waved and then fell through his door, sitting down in the doorway for a moment before picking himself up.

"Maybe another nigh'," he mumbled apologetically.

He awoke at six the next morning and lay for a moment looking up at the bedroom ceiling. He had fallen asleep with the light on, but seemed somehow to have shed his clothes, for they were festooned in odd twisted shapes around the bed. Now the late July sunlight streamed in through the window and made a long shadow from the African mask on the wall. His mouth tasted horrible and his head felt thick. He got up and went into the kitchen, where he drank a pint of water and switched on the kettle. Then he stood under the shower for fifteen minutes. There was not much food in the house except eggs, but he was ravenous so he made an omelette, adding spring onions and a red pepper and cheese that he found in the fridge drawer. He made a large mug of fresh coffee.

When he went into the studio to eat he remembered the broken window for the first time. The canvas crudely tacked across the opening kept out the morning air but allowed light to leak through the cracks at the sides. The effect was to make the room oddly dark, yet striated with shafts of light in which motes of dust danced. He switched on the light that hung over the dining table, then slumped down in the armchair where he had drawn Lucy and ate his omelette there.

The glazier came promptly at eight and was extremely efficient – he had installed a new pane of glass in the window by nine thirty and was gone. Will was now alone in the studio and found himself wondering why he had not heard from Lucy, who he thought would have called him by now. But as if on cue the phone rang and he answered it.

"Mr Bentley? It's Hugh Davies here, from the Met. I'm sorry to call you so early after what you've been through, but have you got a moment to talk?"

A series of emotions went through Will. The first was disappointment that it was not Lucy. The second was a desire to tell the policeman to stuff it. But the third was weariness with the whole business. He wanted an end to it all so that he could go back to painting. Life had been simpler then.

"What is it?" he asked reluctantly, keeping his voice even. "Have you caught them yet? I haven't heard a word from Lucy."

"No further arrests I'm afraid," Davies said, sounding more Welsh than usual as he did when he was concerned. "But it's Lucy that I'm calling about, as it happens. I spoke to her yesterday and she was going off to get a painting tested. She promised she was going to call me when the analysis was done, but she never did. I was rather hoping she might be with you, so to speak."

"She's not here," Will said in alarm. "When did you talk to her? Have you tried her flat?"

"I talked to her yesterday afternoon at about two. I've tried her home number several times since then but there's no answer. I can't get an answer from her mobile either."

"What does her office say?"

"I spoke to her secretary this morning: a Miss Vicky Bowles," Davies said, obviously consulting a notebook. "She told me that Lucy hadn't come in to work, which is odd because she was due to collect a replacement car. Miss Bowles suggested that I check with you."

"Well, as I say, she's not here and I haven't heard from her. But if you *do* find her I'd appreciate you letting me know."

"I'll do that," Davies promised, and disconnected.

Will paced up and down the studio, feeling a growing sense of disquiet. Lucy had been investigating Alfred's message and now she was nowhere to be found. Knowing the people they were dealing with, it was worrying to say the least. He tried calling her mobile and her home number but there was no reply. Then the phone rang again.

"Lucy?"

"Mr Bentley, it's Hugh Davies again," the detective said, sounding much more sombre this time. "I'm afraid I've got some bad news. Lucy *did* take the painting to a test lab called Marcello's yesterday as planned, but I've just discovered that the lab burned down late yesterday evening."

Will swore.

"Have they found any sign of her?"

"I spoke to the dispatcher five minutes ago," Davies said. "The place was apparently full of inflammable chemicals so they've been trying to put it out all night. He said they've found a body in the wreckage but it's too burned to be identified. Apparently the place was totally gutted, so it's not easy. All I'm saying to you right now is that it doesn't look good for Lucy."

Will felt as if his brain had ground to a halt. A *body in the wreckage... doesn't look good for Lucy.*

"Are you still there?" Davies was saying in his ear. "Mr Bentley?"

Will couldn't speak. Davies didn't say anything either and the silence lengthened as both men listened to the silence at the other end of the phone. Will suddenly realised that the policeman was as upset as he was, and somehow that unlocked his tongue.

"I can't just sit here in Cambridge waiting for news," he said. "I'll go mad. Where's this lab which burned down? I think I'd like to go there."

"I was going to go over myself, so I'll see you there if you like," Davies said, and he read out the address.

Will went down to London on the Bonnie, and in an hour and thirty minutes he was driving through the streets of Richmond, looking for the little street he needed. It wasn't all that far from Lucy's flat. He found it quickly enough, but the road was cordoned off with tapes and there were two policemen standing guard in yellow reflective jackets. He turned round and parked the Bonnie on the pavement close to a tiny Italian café called Luigi's, then locked up the bike and walked back down the road to the factory. He was let through the barrier when he explained that he was meeting Hugh Davies from Art and Antiques – Davies had already passed through and they remembered him.

Whatever building had been on the site was gone, now just a pile of blackened rubble almost levelled to the ground. Will threaded his way through the emergency vehicles until he reached the gates of the factory, which were wide open. There was a terrible stench of burning in the air. Firemen walked back and forth, stowing away fire-fighting equipment, looking tired and streaked with dirt. He spotted Davies at the same moment that the policeman saw him, and they walked over to each other. After a moment's hesitation they shook hands awkwardly.

"They've found one body so far," Davies said, gesturing at the forensic officers who were working their way systematically through the building. "No idea whether it was Lucy or someone else, but it turns out that one of the technicians stayed late last night to let Lucy in, and he never returned. I've spoken to his wife."

"So the body could be his?"

"Yes," Davies said grimly. "I saw them take the body away, and I've seen some pretty bad sights in my time but it was horrible. You could only just about tell it had been human."

"Will they be able to identify it, though?"

"Oh yes, dental records maybe, but DNA for sure. They'll run the tests immediately and let me know."

"Have you checked her flat?" Will said, clutching at straws. "She might just be sleeping in late while we're panicking."

Davies shook his head.

"She's not there. We sent a locksmith around in a patrol car and he let them in. There was no sign of her. I spoke to her boyfriend too."

"Rupert Angel?" Will said in such a sour voice that Davies looked at him.

"That's the one. A smooth character."

"Smarmy bastard I always thought."

Davies managed a thin smile.

"He *was* a bit smarmy, as it happens. He said he hadn't seen her and that they'd been out of touch for several days. He said they'd parted with a bit of a row but he hoped that didn't make him a suspect."

"That sounds like him," Will said, rolling his eyes. "So he's another dead end. What about Hoffman and Courtland?"

They walked together across the car park. There was a car still parked there which was now a burned-out shell. It gave Will an unpleasant reminder of the wreck of Lucy's car outside his studio. They stepped over fire-hose snakes as they went, and stopped when they got to the rubble at the border of the outer wall.

"I'm visiting Lucy's company this afternoon," Davies said. "I haven't had time to do more than speak to the secretary so far, but I want to interview them all in person, to see what they've got to say."

"You've got the clue we were following up on?"

"The Triumph of Good over Evil by Procaccini," Davies nodded. "She told me, but what I *don't* know is where it came from. Lucy dodged the topic."

"You're not going to arrest me if I tell you?" Will said, looking at him to judge his reply.

"I've already made that mistake," Davies said simply.

So Will told him about the magazine subscription to Renaissance Artist, and sketched over the means by which they had obtained Alfred's entry on the database. He explained how they had gone to the house in Burnham-Overy-Staithe, gained entry, searched it from top to bottom and eventually found the message.

"You've been busy," Davies said when Will finished the account. "Let me have the Norfolk address so that we can have a look over it, though it sounds like you've already had a peek in every corner."

Will dictated the Burnham address to the policeman, who wrote it down in his notebook. Then they turned in unison and walked back to the gates.

Davies' phone rang and he listened for a minute before disconnecting. Then he turned to Will, his face bearing witness to more bad news.

"I asked for a trace on Lucy's mobile. They can tell what cell area the phone was in by looking back through records."

"And the answer is?"

"The phone was in this cell yesterday evening but the signal connection went dead when the fire started."

They stood and looked at each other but didn't say anything, each seeing the pain in the other's face.

"I wish I'd gone with her," Will said quietly. "Normally I would have, but then the bomb went off outside the studio and it frightened her badly. It scared the hell out of me as well, but I was already at home. Anyway, she jumped on a train down to London and that's the last I saw of her."

"On Sunday night?"

"Yes," Will said, and his mouth twisted. "One of Carter's coppers gave her a lift to the station in case you need corroboration."

"No, no, I believe you," Davies said hastily.

They walked out of the gates and down the street, stopping where Davies had parked his car.

"Can I offer you a lift?" he asked, but Will shook his head.

"I'm on a motorbike," he said. "Will you call me when the DNA tests come in?"

Davies agreed he would and then departed. Will walked back to the Bonnie, feeling utterly despondent. He remembered Lucy's little frown of concentration when she was thinking; her giggle when he said something funny. The velvet touch of her lips. He walked past the bike without realizing and had to turn round and go back to it.

He felt he ought to eat something so he bought a Panini and a coffee in the little Italian café where he had parked the bike, and crossed the street to consume them in a small park set about an ornamental pond with a beer can floating in it. He was joined by a squadron of hungry pigeons. He ate half of the Panini but had no appetite for the rest, even though it was well past lunch time, so he tore it into small chunks and fed it to the birds. When it was all gone they deserted him. He sat and stared into the water, wondering if Lucy was alive or dead. Images of her continued to run relentlessly through his mind. Her hair whipping his cheek in the open-top Roadster on the Isle of Wight. Her comical expression after the fish and chips when she realized she was supposed to be going out to dinner. Her dreaminess as she came sleepily awake in his armchair at the studio.

He felt tired, defeated and hopeless. He had no idea what to do next.

RICHARD JOHN MITCHELL

FIFTY-SIX

All the old knives That have rusted in my back, I drive in yours.
PHAEDRUS

Rupert was in his study in the London house, pacing up and down because he was too angry to sit still. It had started when he had returned to the house in the early hours to find Mrs Morris waiting for him. She was unexpectedly furious that he had got rid of Lucy Wrackham and she had threatened to *leave* – an event which was unprecedented in his long relationship with this extraordinarily efficient and cold-blooded woman. He had thought she would have been pleased that he had fixed the problem, for she was obviously jealous of Rupert's liaison with Lucy. Instead she had been vitriolic; flushed with anger; accusatory and bitter.

He went through in his mind how it had happened, principally to justify to himself that he had made a sensible decision. He had left Mrs Morris at Marcello's the previous evening so that she could "clean up", to use her own words. He had driven back with Lucy unconscious in the back of the Rolls. At some point during the journey, when admittedly he had been feeling very agitated, the man they called the Collector had called him for a progress report. Rupert had still been in a state of shock and had said more than he should. He had reassured the Collector that the security breach had been fixed, apart from one thing: they had a prisoner in tow; the beautiful insurance agent Lucy Wrackham.

The Collector had been silent at first. He had already seen Lucy twice before. He had arranged for the meal at Le Gavroche and paid for Rupert's dinner with Lucy, simply so that he could sit at a nearby table and watch her. And he had so liked the vision of Lucy in her strapless blue tulip-shaped dress that he had followed up with a pair of opera tickets, couriered to Rupert's door, so that he could again be lost in the crowd and yet have the chance to observe the beautiful Lucy from a discreet distance. Rupert had felt obliged to humour him since the man was paying the bills, though neither the luxurious restaurant nor the opera had been a hardship. The fact was that the Collector enjoyed not just the paintings themselves, but the adrenaline rush that came with acquiring them. It had always been that way – Rupert had been required not only to hand over each painting, but to recount in detail the method of its acquisition so that the Collector could enjoy his private moment of glee.

It was with this background that the Collector had offered Rupert the perfect solution: *he* would have Lucy Wrackham. He had the perfect place to keep her, away from the eyes of staff. She would become his property and his problem, not Rupert's.

The Collector had been persuasive. She could be his first *live exhibit*, he had quipped. Rupert had come to a sudden decision and had changed direction away from his London house, driving west out of the city towards the vast Oxfordshire mansion. He had arrived there very late and in pitch darkness. The still-unconscious Lucy had been placed in a wheelchair and removed from Rupert's life. It had seemed the perfect solution until he had recounted events to Mrs Morris.

Mrs Morris had said that he must have lost his reason to leave Lucy in the charge of the Collector, who she referred to as an old fool with too much money. Rupert felt exasperated by the whole business. First Alfred Smith had betrayed him by painting his likeness under the Procaccini; presumably to cover his back. Then the hidden portrait had been discovered by none other than *Lucy*, which had been completely mortifying. The kidnap of Lucy had made it worse still, though there had been no alternative. Then he had driven all the way to the Cotswolds and back in the middle of the night, and when he had returned, Mrs Morris had told him that she had burned down the factory and *killed a witness*. It could not get any worse.

He shook his head wearily, his eyes feeling leaden. He urgently needed sleep. He poured himself a glass of scotch from the decanter and downed it in a gulp which burned his throat. He *had* been desperate, it was true, but had he simply accepted an easy way out as Mrs Morris had so acidly described? He thought not, and his neck flushed red with anger. He considered it was partly *her* fault. He knew that she would have returned from Marcello's and wanted Lucy dead. In a way, *she* had precipitated him into this. She would have proposed swift action to rid them of a prime witness; perhaps a smothering while Lucy was still unconscious, followed by a night-time burial. Instead, Mrs Morris had made it plain that she thought Rupert had sold out by handing Lucy Wrackham over to the Collector. She had called Lucy a time bomb waiting to go off. Rupert had explained his own logic that it was an elegant solution to the problem. She had countered that if the Collector were caught then Lucy would be found and their own arrest would follow swiftly. They had exchanged further strong words and Julia had stormed upstairs, where no doubt she was confiding the whole story in a distorted fashion to her witless and pathetic offspring.

The phone rang and he glared at it. *What now?*

"Mr Angel? It's Charles Winton."

His blood froze.

"Charles!" he hissed. "Why are you calling me here?"

Winton was his man inside the National.

"It's all right, it can't be traced to me," came Winton's voice, sounding a little surprised at the acerbity in Rupert's voice. "I have some news that won't wait. They've *moved* the Botticelli."

"The Venus and Mars?" Rupert said stupidly. "But you said they weren't due to move it for cleaning until next month. We can't do the exchange yet. The – other article – has not been baked."

"If it's touch dry then it'll have to do," Winton said. "Is it?"

Rupert thought for a moment.

"I suppose it *is* touch dry, but we can't–"

"You don't understand," Winton interrupted, anxious to make his point. This is our *only* chance. The painting is in the Conservation Department under review. Then Photographic is due to take a full set of new pictures, front back and sides. Then it's shipping out over the weekend to the Uffizi. It's right here on the computer log."

"To Florence? But why–"

And then in a rush of realisation Rupert *saw* why. The Uffizi was planning an exhibition of Botticelli's work. Famous pieces were coming from private collections and museums all over the world. He had read about it in one of the trade journals but had never imagined that the National would allow the Venus and Mars out of the country. He swallowed, seeing their carefully concocted plan going straight out of the window.

"I see," he said with a sigh, sitting down heavily in the chair. The door to the study opened and Mrs Morris came back in, presumably to continue the argument about Lucy Wrackham. She stopped and frowned when she realised he was on the phone.

He held his flat palm towards her and covered the phone with his hand for a moment.

"Winton," he said in a voice hardly bigger than a whisper. "The Botticelli has been moved early."

He uncovered the phone again and put it to his ear.

"Charles," he said in a weary voice. "I was expecting more warning than this."

"I couldn't possibly have known before now," Winton said. "They don't tell me everything; I only managed to find out at all by accident. The fact is, once it's out of here it'll be under armed guard all the way to the Uffizi. They won't take any chances, and then it's there until November."

Rupert hesitated for a long moment.

"Well, what do you say?" Winton said impatiently.

"We'll do it," Rupert said at last. Exactly as we have planned."

Tuesday brought a second day of heat – not sweltering, for there was a slight breeze and it was only twenty five Celsius. A security van drew up at the service bay entrance to the National Gallery at just gone four. It was let through the barrier by Ted Dobson, the security man who covered the rear bay. He raised the barrier with a button on the console in front of him, next to a computer screen which still sported two tiny plastic St. George's flags left over from the last World Cup. The van backed up to the rear bay doors and two guards got out and walked up to the security man's service hatch. One of them extracted a sheaf of papers. Ted Dobson's cubicle was open at the back, inside the building, and a fan was blowing inside it, making his sparse hair flutter about.

His electronically amplified voice said, "Afternoon. What can I do for you gentlemen?"

"I've got an Art and Antiquities crate in the back for you," the first guard said, his voice slightly muffled by his helmet. He flourished the paperwork, took out a pen and marked crosses in three places on a form. "Big bugger but not too heavy. You'll need to sign for it here, here, and here."

Dobson took the form, which was of a type he had seen hundreds of times before, and scanned it quickly.

He mouthed the figures of the Job Number as he typed it into the terminal in front of him. The security guard raised his mouth shield and breathed the fresh air.

"Bloody hot," he said. "No air conditioning in the front of the van. They cool the cargo but they don't cool the bloody workers."

Dobson nodded.

"You could fry an egg in here too," he agreed. "The sun beats right down on this window for most of the day. He frowned at the screen. "I can't find this job number."

"Typical," the helmeted guard said. "They've probably cocked it up. They said it was a last-minute rush. It has to go to the Conservation Department straight away, apparently. Your boffins must want it for something."

Dobson shrugged. "Art Handling are usually pretty good, but I can't find it. Anyway, I'll let them sort it out."

He smiled to himself at the thought of Derek Bullrode's face when he told him that his department hadn't registered an incoming artwork. Bullrode was a snotty bastard and it would be good to put one over him for a change. He was always lecturing Dobson about security. Damn cheek.

The van driver nodded and turned round to his colleague.

"Okay," he called. "Open it up."

The other man nodded and opened the rear doors of the van wide, then stepped up into it.

"I'll give him a hand if you could open the bay doors," the guard said, and went back to help his colleague. Dobson opened the doors and his young assistant Tony emerged blinking into the sunlight, fetching a specialist trolley when he saw the size of the flat crate which the security men were lifting down from the van. He helped them manhandle the crate onto the trolley and they lowered it very carefully, and then adjusted the supporting bars on the sides so that it wouldn't shift about. Tony tightened up the webbing straps around the crate. You couldn't be too careful. Half the stuff going in and out of the bay was as old as the hills and worth a bloody fortune, Ted said.

He checked the label on the box which the guard pointed out to him, which said "National Gallery," followed by the address and a job number. He gave the job number to Ted over the radio, who gave him the thumbs up through the glass. Dobson took the proffered yellow copy from the van driver, and the driver thanked him and walked over to Tony.

"Your gaffer's got the Delivery Note," he said. "They said mind you get it down to the Conservation Department straight away. Apparently they're waiting for it."

"I'll take it along right now."

The van left and Tony wheeled the crate across the bay and down to the service lift. It took him ten minutes to get it up to the Conservation Department and it turned out that the two boffins inside weren't expecting it at all. They looked at it with disinterest and suggested he put it in the storage area, then went back to the large picture they were fiddling with.

He wheeled the empty trolley back to the service bay and parked it, then knocked on the cubicle. Ted was reading the Daily Mirror.

"I took that crate up there and left it in the storage bay, but they weren't waiting for it as far as I could see."

Dobson tutted.

"Like I've said before, Tony my son," he said darkly. "Half of them professors don't seem to be in the real world. I'll have a word with our friend Derek when I see him."

Rupert's mobile rang and he put it tensely to his ear, listening for a moment before he disconnected.

"That's it," he said to Mrs Morris. "Winton says the crate is in position and so is the bag."

"Shall we take in some culture?" she said with irony. In the back of the car, a single nervous intake of breath betrayed Lawrence's presence.

The three of them crossed Trafalgar Square at five to five and mounted the steps to the National. Lawrence was substituting for Morton. Once inside they threaded their way through the galleries, past wave upon wave of great paintings; the wall of Van Gogh; the huge Seurat picture of river bathers; Stubbs's large painting of the rearing racehorse, Whistlejacket. They headed towards the corridor leading to the Sainsbury Wing. When they had made their way along the connecting corridor they went down the steps instead of entering the wing itself, and entered the toilets. Jammed into a space behind the waste bin was a grey holdall secreted there by Winton. They emerged after ten minutes, now wearing the uniform of the National Gallery security staff, including laminated cards on chains bearing their pictures. They went down another level with Rupert speaking into his mobile phone, then a side door opened and Winton appeared, holding the door open for them. There was no-one in sight and they disappeared through the private door after him.

"So far so good," Winton said quietly to Rupert. "It's not far, just a few minutes. Let me do the talking if anyone asks us where we're going."

But no-one asked them anything. In four minutes they had reached the door of the Conservation Department, which had a large plate glass window in case anyone should suspect that the restorers were not restoring.

Inside the room two restorers *were* working – a man and a woman hunched over a bench. Rupert stared, his heart missing a beat. The real Botticelli was laid out flat on the bench in front of them and they were in the process of examining it. The woman looked up and saw them. She said something to her colleague, who glanced through the glass at them and then looked at his watch. He stood up and came to the door, pressing the button on the inside which unlocked it.

"We're just off," he said to Rupert. "We're not going to finish tonight anyway."

Rupert nodded and ignored Winton's advice to stay silent.

"No rush sir," he said. "We just need to make sure that everything's secure, given that you have the Botticelli in here."

The man nodded earnestly.

"Quite right," he said. "It's in *marvellous* condition; Dr Lindholm and I have just been examining it. Late fifteenth century, but you wouldn't think so. Give us a few minutes."

They waited outside in a nervous huddle for five minutes and then the man and the woman came out. He was short and had the beginnings of a paunch. She had blonde hair tied primly in a bun and wore black-framed spectacles. She had removed her white coat and put on a long grey jacket. Rupert gave her the full wattage of his smile and she blushed as she held open the door for him.

"You need to go inside?" she said with raised eyebrows, her voice rising in a question at the end. She had a Swedish accent.

"Just for a few minutes to check the security," Rupert nodded and stood aside to let her pass. "There's no need for you to wait."

"There are rather a lot of you," she said, surveying the four of them in surprise.

Winton gestured to Mrs Morris and Lawrence.

"These two are new and I'm just showing them what to do, but they can wait outside if you'd prefer?"

"That's all right," she said, shaking her head. She turned to Mrs Morris and Lawrence. "Please be very careful not to touch anything on the work benches."

Mrs Morris assured her that they would take the utmost care and then she and Lawrence followed Winton and Rupert. The door closed and it was as easy as that – the four conspirators looked at each other.

"Not bad," Rupert said with barely suppressed glee.

They walked over to the bench as if drawn to it by a magnet. On the flat surface, dull now under the dimmed lights, was the painting by Alessandro di Mariano di Vanni, known as Botticelli, of a post-coital couple – the warrior Mars and the beauty Venus. The painting was composed to interpret Lucian of Samosata's description of an ancient and lost painting by Aetion, *Nuptials of Roxana and Alexander*. In it Lucian describes two cupids carrying Alexander's heavy spear, while another plays in his abandoned breast-plate as he sleeps naked. In Botticelli's version, Mars lies back in the sleep of the "little death", his load spent, his mind elsewhere, while satyrs play with his armour. Venus sits in an ornately decorated robe, not only fully dressed but looking intensely into the near distance; in control, as if representing the domination of love over war.

Rupert looked at the large painting, which was almost immaculate despite traversing half a millennium. Botticelli was putting the finishing touches to this picture eighty years before the birth of Shakespeare.

"What an awesome sight," he said, and it was not clear whether he meant the painting for its own sake, or the money that it represented.

"Let's *steal it*," Mrs Morris said, her eyes glittering. For some reason the sight of such a priceless painting made her feel sexually aroused. She had an insane urge to offer herself to Rupert right there on the floor, but she could not do so with spectators, especially since one of them was her son.

"Th-that looks like the other one," Lawrence said, blissfully ignorant of his mother's fantasy, pointing to the back of the lab where a crate leaned against the wall. The boy was beginning to develop a slight stammer, Rupert noticed with a sneer.

They went over to the crate and examined it, confirming that it was the one they had packed earlier. Winton was becoming increasingly agitated and went to stand by the window on one side, peering around the edge so that he could see the corridor in both directions without being seen himself.

"Open it," Rupert said to Lawrence, who began to fiddle with the end of the crate, trying to find the quick-release tab that they had arranged. Rupert noticed that his fingers were shaking. He didn't seem to be able to locate the tab.

"Let *me* do it," Lawrence's mother said, elbowing him out of the way impatiently.

"Can't even open a box," Rupert muttered, and was surprised by the sudden look of venom that Lawrence shot in his direction.

Mrs Morris found the fishing-wire loop and pulled it so that the wide tape sealing the end of the box was torn open in a perfect cut, like opening a cellophane packet. She inserted her fingers into the exposed edge and pulled. The end of the crate came loose and swung open on hinges. Inside there was a small roll of tape and a length of foam packaging which she removed, exposing the frame of Alfred's copy. It looked identical to the frame of the Botticelli lying flat on the workbench in front of them. She placed the roll of tape on the table with exaggerated care.

Rupert gently pulled the end of the frame while Lawrence and his mother stood on either side of the crate and held it steady. The picture slid out on little hard foam rollers set into the bottom of the case.

"Do you want a hand?" Lawrence said, coming round to help.

"What, and have you drop it?" Rupert said. "Julia – take the other end."

Lawrence went red in the face but said nothing. Rupert and Mrs Morris carried Alfred's fake over to the bench and leaned it against the back of the work surface, facing away from the window. For a few moments they stood and looked at the two paintings. Alfred's copy, and the frame in which it was located, appeared to be identical in every single detail, as if it had just emerged from some futuristic cloning machine. Rupert shook his head in wonder.

"I don't know how the old man does it," he said in awe.

Mrs Morris was about to reply but they were interrupted by a warning hiss from Winton, who had left the window and was running towards them in a panic.

"Head of Art Handling on his rounds. Everyone get out of sight!"

He followed his own example and vanished into the store room at the back of the lab, closely followed by Rupert and Mrs Morris. Lawrence stood for a moment in ghastly indecision, as if rooted to the spot.

"Lawrence, get *down!*" his mother hissed and Lawrence caught one last sight of Rupert's furious face as the door closed on them. At the last possible moment he came suddenly to life and dived under the huge workbench. He crouched there shivering, his heart pumping the blood in his ears. He realised that he could be seen through the window by anyone giving more than a casual glance. Almost instantly the shadow of Bullrode fell on the window, but he was in a hurry and looked neither left nor right; just moved swiftly on and was gone in seconds. Lawrence banged his head on the underside of the metal workbench and muttered under his breath. Then he crawled out from beneath the table and stood up. The store room door at the back was still closed. He went over to the plate-glass window at the front to see if anyone was outside, but the corridor was deserted. Then he turned back and looked at the two paintings. It was a remarkable sight, as they appeared completely identical. He smiled beatifically.

FIFTY-SEVEN

History is a gallery of pictures in which there are few originals and many copies.
ALEXIS DE TOCQUEVILLE

"We should never have brought him," Rupert was muttering to Mrs Morris. They were at the back of the store room, crouching behind a stack of boxes. Mrs Morris' knees were aching abominably but she would die before admitting it. Winton was behind the door. The only light in the room came from the screen of a computer which had been left on, bathing the room in a blue glow.

"The boy's an idiot," Rupert continued. "I'm sorry, Julia, but he's a liability."

"We planned it for three of us and we needed a substitute for Edward," Mrs Morris sighed. "But I must admit, sometimes it seems like he's half stupid."

"More than half."

"Keep your voices down," Winton said nervously. "If we get caught in here we're done for."

"Or if Lawrence gets caught," Rupert muttered. "I hope to God he got out of sight."

"He must have done," Winton said, "or we would have heard something by now. It was the head of Art Handling, Derek Bullrode; and he's a stroppy bastard. They're the ones who handle picture shipments. If he saw anyone in here he didn't know he'd be in like a shot to poke his nose about. He's always on at us in VS and S."

"What?"

"Security. He thinks it ought to be part of Collections. Always picking holes."

Rupert smiled.

"Well, he does have a point."

"Anyway, surely he can't have seen Lawrence," Mrs Morris said placatingly, "or we'd know by now." She patted her pocket absent-mindedly, where there was the reassuring outline of her loaded syringe in its small case.

"Shall I have a look?" Winton asked.

"Let's just hold on here," Mrs Morris said. "Lawrence will come and tell us when the coast is clear."

Almost immediately there was a barely perceptible tap on the door. They all looked at each other, wondering whether Bullrode was about to stride in and switch on all the lights. But the door opened a crack and Lawrence poked his head through.

"Um, he's not here," he said. "I mean, he's gone."

Rupert stood up from behind the packing cases and brushed dust off his trousers.

"Thank God for that," he said fervently. "You're sure he didn't see you?"

They all emerged into the main room to join Lawrence, looking about them warily.

"Definitely not," Lawrence said. "I hid under the workbench."

"You should have come with us," Rupert said shortly. "Winton, get over to the window and keep a look out again. Lawrence, if anyone else comes along I want you to get into the back room as fast as your legs will carry you."

Lawrence just looked at him.

"Would you like a hand moving the pictures?" he said in a wooden voice.

"No," Rupert shook his head. "Your mother and I will do it. Come along Julia, we need to get out of here."

With infinite care they gripped the painting on the workbench and lifted it. They aligned it with the open end of the crate and slid it in, Lawrence quietly helping even though Rupert had refused his aid. With perfect precision the ancient panel slid into the crate on its foam rollers. When it came to a gentle halt against the protective foam at the far end of the crate, Rupert picked up the strip of foam packaging from the floor and inserted it with care into the box, where it fitted snugly around the frame. He nodded approvingly. Then he closed and sealed the box as it had been before, using the roll of spare tape to close the end. When he had finished he slipped the tape spool into his pocket and nodded to Mrs Morris.

She took out a thin cardboard tube containing a new label for the crate. It was identical in style to the existing crate label except in one respect – instead of the National Gallery, the address now read *Conservation Department, Royal Academy of Arts, Burlington House, Piccadilly*. There was a name and a telephone number provided in case of any queries with transportation. Mrs Morris peeled the back off the label and stuck it carefully on the other end of the crate. Then she located the original National Gallery label and lifted the corner, tearing it a little so that it looked old, as if someone had tried but failed to remove it. She took a pen from her pocket and put two lines across the label, scrawling "Written Off" across it. The colour of the ink was pale blue and difficult to discern. Finally, she took out a small plastic box, snapped off the lid and poured a little dirt into her palm. She rubbed her hands together and then smoothed them across the label, making it look old.

"Hurry up!" Winton called from the window with agitation.

Rupert and Mrs Morris looked at the labels.

"That's perfect," Rupert pronounced, and they hurried with Lawrence over to the door. Winton looked but there was no-one in sight, so they switched off the lights and went out. The electronic door lock clicked closed behind them. Winton had not even used his security pass to get in because the restorer had held the door open for Rupert.

There followed a tense few minutes while they walked back, for they were late – it was already five past six and the gallery was closed. They emerged from the side door into the public section and Winton disappeared immediately into the bowels of the building without a backward glance. Rupert, Mrs Morris and her son ducked back into the lavatories and changed. They were let out of the building by a young man on the door who didn't even give them a second glance.

Ted Dobson was feeling irritated but managing to remain polite. The woman on the telephone sounded very posh but very annoyed.

"I realise it's not your fault but I would have thought you would have checked it more thoroughly. Apparently there was an old label or something from the last time the crate was used. I shall not be using *that* security firm again – *completely* incompetent. Please would you go and check immediately to see if it's there and call me back if so. My office number is on the label so you can use that number. And mind you find the RA label, not the old one. Now if I don't hear from you in thirty minutes I shall call you back. Do you have a direct dial number? It took me fully ten minutes to get through your switchboard."

"Yes madam," Dobson said long sufferingly. "Could I take your name again?"

"Celia Billington-Ford," she said impatiently, "and on second thoughts, let me give you my mobile number in case you can't find the label or something." She said this last in a particularly disparaging voice.

Dobson clearly remembered the crate coming in earlier and he had not checked the label himself – he had let Tony do it. He called Tony in and explained the situation. Then he got the young man to watch the gate while he went up to the Conservation Department. He knew trouble when he saw it, and the Billington-Ford woman was trouble. If he could prevent that smarmy Bullrode from having a go at him about it then he would. The department was closed and dark but he opened the door with his passkey and switched on the lights. The crate in question was in the storage bay and he went over to have a look. He confirmed that it had two labels almost immediately, just as the woman from the RA had described on the phone. He mouthed an obscenity under his breath. The National Gallery label was obviously an old one and when you looked closely it had actually been written off, though you couldn't see it very well. He decided that it was an easy enough mistake to have made, which pleased him because he placed a lot of trust in young Tony and felt that the lad was vindicated. Besides, he knew that he himself shouldn't have booked it in without finding it on the computer.

He checked the box to make sure that it hadn't been opened, as there would be a right fuss if the boffins had already been in it. But all was still sealed, he noted with relief. He examined the other label and confirmed that the crate was supposed to have gone to the RA. It had the Burlington House address and *For the Attention of Mrs C Billington-Ford.* He checked the telephone number and it was the same as the one on the slip of paper in his hand. He used the phone on the desk, got an outside line and dialled the number.

It answered after three rings.

"Billington-Ford?"

"Ah yes, Mrs Billington-Ford," Ted Dobson said in his most ingratiating voice. "I'm pleased to tell you that we've found your missing crate."

"You *wonderful* man, thank Heavens for that!" she said on the other end of the line, her voice much warmer. "Can I send one of our vans around to pick it up?" She lowered her voice and suddenly there was a conspiratorial hint to it which made Ted think this might work out all right. "You see, no-one yet knows of the error, and I don't want them to, er, shoot the messenger."

He grinned.

"As a matter of fact, madam," he said. "No-one knows about it here either because it hasn't been opened. So it would suit me fine if your lads came and took it away, if you know what I mean."

"Perfect," she said. Thank you so much, Mr, er…"

"Dobson," he said. "I'll be on the service bay gate if they get a move on."

"Perfect," she said once more, again with that hint of sexiness. "I'll have them there in thirty minutes. They'll be in one of our vans and I'll send you a copy of the paperwork, so if you could just check that before you hand it over I'd be grateful."

She disconnected and Dobson breathed a sigh of relief.

In half an hour the RA van appeared at the gates and was duly let through by Dobson. He checked the paperwork carefully and made sure that it was correct, then Tony gave the security guards a hand to load the crate into the back of the van and he breathed a sigh of relief as they went off. He looked about to make sure that Bullrode wasn't hanging around, but for once in his life the nasty bastard appeared to have gone off to irritate someone else.

Mrs Morris was feeling extremely pleased with herself. When Morton's two lads came back in the white van and pulled into the driveway of Rupert's London house, she and Rupert met them on the steps. The crate was removed from the van and carried into the house. The RA logos were peeled off the sides of the van, leaving it plain white once more. She went round to the back of the house, taking from her pocket the mobile phone she had used for the calls to the National. She put it on the back step beside the bins and smashed it to pieces with a stone. Then she gathered up the bits, threw them in the bin and went inside. Rupert was in the study with the sizeable crate. He had opened the end of the box and had pulled the picture out about a foot. You could see half of one of the satyrs at the bottom, and Mars' elbow, while at the top a few wasps were visible, thought by experts to pay homage to the Vespucci family, Botticelli's great patrons – the Italian for wasp is *vespe*.

Lawrence came in, but even his appearance did not interrupt Rupert's triumphant mood.

"Lawrence," he said easily. "We've done it. Be a good chap and open the champagne, would you? I think we deserve a little celebration."

FIFTY-EIGHT

Here is where people,
One frequently finds,
Lower their voices
And raise their minds.
RICHARD ARMOUR

Will walked back from the little London park after he had fed the pigeons the remains of his Panini, and stood by his bike for a while, staring sightlessly into space. The café was empty and the Italian owner came to the open door and waved him inside.

"Hey, meester," he called. "You look like you have a bad shock, uh? You come in and have espresso. On the house."

Will smiled emptily at the man but followed him inside. An old Coldplay track was playing over the speakers: "Fix You". He sat listening to the words, and in the midst of his thoughts about Lucy they seemed to mock him. *He felt broken and in need of fixing.*

The man brought him an espresso and Will thanked him. Somehow he couldn't get the smell of the burned laboratory out of his nostrils – even the coffee reminded him of it. Davies' words rang in his ears, describing the body that had been carried out. *You could only just about tell that it had been human.*

His phone started to ring in his pocket. He hauled it out and looked at it. It was Davies – he remembered the number. He stared at it as it rang, afraid to answer it. Finally it stopped ringing. He put it back down on the table, picked up his coffee and drained the cup. The man behind the counter watched him but said nothing. The phone bleeped twice to signify a text message. Davies had left him a voicemail, so he wasn't going to escape that easily. Now the phone would bleep at him until he listened to the message. He sighed and picked it up, dialled and listened.

"Mr Bentley? It's Hugh Davies here. I'm sorry I missed you but I wanted you to know the latest. They've checked the body and they know it *wasn't* Lucy; it turned out to be that poor chap Ellis when they checked his DNA. They've searched the rest of the building and they didn't find anyone else. So in other words we don't know where Lucy is, but we know she's not burned to death. Well that's about it, really, so I hope you get this message. Obviously I'll give you a call if I find her."

The message ended and Will found himself staring at the phone with an idiotic grin spreading over his face. *She wasn't in the fire!* He pressed the button and listened to the message again, twice. Then he looked up at the café owner.

"Give me another of those excellent coffees!" he said, "and two of those little cakes. I need to think." He brought out some money.

"Good news?" the man behind the counter asked.

"Could be," Will said. "Certainly not bad news, anyway. I've just got to find a girl."

"Ah, a *girl*," the man said with a sympathetic shrug. "They drive us crazy but we love them, uh?"

"That's about it," Will said with a grin. "Tell me; is there a library around here? I need to look something up."

The district library was in the High Street, about halfway along. He glanced at his watch as he reached the entrance – it was twenty to four and the library didn't close until five thirty, so he had plenty of time. He went up the steps of the old building and found a modern library inside. People were sitting at tables reading newspapers or books. There were many computer terminals, all occupied. As he went in there was a counter area with several library staff within it, dealing with people returning books or taking them out. He leaned over the counter and waited. A pretty young librarian came over to him.

"I was wondering if I could get access to the Internet," he said.

"Hang on," she said. "I'll check." She frowned at a screen for a few moments. "Number 16 is free in a quarter of an hour, if you don't mind waiting?"

"I don't mind at all."

"All right then. I'll need your library card."

He looked nonplussed. "Well, I'm down from Cambridge for the day," he said, "but I need to look something up. "I've got a *Cambridge* library card but I don't suppose that'll be much use to you?"

She smiled ruefully. "Not really," she said. "Are you on holiday here?"

"Not exactly," he said.

"Because if you were I could book you in as a temporary visitor."

"Well I *could* be," he said, leaning in over the counter and looking her in the eye. "The locals seem very nice."

She looked back at him, blushing slightly, unused to having men quite as gorgeous as this come into the library on an otherwise average Tuesday afternoon.

"Yes, well," she said a little breathlessly. "I'll tell you what; I'll log you in on my card as a guest. Come along. The terminal's free now."

When she had logged him in and left him to it, he stared at the browser for a moment, then loaded the search engine and typed *Triumph of Good over*

Evil Procaccini. He got 136 hits, and pressed Images. Seven hits, all different views of the same picture. It was too hard to see what it was so he clicked on the thumbnail image and waited for a larger picture. Now it was extraordinarily familiar and he was casting about in his mind's eye to recall where he had seen it.

Then he remembered.

It had been in the long gallery of paintings in the house on the Isle of Wight, where he and Lucy had gone to look at the suspect Hammershoi. This painting had been right there, on the wall in the centre. But surely that was too much of a coincidence? Well, here it was, coincidence or not. Perhaps the forgers had some kind of a connection with Sir Philip and Lady Felicity Hall? He thought back, staring into the middle distance. It seemed like weeks since he had been there, for so much had happened in between, but it was less than two weeks. Not the Sunday just gone but the previous Sunday. He remembered Lucy there, sitting in the chair in the reception room with her pretty legs on view. And then with a pang he remembered again that she was missing and that he had better concentrate on whatever clue this painting could give him. *What had Alfred been trying to tell him?* He selected the largest image of the painting that he could find and stared at it for several minutes, trying to discern something from it.

It was no good: he couldn't think of anything at all.

He wondered if he could ring the house in the Isle of Wight and took out his phone to do so, looking around furtively. He decided that the library was noisy enough for no-one to notice. He dialled and gave the name and address, and by some miracle the Halls were not ex-directory.

"Brighstone Manor," a female voice said after a few rings.

He didn't recognise the voice.

"Could I speak to Sir Philip or Lady Felicity?" he said. "My name's Will Bentley and I visited them a couple of weekends ago."

"Just a moment."

Lady Felicity came on the line.

"Mr Bentley, thank you so much for calling! Is there news about the picture?"

He was discombobulated for a moment.

"Er, you mean the Hammershoi?"

"Oh no, Mr Bentley. I'm talking about the Procaccini."

"Yes, well that's what *I'm* calling about," Will said, beginning to feel rather confused.

"Lucy called us and had it picked up by courier yesterday. She said she was certain that it was a forgery and under those circumstances the insurance would be invalid unless it could be tested and found to be the genuine article. She was *very* insistent."

He could tell from her voice that she wasn't at all happy about the removal of her beloved painting.

"Lady Felicity," Will said urgently. "Lucy Wrackham has disappeared and the police are looking for her. We fear something bad may have happened. Can you tell me exactly what she said?"

"Something bad? Oh I do hope not: poor Lucy. I always worried that she was forever chasing after shady characters. It's not a very suitable job for a woman, you know."

"When did she call?"

"Early yesterday I believe. I wasn't in, but my husband spoke to her and she told him all this. She promised to have the painting tested yesterday evening and to call us this morning. That's what I thought *you* were calling about, because we haven't heard a word from her. What do you mean, she's disappeared?"

"She's nowhere to be found. And the people we've been trying to find are very nasty. Did you read about the bomb in Cambridge?"

"Oh *yes*, it was on the news," Lady Felicity said. "And Philip saw it too. That's why he let Lucy take the painting away for testing. I'm afraid I don't for one moment think she's right, though. I know my own painting when I see it. But Philip said she was *adamant* that it was a copy. She said these frightful people have to be stopped, and that's why he agreed to let her have it. I'm sure he was right to do so, even though I was cross at the time."

"I'm sure he was too," Will said, racking his brains for some kind of a clue. "So she didn't say anything else?"

"Not that I know of. Hold on a moment." He heard her speak with Philip for a few moments.

"Philip's right here. He's hoping he's done the right thing. Where *is* our painting, Mr Bentley? Is it with Lucy?"

"I don't know," Will said, deciding not to mention that Marcello's had burned down the previous evening and the Procaccini had most likely gone up in flames with it.

"Oh dear," Lady Felicity said, sounding extremely troubled.

Will had a sudden thought: there was someone else in Brighstone Manor who knew the painting extremely well.

"Could I have a few words with your granddaughter?" he said. "She was in the gallery when I was looking at your pictures, and we had an interesting talk about the Procaccini. Elizabeth might give me an idea if I could just speak with her."

"Of course you can," Lady Felicity said, sounding even more surprised. "But I really can't imagine that *Elizabeth* will be able to tell you anything of use. She's going through a bit of a…you know…"

"…difficult patch," Will finished. "Yes, I know. But we did have a good talk about the picture."

This time he waited fully five minutes before Lady Felicity came back and said she was transferring him. Then he heard the young girl's voice again. He imagined her in black with her skull-shaped rings and black-widow earrings.

"Yes?" The voice was hesitant.

"Acid Tears?"

There was a long pause.

"Who is this?" came the girl's voice again uncertainly, sounding less like a Goth and more like the vulnerable young girl beneath the facade.

"I'm the painter that you met in your gallery. I was looking at the Procaccini and you were sitting in the throne at the time."

There was another long pause.

"I *do* remember you," she said at last. "You knew about art. You told me all about the Vesica Piscis. I looked it up after you'd gone."

"You know the Procaccini has gone to London to be tested?"

"Yes," Elizabeth said, a note of bitterness entering her voice. "There's a horrid space on the wall. I hate them for sending it away."

He ignored that.

"Do you remember anything *odd* about the painting? You talked about one of the angels not having a halo."

"Yes, but we got interrupted, so I never told you the weirdest thing about it."

He waited.

"The weird thing is, the angel I pointed out to you *used to* have a halo, just like all the others. Except that after the picture came back from an exhibition in London, the halo wasn't there anymore. That's why I was asking you about it. And you said maybe it was because that one was a bad angel. It stuck in my mind. I thought maybe the halo vanishing was a sign from the devil or something, but I suppose that was stupid."

Will never heard her remark about a demonic sign because something else she had said was ringing in his ears.

"The painting went to an *exhibition*? Your grandparents never mentioned that, though I suppose there's no reason why they should. And when it came back the halo had mysteriously vanished."

"But why would they paint out the halo?" the girl said.

"Sometimes details change on a painting if it is cleaned," Will said. "The removal of a layer of vanish can remove details added by later artists. Someone long ago may have objected to a demon in a nativity scene. They were a superstitious lot."

"But nothing else changed," the girl objected. "And anyway, they've got a cheek even *touching* our painting. It was only supposed to be on display, not being cleaned. Granny says it's an heirloom."

They talked for a minute more but he learned nothing new, so he thanked her profusely, disconnected and sat thinking. One way that the halo could disappear would be if it was *never painted in*.

If the painting had gone to an exhibition and Alfred had somehow swapped it with his own perfect copy, then the halo could disappear if he chose to leave it out. Will felt certain it wasn't simply a mistake, but Alfred might change it if he thought it would be an improvement. The old man had often pointed out to him errors in the paintings of the masters. He had a sudden recollection of Alfred showing him a picture of Caravaggio's Supper at Emmaus in *Renaissance Artist*. One of the disciples had widespread arms and the hand in the background appeared too large – out of perspective. Alfred noticed things like that because of his intimate knowledge of the masters and their techniques. He didn't believe that passing years and fashion turned a bad painting into a good one, or in this case corrected an error on the otherwise masterful Caravaggio. He believed that if the error were pointed out to the original painter, he or she would take up their brushes and fix it. But with the passing of centuries, it is difficult to imagine a Caravaggio or a Rembrandt being *fixed*. Such paintings attain iconic status, etched as they are by time. Even if the original master could somehow be conjured from the past, how would we feel if they changed that image which has become so familiar to us? If Monet decided that the poppies were too obvious and painted them out. If Vincent donned his new glasses and cleaned up the perspective on that crooked old bedroom. If Leonardo laughed at us for saving an unfinished drawing, and tossed it in the bin.

Will shook his head, still puzzled. It didn't add up. Alfred might omit the halo on a rough copy, but surely not on a perfect forgery? It was too obvious. He leaned back from the computer screen and furrowed his brow in thought. After another minute he concluded that Alfred had done it deliberately. *That* must be the clue. It was a damn subtle clue though. Will typed "missing halo" into the search engine and scanned a page or two of results without being any the wiser. Then he typed "bad angel painting" and scanned his eye down the results: ringtones; lyrics; a Biblical reference. It was the fourth entry that paused his eye:

Angel Gallery – *"...no such thing as a bad painting," said Rupert Angel, managing director of the Angel Gallery.*

For a second he thought it was just a coincidence, but then it was as if silver levers aligned in some complex mechanism, unlocking the secret.

The 'bad angel' could be *Rupert Angel*. An angel without a halo. He was a prominent gallery owner and would be able to dispose of Alfred's forgeries easily enough. Will pursed his lips, wondering if jealousy was distorting his reason. He didn't *like* Rupert Angel, but that didn't necessarily make him a criminal. And there must be something else because a missing halo was not enough to point to the man. Perhaps Lucy had found some other evidence pointing to Angel when she had tested the painting. She would be livid if she discovered that Angel was part of the whole thing and had been spying on her. She might do something rash. What if Angel had been keeping close to Lucy so that he could learn the latest twist in the investigation? After the attacks in Cambridge, Will had felt mystified that the villains always seemed to know what was happening and where to find him. He had never told *anyone* that they were searching for Alfred Smith, for example, but the man with the axe had known about it.

His phone bleeped a message on the desk beside him and he snatched it up. He was popular today.

got u on ring back. i looked up exhibition it was leander gallery in london. elizabeth x

He stared at this new item of information with a frown. Did it mean anything? He typed the name of the Leander Gallery into the screen in front of him, followed a false trail to Henley-on-Thames for a moment, but then found the proper London reference and brought up the website. It was fine art, all extortionately priced. Will clicked the "Founders" link and suddenly found himself staring at the fact that *Rupert Angel was a director of the Leander Gallery*. In fact, it was an offshoot of the Angel Gallery. Will shook his head slowly, remembering the smooth bastard in his silver Merc dropping off Lucy at her apartment; kissing her goodbye. Somehow Angel had persuaded Sir Philip and Lady Felicity to let him exhibit the Procaccini and he had swapped it for Alfred's copy. But by then Alfred had seen through his partner in crime and had decided that he needed an insurance policy – and what more apposite way for him to make an insurance policy than to paint it?

Will sat and thought it through. Lucy must have found some kind of proof in Alfred's painting which pointed unwaveringly to Angel, and somehow he'd found out that he had been exposed. Will quietly thought to himself that if Lucy was hurt or worse, Rupert Angel would learn the meaning of revenge. But in the meantime, what now? If he called Davies and the police handled it clumsily, he could be signing Lucy's death warrant. He could imagine Angel covering his tracks and denying everything, and who would they believe: a prominent London gallery owner or an ex con? He knew he needed to find out more before he made any accusations, but it would be difficult because he didn't even know where Angel lived.

"How's the research going?" said a voice behind him, and he turned to see the pretty librarian, slightly pink-faced.

"Not too bad."

Then it occurred to him that she could probably help.

"Is there any way I can find the address of a company director?" he asked.

"I expect so," she said. "Is it a public company?"

"I should think it must be, but I don't know for sure."

"Let me try."

The terminals around him were emptying as the afternoon lengthened, and she sank into the vacant chair next to his and slid across. She smelled nice. A lock of her hair fell across her face while she worked.

She quickly found a database of companies that led her to 'Angel Holdings Ltd', listing Rupert Angel as a director.

"We're lucky he's not called John Smith," she said, with her brow furrowed in concentration.

She clicked on Rupert Angel's name and the database spewed out a registered address for him.

"There we are," she said, smiling. "That'll be it. It has to be kept up to date for legal reasons, and you don't even have to pay for the report unless you want the financial details."

When she had gone to help close up the library, Will wrote Rupert Angel's address down on a piece of paper. As an afterthought he loaded the postcode into an online map and looked at the street view of where Rupert lived. The house was in London and backed onto the River Thames, so it must be worth a pretty penny. It had a sweep-in drive and he could see the silver Mercedes parked in front of it. Will supposed that it would be easy to afford such things if you went around stealing Procaccini's and Hammershoi's.

The library was closing and the young librarian had disappeared. He hurried down the steps and set off at a fast pace back to the bike, thinking hard as he walked. He felt positive about this strange turn of events. An hour or two ago it had seemed as if there was no hope, but now he had a target in his sights. He reached the Bonnie, saluted the Italian café owner and started the engine with a roar. It was time to find Rupert Angel and discover if his halo was missing.

FIFTY-NINE

*In life there are meetings which seem
Like a fate.*
LORD LYTTON, Lucille, writing as Owen Meredith

Will parked the Bonnie two streets away from Rupert Angel's house and walked there. It was seven-fifteen as he approached and he heard The Archers playing on somebody's radio as he passed their window. He had a crumpled map in his hand which he had printed in the library. He wore an old red bobble hat that he had purchased from a delighted homeless man for ten pounds. The houses were becoming more stately and were set back from the road behind gates with intercoms. The road was lined with plane trees and the gardens filled with rhododendrons. It was a hot and oppressive July evening and he carried his jacket over his shoulder and hummed to himself as he walked, happier now that he was once more on the trail and had something to do. When he got close he stopped humming and walked quietly, conscious of his presence every time a car went past, though nobody took the slightest notice of him. He reached Rupert Angel's house and it had tall wrought-iron gates which stood open. There was a white van without markings parked in front of the house. He turned his head away as he passed the open gateway in case anyone was observing from the house. On the gatepost there was a bell push and a name plate bearing the word 'Angel'. The house looked smart and respectable, giving him a sudden doubt. He walked past, feeling as if his whole theory was built on a tower of cards which might collapse at any moment. It could just be a coincidence that the Procaccini had been exhibited at the Leander Gallery. His notion about the "bad angel" suddenly seemed preposterous.

Further on there was a public footpath that led down to the river, running between two tall Victorian houses. He took the path and emerged suddenly onto the Thames. The sun was disappearing behind gathering cloud but he reckoned it would be another hour or two before dusk, and he was reluctant to approach the house in daylight. He walked up the river. Each of the houses had its own mooring, and some houses had private backwaters that went literally into their back gardens. The commercial pleasure boats had already stopped plying the river, but other boats went up and down. Rupert Angel's house had its own backwater and a heavy old wooden gate painted black and bearing the house number. The backwater went in beside the gate and there were spikes radiating out to prevent intruders from gaining easy ingress. Will walked swiftly past the house. A few hundred yards on was a pub with outside tables and a bank sloping down to the water. It was full of people, overflowing from bench seats onto the grassy riverbank, talking and laughing; some smoking. He went in and ordered himself a pint of orange juice and lemonade. He wanted his head clear for what lay ahead. Then he sat down on the grass beside the river and dangled his feet over the edge of the bank. He made the drink last while the cloud thickened and finally the sun emerged briefly before extinguishing itself in the river. The sky was looking increasingly stormy and his skin prickled with static electricity. After a second pint of juice it was suitably dark. The family drinkers had departed for supper and now a younger more sophisticated and moneyed crowd filled the place. He had a side-table now and was entertaining himself with a small pocket sketchbook, doing quick pencil drawings of the people that sat around the tables laughing and gossiping and chatting. Occasional boats on the river sported red and green lights. He glanced at his watch. It was nine-thirty and he felt as if he had waited long enough. He drained the last bit of his drink and went into the pub to return his glass. When he emerged, people were groaning and laughing and getting up because there was a sudden pitter-patter of raindrops, turning the dust into little muddy rivulets as it gathered momentum. He didn't mind – rain would help conceal him. He walked back along the river with the pub's music and sounds of laughter slowly receding behind him. When he reached Angel's gate he looked up and down the river path but no-one was watching. It was dark and the rain was growing heavy; large droplets of water were beginning to soak his shirt. He put on his black leather biking jacket. Then with a last furtive look around he went up to the spikes protecting the backwater, grasped them and used them to swing himself out carefully into space. The spikes were wet and he almost lost his grip and fell in, but just managed to retain his hold and swung past them, stepping back onto the brick path on the inside of the gate. Beside him the backwater was jet black, but its mirror surface was perturbed by the rain into concentric circles that blurred into each other as the rain intensified.

    He looked around. There was a long back garden, paved where he stood. A sleek white boat was moored in the backwater – Angel certainly didn't stint himself. There was a shed which was unlocked and contained garden implements and boating gear. The storm was releasing its static charge in the form of sheet lightning, which flickered over the clouds and was followed at intervals by dull rumbles. The rain intensified into a rod-like summer downpour which quickly saturated him. It was surprisingly noisy, but one thing was certain – nobody would be out in the back garden taking the night air.

    He could see the lighted rear windows of the house now; large yellow oblongs which looked welcoming but in reality were not. He knew he had to be very careful. The bearded man had conveniently blown himself up, but Will didn't want to meet any of the other men that had tried to hang him from his own studio beam. He reached the back of the house. There were French windows opening onto a small patio, but the room inside was in darkness and the handles of the French windows did not yield to his touch. There was a back door and he twisted the knob but it too was locked. There was a big window on the first floor, but the house was tall and the window was quite a way up. However, there was a large green rubbish bin which would help him gain height, and he could see a sturdy drainpipe halfway up the rear wall. He spotted a heavy-duty bucket near the back door which already had two inches of water in it. He emptied it out and upturned it on the flat top of the green bin, then climbed up. When he stood on the bucket he felt extremely precarious but the drainpipe was now within reach. He hauled himself up until he reached a sturdy cast-iron rain catcher which was gurgling with water. The drainpipe angled up at a slight slope towards the window, and another pipe descended vertically, so he had something to walk along and something to hold onto. It felt like suicide but he edged carefully towards the lighted window until he reached it and was able to grasp the window ledge. His hair was plastered to his head and the rain was bombarding him. On the path below, raindrops were hitting the bricks with intensity and bouncing up again two or three inches. The drainpipe he was standing on had been made to last; it remained solid as a rock as it supported Will's weight. He clung to the window ledge; his fingers hooked into the ridge of wood on the side of the frame, and leaned across until he could peer into the room. Alfred Smith was dozing in an armchair.

RICHARD JOHN MITCHELL

SIXTY

The inexpressible comfort of feeling safe with a person – having neither to weigh thoughts nor measure words, but pouring them all right out, just as they are.
DINAH CRAIK

Will nearly fell off the drainpipe with the shock of seeing his old friend after such a long search. He worked his way forwards a little more until he was able to see into the whole room. It had been set up as a large studio, complete with a professional-grade easel and a table full of paintbrushes and tubes. There was no-one else in the room so Will tapped on the windowpane. The old man opened his eyes and looked at the door warily. Will tapped again on the glass more urgently, feeling precarious on the drainpipe. Alfred looked over at the window and at first didn't react. Then he started up as he saw a pale shape through the glass and came across to the window. For a moment he didn't recognize Will and looked alarmed, but then he realized who it was and opened the casement cautiously, trying to contain his astonishment.

"Shouldn't you have brought an umbrella, old boy?"

"You should see what it took for me to get up here," Will said, hanging on grimly and indicating downwards with a flick of his head.

Alfred leaned out until he could see the wet gutter that was supporting Will.

"You'd better come in," he said in a low voice. "It's quite all right; they won't disturb me now."

"I'm a bit damp," Will said in magnificent understatement as he heaved himself up over the sill. He dropped down silently into the room and closed the window, water running off him. He held out his hand to Alfred and they shook hands with genuine pleasure at seeing each other again.

"You look as if you swam here," Alfred said, keeping his voice low as he handed Will a towel.

"I feel like I did," Will said quietly, drying himself vigorously. "You don't seem very surprised to see me,"

"Rupert Angel let slip in the Burnham studio that you were on my trail, but by then I didn't trust him an inch so I decided to leave you a small clue. To tell you the truth I was beginning to worry that he might have his man Morton bump me off. We're almost at the end of this little game."

"Does Morton have a beard, by any chance?"

"He did have, but he shaved it off. I haven't seen him for a couple of days, though, which I don't mind a bit. He's a nasty bastard."

"He's not a nasty bastard any more. He managed to blow himself to bits."

Alfred looked at him in surprise.

"Did he indeed?" he said in a normal voice and then looked guiltily around and carried on almost in a whisper. "That would explain why everyone in the house is so edgy. And how did he manage to do that?"

"I think he was trying to get rid of me and a friend of mine called Lucy. I don't know exactly what happened but some kind of bomb went off."

"Good Lord, it sounds very dramatic. I think we need some tea."

Will followed him into the kitchenette and dried his hair as Alfred filled the kettle.

"I saw you in a red car with a very attractive young woman when we were doing a bunk," Alfred went on. "Would that have been Lucy?"

"Yes it would!" said Will, astonished. "She's an insurance agent, and somehow she talked me into looking for you. But just as I was about to give up, your man Morton and his people started trying to frighten me off."

"And knowing you, it had the reverse effect."

"I was pretty mad, but it wasn't through any bravado on my part," Will said with a smile. "To tell you the truth I was a bit worried about the people you'd managed to get yourself mixed up with."

"Rightly so, dear boy." Alfred reached into a cupboard and brought out a red teapot.

"So where did you spot Lucy and me?" Will asked.

"We had just left the Burnham studio and we passed you in the lane. If you'd been five minutes earlier you would have caught us there, though it's probably just as well that you didn't. Morton had a couple of his heavies there to make sure I didn't decide to slip away."

"You're not at liberty, then?"

"I was at first," Alfred said grimly. "But Angel is getting increasingly nervous, it seems to me. A few days ago he sent the two morons up to keep me company, and then I was brought down here with no choice in the matter. And now I'm a prisoner. When they took my latest painting this morning they locked the door and they've only opened it once since then to provide food."

"We need to get you out of here," Will said. "And I need to find Lucy, because she's disappeared. I'm hoping to God they haven't done anything to her. We did go to the Burnham studio just as you said, and we eventually found your Procaccini clue. It was the Renoir reference that pointed me in the right direction."

"I was hoping you'd see it," Alfred chuckled. "I had to be bloody subtle because Angel was there and I was afraid he'd notice. So you followed up on the clue?"

"I didn't, but Lucy did," Will corrected. "She came down to London, got the painting from the owners and had it tested in the labs. At least I *think* she did. The next thing we knew she'd disappeared and the lab had burned down. The lab technician was killed so there's a murder charge waiting for whoever pulled off that particular stunt."

The kettle clicked and Alfred made the tea, shaking his head and looking very grave.

"I think I've been rather foolish," he said apologetically. "Angel seemed such a good bet in the beginning, but it turns out he's in league with some people who aren't just villains – they're plain evil."

He handed a cup of tea to Will and then poured some of his own tea into his saucer and sipped it thoughtfully. Will watched his friend and remembered this peculiar habit with affection. It was wonderful to see him again, albeit in these difficult circumstances.

"So how on earth did *you* manage to find me without the actual Procaccini?" Alfred asked.

Will explained about the missing halo and the old man smiled in memory.

"I left it like that for a bit of fun," he said. "Fancy their little girl noticing it."

Will asked him if there had been another clue, so Alfred told him about the portrait of Angel beneath the top layer of paint.

"You'd be able to see it on an X-Ray test easily enough," he said. "It was my insurance policy. I didn't trust Angel any more, even then. He started out pleasant enough as I say, and paid me a good deal of money for my services. I needed a nest-egg and he provided it. The old Smith hands are getting stiff. I thought I might not be able to paint in a few years time and then I'd end up on the breadline. I suppose I didn't want to be a burden on my sister, as I get on rather better with her these days."

"Because her husband Brian died," Will said. "I met her."

"You met Gillian?" Alfred said, looking astonished. "Good Lord, you've certainly been doing the rounds."

"You are quite elusive."

They leaned against the table in the kitchenette while Will told him in low tones the events that had brought him to the drainpipe outside the window.

"Very enterprising," Alfred said when he had finished. "This Lucy of yours sounds like a good catch."

"Have you seen her here? Is she in this house?"

"I haven't seen her here, though she may be," the old man said, shaking his head. "But I can make a good guess where she is. I heard Rupert and Mrs Morris yelling at each other this morning."

"Mrs Morris?"

"Julia Morris. She's Rupert's executive assistant and arranges all Rupert's dirty work for him. Utterly ruthless bitch, to put it mildly. She'd top the lot of us if she thought she needed to. Anyway, I've never heard her as angry as she was this morning. She was yelling at Rupert about your Lucy."

"Is Lucy all right?"

"I don't *know* that she's all right," Alfred admitted, "but I have a feeling she is at the moment. And as I say, I think I may know where she is."

Will opened his hands and nodded in encouragement.

"Well?"

"You'll be amazed when I tell you," Alfred said, apparently relishing the moment.

"I'm sure I'll be stupefied," Will said in exasperation. "Tell me!"

"She's at the house of a man they call the Collector. He's the chap who pays for all of this lot," Alfred said, waving his arms to encompass the studio. "He bought most of the originals from Rupert. I presume you've worked out what the game is?"

"You steal an original, copy it and put the copy back?"

"That's it exactly, dear boy. And the Collector buys the original works. He's been doing it for years. Before they had me as the forger they had another chap who was quite handy with a paintbrush."

"Is this leading somewhere?" Will asked.

Alfred smiled at him over the top of his tea cup.

"Bear with me," he said. "You'll never guess who the other chap was."

Will cast his mind back to prison, but he couldn't think of anyone obvious.

"I give up."

Alfred took another sip of tea, his eyes twinkling.

"*You*, dear boy. The first forger was you."

Will stared at Alfred as if he had suddenly gone mad.

"*Me?* But I didn't do it; I always told you I didn't do it. Don't you believe me?"

"Oh yes, I believe you, dear boy. But you see, you were doing perfect copies and they were playing exactly the same game back then. They were having your copies signed and aged and putting them back in the place of originals. This Collector chap was buying them all at a fraction of their real worth and spiriting them away in his mansion."

There was a silence for thirty seconds as Will's mind raced back to those days. He had been so naïve then. Prison had changed him so much – in a way it had forced him to grow up. He had been engaged to the beautiful Fiona and happy enough, before it had all gone sour. He thought of the days in court and Fiona's father with his face like thunder and the jury's grim faces and his own cockiness that had helped turn them against him.

He looked at Alfred incredulously.

"You don't mean–?"

Alfred nodded gravely.

"I only discovered a month or two ago, and the irony was not lost on me, dear boy. The Collector is the man who almost became your dearly beloved father in law. He is Lord Ruskin."

An hour later Will had once more descended into the back garden. He took one last look up at the lighted window which framed Alfred's silhouette, then ran back along the brick path on light feet. The rain was beginning to ease off. He felt more elated than he had felt since he had kissed Lucy in his studio. *He knew where she was.* He swung around the spikes that guarded the rear entrance to Rupert Angel's domain and rejoined the river path, dodging the puddles. He didn't want to pass in front of the Angel house again so he set off left along the riverbank, passing the now-closed pub, looking for another way through.

At first he had tried to persuade his old friend to leave with him, but Alfred couldn't climb down a drainpipe at his age, and his studio door was locked. They had also both been worried about Lucy's fate if Alfred suddenly vanished.

"Mrs Morris would do away with the poor girl as soon as look at her," Alfred had said. "Sadly I think the game is up for me, dear boy. "I'm too old to run and too tired. All I can hope for is a bit of clemency if I give you a hand to catch these people. They've treated me like dirt, and I'd like you to get your Lucy back. But I've had plenty of time to think and I have the makings of a plan."

The old man had gone on to tell him about the copying of Botticelli's Venus and Mars.

"I don't want to blow my own trumpet, but it's a good one," Alfred had said to him. "Front, back and sides; you know. I put it on an original panel from a *cassone* and I tried to make it my finest hour. That's why I was bloody furious this morning when Rupert took it away before it was properly baked."

Will smiled at the look of indignation he remembered on Alfred's face. He came to a street lamp and squinted at his watch, wiping the rain off it. The time was ten past midnight. He didn't have his phone on him – it was switched off and locked in the pannier of the Bonnie. He found an alleyway and went up it, hurrying the more he thought about Lucy. He reached the Bonnie after ten more minutes, started it up and cruised away as quietly as he could, his head soaked inside the helmet, his visor steaming up. When he came to a railway bridge he stopped underneath, took out his phone and switched it on. He stared at it for a few moments, astonished at what he was about to do. Then he found Davies' number and called it.

The phone kept diverting to voicemail, and he kept disconnecting and then calling again, with increasing worry and frustration. The sixth time he did this the phone was answered almost immediately by a sleepy Hugh Davies.

"It's Will Bentley," Will said into the phone. "Are you awake?"

"Not exactly," Davies said. "What's happening? Have you got news of Lucy?"

"I know who kidnapped Lucy and I know who funded this whole deal. It turns out it's not just a few paintings; it's dozens. I have a plan worked out but we don't have much time. Are you awake yet?"

There was a rustling of bedclothes.

"I'm wide awake," Davies said, more crisply. "How do you know all this? Tell me everything."

I think Lucy is alive but in danger so we need to prepare right now – tomorrow will be too late. First thing tomorrow the kidnapper is taking the final painting to the man with the money. After that it's all over. Deal done; they disappear and cover their tracks."

"Give me their names," Davies said, wide awake now.

"I'll give you the names when we meet," Will said. "I can't risk anything going wrong with this one."

"What if something happens to you the way it did to Lucy?" Davies said in frustration. "Just give me *one* name then."

"All right, but I want your word to do nothing until we meet, and in turn I swear to you that this is stone-cold certain, there is *no* doubt. I just spoke to Alfred Smith for two hours and he is locked in the kidnapper's house right now. That's where I met him."

"You have my word," Davies said, his mouth dry. "Who is it?"

Will told him.

There was a long pause.

Then Davies said, "I'll need thirty minutes. Where are you now?"

RICHARD JOHN MITCHELL

SIXTY-ONE

By prevailing over all obstacles and distractions, one may unfailingly arrive at his chosen goal or destination.
CHRISTOPHER COLUMBUS

It was ten past eight on Thursday morning. The rain had finally abated and the sun was already high, steaming the pavements dry. Neither Will nor the various policemen had slept so they were all tired, but everything was in place. They were in an innocuous green van not unlike the one which had been used for covert observation of the brothel outside Will's studio, except that this van was loaned by the security services so it was more technically advanced. In the van were Will, Davies, two security services men who had introduced themselves as Ben and Harry, and two uniformed policemen covered in radios and equipment and carrying slung weapons. There were two more vans parked around the corner which could be summoned in a minute or so, but they weren't surveillance vehicles; they were fitted with seats and tightly packed with armed police officers. After the bomb in Cambridge no-one was taking any chances.

The green van was two hundred yards away from Angel's London house and had been positioned so that it had line of sight to the front door and the white van parked in front of it. They had just filmed Rupert Angel, Mrs Morris and a lanky young man loading a large painting crate into the white van. Background checks had swiftly identified the lanky young man as Lawrence Arthur Morris, the son of Julia Eunice Morris, both assistants of Rupert Angel. A computer screen showed information about the three individuals. Will could see driving licence pictures, passport photographs, bank account details, credit details, phone number calling records, mobile phone usage records, card purchases, property holdings, vehicles owned, travel patterns for the vehicle registrations owned. He shook his head, both impressed and alarmed at the speed and efficiency with which this data had been assembled. But in the end all he cared about was Lucy – it would be satisfying to see Angel and Ruskin get their just desserts, but it would be in vain if anything happened to Lucy.

He was also impressed by the quality of the recording, which was a glimpse into a different world. The screens were not showing a distant monochrome view of figures that might or might not be the guilty party. The sound didn't hiss and splutter like a spy's microphone in an eighties film.

They had two perfect full-colour camera views, one framing the figures and the other close up on their heads. One of the security men sat with headphones and a console, guiding the cameras.

Sound came from directional microphones concealed in the rhododendron bushes to one side of Rupert's drive, transmitting their signal over a closed frequency channel to the van. There was no wind noise or other background sound; just three voices conversing as if they were in a television play. The security man on sound was Harry. He held up his hand for silence as Mrs Morris began to speak.

"Lawrence can go with you and give you a hand with the Botticelli," she said. "It's easier with two."

"Not if one of them is Lawrence," Angel said sourly.

There didn't appear to be much love lost there. Lawrence looked as if he were going to speak but then turned abruptly on his heel and went back into the house.

"Very well then," she said with a look of exasperation. "Did you speak with Ruskin?"

"Yes. He's very excited."

"So he should be," Mrs Morris said tartly, "but I don't mean about the painting. I mean about the girl."

"I know exactly what you mean, Julia," Angel said shortly. "You have made yourself very plain. I will talk with him on the subject of Lucy."

Davies caught Will's eye and they mimed a slow-motion high-five.

The camera panned to Mrs Morris's face in anticipation and Will looked at the shot, reading her expression. She looked furious, he thought. Alfred had said that she and Angel had argued. Presumably they hadn't yet settled their differences.

"The situation with that woman can't be allowed to continue," she said in a clipped voice.

Angel looked exasperated but didn't reply. Apparently the conversation was over. He got into the white van and started the engine, the sound of it oddly large in the surveillance vehicle. The white van emerged from the driveway and drove past them. Will got a sudden view of Rupert Angel in the driving seat. The other camera zoomed back from close up and watched Mrs Morris in the doorway of the London house for a moment before she went back inside. Their own driver started the green surveillance vehicle and they moved off in pursuit. After a few seconds, Harry switched their screen view to the inside of the white van being driven by Rupert Angel.

Security services engineers had accessed the white van in the darkness. Working with night-vision goggles and equipment more usually found in the pocket of a car thief, they had opened the van and wired it for sound and vision. They had also installed a GPS tracker which told them exactly where the van was. Will could see Angel on the video monitor as he went on his way. The view seemed to be coming from somewhere on Angel's dashboard. It was a little distorted as if passing through a fish-eye lens, but Angel was perfectly recognizable.

"How come he doesn't see the camera?" Will asked Harry.

"It's too small," Harry said. "It's just a fibre-optic thread with a polished end and a lens and transmitter on the other end of it. It's like a tiny little hair inside the heating vent. You wouldn't see it even if you were looking."

Will nodded, feeling more at home in the world of paint than in the world of high-tech gadgetry. He thought about the next part of the operation: the critical part; the part at his old enemy's mansion.

"Do you need to change the tapes or something?" he said. "Put in some fresh ones?"

"It's all right," Harry said. "It's all flash memory."

It was evident that they knew exactly what they were doing so Will lapsed into silence and stared into space. Although the van's rear section was closed off, he could see where they were going on one of the screens. However, he wasn't that familiar with London so he didn't know their exact position.

"We're going to get a little ahead of him," the security man said after a while. Will noticed that he had an earpiece in his ear. "The other cars are maintaining visual, so we're going to take another route and he'll get snarled up in the traffic."

"What if he doesn't get snarled up?" Will said.

"We know where he's going, and he's got SatNav in his vehicle so we know how he's going to get there. You can see that he glances across at it now and then."

"He still might get there first."

"I don't think so," Harry said conversationally. "The road he's on has got variable-speed signs to control traffic flow. We just took it from 70 down to 30."

"You can *do* that?"

Harry winked.

Luxley Park was the Oxfordshire residence of Lord Charles Geoffrey Lovell Ruskin, and they arrived in the vicinity at five past ten in the morning. Will felt an odd tightening in his chest as they went through the little village of Lower Stoke and he recognised quaint buildings that he had not seen in a long time. It was a pretty black-and-white village that should have gladdened his heart, but instead made him remember too much. He glanced sideways at Davies and thought he too looked uncharacteristically grim faced. Will realised with surprise that he now thought of Davies as a friend. They were on the same side, which was a new experience in itself. After Will's arrest for forgery and the subsequent trial, his trust in the law had declined to zero.

Ruskin had employed a top Queen's Council to run rings around Will's own feeble representative. Will had therefore gone to prison, an institution not renowned for its sympathetic attitude, where he had been further alienated by the heavy-handedness of the establishment and the violence of a few inmates.

The van lurched and Davies' knee bumped against Will's. The policeman caught his eye for a moment and smiled, saying nothing. Will supposed that the world of Art and Antiquities was normally a quiet backwater of the police force, more cerebral than action-oriented. He imagined that it was probably rare for Davies to get involved in such a dramatic operation, especially one that would reach a high profile in the media once the news got out. The papers were hungry for more information after the hanging and then the bomb, and now they were going to get it. The events of the day had everything; art fraud, money, wicked villains, bent aristocracy and a pretty girl. Will grimaced to himself, unnoticed by anyone, as he thought about the pretty girl in particular and hoped that she was all right.

A feeling of dread stirred in him when he saw the familiar gates of Luxley Park. He remembered his previous visits when he had painted *trompe l'oeil* for Ruskin and had courted his daughter; the lovely but spoiled Fiona. All the lies and betrayal flooded back. He had a sinking feeling in his groin.

The gates were large and imposing and open. There was no technology apparent – no CCTV on stalks, no intercom at the entrance. This was a traditional English mansion which had miraculously evaded the National Trust and stood solid and proud in 287 acres of prime English parkland. It must be worth a vast sum, and cost a further fortune to maintain, but Will knew that Ruskin had the necessary funds. His was not an impoverished family of diluted royal blood, unable to maintain a good table. His grandfather and father had been financiers who had made their money in South African diamonds, and Ruskin too had invested and traded wisely, continuing the family tradition of financial prudence.

The police driver ignored the main gates and swept past, pulling off into the woods at a spot which Will had suggested. Two more unmarked vans turned in behind them and they drove over rutted tracks until they were out of sight of the road. Then they disembarked and the woods seemed suddenly full of policemen. Will looked at them and felt an unexpected calm. Up until now a part of him had been worrying that he had involved the police, after all the stories in the press of them blundering about and shooting the wrong people. But these men were calm and friendly and very professional. They exuded confidence. It made him feel odd that he was now on their side, having spent so long despising them.

Everyone wore flak jackets, including Will himself. The uniformed men had the usual multitude of leather pouches containing unidentified gadgets. Some of them carried Heckler and Koch MP5 Submachine guns for use in close-quarters battle. They wore black earpieces and would occasionally speak into radios on their shoulders. It was disconcerting because Will could only ever hear one side of the conversation, and their talk was peppered with so much jargon that it was for the most part incomprehensible.

He led them to the house from the side and they got up close to the imposing gravelled sweep at the front of the property. The house was even bigger than Will remembered, with a round tower at each end and a dome in the middle, built of honey-coloured Cotswold limestone. The white van had not yet arrived, but they were hurrying now because it would be there in ten minutes and they had not yet set up the cameras. There was a flurry of activity; equipment being switched on and connected to portable power units; parabolic-reflector microphones being aligned; lenses being pointed.

The white van finally arrived at a few minutes before eleven. Rupert Angel emerged from it and looked around but didn't appear at all suspicious; it was just a casual glance around. He looked at his watch. The doors of the house opened and two men came down the steps. They helped him get the large crate out of the van and carry it into the house. At ten past eleven they had finished and closed the rear doors of the van and disappeared through the imposing double front doors.

One of the policemen was speaking into the radio, coordinating movements around the house. He nodded and turned to Davies.

"Ready when you are, sir."

"Okay," Davies said. He looked at his watch. "We'll go in on the dot of quarter past, and tell London to do the same." He got the warrant paperwork out of his pocket.

It took a further ten minutes for them to enter the house through an unlocked back door and secure the building. There was no resistance. They found a cook and three maids, a housekeeper and a butler. There were also four gardeners that they had rounded up in the grounds, who were sitting somewhat bemused in a police van.

They had *not* found Rupert Angel or Lord Ruskin. The front drive was now full of police vehicles and there was the distant roar of an approaching police helicopter. Davies and a posse of armed policemen were with the butler in the grand main entrance hall, having worked through the house from the rear.

"His Lordship said that he will be in the chapel and has asked not to be disturbed during his worship," the butler said rather imperiously.

"I can't help that," Davies said crisply. "Take us to him please."

The butler looked as if he were going to argue for a moment, but then he took in the faces of the men before him and capitulated.

"If you'll follow me, sir."

They went down a long gallery which was lined with doors and ageing portraits. They made a curious procession. First came the butler in his black tailcoat, white shirt and black tie. He marched along with his head held high and one hand held behind his back. Then came Davies, wearing dark clothes and a flak jacket bearing the single word 'Police' over the heart. After him came a number of policemen in uniform bearing weapons. Last of all came Will, because he had been told to stay at the rear of the action at all times. He had only been permitted to attend because he had first-hand knowledge of the inside of the house – and perhaps also because Davies was bending the rules a little. They marched down the gallery and the policemen's boots echoed on the marble floor. Dark portraits of Ruskin's forebears glowered at them.

The chapel was a round room in the bottom of the west tower. It had a heavy wooden door which was closed. The butler knocked on it. It was the sort of knock that a butler uses when he is standing just outside his master's door with a platoon of policemen; polite but unquestionably insistent. To compound the indignity, Davies stepped forward, grasped the handle and pushed the door open without further ceremony. Lord Ruskin himself came immediately into view, hurrying towards the door from an ornate gold-coloured altar. He stopped in amazement when he saw the assembled multitude.

"Some gentlemen to see you, my Lord," the butler said with admirable restraint, and then was carried forward as the horde of policemen surged on down the steps and into the chapel. It was a large circular room but they practically filled it, even though some of them stayed outside. Will came down the steps last and paused at the top, unable to resist savouring a moment of triumph at the sight of his old enemy surrounded by policemen in his own house.

"What the devil?" Ruskin began. Then he caught sight of Will on the steps and turned visibly pale.

"You!" he said incredulously. "What are *you* doing here?"

"I'm watching justice being done," Will said evenly.

"You're supposed to be locked up," Ruskin spluttered. "Look here, who's in charge?"

"I am," Davies said. "We have a report that you are holding a Mrs Lucy Wrackham here against her will, sir. And that you have some paintings on the property that have been acquired through illegal means. I therefore have a warrant to search the premises which you may inspect and a copy will be provided to you. Would you care to comment on the serious charges that have been made, sir?"

"Absolute rubbish," Ruskin said, but Will could tell that he was severely rattled. He knew the man well and his memories were flooding back as if they had been locked in some frozen vault of suppressed synapses, awaiting service until this moment. Ruskin tried to regain his composure.

"Look here, officer, this man went to prison for forgery," he said in an easier tone, pointing an accusing finger at Will. "I was instrumental in making sure that justice was done. He bears a grudge against me, so I don't know what he's been telling you but I can assure you that it's nonsense."

Will felt relieved that it wasn't just on his word that they were here: they already had the conversation recorded outside Angel's London house, linking Lucy to Ruskin.

"There is a white van parked outside on your driveway, sir," Davies said. "I wonder if you could identify the owner of it?"

"The owner?" Ruskin said, clearly wondering what to say. "Ah yes, the white van in the driveway. I have a visiting London art dealer here at the moment. Nothing unusual about that."

"Could you tell me the dealer's name, sir?" Davies said.

"His name," Ruskin said uneasily. "Yes, well, his name is Mr Angel, of the Angel Galleries."

"Mr *Rupert* Angel, sir?"

Ruskin was looking distinctly alarmed.

"Er, yes."

"And did Mr Angel bring anything with him, sir?"

"No, no, nothing at all," Ruskin said, making his first serious mistake of the proceedings. "He's just come up to Luxley Park to value a few of my pieces."

Davies took out a pad and began to make notes on it.

"So Mr Angel has just come here today to value some of your collection, sir?" he asked in confirmation.

"Yes he has," Ruskin said rather testily. "Now what is *your* name, officer? I shall be needing it when I speak to the Chief Constable today about this extraordinary invasion."

"I'm sorry you feel that way, sir," Davies said, becoming more polite as Ruskin became less so. "I'm Detective Inspector Hugh Davies of the Metropolitan Police's Art and Antiques Unit. Now back to the gentleman that came to value your collection, sir. Where is he?"

Ruskin looked around the chapel and waved his hand vaguely.

"Well, somewhere around I expect," he said. "Somewhere, er, valuing items. It's a large building, inspector."

"It certainly is, sir, but we would like to find Mr Angel and talk with him immediately. We have been unable to locate him in the house and we want to clear this matter up."

"I'm not sure I know what you mean," Ruskin said sourly, beginning to look increasingly like a cornered rat. "What matter?"

"The matter of the large crate that Mr Angel unloaded from his van and carried into the house with the assistance of two of your staff," Davies said in the same unfailingly polite tone. "I was wondering why Mr Angel would be bringing in such a crate when he is merely here to value a few pieces in your collection."

"Are you trying to trip me up?" Ruskin said, every inch the lord and master of his domain now. "Mr Angel and I frequently conduct business, and I expect he brought a painting back from cleaning or something like that."

"I don't believe I mentioned it was a painting, sir," Davies said. "But the matter will be quickly cleared up as soon as we talk with Mr Angel and examine the contents of the crate."

He turned to the butler.

"Do you know where Mr Angel has gone?" he said abruptly.

The butler looked alarmed now.

"Well sir, I couldn't possibly say."

"Why not?"

"Well, that is – I had thought the gentleman was with his Lordship in a private meeting, sir."

"Conducting a little private prayer together, perhaps?" Davies said with a trace of sarcasm now in his voice. "I believe you said his lordship was in this chapel alone for worship, and now you say that Mr Angel was in a private meeting with him."

Ruskin started up again, his voice a braying sound like a donkey.

"Now look here, I must ask you to stop cross-examining my staff."

The butler looked more harassed than any butler is supposed to look.

"Must you?" Davies said icily. "I'd like to meet Rupert Angel and I'd like to see inside the crate he brought immediately. Perhaps we could stop playing games and get on with it."

Ruskin held his gaze for a long moment but then dropped his eyes.

"You'd better follow me and we'll go and look for him," he said. "Perhaps he's in the gallery."

Will stepped aside, watching the man with an artist's intensity. Ruskin's eyes flicked sideways to the altar for a moment and it was that fleeting look that reminded Will of something. He frowned. Ruskin went up the steps and Davies followed him closely behind. Some of the policemen were already outside, some in the room.

Then Will had a sudden epiphany and he smiled.

He's leading them away from the centre of the action.

SIXTY-TWO

*On the touching of her lips I may
Melt and no more be seen.*
PERICLES

"Mr Davies!" Will called out loudly.

Davies stopped at the top of the steps, and Ruskin halted and turned too, his face frozen.

"A long time ago there was a man called Nicholas Owen," Will said animatedly. "Pope Paul canonized him in 1970 – he was one of the forty martyrs. I read a book about him."

"What are you talking about?" Davies said, mystified at this obscure interruption.

"Nicholas Owen," Will repeated. "He travelled the country in the late sixteenth century building priest's holes."

"He built *priest's holes*?"

"Yes, for the safe harbour of catholic priests. And he built one right here in this chapel," Will went on. "When I was working for Ruskin I painted this chapel for him." He pointed to the paintings on the walls. "See those? The Crucifixion, the Resurrection and the Ascension, and you'll find my signature on them. Now Lord Ruskin here once told me that there was a priest's hole concealed in the chapel. It was so well hidden that they only found it in 1963. Anyway, Ruskin never could resist any opportunity to impress, so he showed me where it was."

He walked over to the altar.

"The trigger is somewhere here," he said. "Though I can't immediately remember where."

Davies came back down the steps slowly, and turned back to Ruskin.

"Perhaps you'd be good enough to open the priest's hole, sir?"

"I haven't opened it for a long time," Ruskin said, swallowing. "I can't immediately think, er…"

His voice tailed off and he waved his hand vaguely. Will shook his head and knelt down to reach underneath the altar.

"I think it was somewhere under here," he said, his face jammed up against the altar cloth. Then he pressed something and there was a click. One of the painted panels in the wall had opened slightly, floor to ceiling.

Will straightened up and brushed himself down, then walked over to the panel and pushed it open, waving his hand with a grin.

"Ta-da!"

He waited for Davies, who came down the steps and approached him while Ruskin stood surrounded by a grim phalanx of blue serge.

Will stepped back to let Davies in, and the policeman went through the open panel, giving Will a barely perceptible wink as he went. Two policemen followed him with guns. Will hesitated for a moment and then followed them. Beyond the panel a short corridor led to a stone room. It had no windows but was illuminated brightly with modern spotlights. The far wall was part-panelled and there was an ancient oak table and a chair. Will could imagine a frightened priest sitting there while Oliver Cromwell's brutish soldiers searched the house in vain.

Ruskin was summoned by Davies and in a few moments he came through the door, angrily shaking off the hand of a policeman on his arm.

"You can see there's nothing here," he said, his arms folded in front of him, his eyes down. "It's just a little cupboard room, nothing more."

He was sweating profusely.

Will examined the room.

"Another practice of Owen's was to build a second exit," he said thoughtfully. "Especially in these big houses where they had plenty of money. The poor old priest might have been stuck in here for a week so he'd need an escape hatch or he'd die of thirst."

Davies walked up to the panel at the back of the little room.

"Well it could be here somewhere," he said, and turned to Ruskin again. "I don't suppose you can save us some trouble by telling us where to look?"

"This is ridiculous," Ruskin snapped. "Complete fabrication. I shall be calling my lawyers immediately. Bentley's making it all up and you're swallowing the whole story. He's a criminal with a grudge."

"Not a criminal any more, sir," Davies corrected him. "He's served his time. And in the meantime someone has threatened to chop his hand off with an axe, tried to hang him, and blown up a car in a busy street outside his property. Now *that's* what I call criminal activity."

Ruskin's skin was now so mottled that Will wondered hopefully if he might be going to have a cardiac arrest. Davies ignored Ruskin and began to rap the panels. Will and various policemen joined him in this effort.

After several minutes of pushing and prodding and tapping, one of the constables discovered that the entire back wall panel simply slid to one side. It revealed a large steel door with a businesslike combination lock, making it look like a huge safe. Unexpectedly it opened when Davies tried the handle, as if the last person to pass through it hadn't had time to spin the lock. There was a further corridor and the hum of air conditioning could be heard.

Davies nodded to his sergeant and Ruskin was held firmly.

"Search him for concealed weapons just in case," he said. "Tell the lads not to take any chances with the rest of the staff, and bring in some more back up from the local nick."

He turned to Ruskin.

"It seems you're not telling the truth," he said brusquely to Ruskin. "I'm going to go through this door and I'm going to require you to remain with these officers and submit to a search. If you're not prepared to do so then you'll be arrested. If there's anything you need to tell me at this time that might avoid hostilities then it'll be better if you say it now."

He expected an angry riposte but Ruskin looked pale and somehow diminished; shrunken and older.

"There's hardly anyone here," he muttered, "and anyway, it's all over now. I need to call my lawyer."

"All in good time," Davies said grimly. He went through the steel door, followed by three armed policemen. Will stepped through the door behind them and no-one tried to stop him. There was a short corridor and then they emerged into a huge underground cellar beneath the house. It was suddenly clear why Ruskin had said that it was all over, for the cellar was not empty. It had glass screens interspersed through it and dozens of pictures were hanging on them.

The glass screens reminded Will of the upstairs room at the National Portrait Gallery; the one with all the writers and politicians and painters. But this vast cellar had a different feel; its low vaulted ceiling and supporting pillars lent it a gothic appearance. Davies caught Will's eye.

"Well I think Ruskin is well and truly nicked," he said with a ghost of a smile.

They walked down the rows in awe, immediately recognizing several masters. It was like a Nazi hoard. Will stopped for a moment, looking at the painting before him on the wall. It was the real Procaccini: The Triumph of Good over Evil. It appeared identical to the one he had looked at previously, except that his eyes went to one particular spot and confirmed that this picture's angel had its halo intact. He walked on, his head raking from side to side like one watching tennis.

He stopped at the original Fran Snyders: *Fruit in a Bowl on a Blue Cloth*. It looked identical in every way with the one that he had examined so closely in the sitting room of Brighstone Manor. He chuckled. This at last was the incontrovertible factual evidence which Lady Felicity required.

He walked on but paused again in front of one of Edvard Munch's versions of *The Scream*, famous in part for the number of times it had been stolen. He didn't personally think much of the picture, but the Norwegians would certainly be pleased.

He reached the end of the row. Davies and a policeman were there beside the wooden crate that they had seen being unloaded from the white van. Davies was speaking on the radio, summoning more men to conduct a thorough search.

"No sign of Angel or Lucy," Davies said to him as he came up. "Did you see the Renoir?"

"Renoir? Jesus, no I didn't, but I saw *The Scream.*"

Davies shook his head in amazement.

"The old bugger's going to get locked up for about ten thousand years," he said, pulling on plastic gloves and addressing his attention to the crate.

But Will wasn't interested in Venus and Mars just then; they could lie in their post-coital bliss for a little longer. His eyes had moved to the left, into the furthest corner of the gallery cellar, where there were two doors. He left Davies and walked over to them. One of the doors was the same heavy steel design as the entrance door, with the same combination lock. It was closed but this time the stainless steel handle refused to budge when he tried to move it.

The other door was made of stout oak and led to some kind of storeroom. He twisted the key and swung the heavy door open, its hinges screeching. Sitting on a single chair and looking at the door defiantly was a familiar blonde figure.

"I can't leave you alone for a minute, can I?" he said, with his hands on his hips. Lucy stood up and slowly unclenched her fists as she saw it was him.

"I suppose you can't," she said, and suddenly realized that she couldn't speak because if she did she would cry and she didn't want to look ridiculous. Her eyes were filling with tears and she blinked furiously.

"They said they'd already burned the Procaccini," she said, shaking her head. "They said no-one would ever find me. Ruskin's completely bonkers. He told me I was his latest exhibit and he was going to put me in a *cage*, for God's sake. And Rupert just let him get on with it, the bastard."

"They *did* burn the picture," Will said, "but eventually I stopped feeling sorry for myself and figured out the clue anyway."

He took her hands with concern, seeing how close to tears she was. "Are you all right?" he asked. "Because if they've harmed just one hair of your pretty little head…"

She giggled but it turned into a strangled sob and a huge shudder went through her.

"I can hardly even speak," she said, lifting her face to his.

When he kissed her, her lips tasted of tears.

RICHARD JOHN MITCHELL

SIXTY-THREE

To run away from trouble is a form of cowardice.
ARISTOTLE

Rupert Angel felt both incredulous and bitter that the police had dared to raid Luxley Park. As soon as he and Ruskin had seen the uniforms on the monitor screen in the secret gallery, he had known that their whole enterprise was over. Ruskin had gone to try and brazen it out, while Angel had watched the scene in the chapel with a sinking heart. He had seen the Welsh detective before on the news. Then he suddenly recognized Lucy's friend *Bentley* at the back and an intense hatred surged through him. It was Bentley who had survived all attempts to kill him; Bentley who had somehow brought the authorities here, and Bentley who had stolen away Lucy's heart.

As he watched, Bentley came forward and started to fiddle with the altar. Jesus, now the confounded man was looking for the *priest's hole*! They could be in here in minutes. Angel looked around in desperation – he would have to use the rear exit. He looked at the wooden door behind which Lucy was imprisoned, and wondered for a wild moment whether he should take her with him as a hostage. Then he dismissed the idea: she would fight and kick and scream and he had no stomach for it. If the truth be known, he couldn't bear the look of contempt he would see in her eyes. He shook his head and decided simply to walk away from the scene.

He snatched up his jacket and put it on; his eyes flickering fearfully back to the monitor screen. *They were entering the priest's hole.* He needed to get out very fast or they would catch him. He had a sudden idea and grabbed Ruskin's keys. Ruskin would have no need for them now. His eyes fell on Botticelli's painting of Venus and Mars, freshly removed from its crate and wrapped only in muslin cloth. The muslin cloth had been pulled back at the top by Ruskin only minutes earlier, so that you could a red cushion and bit of Venus's elbow. On impulse he decided to take the painting with him – if he escaped then it would be his ransom. He wrapped the cloth back around the ancient panel. Then he unlocked the steel door next to Lucy's temporary cell. It had the same combination as the door from the priest's hole. It sickened him to leave Lucy there to reveal all, but it was only a matter of time before they found her.

It took him longer than he expected to get the Botticelli into the narrow corridor beyond the door, and he grazed his elbow badly on the steel frame as he tried to manoeuvre the six-foot long painting through a space never designed to accommodate it. The narrow corridor was designed for fleeing Catholics, not large paintings. As he closed the steel door carefully behind him, he gave the combination lock a spin so that cutting equipment would be needed to get through it.

He had only been in the tunnel once before. The air in the passage was earthy and damp and lit only with occasional naked bulbs – no air conditioning in here. It took him ten careful minutes to reach the other end, and he had no idea whether he was going to emerge into the arms of the police. However, he couldn't stay in the passage for a moment longer so he had to risk it. He put down the painting and looked through the spy hole. There was no one in sight. He slid the two locking bars an inch to the left and a wooden panel unlatched itself and swung open. He looked through the gap cautiously, seeing no-one. Then he stepped through the panel and emerged into the mausoleum at the edge of the gardens, having passed beneath the lawns.

The last time he had been there was when he had slipped in from the Summer Concert and been followed without his knowledge by David Wrackham. Wrackham had trailed him all the way to the underground gallery and had seen everything for a few moments before Morton had extinguished his life with a blow from behind with an iron bar. The squelching sound of the shattering skull still sometimes haunted Angel's dreams and made him start awake in a cold sweat, staring into the dark.

Angel collected the painting from the tunnel and closed the panel behind him, then went across to the heavy oak doors, his arms and back already beginning to ache with the weight of the panel and the strain of preventing it from knocking into anything.

Now for the moment of truth. There was no spy hole here so he simply had to unbolt the heavy doors and open them. When he did so his heart was in his mouth but there was no one to be seen. The police presumably had the house surrounded but it would be impossible to cordon off the entire grounds. The path in front of him was screened by a dense thicket of rhododendrons and was deserted. He emerged cautiously from the mausoleum, clutching the cloth-wrapped painting, pulled the doors closed and began to hurry down the wide, shallow steps that led to the river, his breathing smooth and easy. *Still* there was no shout of surprise and no chase! He heard the sound of a helicopter and pressed himself against the dark bark of a Holm Oak until it had moved on. Then he carried on down the steps with a wide, loping gait. At the bottom was the landing stage and Ruskin's sleek white cruiser. Angel tripped on the bottom step and went flying, dropping the painting so that it skittered across the gravel in its thin cloth.

He swore quietly, got to his feet, ignored one knee that was cut and bleeding and pulled back the muslin cloth to look inside. Botticelli had picked a good piece of wood: Venus was still languid and Mars was still sleeping. He exhaled slowly and gathered the painting up again with exaggerated care, carrying it over to the boat.

The controls of Ruskin's boat were similar to his own and he fumbled in his pocket for the man's keys. The diesel engine started immediately. After he had the Botticelli on board it took him only a minute or two of fiddling with ropes before he was able to engage the drive and cruise slowly away down the river. By the time the Environment Agency found the abandoned boat several hours later, Rupert Angel was long gone and there was no sign of Botticelli's Venus and Mars.

SIXTY-FOUR

Sometimes I've believed as many as six impossible things before breakfast.
LEWIS CARROLL

That morning, Mrs Morris had watched Rupert Angel pull the white van out of the drive and raised her hand in farewell, though in reality she was seething inside. Overnight she had concluded that he was too weak to be in charge; he couldn't make difficult decisions when needed. Not that she would have regarded the disposal of Lucy Wrackham as a difficult decision – more a necessity. For him to have simply handed the woman over to Ruskin was beyond belief. Ruskin was no better, all puffed up with hot air and his father's fortune, and mad as a hatter. Quite what he got out of owning so many old paintings she would never know, for he had paid Rupert a fortune but could never show them off to anyone. She herself enjoyed luxuries, but if she had a gold bracelet she would want to wear it, not lock it in a closet and gloat over it.

She turned to Lawrence as they went inside and was surprised to see a smile on his face.

"You're very chirpy," she said, "considering he was damn rude to you as usual."

"Perhaps I'm just glad not to be lugging paintings around for him while he treats me like dirt, mother."

She was surprised. Lawrence rarely spoke his mind. Perhaps the boy was getting a personality at last. He had always taken after his weak-willed father, but she had never given up hope that her own strength of character might begin to flower in him.

He went up the stairs two at a time and she hesitated, then went into the study. She needed to think. She sat down in the armchair to analyze the situation.

First, Lucy Wrackham had to go, because she could put them all in jail. Ruskin apparently wanted to keep her as some kind of pet, so he'd obviously lost his marbles. The only way out of it seemed to be that she herself would have to go to Ruskin's estate and deal with pretty little Lucy Wrackham. Her mouth curled into a smile. They wouldn't fancy her quite so much when she started to rot. Then she laughed out loud: Rupert wouldn't anyway, but she wouldn't be so sure of his lordship.

Second, Alfred Smith would have to go. If they let him out into the wide world he might get drunk and talk about the whole affair, or he might come back and attempt to blackmail them once he ran out of money, or he might be caught on some other charge and this could all come out.

Third, there were three of Morton's men remaining. Four others had taken off – they could smell danger a mile away and they simply were not there one morning. Were they a problem? Technically she would have liked to dispose of them too, because they all knew too much, though they certainly didn't know the whole story about Alfred Smith or the Wrackham girl. The trouble was, they were big brawny louts and she certainly wouldn't want anything to go wrong if she did decide that they had become redundant, because if they survived they would turn very nasty. She didn't want to become a victim herself, and she had only survived as long as she had by anticipating problems and not expecting everything to go like clockwork. She decided simply to let them go.

Fourth, there was of course Rupert himself, and Ruskin. She had worked for Rupert for too long and she couldn't contemplate doing anything to *him*, though she was certainly beginning to wonder whether she should split from him once she had her share. And Ruskin? It would probably be best to leave him alone as well. He was protected by his title and people's respect for the upper classes, and had too much to lose ever to say anything. An amusing thought entered her head; it wouldn't be difficult to subdue the old fool and his staff and steal the entire store of paintings in what he called the Secret Gallery. He would never be able to report them stolen! She liked this idea very much and went to the drinks cabinet, where she made herself a gin and tonic, even though it was still before nine in the morning. She caught sight of herself in the mirror and toasted herself. It had been a long day yesterday, followed by an angry row in the evening and then a night in which she had lain awake. Considering all this, she didn't look bad at all.

There was a knock on the study door and a shaven head appeared around it – one of Morton's louts.

"The old man's asking for breakfast," he said.

Her eyes glittered.

"Tell him we'll rustle something up."

Forty-five minutes later, Alfred was tucking into the hearty breakfast that Mrs Morris had prepared for him, feeling astonished that she had bothered. In fact, she'd been quite charming. She wasn't bad looking either, it had to be said. When all was said and done he wouldn't have minded a leg over. And she could cook: he had bacon, sausages, two fried eggs, tomato, mushrooms and toast. Best bloody breakfast he'd had for a long time. She had to keep him locked up on Rupert's orders, she'd said. Then she'd told him *she* thought it was bloody ridiculous and Rupert was just being paranoid. She said she'd let him out if she had her way, but Rupert wouldn't let her, and besides, Morton's heavies were still hanging about. He chopped a sausage in half, spooned egg onto it and popped it in his mouth.

He pushed the plunger down on the cafetière of coffee that the Morris woman had provided. Perhaps he'd got her wrong – she'd always seemed a complete bitch but she'd certainly been pleasant enough this morning, even a little flirty, he thought, and he'd smelt gin on her breath.

He finished off the meal and used the last piece of toast to mop up the egg. Absolutely excellent! He almost regretted telling all to Will, but when all was said and done he was still a prisoner here, and he'd had enough of being a prisoner. He wiped his mouth and poured a mug of coffee. He added milk and two sugars; all this talk about heart attacks was a load of bloody nonsense. When it was your time, you went. He took a sip of coffee and savoured it. He had known too many pious bloody people who exercised and didn't smoke or drink and ate sensible food, then they'd drop dead one fine day. Gillian's frightful husband, Brian, for example. Nobody could be a more pious prick than him, and now look at him – sitting in an urn on her bedroom window ledge.

He wondered how Will was getting on. He liked the lad very much – well, not such a lad really – and he hoped he would find the girl he was looking for. What was her name? Lucy. Pretty girl: there was no doubt about that, even though he had glimpsed her only for a second in that car. Of course, Will himself was a good-looking lad and that's why he had probably got into such trouble in the joint, until that chap had started looking out for him. What was his name? Couldn't think of it. Alfred finished the coffee and wondered whether to have another one. No, he would save it until later and warm it up in the microwave. It wasn't every day that he got fresh coffee made for him.

He had no way of knowing what Will had been up to, and that was frustrating. He wanted to start a new painting, but it was hard to concentrate with all this going on. He was still angry with Rupert for taking the Botticelli away before he had finished drying it. It had been bloody ridiculous anyway trying to dry it with a hair dryer, but they'd left the oven in Burnham so that was that.

He stood up and stretched, feeling very tired. He hadn't slept well last night, after the unexpected visit from Will. He went over to the window and opened it, leaning out and inspecting the drainpipe in the daylight. The rain had stopped now and the sun was out, but everything still bore a coating of raindrops that coruscated in the sunlight. There was a bejewelled cobweb just below his window, across the top of the drainpipe funnel that Will must have stood on to reach him. The birds were out in force this morning, singing their hearts out. He inspected the distance to the ground and was glad he hadn't agreed to Will's damn-fool suggestion that he try to climb down there himself. Probably would have broken his bloody neck! He stumbled slightly against the side of the window and righted himself, surprised. Shook his head. Yes, the lad must have stood on those bins and then clambered up onto the drainpipe somehow. He couldn't see how he had reached up but he'd done it. Alfred remembered doing things like that when he'd been a lad himself. He'd climbed on the school roof to get a ball once, and there had been a load of balls up there, all shapes and sizes, so he'd chucked them all down for his classmates, and then Old Beaky had caught him up there and given him a bloody good caning, the old sod. He chuckled at the distant memory and rubbed his eyes, because the room was slightly out of focus. He'd have to find his glasses. He turned back into the room and fell down on one knee, stumbling forward so that he landed with his weight on his outstretched hand, hurting his wrist.

What was happening? He felt all woozy. Bloody room was swimming around. Be a pretty fine thing if he went and pegged out now after such a hearty breakfast. Perhaps he was the condemned man! He went on his hands and knees over to the table, intending to use the chair to pull himself up, but he fell over and upturned the tray so that the plate went flying and the half-empty cafetière tipped over and soaked its precious cargo into the carpet. He was so sleepy, he couldn't keep his eyes open, just lay there with his jaw slack and the cafetière on its side a few inches from his face. Then a dim and distant thought penetrated his brain. The Morris woman. Had made the breakfast. Had made…

He closed his eyes, just for a moment.

Mrs Morris waited until eleven and then listened at the door. She had sent the guard away and told him she'd take a turn. He'd been too stupid to think anything of it. She couldn't hear anything, so she knocked. Still nothing. She opened the door and saw Alfred spread-eagled on the ground, snoring slightly. She had put enough Ketamine in the coffee to knock anyone out. She went into the room and closed the door quietly behind her. Then she opened her bag and took out the little plastic case with her syringes in it. She also removed a small bottle with a rubber cap, took one of the syringes and emptied it into the bottle. Waste not, want not. She pulled the syringe open again so that it was full of air, and walked over to Alfred. He was definitely unconscious. He had spilled the coffee, but she could see his mug was dirty, so he had definitely had a cup. She felt for the vein at the side of his neck and pricked it with the needle. Then she emptied several centimetres of air into Alfred's blood stream. She withdrew the syringe and did it twice more, but as she was doing the third one he tensed and shuddered and then stopped breathing. She waited and watched, holding her own breath. Then she felt for his pulse and confirmed that there was none.

"Ashes to ashes, dust to dust," she intoned over the body, and inside the old man's head at her feet, all those years of acquired knowledge and skill began to unravel as the electricity of the brain ceased, like mist evaporating in the morning light.

She heard a sudden tremendous commotion downstairs, a huge banging sound and men shouting. She stood up, the syringe in her hand, but before she could move, armed policemen crashed into the room and raised their weapons at her and screamed at her to get down on the ground. For once in her life, Mrs Morris couldn't think of a thing to say. She just stood there, until they realised that she wasn't going to move and wasn't holding a weapon, apart from the syringe. She was arrested and body searched by WPCs. The syringe was taken from her and dropped into a plastic evidence bag. Like a woman in a dream, she was taken out to a waiting police van. As she came down the steps, paramedics ran past her, heading too late for the room where Alfred's body lay stretched out.

Will and Lucy were sitting in the back of an unmarked police car, holding hands. Lucy had told the authorities that she was perfectly all right and didn't need to go to hospital for a check up; she just wanted a shower and a change of clothes. It made Will smile because that was exactly what *he* had said after Morton's attempt to hang him. When you'd been through an extreme trauma, you didn't want fuss. You wanted to be among your own things and your own friends and away from officialdom.

Davies had agreed to her going home but had detailed four officers to go with her and mount guard over the flat; two women police officers inside, plus a man at the front and at the back. Rupert Angel had not yet been recovered, though they were combing the house and grounds for him, taking no chances.

"Do you want me to come with you?" Will said worriedly.

She snuggled up to him.

"That would be very nice," she said. "But I'd quite like to get cleaned up and into some fresh clothes, then spend some *normal* time with you, if you know what I mean. Not work time, and not being hanged or blown up or kidnapped; just normal time."

"How much cleaning up time do you need?"

She smiled.

"Just tonight. Then I suggest we go away for a few days. We'll only tell Davies where we are."

"We might have to make a statement or something."

"Well, we'll do that and then scoot off somewhere the media won't find us. I just want a bit of peace. You need to go home too and pack your toothbrush."

"And you'll do your best not to be kidnapped?"
Then she kissed him and it was as electrifying as before.
"I won't get kidnapped if you don't get hanged," she said.
They said goodbye and Will stepped out of the car. He needed to go back with Davies to pick up the Bonnie from the car park of the Art and Antiques unit. The car started up and moved down the drive, and she wound down the window and waved.

Someone crunched across the gravel towards Will and he turned to find Davies.

"A fine woman," the Welshman said, looking considerably more subdued than Will.

"She certainly is." Will said, his heart singing. Then he caught the look on the Welshman's face. "Are you all right?"

"The thing is, Will, I've just had a bit of terrible news about your friend Alfred Smith and I wanted to be the one to tell you. I'm afraid he's dead."

Will looked at the policeman dumb-founded; unable to believe it.

"But I was only talking to him last night," he said disbelievingly.

Davies went on in the same measured tone.

"Rupert's assistant Julia Morris did away with the poor bloke just before our boys burst in. The medics tried to revive him for twenty minutes but he was already dead. The woman injected him with something but they won't know what until the post mortem. I'm ever so sorry."

They stood there like that as seconds went by in slow motion, then Will shook his head, his eyes filled with tears. He lowered his head and gripped Davies' arm tightly, and the policeman stood and said nothing, feeling the man's pain; having nothing to say that would help.

"These people," Will said bitterly. "These *unbelievable* people."

SIXTY-FIVE

How silver-sweet sound lovers' tongues by night,
Like softest music to attending ears!
WILLIAM SHAKESPEARE, Romeo and Juliet

Will was completely exhausted by the time he got back to the studio late on Wednesday afternoon. He parked the Bonnie in the back and let himself in, feeling as if he could sleep for a month. He hadn't slept at all the previous night and had followed it with the most eventful day of his life. His emotions were in turmoil: delight at finding Lucy but misery at losing Alfred.

He was cautious when he opened the door into the hall. He picked up Lewis's baseball bat, which was leaning against the bottom stair post. Angel was still at large after all, though Davies felt it unlikely he would be free for long. Will went up the stairs and prowled around the studio, checking his kitchen and bedroom to make sure that no-one was about to leap out on him. When he found it empty he felt a little foolish. He discarded the bat, put the kettle on and spooned coffee into the cafetière. While it was coming to the boil he walked back out into the studio and stood in front of the large painting of Sandy that he had done – the one with the black eye and the shadow of her old boyfriend falling across the crimson dress. The paint was touch dry when he tested it with his finger. He inspected the image critically. It was good, though the hair was weak and needed some finer lines that he could do now that it was no longer wet.

There was a sound like a moan from somewhere behind him, making hair follicles stir along his back. With horror he realised that the door to Lewis's room was closed, and it had definitely been open when he left the studio. He *always* left it open in case Beauty or the Beast were asleep under the bed and got shut in. With exaggerated care he retrieved the baseball bat and cautiously approached the door. When he reached it he threw it open and rushed in, brandishing the bat.

Lewis was in bed, sitting half up on stacked pillows, with a small bandage on his arm and a larger white bandage like a bandolier across his bare chest. His knees were raised. He appeared frozen in horror when Will burst in, but then the bumps under the coverlet began to move and Sandy's head emerged. Then an arm and a naked breast, her hair tussled. She looked at Lewis and then followed his eyes to the doorway in which Will stood framed.

"Oops!" she said, beginning to giggle. "Sorry, Will. They let Joe out of hospital today and I was just making sure everything's in working order."

Will backed out of the room grinning.

"And there was me worrying about whether they were treating you well in the hospital," he called. "I think I shall go out and buy a paper. I expect I shall be about half an hour."

There was the sound of the studio door closing noisily, and Lewis looked at Sandy.

"'Alf a bleedin' hour," he said, his voice somewhat hoarse.

Sandy reached her mouth up to his and kissed him. Then she slid on top of him.

"Better be quick," she said.

That evening there were five people around Will's table. Lewis and Sandy were present and now fully clothed. Lewis held Sandy's hand and it looked tiny in his. George and Anna had come round as soon as Will had phoned them, bearing salad and ingredients to make paella. Will had stocked up with wine and beer and the atmosphere was at last merry. He regretted that Lucy was not there, but the wine was anaesthetising that particular pain and he certainly had a remarkable story to tell. The death of Alfred remained as a dull ache. He had told them about the call from Davies the previous morning, and his reckless drive south on the Bonnie to find the smoking remains of Marcello's. He had told them of his despair when it had seemed that the burned body might be all that remained of Lucy, and his relief when it had turned out not to be. He'd told them about deciphering the halo clue, going to Angel's house, and his feelings when he had at last found Alfred. He had recounted the police operation in which Ruskin had been captured and Lucy recovered unharmed, and finally of the death of Alfred.

"So this Angel bloke got clean away then?" Sandy asked.

"He has for now," Will said, picking up a breadstick and snapped it into quarters. Then he grinned. "That's why I had forty fits when I came in and heard someone groaning in Lewis's room."

"Who was groaning?" George said, mystified, coming back into the conversation from a mile away. Anna gave him what he referred to as 'one of her looks' and Sandy went a little pink.

"Lewis's battle wounds tweaking him a bit," Will said gravely. "So the police need to find Angel and we need to keep our eyes open just in case. Hugh Davies phoned me earlier to say that they'd checked out Lucy's apartment before they would let her go in. He said it was fine, but she *was* a bit worried that Angel might turn up so she's staying the night with her friend Millie."

"So the only really horrible thing to have happened is your poor friend Alfred," Anna said soberly. "When's the funeral?"

"It's too early to say, yet," Will said. "He'll need a post mortem. I rang his sister and told her the bad news, and she was very upset. She's a prim old dear but I think she was secretly very proud of how well he could paint, even though she disapproved of his wayward habits. He never even told her he'd been to prison, though I expect it will all come out now."

"That Morris woman sounds like a complete nutter," Sandy said.

"It gets worse," Will said. "Davies says they have her on CCTV walking away from Marcello's just before the fire went up, so it looks like she did that as well. That means she's probably guilty of killing the lab tester as well as Alfred."

The jovial atmosphere around the table had evaporated, so Anna stood up and tinkled her glass with a teaspoon.

"I suggest we make a toast to Alfred Smith and the other chap – John Ellis," she said soberly. So they got to their feet and raised their glasses.

They turned in early. Will was exhausted and Lewis regretfully made his excuses; he had to return to the hospital first thing in the morning to get his dressings changed. Sandy disappeared with Lewis, and Will couldn't help wondering exactly how much sleep Lewis was going to get. George and Anna went home, with George asking Anna in a sibilant whisper if she'd seen where Sandy had gone, and Anna begging him to shut up.

Will climbed into bed. He wondered if he should call Lucy but fell asleep instead. He was awoken by his mobile phone ringing at midnight. He fumbled around in the darkness, but by the time he had turned on the light the phone had stopped ringing. He picked it up and looked at it – the missed call was from her! He pressed buttons and lay back on the bed, staring at the ceiling, blinking to get the sleep out of his eyes. She picked up immediately.

"Lucy?"

"Hello Will. I simply had to call. Hugh told me about poor Alfred, but I wanted to speak to you anyway."

They talked for a bit about the old man they'd both been seeking for so long.

Then at last she said, "So how are you? Are you all right?"

"I'm fine. Are you okay? Managed to avoid being kidnapped?"

"I'm all right," she said with a giggle. "I came round to my friend Millie's. I know it's ridiculous, but I suddenly felt too scared to stay at home with Rupert on the loose."

"It's not ridiculous at all. Is Millie looking after you?"

"If you mean giving me too much to eat and drink, then yes. I feel like a barrage balloon. A drunken barrage balloon. Oh, that doesn't really work, does it? Anyway, we've been talking for hours and Millie said I should call you before I went to sleep. So here I am, all curled up in bed and talking to you."

"Well I'm all curled up in bed too."

There was an awkward silence.

"Will?"

"Mmm?"

"Thank you for today. I don't like to think how long I might have been stuck there if you hadn't found me."

"That's all right. What actually happened when you got abducted?"

She told him about the visit to Marcello's, courtesy of Rupert Angel and Mrs Morris.

"When the image of Rupert came up beneath the Procaccini, at first I couldn't understand it at all. Then I suddenly realised what had been going on – he'd chatted me up from the very start because I'd mentioned the investigation. I felt a complete and utter fool."

"Pretty bad luck in the first place that you happened to mention it to *him* of all people."

"Yes," she conceded. "So I was *furious*. I left poor darling John Ellis and ran out to the main entrance, where Rupert was waiting for me, no doubt on tenterhooks in case I discovered something. I yelled at him and waved his stupid picture in his face and then I can't remember what happened next."

"He must have whacked you."

"I don't know. It might have been that frightful Morris woman. She was behind me. Anyway, I woke up with a splitting headache in that store-room where you found me, but I didn't seem to have any bumps on the head or anything. I just can't remember what happened."

"You were lucky they didn't simply finish you off."

"I suppose I was," she said after a pause. "I don't really know why I got away with it."

"Angel probably couldn't bear to do it," Will said. "Anyway, I'm tired of talking about him, so let me ask you a question. When are we going to meet, or am I destined to pine away forever while you go gadding off somewhere?"

She giggled again.

"Do you miss me? I'm all snuggled up and thinking how nice it would be if you were here too. Do you know what I'm wearing?"

Will swallowed.

"Well not exactly."

"Absolutely nothing. I'm completely naked."

Will swore under his breath.

"And where does this friend of yours live?"

"Oh I couldn't possibly tell you. I've had far too much to drink and you might take unfair advantage of me."

"Maybe I could take unfair advantage of you tomorrow?"

She stretched and took a deep breath and gave a languid sigh. It was the most erotic sound. It made his spine tingle.

"Actually, I *was* planning to come up and see you tomorrow," she said dreamily.

"You *was*? I mean: you are?"

"Yes. Millie's very cross because she wants to meet you as well, but I don't feel I've had any proper time with you myself yet. So I'm coming up to kidnap you and take you to a hotel, if that's all right."

Will started to speak but had to clear his throat because his voice unaccountably came out as a croak.

"It'll be grand," he said. "I'll make some strong coffee."

"And get out the headache pills."

"And I'll paint you with black rings under your eyes."

"I can hardly wait. But remember I don't yet have a car so I'll come by train. You can expect me about noon tomorrow. I mean *today*. And in the meantime I want you to go to sleep and have *very* disgusting thoughts about what you'd like to do to me."

Will nodded thoughtfully to himself as he put down the telephone.

"I think I can manage that."

Will slept in until nine thirty and then awoke with a start. Everything that had happened the day before flooded back to him. In particular, last night's conversation with Lucy Wrackham was burned into his memory and he lay there for a while, savouring every word. When he remembered that she'd be arriving at midday he looked at the clock, discovered that it was already twenty to ten and leaped out of bed. Lewis and Sandy had left for the hospital. There was a note on the table in Sandy's rounded hand, telling him they'd be back soon. He showered and shaved. Then he cleared up things left out the night before and made coffee. When he heard the knock on the door at five to twelve he bounded down the stairs two at a time and threw open the door to welcome Lucy.

Rupert Angel was standing there with a double-barrelled shotgun in a cloth bag. He tugged off the bag, raised the weapon and pulled the trigger.

RICHARD JOHN MITCHELL

SIXTY-SIX

It is sweeter far than flowing honey.
HOMER

Angel had ditched Ruskin's boat a few miles down the river. He moored it next to other similar boats, retrieved the Botticelli masterpiece and walked away unobserved by anyone except a small white dog on an adjacent boat. There was an old hay barn in a field by the river and he hid the painting in it. It was a risk, but he couldn't walk down the street carrying such a large object without attracting immediate attention. Thus unencumbered he walked up the river, passed a pub where all the boat owners were drinking, crossed a bridge and entered a village. He used a cash point in the bank and found that his cards were miraculously still working, so he withdrew his full limit on three different cards. Then he caught a train into London.

He needed transport so he went to his gallery, but there was a police van parked on double yellow lines at the front. As he watched, a policeman emerged from the door of the Angel Gallery bearing two black bin bags. They must be collecting evidence, so the staff would know the truth by now. They'd probably be off as soon as the police had gone, taking anything that wasn't bolted down. He shook his head helplessly. It had been so good while it had lasted. It seemed impossible that he couldn't simply walk in and take command as he always did. Instead he went through the side alley to the rear parking area. The gate was open and he could see his Mercedes. If he didn't take the risk now he felt sure there would be more police and he would never again get the chance. He made up his mind and walked swiftly across the road, suddenly conscious of his rough appearance: a grazed elbow with the torn sleeve flapping; his shirt dusty from Nicholas Owen's hidden passage; a wisp of straw on his trousers from the hayrick. He took out his keys and unlocked the car remotely. In a few seconds more he was in it and driving sedately away.

He went to the Mercedes garage he used and looked for a silver Mercedes like his own. There was an identical one for sale on the forecourt so he noted the number plate. Then he drove to a small garage and ordered a set of plates with the registration he had recorded. They asked for vehicle identification but he apologised that he had not brought it with him and hoped that a cash bonus might justify them taking the trouble. It did. He bought a screwdriver and fitted the new plates in a quiet cul-de-sac. Finally he went to a man's outfitters and bought a black shirt and a dark jacket and trousers so that he looked respectable again.

When he was on his way back to the car he passed a TV shop and stopped in shock as he saw his own face staring out of the screen. The image was a recent one which had been on the wall in the foyer of the Angel Gallery. He hurried away, aware that anyone on the street might instantly recognize him. He went into a chemist and bought a pair of old-fashioned black-framed reading glasses with a weak prescription. They were completely hideous but changed his appearance significantly. He also bought hair gel, a comb and a packet of razors. Back in the car he gelled his hair and combed it differently, then scraped off his stubble but left the beginnings of a moustache. Finally he shaved his eyebrows to make them thinner.

He had a sudden panic that the police would be able locate him through his mobile phone, so he switched it off and dropped it down a drain, watching it sink into murky water. His credit cards followed – they would certainly be blocked by now.

Then he returned to the Mercedes and thought about the next stage of his plan. He needed a weapon, which was ironic because Morton had kept an arsenal in the basement of the London house, but now it was beyond his reach. However, he had once accompanied Morton to an army surplus shop in South Tottenham, which traded guns illegally in a dingy back room. Morton had picked three weapons and Angel had paid cash for them. Today he had plenty of cash in his pocket, surely sufficient to acquire something lethal, but the challenge lay in finding the shop again. He set off for Tottenham and after various false starts found what he was looking for, but to his dismay discovered that the shop was closed. He rapped on the door impatiently but no-one came. A card in the window announced that the shop opened at eight in the morning. Beneath it was a telephone number which he called from a phone box on the corner. A man answered and told him what he already knew; that the shop didn't open until eight. He said who he was and mentioned Edward Morton's name in connection with what he wanted.

"You're bloody red hot, mate," the man said. "The old bill's after you and I heard on the grape vine that Morton's snuffed it. I can't deal with you."

"I've got plenty of cash," Angel said, holding the smelly handset away from his mouth in distaste. "Do you want it or shall I go somewhere else?"

There was a long pause.

"Come along at eight and I'll see what I can do," the voice said at last. "But put a bleedin' paper bag over yer 'ead or someone'll spot you in the street."

"I'll be there," Angel said. When he put the handset back in its cradle he realised he had made it wet with sweat. He was not sure how long he could keep this up. It was not glamorous being a fugitive – it was frightening – but he was going to stick to his plan. First he would have his revenge on Bentley.

Then he would ransom the Botticelli. After that he would disappear until the media lost interest.

He stayed the night in a seedy hotel under a false name, paid in advance for his room with cash and left unobserved by a side door in the morning. He was outside the Tottenham shop again at seven-thirty. He looked around carefully but there was no-one suspicious; just people going to work. He cruised by and parked further down the street just in case. He had purchased hair dye the previous night and coloured his hair and moustache hairs black. He bought three newspapers at a corner shop and sat on a bench to read them. They all had pictures of him but he hadn't made the front page; that had been reserved for a picture of Lord Ruskin, which made him feel slightly piqued.

At eight o'clock he put the newspapers in a bin and walked across to the shop. A man unlocked the door from the inside and ushered him in.

"Come out the back," he said. "It'll be quiet for a bit yet."

Fifteen minutes later Angel emerged with a tent bag containing not a tent but a double-barrelled shotgun and twenty cartridges. The shop owner had hurriedly shown him how to load the weapon, arm it and fire it. Angel walked down the street feeling as if everyone's eyes must be upon him, but the residents of Tottenham never looked twice at the man who had risen early to buy a tent from the army surplus store. He made it to the Mercedes, put the tent bag in the back, started the engine and drove away. If he had been more experienced as a fugitive he might have noticed the unobtrusive dark blue Maestro that followed him, but his eyes were on the road ahead. Every time he passed a police car he had to fight an urge to turn off or swerve away.

He drove as fast as he could to the Thames near Oxford and retraced his steps to the hayrick. The Botticelli was safe and he breathed a sigh of relief. He carried it over the footbridge, still wrapped in its muslin cloth. One or two dog walkers eyed him curiously but he ignored them. He reached the Mercedes without incident, put the seats down and slid the painting into the back. Then he got on the road to Cambridge. As he drove he listened to the radio and became angry as the media enlarged upon and exaggerated the story. How the British public liked to see a rich and successful man put down. He learned new things: Julia Morris had been arrested and charged, as had all the other occupants of his London house. He chuckled mirthlessly at the thought of Lawrence being banged up. He was probably wetting his pants.

He arrived in Cambridge at a quarter to twelve, parked in a disabled slot just down the road from Bentley's studio and set off with the tent bag. The gun was loaded and ready; he just had to snap off the safety catch and it would fire. Bentley's street was not busy. Lucy's burned-out vehicle had been taken away by the police for forensic analysis, though he could see the scorch-marks on the road. He waited a few minutes until the street was empty of pedestrians, then knocked on Bentley's door and waited, opening the neck of the tent bag and reaching inside. Could it really be this easy? What would he do if Bentley wasn't there? Then he heard someone coming down the stairs rapidly and the door was flung open by Bentley himself. He had obviously been expecting someone else because he his expression of delight turned to horror as he realised who was on the doorstep. Angel let the tent bag fall away and raised the shotgun as Bentley tried to slam the door on him. The gun went off as Bentley dived sideways, missing him but blasting a satisfyingly large chunk out of the ceiling. The sound of the blast was deafening. Angel was astonished at how much the gun kicked in his hands – he normally let Morton do this sort of thing. Bentley didn't manage to get the door closed because he was too busy running for his pathetic life. Angel kicked it open and went in, slamming it behind him.

Various local residents stopped what they were doing and wondered if they had really heard a shot. One of them had sustained minor injuries in the bomb blast and she had not slept much since. She went to the window and looked out worriedly, wondering if she should phone the police, but there was no-one in sight.

Will literally felt the wind of the shot rush past his face. A split second earlier and it would have taken his head off. He didn't stop to look but sprinted up the stairs, which was the only escape route he had. Angel came in behind him and emptied the second barrel up the stairs as Will disappeared through the upstairs door. A second near miss and Will was in the studio now, looking desperately for any kind of a weapon. He grabbed the armchair and slid it across to block the studio door.

Angel mounted the stairs slowly, breaking open the shotgun and feeding two fresh cartridges into place, fumbling a little because he wasn't used to handling weapons. He reached the door and tried to open it, feeling resistance. He leaned heavily against it and the blockage moved away easily enough. The door opened but there was no sign of Bentley. He pushed the armchair back against the door to block the escape route and looked around the studio, the loaded shotgun in his hands. Where was the bastard hiding? There were various doors leading to other rooms and he would have to check them all. However, the gun in his hands made him feel supremely confident. He went through the rooms one by one, finding no sign of his quarry. He was moving faster now, conscious of the surprisingly loud sound the shots had made. He needed to finish Bentley off and get out fast. When he came back into the main studio he caught sight of a movement over by the easel and fired in that direction, blasting a large hole through a picture of a girl in a red dress before he realised that he had fired at his own reflection in a mirror. His hands were shaking with nerves now, but there was a sudden sound of something being overturned in the dark recesses at the back of the studio.

He moved across the studio and Bentley appeared and rushed up a black spiral staircase tucked away in the corner, disappearing through a trapdoor which must lead to the roof. Angel managed to halt his finger on the trigger this time, as he knew he would have to reload if he loosed off another shot without hitting his target. He was pretty sure he had Bentley trapped on the roof. He walked across the room and up the stairs, cradling the gun on his chest. At the top of the little staircase a baseball bat came slashing down and narrowly missed his head, glancing sideways off the frame of the trapdoor and ricocheting onto his cheek. Pain exploded in his face but he snatched at the bat and pulled. Bentley lost his grip on the bat and Angel flung it savagely behind him as he emerged onto the roof. He stopped and stared at the Gaudi-like decoration for a moment, then looked around for Bentley.

There was nowhere for Will to go – he was cornered on the roof. There was no fire escape and if he jumped from this height he would break his neck. His last desperate attempt to get Angel with the baseball bat had failed. He saw Angel's head and shoulders appearing through the trapdoor, and any second now he would turn and fire at point-blank range. Will dived for the chimney breast just as Angel turned and saw him. The man brought his gun up and Will just made it to the cover of the chimney breast as Angel fired. Except that he *hadn't* quite made it, he realised with shock. A few stray pellets of buckshot had struck him in his side, and when he reached his fingers there he found blood welling from multiple tiny wounds. Several of the Gaudi tiles fell off the chimney breast, smashed by the blast. He swore and wiped blood-wet fingers on his torn white shirt. He was able to move but his side was already hurting like hell. He risked a look around the chimney and saw Angel feeding more cartridges into the shotgun. He knew nothing at all about guns but he could see that this one had two barrels and Angel was reloading after every two shots. That meant he had just a few seconds left. He looked over the short parapet wall and saw the roof of the brothel. An image of the drunken party long ago popped into his mind; his friend clinging on desperately after jumping across. Will had always said that only a madman would be suicidal enough to try it. But he had no choice so he didn't allow himself to think, just gathered pace and charged across the roof to the parapet, launching himself with a huge leap into space. He didn't make it to the opposite roof but landed heavily with his arms hooked over the parapet wall of the brothel, just as his friend had once done. His felt as if his back had a round target painted on it. He almost lost his grip, but adrenaline fuelled his muscles and he clung on with fear and desperation. His side was stinging and his arms were throbbing. He scrabbled with his feet to get a grip.

Angel was reloading the shotgun but in his haste he dropped the second cartridge. It didn't occur to him that one cartridge would be enough – he was passing from anger into shock and his brain seemed to be stuck in treacle. He watched Bentley's insane leap. Then he fumbled out another cartridge, cursing all the while, and thrust it into the breech while he watched Bentley only a few feet away trying to pull himself up.

Will's boots found a toe-grip on a line of lead that ran round the edge of the roof, and he hauled himself up the wall, seeing the alley far below. He left bloody smudges on the bricks. As he dropped over the parapet the edge of the bricks ground into his side and he cried out in pain. He saw the silhouette of Angel and the gun before he let himself fall flat onto the gravel, knocking all the air out of his lungs. The gun went off again and peppered the top of the parapet wall uselessly. That meant Angel had one more shot. Will didn't know whether the man would jump over but it seemed a fair bet, and he might make it where Will hadn't. He forced himself to think. He needed a decoy. He unbuttoned his shirt and took it off with difficulty. He shimmied several feet along behind the wall and then risked a quick look. Angel was standing with the gun aimed where he had been and he swung the gun around as Will ducked again. But he didn't fire. Will bunched his shirt up into a ball and threw it upwards. This time the shotgun crashed and the shirt was torn to ribbons a few inches from his face. Now he had a few seconds! He jumped to his feet and saw Angel frantically reloading the gun. He ran to a trapdoor like the one on his own roof and grabbed the handle, hauling it open and almost losing his footing. There was a narrow staircase and he practically fell down it. Angel never loosed off another shot.

RICHARD JOHN MITCHELL

SIXTY-SEVEN

Nothing in his life
Became him like the leaving it
WILLIAM SHAKESPEARE, Macbeth

Rupert Angel watched in horror as Bentley disappeared from sight. He heard shouts from below and leaned out. People were pointing up and he could hear a distant police siren. Not only had he failed to get his victim, but he was about to be caught for attempted murder. Fear gripped him – he had to escape. It was too late to get Bentley now; he needed to save his own skin. He dropped the shotgun on the ground and ran for the trapdoor by which he had entered. He sprinted down the stairs and across Bentley's studio, dragged the chair away from the door, then went down the next set of stairs and out of the front door. People turned and someone shouted. He left Bentley's door open and took to his heels. He regained the Merc, scrabbled for his keys and fell into the driving seat as people chased him. He started the engine and skidded away, locking the doors as a great brute of a man reached the car and beat a ham-like fist on his side window, making a starburst of fractured glass. The Mercedes slalomed into a lamp-post and knocked it into a diagonal, deploying the airbag so that his vision was momentarily obscured. He punched it out of the way and then straightened the vehicle, with his driver's-side window now completely shattered and a buckle in the silver bodywork. The Botticelli painting was rattling around in the back in an alarming manner, but it was too bad. There was a red Clio in the street with its door open and he swerved to avoid it. The big man who had tried to get into the Merc was pursuing him on foot. Angel accelerated down the street, making pedestrians leap out of the way. As he reached the corner and turned it he saw none other than *Lucy Wrackham* standing at the open door of a taxi, her mouth open. Their eyes met for an instant and then he was past her, stamping on the throttle so that the powerful car accelerated away.

Will was in a corridor running past closed doors. A young woman in a skimpy top appeared as he sprinted past.
"We got trouble Darren!" she screamed, imagining Will to be a client. He went down the corridor and emerged into an anti-room. A large overweight man emerged from an office and said "Hey!"

"Where's the way out?" he yelled at the man. He must have been quite a sight, naked from the waist up and with blood on his side and his face.

"Now just a minute..."

"Where's the fucking way out?" Will screamed, his arms spread, and the man pointed mutely at a door. Will tugged open the door and found the stairs. An older woman came out of the office ready to do battle but he ignored them both and plunged on down. There were three women coming up and he yelled at them to get out of the way. They flattened themselves to the side as he went down two stairs at a time and emerged into a large reception area gaudily tricked out with chaises longues and erotic photographs. There were two men in the room. One leaped to his feet and looked as if he was going to run for it, but the other man just sat and looked at him in astonishment. There was a young woman with each of them. Will made for the hall, tugged the front door open and fell into the street, looking around wildly. Rupert Angel was running down the street away from Will. Sandy's red Clio had turned up and Lewis was getting out of the passenger seat with more haste than an injured man should. He hadn't seen Will, but he took off after Angel and Will went after them both. Angel made it to his car and managed to evade Lewis. He lost control and smashed a lamp-post but then went off down the street, never even spotting Will and narrowly missing pedestrians. Lewis was climbing back into the Clio and Will ran up to it and threw himself into the back seat.

"That's him!" he yelled urgently. "That's Rupert Angel."

"Bloody bastard," Sandy said grimly, and restarted her engine with a roar, crashing it into gear and giving chase. She skidded to a stop at the corner and Will couldn't see why until the back door was snatched open and Lucy fell into the seat beside him.

"Oh my God," she managed to say as she saw Will's shirtless body seeping blood, but then Sandy was off again; a woman with a mission, leaning on her horn to get people out of the way. There was something very comical about the four of them crammed into the Clio, especially the huge bulk of Lewis, and Will began to chuckle so that Lucy looked at him strangely. The Mercedes was far up the road with a blue Maestro between it and them. It seemed unlikely that they would catch it but Sandy put her foot down and the little car lived up to its agile reputation and bounded forward.

Angel wasn't going to stop at the lights but he had no choice because they had turned red and the traffic was a solid wall before him. He looked behind him and saw the pursuing Clio far down the road. The lights were changing and the cross flow was clearing – he was going to make it! A large lorry jumped the opposing lights on yellow and crossed in front of him. He readied his foot on the accelerator and glanced sideways through his broken window. There was a man in a blue car next to him pointing something. Then a 9mm jacketed soft-point bullet hit Rupert Angel in the head and blew the back of his skull off, spraying brains and blood across the passenger window.

His foot clamped down in reflex and the Mercedes surged forward into the moving lorry. It plunged into the side of it and the rear wheels of the lorry mounted up and dragged its whole thirty-ton weight over the Mercedes, crushing it flat. The five-hundred year-old panel of wood in the back was bent into a slight curve before it shattered, and then the wheels of the lorry went through the middle of it. The lorry slewed sideways and hit three cars before it came to a stop against the traffic lights, canting them over at a crazy angle. A mother snatched up her four-year old and stood white-faced against a hedge while her little boy started to cry. People were running from all directions and the first distant siren could be heard, already summoned by the earlier sound of the shotgun blasts. Sandy had stopped the Clio in the middle of the road. The only car that was still moving was a blue Maestro, which turned right up a side road and drove sedately away. Inside it, a man in the back seat was making a mobile phone call. It answered after a few seconds and he told Mr Harold that it had taken a little time but honour was satisfied.

Everything was mayhem at the Cambridge road junction. The lorry driver was climbing shakily down from his cabin, and people stepped forward to give him a hand. He was saying it wasn't his fault and people were taking his arm and reassuring him. A young man was filming the scene with his mobile phone.

The first police car arrived and killed its siren, leaving its blue lights rotating. Two officers piled out of it and started calling in urgent situation reports, while other sirens could be heard in the distance. Will and Lucy climbed out of the Clio and hugged each other. Then Will looked over Lucy's shoulder and realised what he could see sticking out of the shattered Mercedes – a bloody arm.

He went over to the twisted wreckage. Rupert Angel was clearly dead but the sight of the twisted body made Will feel more sick than victorious. Lucy walked up and stood beside him, looking at the bloody remains of Rupert. With a gut wrench she realized that he was wearing the same pale blue suit he had worn to *Le Gavroche*. She remembered telling him that she always got her man, and him promising on his life to keep silent if she told him the story.

"I held you to it," she said softly, and Will looked at her, wondering what she meant. But then he was no longer listening, for in the back of the twisted car he had spotted a fragment of broken painting, only a few inches across but instantly recognizable. It was the face of Venus, looking ahead in thoughtful contemplation. He pointed and Lucy gripped his arm very tightly.

She reached in and picked up the broken piece of painted wood, while pedestrians urged her back and one of the policemen shouted at her.

STEALING VENUS

"He was stealing Venus," she said, hearing her voice as if it belonged to someone else.

She stepped away and handed the fragment of Venus to Will, who took it like an automaton. As he turned it the right way up, the broken edge of the painting left a line of paint on his hand. Then a policeman arrived and ushered them back.

SIXTY-EIGHT

If you could say it in words, there would be no reason to paint.
EDWARD HOPPER

Yesterday had been Alfred's funeral, a month after his death. With no wife or children it had fallen to his sister Gillian to choose where to bury him, and she had selected her own church; St. Andrews in Hastings. Will and Lucy had stood at the edge of the grave with a small crowd of people; black-clad figures either silent or weeping. Lucy was one of the dry-eyed ones who simply stared, and Will had struggled to keep from tears as the coffin was lowered. After only one covert conversation in Rupert Angel's house, the next time he had seen his old friend had been to identify the body.

Gillian Heath had looked tired and old. She had done a reading and said that Alfred was in the arms of the Lord now. Will hoped that she was right. He had spoken to her after the service, saying that her brother was already recognized by experts as a painter of genius. The Angel Gallery had been closed since Rupert's death, but now there was talk of a consortium buying it and using it to display Alfred's forgeries as a permanent exhibition. The notoriety of the whole affair and the paintings themselves would make it a major new London attraction.

After a reception in the Church Hall with thimblefuls of white wine and wrinkled cocktail sausages on sticks, Will and Lucy had gone to a pub with George, Anna, Sandy, Lewis and Davies. Lewis wanted to move up to Cambridge, for there was plenty of security work there and he and Sandy were closer together than ever. Davies had come down to the funeral that morning, uncomfortable in his black suit, and they had teased him gently for looking like an undertaker's assistant.

It had been a strange day; a day of putting Alfred Smith to rest, but also a day of assembly for this unique group of people that had been involved in the whole affair since the beginning. When they had been about to leave the pub, Gillian Heath had walked in and tried to bolt out again when she saw them. But they had seized her and bought her a small whisky and ginger ale at her request. She had sipped the whisky slowly and looked at them all in confusion: the painter and a pretty girl who was something to do with insurance; a nice-looking couple she didn't know; a pretty young woman who seemed a little common, and a big brute of a man that she didn't much care for, though he seemed polite enough. There was also a Welsh policeman, who wasn't wearing a uniform so he must be a detective or someone very high up. She supposed that he must be off duty because he was drinking a pint of beer.

That had been yesterday: a funeral and some tears. But today Will was happy. On his arm he had a pretty girl who was something to do with insurance. They were in the Sainsbury Wing of the National Gallery, where they had been staring for the last ten minutes at Sandro Botticelli's Venus and Mars, newly returned from its cleaning.

The National Gallery had unpacked it when they had been told it was a forgery, but after a day of tests they had remained certain that it was the original. This had been confirmed for sure when the fragments of the broken painting from Rupert's shattered car had been analysed – the paint was still a little wet at the broken edges of the panel, because it had not been properly baked.

Lawrence Morris had given the police a detailed account of the break-in at the National, including a five-minute period in the Conservation Department when he had been left alone with the copy and the original masterpiece. He had swapped them around and then smugly watched his mother and Rupert Angel swap them back, paying them back in the most painful way he could think of for their endlessly scornful treatment of him. Because of his actions he was likely to get only a suspended sentence, and when the legal proceedings were over he planned to seek a job as an interpreter.

When Will and Lucy had looked enough at the Venus and Mars picture they turned and walked away, through the galleries, down the steps and out into Trafalgar Square. There was a news-stand on the next corner with a placard announcing the discovery of a new Whistler, but they didn't look in that direction.

RICHARD JOHN MITCHELL

ACKNOWLEDGEMENTS

With thanks to my wife Viv, who put up with my long absences as I wrote this novel, and helped whenever I needed to talk about it. Thanks also to Robin Churchill, Nick Morgan, Daniel Langley, Matthew Shooter and members of my family for their careful proof-reading. Thanks to Le Gavroche in Mayfair, who were kind enough to invite me into their inner sanctum and let me see their beautiful restaurant. Thanks also to an administrative lady in HMP Ford who helped me out on all things to do with open prisons.

RICHARD JOHN MITCHELL